Season of the Heart

ALSO BY CLARE BARROLL

The Iron Crown

SEASON OF THE HEART

Clare Barroll

CHARLES SCRIBNER'S SONS / NEW YORK

Copyright © 1976 Clare Barroll

Library of Congress Cataloging in Publication Data

Barroll, Clare.
     Season of the heart.

     I. Title.
PZ4.B2768Se [PS3552.A7369]   813'.5'4   76-28797
ISBN 0-684-14811-0

3 5 7 9 11 13 15 17 19   v|c   20 18 16 14 12 10 8 6 4 2

Printed in the United States of America

Love knows no rhyme or reason,
Or any season . . .
Except the season of the heart

(From a song of Peter's)

For the medical details of the frozen man, Christer, I have followed the report of Dr. Samuel Naucler, published in the *Kongl. Vetenskaps Acadamies Handlingar,* 1756 (the Proceedings of the Swedish Royal Academy of Science). I have gone beyond this report to give Christer his name, his place in life, and his past. The man reported on by Dr. Naucler was a poor crofter of the islands. There are a number of instances like this of frozen men in arctic annals, particularly in Scandinavia and in Russia.

Season of the Heart

Chapter 1

What is a priest to do, when he sees that murder is to be done? Murder most foul, of a most gentle lady, more gentle than any I have ever known. I saw that Lord Ivar hated her now, his wife, his proud possession. He hated her, my lady Donna; he would bring her to kneel before him in humility, to confess to a crime she did not commit, a crime for which the only punishment is burning. Burning awaits some of us, perhaps, in the afterlife. But burning alive . . . this is the penance of the witch.

To think of it, and of Donna, is like a sword thrust to the heart. The raised platform, the piled faggots, the quick, licking flame. And the crowd in the cobbled square, pushing and jeering . . . some throwing stones, and most throwing ugly words. And my lady Donna in the grey prison shift, white arms bound, white throat bare, the cloud of dark hair loose upon her shoulders.

In the crowd there would be churchmen, with swinging censers, chanting psalms to ward off evil, for the soul of a witch may escape in the rising smoke to bring baleful fate upon those who stand too close. The smoke is very rank and dense, for whale oil is thrown upon the flames so they are high and quick. Men-at-arms would move among the crowd, Lord Ivar's men in iron armour, bearing his banners.

And my lord himself? Though this would be the murder of his lady, at his bidding, he would bear no blame. Men would shout applause, he would win citation from the King, and a great reputation in Stockholm. For so it is when a man has captured and caused to be burned a witch.

I know my lady Donna; I have been her confessor. She was not a witch, though she was not blameless. Her sin was love. And is it so great a sin?

I must set down my own shame, too, from the beginning. My sin against my gentle lady, as great as Lord Ivar's sin. I must write of it, though nothing can ease the burden on my heart.

I will begin with the night when I first saw her. And Kurt first saw her, too. The night when the Unknown came to the village, the dead man brought in from the ice.

And some of what I write has been told to me; and much I have guessed. But much I have seen for myself . . . and not least, Donna's love for Kurt, and his for her, from the beginning.

Chapter 2

———◆••◆———

I was on unwelcome duty. It had been a hard, cruel winter—
in the year 1430 we had such weather, which the village folk
call a "wolf winter," for then the wolves come down even to
the edges of the mine pits, where fires are burning. And last
year was no better; this year, even in April, the road was
hard-packed with snow, and I rode between walls of snow
away from the village. The old mare snorted and stamped;
her blanket was stiff with frost, her haunches silvery. I rode
close by the inlet, ice-bound now; then the road dipped into a
grove of black pines, weighted with snow.

The road grew narrow, only a track; it shone with streaks
of ice, and the mare stumbled now and then. The cold stung
and pricked my eyes, and my nostrils; and I wished I were
not the youngest and the most humble of all the brothers at
the monastery, for such duties often fell to me.

The Church rules strictly that a lay brother may not per-
form the office for the dead, but our Abbot was liberal. "Let
the comfort of God be brought," he would say, "if only by a
lay brother, so long as he is devout." The Abbot was most
inclined to this view in bitter weather when our old monks
complained of ague and cramp, and the Abbot was loath to
send them out in the cold.

Word had been brought that a newborn child lay dead, in a croft beyond the inlet.

The wooden hut was drifted deep in snow. Old Nilsson met me; his wife was dead, but he gave me watered beer to warm me and took the mare to the shed. His daughter had given birth two days before, but the child was dead. The mother wept piteously, with distraction, and held her hands to the swollen breasts under her woolen shawl. Breasts full of milk which the child would never suck. Yet she wept so that I wondered. I have seen grief, the kind that stuns like a sleeping draught.

I am country bred; I was born here, near the inlet. I know there are roots to be dug, there are bitter berries . . . and potions of these which offer an easeful death. I know these are used when there is no room for a child, and no bread but the sour loaf they bake from birch or pine bark. Here there was no room for a child and no known father.

I thought it might be that the mother wept more from guilt than from grief.

But it was not my duty to judge such things.

I did my duty. I said the words over the grave. Jens Stenman had come from the nearest croft; men had cleared the snow and warmed the frozen ground with straw fires and opened the earth with a heated hay fork. The grave was in the forest, behind the barn. The grave was shallow even for so small a box of splintered pine; they covered it with stones. So the babe was laid to rest where perhaps, under the pines, he had been conceived.

I had brought bread and cheese, a sausage and wine, from the monastery. I knew they could not afford to share it with me; I left them and took the snowy road again.

The long blue shadow of pines lay across the snow as I rode back. Where the way skirts the inlet, the ice lay in sheets, roughened and piled by wind. Beyond was the blue glint of the bay, dark water stroked with shining white.

But close in-shore the ice was smooth, and upon it was a thin finger of fire, built of brittle water rushes; I thought to stop and warm myself. There were torches stuck in the piled snow, and tethered there, a horse, poor beast. And a sledge on heavy wooden runners.

In the still, wet pools upon the ice, light was caught, the light of the late red sun. And there upon the ice, there was blood too, and two great dark shapes. Close by these lay an oaken club, spiked with iron.

I had gone out, as a boy, to club the seals, when the first free water piles the ice cakes up, leaving the beasts stranded. One of the seals was dead, but one still lived; he heaved his great bulk, and turned, and then was still.

Where were the men? Out on the ice beyond the rocks? I climbed, slipping and catching myself, grabbing a stunted branch of pine. And then I saw them below me. Two of them. I knew them: the young son of Sven Mattson and old Rolf. They were bending over another seal, but their clubs lay beside them on the ice.

I hailed them. Young Sven looked up and scowled. I saw that he had a knife.

"God's blood," said Sven. "Whatever the bounty, the Church must share in it."

"No," I said. "I would only share your fire."

But he cursed me. I saw that he was full of that fiery raw spirit which they distill from wood. But the old man spoke to him. Then Sven stood quiet, but surly, fingering his knife. The old man gave me greeting; I had sat by his wife a month ago when she lay ill of fever.

"Peace," I said again. And then I saw that the dark shape on the ice was not a seal, but the body of a man. A stranger.

He wore leather boots and a furred cloak. A hood of fine wool, bordered with marten. And soon, in the bitter cold, he would be frozen hard as a ham that hangs in a shed. Already the body was stiff; and the jaws rigid. The eyes were fixed;

the face was pallid and icy cold; on the cheeks, the veins were blackish. One of the hands was gloved, but the other bare. I took the cold hand in my hand; there was no pulse.

I made the sign of the cross. "So," I said, "you would rob a dead man. And leave him here where wolves will find him."

"Where we found him," said Sven. "And we'd not leave him here; we'd drag him to the sea and let the strong tide take him. But he's got no need again for that cloak. Or the belt, or the golden chain round his neck."

But old Rolf said, "That gold chain could hang you, Sven. Be remembering the time when——" He stopped short and I said quickly, "Rolf is right. With a stolen cloak comes a curse. Come, lad, we must get the dead man to the alms-house. He must have Christian burial."

We hauled the dead man into the sledge, and beside him, the heavy bodies of the seals. These were still warm, and their fur was stained with clotted blood. I followed the sledge, urging the old mare on, though she was tired. It was near sundown now; a grey bank of cloud lay low on the snowy hills; there would be, I thought, a fresh snowfall before morning. We came to the cluster of wooden huts at the end of the village; here was the inn.

At the inn the men would stop. There was food and drink and a good fire, and stabling for the horses.

"I'm cold as the dead man there," said Sven. "Hell itself couldn't warm me." But drink would, I knew; and then he would sleep in the inn, stretched out on one of the wooden benches against the wall.

He would have left the dead man in the sledge and come out later, to cut the good clothes from the body, and the fine gold chain. "Come, Sven," I said, "death demands some respect." But he turned his back on me.

Old Rolf helped me. Between us we propped the dead man so that he seemed to walk, though stumbling.

In the inn, a great fire burned on the stone hearth. Shadow and light moved on the plaster walls; smoke hung in the rafters. Yet the room was dim, for Fat Tomas is stingy with his candles. I was glad for that. We moved among the oaken tables; men glanced up from their ale or bacon but paid us no heed, with the shuffling body between us. They thought the dead man drunk.

We got him into the tiring room, the alcove where men of the road sometimes stopped, taxmen or traveling mummers. The rough log walls let the chill in through the chinks, but here on the hearth, a small fire burned. On the pine chest was a candle; there was a bedstead, rough-built of pine, and on it a cowhide and an eiderdown. We laid the dead man out upon the bed. His hood fell back and I saw on the side of his head a grey, swollen bruise.

"I'll watch by him here," I said, "and take him on to the almshouse in the morning. Good Rolf, you've earned a prayer said for you. And a mug of ale." I reached in my purse for a thin coin. "Tell Tomas to bring me bread and wine and cheese." And when he had gone, I opened the dead man's cloak and jerkin and saw on the shoulder another bruise, but then I covered the body, for Fat Tomas came to the door with another candle. Grease gleamed on his lip and wine on his chin. He looked at the body on the bed. "Priest, there's no room for him here. No room for a sick man." Then he came close with the candle. "Christ's help, he's dead."

"In his place, Tomas, you'd be glad of a little mercy."

"Dead. And he'll not rise from the dead, to pay for his bed in hard coin."

"I'll pay, Tomas."

"The room will be tainted. Who knows why he died? They say there's the sweating sickness in Falun."

"No, Tomas."

"There's blood on him. Black blood. They bring that up when they cough."

"Seal's blood, Tomas. He lay in the sledge between two seals."

Tomas set his jaw. "Let him lie there now, in the shed with the seals. Get him out."

"He'd be robbed. And no prayer said for him. No, Tomas. Bring me food and wine. And I'll forget you paid the Church no tithe at Christmas."

Tomas stared at me now, considering. And then he jerked his head. In the room beyond, where the men sat and drank, there was a sudden silence. No sound but the snap and hiss of logs on the hearth. Then the voices of two men, muttering. And silence again.

"What *now?*" said Tomas. "Fighting among them again? By God, they can split each other's heads, but not my furniture. Last time, a trestle table smashed so it was kindling. And four stools . . . a pewter mug stolen in the brawl . . ."

I stood beside him in the doorway. There was no fight. Men sat quiet and stared, their mugs clutched in their fists.

My lady Donna had come into the inn.

She should not have come. This was no place for a lady such as she, a Queen's ward, a great lady of the court. But my lady was willful.

Willful, and young, and very lovely.

Four days ago she had come to the village, to the manor, but no one had seen her, except the manor folk. There were sixty or more there, to keep the place in order, and little enough to do. Lord Ivar came north from Stockholm seldom, once or twice a year. But word had been sent that he would come with the new bride, my lady Donna—a girl less than half his age, wed to him three months. He had left her at the manor; he had to go to Falun on business and was not due back till tomorrow.

My lady had spent four days close-confined in the cold, and now she was restless. She demanded to be driven out in the sleigh; Old Matt could only obey her. She had with her only Kari, the little tiring maid from the manor. And no outrider, but the roads were usually safe by day.

Young Kari was excited by the outing. And I think Donna must have had joy at first as they drove over snowy roads, the sleigh piled with bearskins, and my lady wrapped in furs with warmed stones at her feet; and Kari beside her, her small face pink with cold. It was, said my lady later, like driving through a crystal cave . . . the ice on the road shining like glass, and on either side, the snow encrusted with frost and dazzling in the sun, the bare trees arched overhead and glittering.

But then the sun dropped low behind the snowhills. Here the winter darkness sets in early. Light drained from the snow; in the last, late light, the road seemed like a streak of copper. The dark pines crowded like hostile troops on either side. Old Matt reined in the horses sharply. Two foxes had crossed the road close to the horses' hooves.

And then they saw ahead the small light of the inn, and the smudge of smoke from the chimney. My lady Donna said they would stop. "And warm ourselves and command a hot posset. And ask for torches, to light the way back."

Old Matt looked surly; he said it would be a cold wait for the horses. And Kari said in distress, "My lady, the inn is rough. A lady cannot——"

"Ah, yes," said Donna. "In Stockholm, ladies go to inns."

I doubt that this is true.

And I saw on her face as she came into the rude, smoky room, that she herself felt doubtful. From the long benches, men stared at her; and she had not seen such men, not then. Men from the farms, poor crofters, in filthy sheepskins, hunched over their mugs.

And men from the mines. The old ones are as bent as gnomes, their hands as gnarled as tree stumps, and the black soot of the mines will never leave their faces, so deep is the grime in the horny skin. You would think they spent their days tending the fires of Hell.

There were two young miners, their eyes fierce and red-rimmed in the swarthy faces. Both were drunk. One got to his feet to bow, in surly mockery, before my lady; but his fellow tripped him up, and he fell, and lay where he fell, on the plank floor.

"Come, my lady," said Kari, close to tears. She pulled the grey woolen cloak closer about her, but the hood fell back from her face; and the sun-gold hair was like a torch in the dim room.

But my lady saw me, in the doorway of the little room; she saw that I wore a priest's gown, and she came to me. If she was fearful she did not show it. She moved as she must have at court, the cloak of sable sweeping behind her, her head high. Her sable hood was close around her face, but soft little tendrils of dark hair escaped and lay against her cheek. And Kari followed her, for Donna had taken her hand.

Fat Tomas bowed—difficult for him, for he had a large pot belly. As he straightened, I saw on his face a mixture of emotions. Astonishment that my lady had come, hard envy at her beautiful cloak. And greed. If she had come to the inn, she would leave good money here. And yet I knew of a sudden what he was thinking. She would leave as much as a gold *riksdaler* perhaps. Yet the man on the bed, the dead man, had much more upon him in wealth.

"Stay back, my lady, I beg you," said Tomas. "There's a sick man here."

My lady stood in the doorway. She looked at the body on the bed, at the furred cloak and the fine belt with a buckle of jasper, and the gleam of gold at the neck.

"Stay back," said Tomas again. "There is risk of infection, the sweating sickness."

My lady paused. And she said, very clearly, "This man is dead."

I caught her eye. "Yes, my lady. But I think there is no infection."

My lady said, "I am not afraid of it." She looked at Tomas. "Go. Bring a hot posset. Very hot, with brandy in it, if you have it."

"But, my lady, you do me honour. I would go on my knees to serve you. But I confess, the man *is* dead. Please come no closer. We will take the body out to the shed."

"*Go.*"

So Tomas went.

"My lady," I said. "I am afraid for you. Tomas is right, you must not stay."

"You said there was no infection."

"I have seen no sign on the body. Black plague . . . there are no plague sores. At the throat, no swelling. No sign of pox. Or of the bloody flux, he would be soiled with that, his chest stained, and his clothes fouled. I beg pardon, my lady."

"Good priest, this is a man of noble birth. No matter how he died, he cannot be thrown out in the shed, to lie like a slaughtered pig."

"I have heard much, my lady, of your kindness." I had heard other things about her, too, which I could not believe. Not now, looking at her, her eyes wide and dark with compassion. "I think," I said, "that this man died from cold. He was found on the ice. I think he rode, and stopped by the way, the urge upon him to make water, or to relieve himself. Pardon, my lady."

"Yes, go on," said Donna.

"He stopped, I think, and went down from the road, tethered his horse there, and I think men of the road—there are rough ones in these parts—saw the horse and cut it loose."

"Perhaps he saw them do it, squatting as he may have

been." My lady was very direct, for one so gently born. "Perhaps he saw outlaws come upon the horse and take it. And dared not show himself for fear of murder."

"Yes. And then he walked along the strand, along the ice, for close by the inlet he might have found a hut, a fisherman's cottage. To wander up into the forest would have been worse danger. And he fell, at last, weak with cold and hunger. There's a mark on the back of his head; there are bruises. But no sign of mortal illness."

"Then why is the pig of an innkeeper so afraid?"

"He isn't, my lady. He would only frighten you off, so he can rob the body."

"With you here, good brother?"

"They've small respect here for the monk's gown. Or for the cross. They've more faith, I think, in witch symbols. Besides, I am only one against many."

"Now we are two," said Donna. And she smiled at me, and I knew that I would have served her forever.

Tomas came with the steaming posset. My lady put a gold coin upon the battered pine chest. "Now take the drink to my coachman who waits outside and is near death himself from the cold. And then come back to help the priest. We will take the dead man out to the sleigh."

Fat Tomas stared at her.

"You are slow to do what you're told," said Lady Donna. "Perhaps from disrespect?"

"Oh, no, my lady."

"Then be quick."

And Tomas was quick to snatch up the gold coin from the chest; and then he went, in ill humour.

My lady turned to me. "You will come with me to the manor? And lay the dead man out, and say the prayers? I have small experience with . . . with the death watch."

I saw then that her brave show was false, for she bit her lip and her mouth was trembling.

"I'll ride back with you. Gladly. But I have only the monastery mare. She's old and stiff."

"Tomas shall care for the mare. We can send for her in the morning. There is room in the sleigh for us all, you and . . . the stranger."

But she did not look again at the dead man. She stood quietly, her hands clasped. Tomas came back, to help with the body. We carried it through the inn; men muttered, but made no move to molest us. Most were too drunk to move. My lady walked behind us; her head was high, but her cheeks were flushed. And Kari followed.

We laid the dead man, stretched out and stiff as a bar of iron, in the back of the sleigh. I covered him with a bearskin. My lady told Kari to climb in front with the coachman and then sent Tomas for torches to light us on the dark way ahead. The air was sharp with cold, brittle with it, and yet like an iron wall through which we must ride. My lady stood beside me in the snow and put her hand on my arm.

"You are very good, priest."

"My name is Jonas. Folk call me Brother Jon."

In the black sky the stars were brilliant; the snow itself cast a pale light which illumined my lady's face, small and framed by her dark furs. I saw that she smiled at me, and I felt my heart beat. For a moment we stood without speaking; the night was very still, as if the cold had frozen all sound out of the air. And then I heard on the hard road behind us the sound of hooves, an iron clatter on the frozen road. The coachman raised his whip.

Then Tomas opened the inn door, bringing torches; light streamed out upon the snow.

"Thank you," said my lady. "I will give you——"

Tomas looked at her, like a fawning dog.

"I will give you," said Donna coolly, "some good advice. If you fear infection, burn this inn."

He dared make no answer; he was fixing the torches in

their brackets. And then wild young Sven was in the doorway; the door was filled with the shaggy bulk of him in his sheepskins—Sven who had found the dead man on the ice. He lurched toward us. In the torchlight his ruddy thatch of hair seemed aflame. He was raging drunk.

"Mine," he said thickly. "Dead man is mine. Take him from me, will ye? The rich take it all." He spat in the snow. "Not this time. I take what's mine."

My lady put out a hand in appeal and his fist came down hard and heavy on it. He would strike her out of the way as he would kick a dog.

But I grabbed his arm and he turned on me, slipping a little in the snow. And suddenly beside us were horses, trampling the snow and snorting; the steamy breath of one was over me. The riders reined in, four men in black leather armour. They were hooded and muffled against the cold. I could not see their faces. And one shouted and jumped from his horse, throwing the reins to the man beside him. He came at Sven, throwing the weight of his shoulder against him. Sven went down in the snow, and lay sprawling upon it.

I was glad for that. Yet my heart pounded. Rough riders of the road. And we were defenseless.

Then the tall man turned to me. "A sorry greeting for my lord's lady. We'll ride on with you."

He pulled the leather guard from his face. And I saw that it was Kurt. Kurt Arnison.

"Kurt," I said. "God has sent you."

"Ah, no, Jon. God picks better men than me to do His errands." Then he called to Tomas in the doorway. "Get young Sven into the inn. Though perhaps he'd best lie here to cool himself off."

"It is Kurt," I said to my lady, for still she stood beside me. "We are safe with him." I think of that now. Perhaps she came to think of it, too. We were safe with him then. But soon, with him, we would meet trouble like a raging flood. And great danger.

Now my lady said, "We are glad of a brave escort. You are called Kurt?

"Sir Kurt Arnison."

"How do you know me?"

"Who in Morby would not know you, wife to Lord Ivar? Such a cloak isn't often worn to the village inn." And Kurt's hand in its long gauntlet fell upon my lady's fur, upon the shoulder. She looked down at it and then at him. There was in that moment something between them, as if fire leapt from one to the other. But perhaps this was only my fancy, knowing what I know now. Kurt's face was half in shadow, the deep lines under his eyes etched in black. But my lady's face was rosy in the light; her eyes were dark and shining.

Kurt said, "I ride your way with my men in any case. My land adjoins your husband's. On the east border by the sea."

"You are neighbour to us? My husband's friend?"

"Friend? I think Lord Ivar would not say so. But we meet now and again. We met a month ago. In Stockholm with the King."

"You are received at court? But I have not seen you there."

"I am received. Not welcome. And I think Lord Ivar will not welcome me, yet I hear he arrives tomorrow. I will come then to the manor to see him."

"I will give you welcome," said my lady, and her small face was full of witchery.

Is it true, then, I wondered, what they say of her? I helped her into the sleigh, in front, with Kari. I would ride in back with the dead body. If Kurt was surprised that we carried a dead man as burden, he said nothing. For a moment, I wondered if he or one of his men . . . but no, I could not think that. Yet Kurt had the blood of others on his hands.

Lady Donna was quiet in the sleigh. Kurt's men rode behind us, but he rode ahead on the tall, black horse. His long shadow leapt ahead of him on the road. It was sometimes near, in the flaring light of the torches, and then far and distorted.

And lost to sight in a black turn of the road. Like happiness, said my lady later. Sometimes so close. Then lost to us.

Kurt has always cast a long shadow.

Chapter 3

The tall iron gates of the manor were open. Our torches picked out the gleam of bronze and gilt scrollwork; over the gates, my lord's arms were mounted in pride.

Before the gatehouse, men-at-arms were gathered with many torches; a red glow lay over the hard snowcrust and in it were winking diamonds of light. A troop of my lord's men were mounted to ride out and search the roads for my lady. The horses were trampling the packed snow.

The long approach to the manor winds through the dark pines. My lord's men rode with us. I saw a horse's head lift suddenly, the steam of breath issuing from its mouth; and behind it, a great bough of pine bent and released a soft fall of snow.

In starlight, the great stone pile of the manor was like a fortress. And soon for my lady it would be a prison, during that hard time to come when my lord would forbid her to ride out.

Now from the manor casements light streamed; how many candles, how many torches burned within? But the upper casements were black; I fancied that from those blind windows shadowy faces looked out . . . ghostly watchers, phantoms who in life had walked these stone battlements. So much of life, of love and suffering, has been contained within these walls.

In the great hall there was warmth and light and the bustle of many folk. And yet there was a sense of still, cold chambers beyond the hall, and echoing corridors.

The dead body was brought into the hall and laid out upon the bearskin before the blazing fire.

And Kurt came in to look at it, to look at the waxen face with the black veins upon it. The eyes were fixed and I closed them. Kurt pulled the fur loose from the neck and examined the gold chain. It was of chased work, heavy and very beautiful. From it hung a crucifix set with dark garnets and small enamels.

"Fine work," said Kurt. "Perhaps Italian. Yet the cross is no protection here among our mountain men. There's small welcome for strangers."

My lady was watching Kurt. And I saw him then as she must have seen him, as if for the first time. Kurt—dark of brow, strong of feature, with high cheekbones. A man of stubborn pride, yet gentle, as most of our nobles are not. So I saw him, who had known him so long. I saw too the lines of fatigue in his face. And in his eyes the bitter search for answers; Kurt had always been one who looked for ordered answers. No man ever finds the answers, I know that now. But Kurt was a man who asked the questions. A man who dared.

My lady urged him to stay for a warm fire and a warm brandy, but he would not.

"A long day on the road," he said. "We've come from Arboga. With an hour's ride still before us."

Men did not often say no to my lady Donna. She was not pleased, but she said, in a cool little voice, "Naturally. You wish to be home. Your wife awaits you."

"I am not wed. Not as yet," said Kurt. And he left us.

Donna did not bid him farewell. She stared down at the dead body stretched out upon the bearskin. And Dame Agnes came in to us, scolding.

Dame Agnes looked, in her stiff grey robes and her square headdress, as if she were hewn from a block of granite. She had stiff grey hairs upon her chin, and an iron will. "Oh, my lady, out on the roads so late, on such a night. What can I tell my lord Ivar about you? The evening meal is waiting."

"It will wait upon death," said Donna.

Dame Agnes looked upon the dead man with distaste. And then with respect, for she saw that this was a man of property. Dame Agnes did not fear death, or anything living. Indeed, death would avoid her for a long time, perhaps fearing to take her.

For, once in Heaven, where she had no doubt a reserved place, she would wish to leave it, to visit Hell, where she could order the torments and harry the young devils to stoke the fires properly. Or so my lady has said.

Dame Agnes had come from Stockholm with Donna, unwillingly. But she had done her duty, she would always do her duty; she had seen to it that furs were aired, that tapestries were hung, and a tally made in the larders. She ordered the servants about and quarreled with them, and this was joy to her.

But now Donna took charge. "Dame Agnes, the priest will stay. I will make arrangement for him. And for the body. I will dine in an hour. See to it, please."

So the body was brought to the room they call the chapel. This is the old part of the manor, built two hundred years ago. There are two vaulted rooms, and the chill of years is in them, locked in the stone walls. Beneath the low stone arches, there are the shadows of years. It was here that Lord Ivar's mother died and here that she spent her last years, when after a life of lust and pride, she turned suddenly to penance. I had seen Lord Ivar's mother when she came sometimes to the monastery. At the last, she was wasted in body and racked with sickness of the lungs; still there were traces on her face of the beauty for which she was famed. And of the greed which had ruled her and the harsh pride with which she had ruled others.

In the end she was harsh with herself. As if by mortifying the flesh, she could turn death from her. For these rooms are bare and dark. There is a stone pallet where my lord's mother slept, with a blanket of fiber of thistles to cover her. Fixed in the walls are iron brackets for candles. There is a crucifix upon the wall, carved from bleached wood; the face of the Christ is full of agony under the iron crown. The holy figure had been painted. There were traces of dark grey in the furrows on the face and on the long thigh bones; red stained the hands and feet beneath the iron nails which pierced them.

Below this are two worn steps where for hours Lord Ivar's mother had knelt, until she was too stiff to stand, and her women folk would help her rise and then lay her out upon the stone where she chose to rest. Like the figure upon her own tomb she would lie there, her eyes fixed on the tortured face of the Christ.

On this pallet we laid out the dead body. Candles were brought and set in the iron sconces; and yet the room was dim. I arranged the dead man's cloak and folded the furred hood under his head to shield his bruise from the stone, though he could not feel it. Donna was watching from the doorway; she asked that tapers be brought to set at his head, and the amber light illumined the pallid face. But the jaw was fixed and sunk in shadow. His arms were rigid at his sides. Gold gleamed from the heavy neckchain and the cross on his breast. So he lay, in his dark mantle; the clasp of his belt caught the light, and this was of jasper, a great glowing stone incised with the letter C.

"Was nothing found with him?" asked Donna.

"Nothing. We can never know who he was or what befell him."

"Can you leave him so? Can you come and dine? You have not eaten, I think."

"I'll stay here. Later, some wine, if you will."

"You must eat."

"And you, my lady."

So Donna left me, but men from the kitchens came with hot roast fowl and soft new bread and cheese. And a bottle of German wine with two goblets. These were of dark crystal, a smoky light in their depths.

The meal was laid out in the little anteroom where my lord's mother sometimes sat at work on a tapestry for the chapel. This was unfinished, spread out on a font in the corner, and ragged with loose threads. The room held nothing else but an oaken settle where tapestry silks had been sorted and, before the black cavern of the fireplace, two chairs, high-backed, of carved wood.

Men came to build up the fire and I was glad for it. This room had a window, a small roundel set high in the wall, and I could feel the cold beyond the leaded panes and hear the wind behind them.

I did not eat but drank a little wine; and then I went back to the chapel where the dead man lay and knelt upon the stone and said the office for him.

When it was done, I stood looking at him, brought down by violence to sudden death. I looked up at the face of the Christ upon the wall and in it I saw no compassion. Yet the stranger had been a gentle man; his face was gentle even in death. And he had known sorrow, there were deep furrows under the eyes. I knew nothing of him then, of the excellence, the fullness of his life, of the boon he had brought to the world. A murderer, for all I knew. Yet I thought not, looking at the noble face. A man of consequence. Yet he wore no ring, no seal, and this I thought strange, that the long stiff fingers were bare. Perhaps Sven had pried the seal from the cold hand. And would have taken the gold neckchain if I had not come suddenly upon him.

Whoever he was, whatever his life, the dead man had not asked for his fate. I thought long thoughts on man's mortality. The candles were burning low. They cast moving shadows upon the floor, like small, moving devils about the body. Over it, would I see some primeval struggle for the soul; about it, a beating of dark wings? Yet this was morbid fancy.

The candles were smoking. Shadows stretched and crept upon the walls. There was a waxen smell. And something more. The odour of the crypt, of mould and decay.

And then I heard a whispering of sound. It was not the wind behind the round casement, though I gazed at it, a blank black eye in the wall. And then in the stained glass, small tongues of flame appeared, ruby, emerald, wavering points of light, as if, beyond in the gusty dark, unearthly spirits waited and watched.

The whisper of sound grew closer. I turned and there was Donna in the doorway, her long robe brushing the floor and her taper held high, the five candles waking in the window dancing points of light.

She set her taper down upon the floor, and again the window was black.

"My lady, it is very late."

"I could not sleep. I thought of him." She walked toward the body, though not close; her eyes were dark and a little fearful.

"You are fearful of death, my lady? Do not be. Death is a long sleep and a great peace."

"I . . . I am not afraid, Brother Jon, with you here. Are you warm? Do you wish for anything?"

"You are kind, my lady. But you will take a chill. Come, I will build up the fire."

She followed me into the tapestry room. I piled wood upon the fire, and the great logs blazed. Donna looked at the meal spread out upon the settle. "But you have not eaten. You have barely touched the wine." She poured a measure for us both, into the goblets, and sat before the fire to drink. She wore over her white night shift a long cloak of dark blue velvet; her white throat was bare, but there were pearls in her ears. The lobes of her ears were small and very white. Her hair was loose, tumbled in dark waves upon her back. She did not mind that I saw her so. She did not think of me as a man, only as a priest. She is very young, I thought, not more than twenty; we were of an age, nearly; I am twenty-eight, but I look older in my priest's gown.

"The wine warms me," said Donna, and smiled. "And now I am so hungry. Sit with me and eat. And talk." So I sliced the roasted fowl and gave a legbone to her. She took it up in a linen napkin and began to eat with appetite.

"Best be quick, good Jon, to take the other leg. Or perhaps I shall."

So we sat in firelight, eating and drinking, as if we were long wed. I shall not forget it. I could not take my eyes off her. Her face was small and very sweet. So white was her skin, so delicate her look, I thought she was like an elfin princess. And I saw that her eyes were dark, but not black as I had thought. They were blue, as blue as the wood anemone that stars our grassy slopes in spring.

The manor was quiet, huddled in snow and wrapped in sleep. There was only the noise of the wind and the hiss of the fire. We were alone, in an island of time, and my lady spoke to me in confidence, as men do during long night watches when they have dug themselves into the earth before a dawn attack.

"Pour me more wine, Jon."

"You are not—forgive me, my lady, but you are not—not at all as they say."

"And what do they say?"

I felt colour rise to the roots of my hair. "I . . . I would rather not tell."

"I know, any way. That I am Lord Ivar's wife, who would not have wed him, but I had no choice. That I toy with other men and think only of lively ways, and that I have taken the King himself into my bed. I know what they say, but it is not true. Except——"

"Except?"

"That I married against my will a man I do not love. That is the usual way, isn't it? Lord Ivar is a great catch, the Queen advised me. I had no choice."

"It is the custom. A lady such as you must wed. Or take the veil. If she has no parents to guide her. We have heard that your father died two years ago in a hunting accident. You are a Queen's ward, I know."

"Since my mother's death. I was twelve then. My father sent me to court. The Queen has been kind. A friend during the years."

"I think she must have advised you well. Love is not customary in marriage."

"I have tried to love my lord. But . . . ah, Jon, I would not live my life, my whole life, without love."

"All maidens dream of love."

"Yes. And play false games with men who are gallant to them. But they were games only, good Jon. It *is* false at court. The masques and dances. Hawking parties. Riding out to hunt. We are much together, men and women. There is much wine. There is music."

"Yes, my lady. So you came to the manor to be quiet. Perhaps to think of other things."

"I came because my lord is angry. There had been a little game . . . one of the Queen's captains. It was nothing, an exchange of notes, a touch of the hand. A look, as we danced. Nothing. But my lord is always jealous. There was a music master, too, who is now dismissed. My lord thinks country life will do me good. And the Queen has gone with the King on a tour of the royal manors in Skåne. Or she would have spoken for me. So the horses were saddled, the chests and sleighs packed. And here I am with Dame Agnes to guard me." Donna made a little face, wrinkling her nose. "No one to talk to but Kari. And you."

"I am poor company. I know little of great ways, of the life at court."

"You know of other things. I would be lonely tonight without you. And sad."

"Because of the dead man?"

"Yes. He is so like my father. I cannot forget the night when they brought my father in. He was so still, there was so much blood. He was hunting boar, he was gored."

"My lady, you must not distress yourself."

"I *must* talk." And yet she sat very quiet for a moment; her eyes were deep. The wind was rising beyond the dark casement. "Ah, Jon, how the wind blows. Sighing and crying in bare trees. My mother hated it. She hated the cold, she loved the sun in Italy. And she loved my father. But she was Italian, sister to a Papal envoy. She had spent golden years in Rome. Often she told me of it. She hated Sweden. She was afraid when the long, dark night of the north came on. She would sing to me in her soft, southern tongue, and she longed so for peaches! And apricots. And the soft green twilights of Italy. I am glad I speak her tongue; my father never learned it. They say of the King that he is too kind to me. But truly it is for this, that I speak the Italian tongue. It is crowded at court, always, with missions from the Pope. The King is glad I am there to speak for him. And yet I do not like him."

"There are many to agree with you, my lady."

"But the Queen loves him. I am sorry for her. The King is often away, and she is lonely. She speaks so little Swedish.

She has women with her, her own, from England, but always she knows that the King does not love her. When he is at court, he has many women."

"Not you, my lady?" I could not help myself.

"No. No, I do not like him. He has a square face and a thick body and he is very ruddy from wine and riding. Rough in manner and often drunk. And so many women. Last fall an ice-blonde girl, and later one of Philippa's own maids, an English girl with fair blue eyes and dark hair. Afterwards, the Queen sent her away, but without rancour for she knew the girl could not help herself. Last May Day we were riding out and the King had for once been gay with the Queen and patient with her. She was pleased at his courtesy. We made chaplets of flowers, and the Queen's was ready; but the King rode off after his ice maiden, he wore *her* chaplet. The Queen let the garland fall from her lap. Her hands were hot upon it; soon it had wilted. Her eyes were very sad. When I wait upon the Queen, I bring her jewels to her. She takes them up without joy and puts them down and says, 'It does not matter what I wear. He will not look at me.' "

I was glad when Donna spoke so, of the court and not of her fear. Later, I thought, when she goes to her bed, I will go back to the chapel and tend the candles and wash and anoint the dead body.

But Donna's thoughts turned, with mine. A great gust of wind shook the casement; she shivered. "It is cruel to think of the dead man. Lying there on the stone, so still and cold, and blood upon him."

"My lady," I said suddenly, "do not be afraid. Come with me to look at him. He lies in peace. Come and bless him. And say a prayer. Then perhaps you will sleep."

She put her hand in mine as a child would; her hand was soft and small and in it I felt her heartbeat. We walked into the chapel, into that vault of shadows, and stood beneath the grey wooden body of Christ and looked down upon the dead man. Donna held me more tightly. The candles wavered and flickered; about the body there was the sickly sweet odour of blood.

"So much blood," said Donna; her voice died in a whisper.

"It is seal's blood, my lady. The body lay in a sledge between the seals. Do not fear."

Then Donna bowed her head and said, "Mary, Holy Mother, receive this soul." Then I loosened the dead man's cloak and his doublet at the throat, and she put her hand there where no pulse beat. "God's blessing," she said, and then, in wonder, "He . . . he does not seem so cold."

And I put my hand upon his chest, and there it seemed to me I felt a little warmth. "It is the heat of the candles," I said, but I thought it strange. I felt his thigh, beneath his doublet; it was cold as stone. The body was rigid, the joints stiff. I touched his eyelids, the dead man did not wink. There was no sign of breath in him, or pulse.

And yet there was a little warmth over the heart.

"My lady, there is small chance . . ."

"Warm him, warm him," said Donna. There were tears in her voice and I thought her distracted from wine and weariness.

Yet I would humour her.

And Donna helped me. My cloak lay in the far room close by the fire. It held a little warmth, and we wrapped the dead man closely in it. I pulled off his boots, but the feet were swollen and blackish. I thought if he should live he would lose the use of his legs. Donna chafed the cold hands; she had lost her fear and colour burned in her cheeks. And it seemed that the dead man's colour was better. But perhaps that was only the warm light of the candles.

Then I thought of the goodwives of Morby and how when they have frozen meat or eggs, they put them in cold water to draw out the frost, and these are fresh when they thaw, with no rotten taste about them.

So Donna took napkins from our meal and wrung them out in wine, for a little remained; it had taken on the chill of the room. In the wet napkins we wrapped the dead man's feet. We kept the napkins wet and Donna kept rubbing the dead man's hands. I think we worked for an hour. The candles were sputtering and soon would die. But at last the dead man's stomach began to warm. And his face, in the dying light, seemed made of flesh not wax.

I sent Donna for fresh candles and for maids to help. And I bade her go up to sleep, but she would not go until just before dawn when I could perceive a faint breath, a tremour in the dead man's chest.

Long after dawn I could still find no pulse and I was not able to open the stiffened jaw. I began to despair. And yet I worked. And prayed. And sent for fresh poultices.

And then I let others work, for my hands were numb. I could do no more. For an hour I slept, in the tapestry room, stretched out like a dog before the fire. Then Donna came and waked me. "Dear Jon," she said softly, and took my hand in hers and put it for a moment to her cheek. And I was refreshed.

Together we went in to the dead man. As I laid my hand upon his breast, there was a little pulse. Faint but real.

I took a silver spoon, gently, to open the rigid mouth, and was able to get a few drops of warm wine between his lips. A miracle if the man could swallow. And he had trouble; wine dribbled upon his chin, yet he managed. He gave a strange, sharp cry, like an animal's cry, low in his throat.

One of the maids began to sob. "He has given up the ghost."

But he had not. Sweat formed on his brow and his cheeks took colour.

By noon he began to wink when I touched his eyelids; his body was warm; he moved his arms a little. I gave more wine and a little warm gruel. He swallowed and struggled to speak. At last he opened his eyes and gazed up at the Christ upon the wall. And said, on an indrawn breath, *"Ecco homo."*

"He speaks, " said Donna in wonder. "He speaks in Italian!"

I thought it Latin, but the two tongues are close.

I bent over the frozen man. He was muttering. "Christ . . . Christ . . ." The voice was a sigh. Then he spoke clearly, in Swedish. "I . . . I am . . . Christer." This is a name for Christ among us. One of the maids said fearfully, "He calls himself the Christ."

"He calls *upon* Christ," said Donna firmly. She took up his gold cross and put it between his fingers, but he could not hold it. He sank into sleep, but soon he woke and groaned and turned, as if he suffered mightily from colic. So I kneaded his abdomen, and his back, at the outlet of the bowel, and saw that a small pouch extruded from the bowel. This I extracted. It was of scraped parchment, soft and pliable. It was filled with gold dust. So does a man carry secret papers at times; when he is searched by a stupid guard nothing is found upon him.

When he was relieved of the pouch, the frozen man stirred and turned on the stone pallet, and passed a great deal of wind. He seemed somewhat eased. I showed him the pouch, but he did not speak; he gazed at me with burning eyes. Perhaps he only questioned who I was, or why he was here. But he turned his head as if looking for something.

"Perhaps he seeks to ease the pain in his head," said Donna. "His bruise is black and ugly." She took his hand, and he looked at her and said quietly, *"Bella . . . bella."*

And I showed him his gold cross, but he looked upon it with blank eyes.

Donna sent a man from the manor to search the ice by the inlet. He found a fragment of parchment, caught in a hollow in the rocks. The parchment was hard-frozen; the ribbons were torn and water-stained; the great seals broken. As I touched them they crumbled, yet we saw that one had been stamped with a lion's head and a lily; and one with a coronet. Royal seals? We could not know. I smoothed the cracked parchment. A letter of passage?

We could read only: "Christer . . . Magister . . . Medici . . ."

"Perhaps he has been to the great school at Salerno. And is master of surgery. Or healing drugs and the humours of the body. He speaks Italian," said Donna.

"And Swedish. Christer."

"That is his name, Christer," said Donna. And that was all we knew of him then, though surely he had other names and titles. He must have traveled with saddle bags of clothing and furs, with letters of credit and gold coins in plenty, a great sword and a fine saddle, a rich drinking cup. All were gone now, with his horse. Had he traveled alone? Or had his own men robbed him?

We gave him an egg posset and stayed with him till he slept. He was restless when Donna was out of the room; his eyes followed her. He had, I think, a memory in the dark part of his mind of her touch in the night, her chafing his hands, her gentleness, her voice.

And I would always remember her so, my lady of compassion, though others would call her cruel and of ill repute in the days to come.

Chapter 4

During the day the wind had dropped and the bitter cold moderated. At sundown Kurt came, with Peter, his young squire. They came into the manor hall, stamping snow from their boots, bringing the sharp breath of winter air with them. They stood before the great fireplace; oak logs blazed and crackled, a fire that could roast a suckling pig. Their leather armour creaked in the stinging heat.

I thought it graceless of Kurt to come to the manor so, dressed as if to ride to the inn in Granholm. I knew that he owned wonderful armour, made in Flanders, an undercoat of fine chain mail, the armour of polished black plate, with mountings of bronze oak leaves and silver damascene.

But then I saw that tonight Kurt meant to show himself as one of us, one with common folk. And so he had always been, one of us, we felt it. Yet Kurt is gently born, as much as Lord Ivar.

Kurt and Peter came in to the chapel to see Christer. Christer lay still upon the stone pallet; my lady had covered him with furs. His face was waxen pale in candlelight; his eyes were dark and burning. He looked up at us and murmured *"Freddo . . . freddo . . ."* I took it to mean that he was cold, yet his hand in mine was warm.

Kurt and Peter helped me, for Christer could not help himself. We moved him to a chamber off the solar. A vaulted room with dark paneling. There was a wide bed, of carved oak and curtained with rich blue samite. We helped Christer to the bed; he was weak and shivering and grateful to lie at last upon the crimson eiderdown.

A good fire blazed in the wide fireplace; he turned his face to it. And then closed his eyes with pain. "*La testa . . . il dolore . . .*" He put his hand to his head.

He wore still the dark mantle, stiff and fouled with dried blood, but we cut the stained clothes from his body. Maids came in to help us; they brought tubs of steaming water and linen towels. They washed Christer; he bore it patiently; he said nothing, but I believe he was in pain.

Then we dressed him freshly in doublet and fine wool britches, Lord Ivar's own. I took a kerchief pin and fastened the heavy gold cross to the bed hangings. There against the rich silken blue it gleamed like sunken gold.

We left Christer to rest and went out into the great hall.

Kurt put a hand on my shoulder. "Jon, I'll call on you when I have need of miracles. That will be soon."

"Ah, Kurt, it was the seals. Their warm bodies and their blood. They kept Christer alive. And my lady helped. She worked with me through the night."

And I saw something dark in Kurt's eyes. And then a little flame in them. Donna was descending the stair. She had gone up to bathe and freshen herself; Lord Ivar was expected before the evening meal.

I had not seen her before in court dress. The gown was blue, very dark; and most gracious, sweeping around her feet. The sleeves were slashed with vermilion and bordered with ermine. The bodice was cut very low; the soft curve of her bosom showed, and the creamy throat. And my lady wore rubies in her ears and pendant rubies, Lord Ivar's gift at Christmas. Their crimson fire burned as she came toward us.

Like drops of blood, I thought suddenly, staining the white throat. A curious thought.

She came to Kurt and took his hand. There was a tiny silence between them, as if they needed no words. Then she dropped his hand. "You are most welcome, Sir Kurt. Will you stay and dine? My lord has not yet come."

"I will stay gladly. Though I feel no need of his company."

"Brother Jon is good company," said Donna demurely.

"Ah, yes. How goes it, Jon, with the saving of souls?"

I laughed at him, and Kurt said, "My lady, he has given me up. He knows me too well, we have been friends since boyhood."

We drank mulled wine and waited for Lord Ivar. My lady sat before the fire; there was a glow about her, the curve of her cheek golden in firelight, the waves of dark hair shining. I seldom saw her wear a headdress. She was ever impatient of constraint, ever impulsive. She hated to bind up her hair with coif and veil and netted jewels.

Kurt was smiling, his eyes upon her. His was a strong face, thoughtful, often marked with bitterness, often sardonic. Yet tonight the dark look was gone, for a little time. Until Lord Ivar arrived.

Young Peter had brought his violin. When he played Peter could draw the angels from heaven to dance for him. Even more difficult, he could bring tears to the eyes of the Bishop of Lindhagen. He began with a gay little tune he had heard in Flanders. And he sang of the maiden bewitched and turned into a doe, so gentle and so fleet. "She is safe, no man can catch her."

Then Kari came into the hall, very gay and sweet in a scarlet skirt and a bodice stiff with stitchery, flowers of the field in many colours; she was apt at needlework.

She sat on a stool before the fire; her face took colour as Peter stood before her. These two were handfast lovers, though not churched. "A song for you, Kari," said Peter fondly; then to tease her, he gave us the ballad of little Kari and the wicked husband she wed; and his cruel mother who made her walk nine miles each day to the mill and spin till her small hands bled. And at last contrived to kill her. And she went without delay to the Gate of Heaven and there the Virgin Mother met her.

> "The Blessed Virgin brought out a stool;
> 'Sit down, little Kari, and rest your feet.' "

"Ah, wasn't that a kind welcome from the grand Queen of Heaven?" said Kari.

Then Peter sang:

> "As well I like thy yellow hair
> As apples fair on a bough;
> Blissful he who will have thee;
> God's mercy on him who must lose thee."

"Peter, Peter," said Kari, smoothing her red skirt with small hands; laughing at him and shaking her head so the corn-gold hair fell about her shoulders. "Sing now for the lady Donna."

Then Peter looked from Donna to Kurt and back again, and sang:

> "If I should go to Heaven and find
> No trace of thee among the natives there,
> Then I would sin and sin,
> And seek thee otherwhere."

Kurt lifted his cup then and said, "My lady." And she drank to him. They might have been alone in the room, the rest of us shadows. Then Peter began a dance. And Donna seized Kurt's hand and pulled him to his feet.

"But I am no courtier, my lady. I'm country bred."

This was not true, really. Kurt's blood was blue as Lord

Ivar's, their fathers were second cousins. And he knew courtly ways when he chose to remember them. He bowed, and they danced as great folk do at court, their arms twining, their hands touching, Donna stepping back and turning, her skirts swaying, all lightness and grace.

When it was done, she dropped him a curtsy; and Kurt said, "You are artful, my lady. I should teach you our country dances. The lads swinging the girls so their skirts fly, all stamping and laughing and turning like feathers in the wind. Come, Kari."

It was a wild tune. Kari whirled, her pale hair swinging on her shoulders, her red skirt in a tumult. And Kurt circled her; he lifted her high at the end and set her again on her feet.

Donna was clapping her hands and laughing. "It is like flying . . . so quick, so gay. Let me try, let me try."

But Peter put down his bow. For now there was a great stir in the outer hall, a commotion among the dogs, the noise of heavy boots and men's voices. Torches were being brought and servants were swarming. Lord Ivar had arrived.

He had brought with him the King's bailiff.

Grunting and wheezing, the bailiff lowered his great bulk into a high-backed chair by the fire. A manservant hurried to help him draw off his boots; another was quick to pour his wine.

We had been so lively and now the great hall seemed to fill with frost.

Lord Ivar stood in the doorway. A tall man, though not so tall as Kurt. He bore himself proudly, as was his right. I had not seen him since his mother's death; at sixty he had changed but little, though the thin, sandy hair was touched with white at the temples.

Born to great estate, my lord's face showed it. He had a noble brow; the high-bridged nose with flaring nostrils gave him a look of disdain. The ice-grey eyes were cold and distant; always when he spoke to me, he looked beyond me.

Yet his mouth was full and sensual. A sign of weakness? I never saw him display weakness. Nor did he readily show his feelings, unless of displeasure.

But tonight he was genial. He walked to my lady, and I saw the light go out of her eyes.

He cupped his hands under her breasts and bent to kiss the curve of them and the little hollow in her throat, and then he kissed her lips. "My sweeting, you are lovely. You are wearing the rubies. You did not wear them last time when the King was with us. They become you. Do not leave them off again when I bring guests."

I was watching Kurt. He stood stiff as a lance, and he was scowling.

Lord Ivar nodded to Kurt and produced a cold smile. "Welcome, cousin. If you had not come, I would have sent for you."

My lord went up then to put off his armour, silver-grey and beautiful, but mud-splattered; he had been a week on the road. He came down to us in britches and doublet of moss-green velvet, embroidered with gilt stitchery, a design of acorns and leaves. The sleeves were bordered with marten; his boots were of soft fawn leather, crushed at his ankles and buckled with lump topaz.

We went in to dine, but the meal was not a merry one. My lord kept mummers and dwarfs and men to make music in Stockholm, but none were here to beguile his guests. It was not a feast but a council meeting, though I had never seen such candlesticks or such plate, and we ate as I have seldom done, even when the Bishop visits the monastery. Course followed course. Venison, cream pasties, goose and liver tart; a whole suckling pig; comfits and gingered fruits; galantines and puddings. And many wines. We were midway through Lent, but Lord Ivar despised fish and ignored the Church fasts. I had no choice. I had eaten chicken last night with my lady, now I ate pork with my lord. But I had small appetite, watching the bailiff wolf his food.

The King's bailiff sat by Donna. She made an effort to smile.

This was Joachim Jensen, a piece of rancid pork if ever I saw one. He was grossly fat, his thick jowls were marked with pox; the small eyes gleamed with greed. He spoke with the heavy accent of the Danes, as if he had a mouthful of hot gruel and could not spit it out. But he did not speak much when food was before him. He gobbled and slurped and snuffled; grease dropped from his chin. They said when he was truly hungry he would not hesitate to slaughter a child and serve it up on a spit. So the people say of all bailiffs; these are the King's taxmen and his spies.

Kurt ate sparingly, he fingered his wine cup; he did not look at Donna. I thought she seemed dismayed.

And watching Kurt, I thought of a night when I had looked from the monastery porch and seen beneath me in the snow, in moonlight, a boarhound set upon by wolves. In the sharp blue light their eyes glowed like coals. At first, they were a pack of shadows skulking beneath the black pines, circling and snarling. Then they closed in.

Donna, I thought, Kurt has no time for you now; he is hard beset, like the boarhound; he is fighting for his life.

Kurt sat quiet and cool, and waited.

Lord Ivar said, "You were loud at Council meeting, Kurt. You were above yourself to speak as you did. The King was not pleased."

"I speak for myself. And others."

"You were not asked to do so. You are chosen from this district for council because you have the ear of the people. You are best suited to convey to them the wish of the King."

"He has, I am aware, no wish to hear their side."

"He has indeed no wish to hear what they think, if they think. Their minds are like frozen clods of mud."

"My lord——"

"We will not discuss it. It is clearly their duty to serve their King."

"In a war on foreign shores they must serve under a Danish King, and fight his wars in Holstein? Last time the King's men went round and beat our men—those who resisted. And shackled them like oxen, yoked together with iron chains. Drove them like oxen to Stockholm to take up the King's arms in Denmark."

"War is a bitter fact of life, Kurt. Like poverty. As fated as the wind in winter."

"I am well aware of it. I served six years in Holstein."

"Yes," said Lord Ivar. "And you know the needs of war. You know, Kurt, who served so ably. We need men. We need money. We need iron."

Kurt set down his wine cup. "If His Majesty wishes to take all three—men, and money, *and* iron—from our mountains, he must ask the Church for a miracle. When the best men, the young ones, are sent to fight a foreign war, who is left to work the mines? Only the old. Half blind, they've spent their lives in the dark channels of the earth. Half starved—can a man feed himself on a wage of five coppers? They are crippled from damp and cold, they work slowly."

"We pity them," said Lord Ivar smoothly. "But God has allotted to them their station in life. Do you question the will of God?"

"*Men* can do much to ease one another's burden."

"I repeat, Kurt. It is not your function to represent the people to the King. It is your duty to represent the King to the people."

Kurt's mouth was tight. He looked at the bailiff. "You are here to collect new taxes. Do not ask me to goad the people. Bread from our mouths we give, blood from our veins. But we cannot cut the hearts from our bodies."

The bailiff looked up from his venison and said tonelessly, "The money will be found." He returned to his food.

"Kurt," said Lord Ivar, "in Bavaria you studied hard. You became a master of mining, of engineering. A pity you also became a master of rhetoric. I do not wish to be burdened with this rhetoric. Nor does the King. You have wearied him with grievances. Do not vex him further. Or you may lose the place at court on which your ambition feeds and your pride depends."

"You may depend on it, Lord Ivar, I will bring these matters up again before the Council. Our poverty, our burden, the foreign war . . ."

"Enough, Kurt. We are willing to concede that if men are taken for war service, the mines cannot operate to full capacity. His Majesty has agreed. No men will be taken for six months. And you will apply yourself to what you know best—getting the ore out of the earth. We must double the yield. The forges must work night and day. A double shift of workers. You will hire more foremen. As incentive the wage will be increased. If a man made five coppers, he will now make nine for a day's work."

"I see," said Kurt. "On a wage of five coppers, they paid back two in taxes. On nine coppers a day . . . well, my lord bailiff?"

"On nine coppers, the men will pay four in taxes. They will benefit, we will benefit."

"Speak for yourself," said Kurt acidly. "And the Church will take its share. No. The men must have a living wage. I will bring the matter up again in Council. The men are denied the right to speak for themselves."

"Stones in a meadow should speak?" said the bailiff.

But Lord Ivar said, "I will bring the matter up. If it is necessary." He was growing impatient; his long fingers were tapping the table. "You will not appear at court for a while, Kurt. You are needed here. It is proposed to open the old mine. The men who will work in Hell Gate will receive double in wage."

"They have a choice?"

"Certainly." Lord Ivar was smiling. Not a pleasant smile.

"If they will not go down in Hell Gate, they may serve in Holstein. Put this to them, Kurt, in your best rhetoric."

Kurt was silent.

"I will excuse you now, Kurt. The bailiff and I have had a tiresome week. Day after day, riding in the cold; we spent three nights in an inn, a fleabag of an inn, and the bailiff had an attack of the stone. Last night at Ekelund, at the monastery, all night long the monks were chanting and droning psalms, worse than a pack of hounds after a bitch in heat. I have not seen my sweet wife for a week. I would take pleasure in her." Lord Ivar reached out to fondle my lady's hand.

Kurt rose and lifted his wine cup. "I have not congratulated you on your marriage. I beg leave to drink to your gracious lady." Then Donna took up her cup and drank to him. Their eyes met. The look was like an embrace.

My lord did not notice. I was grateful for that.

"I bid you good night, Kurt. Give thought to what can be done at Hell Gate."

"I have. I have gone down twice since the accident. Only into the first chamber, and a great fall of rock has blocked most of that. The wheel of the windlass sticks up out of the rubble. Across it, stretched as if on the torturer's wheel, there was the body of a man. So rotted I could not tell who it was. In the black, bloated face, I could see the teeth. The old channels are closed, deep in rubble; the water seeps in. The old supports lie deep in mud. Thirty or more men are under the rubble. The smell is foul. Hell Gate is a mass grave. Our men won't go down."

"Use your skill, Kurt. Clear the rubble, drain the water. The old bones must be brought up, a fine funeral arranged. If there are any relatives to attend. New supports . . . you know better than I what must be done. A challenge to any master of mining."

"As you say, my lord. A challenge. I submit that first the

priests must go down to say Mass. So many unblessed bodies. I will go with them. Perhaps some of the foremen. But your prestige, Lord Ivar, is far greater than mine can be. Will you go down with us? So may others be persuaded."

Lord Ivar paused for only a moment. Then he said, "Agreed." But I saw, in that moment of hesitation, that he was afraid.

There are men who bear with courage the stress of battle, who have no fear of a strong winter sea. Even of the plague. Yet they sweat with fear in the black tunnels of a mine, with the rock wall closing in over their heads, shutting out all daylight.

Lord Ivar was strong. I give him credit. He was afraid, but he took up the challenge.

He stood to bid Kurt good-bye. Kurt is like our mountains, I thought, a granite man, veined with iron. Lord Ivar is hard, of rigid self-control, a man of ice.

Ice can split granite.

And iron can crush ice.

Which would it be?

We would go at last to bed. But then one of Lord Ivar's men came to us, to say that a crowd had gathered outside the manor.

We went to the upper gallery; from the casements, we looked out. The air and the sky were grey with moonlight. A wisp of cloud drifted across the face of the moon. Below us we saw them standing in the snow, thirty or more men in heavy sheepskins, dark shapes, silent as sleeping beasts in a field. Some had torches. Behind them under the pines the horses waited, stamping the snow, but patient as the men. The night was windless, so still that the torches seemed frozen; single, steady flames. Grimed faces, dark beards, were touched by the light.

One of the horses whinnied; the sound seemed loud. Still the men were motionless, silent as stones.

"Their mood is not ugly," said my lord. "But this is trespass. I will go down to speak with them."

I went with him. We stood in the manor doorway. Lord Ivar called to the men. "Go to your homes, now, all of you. If any wish to speak with me, I will be free tomorrow. You may come in groups of two, or at most, three."

Some of the men shuffled their feet; two of them touched their foreheads in rude salute. Yet they stood there; none of them spoke.

Then behind us, the bailiff stood in the doorway. He was outlined against the light, his big fleshy frame and his head with the tow-white hair.

Suddenly from the men there was a cry—hoarse, rough, a roar of sound so savage it curdled the blood and chilled the marrow. Like the wolf cry in the night.

Then the sound faded; and sudden and swift as wolves the men made a rush for the horses. They were fleeting shadows under the pines and then they were gone.

Word had spread quickly among them that the bailiff was with us.

Certainly some of Kurt's men had ridden in my lord's wake, all through the week, to learn what they could of his plans and those of the bailiff.

And some of Kurt's men were there with the silent crowd in the snow.

And Kurt himself. I was sure of it. He was with them. He must have told them, "Show yourselves, but not with violence. The time is not ripe for that. Not yet."

Chapter 5

Lord Ivar had ordered a double watch, but we passed a quiet night. The morning was sunny. On the slope before the manor the snow was much trampled; my lord bade Donna stay within doors. By noon, no men had come to speak with him "in groups of two, or at most, three." He proposed to ride to the monastery to see the Abbot.

The bailiff went with him, and I should have gone but my lady begged me to stay. "Do not leave me. Good Jon, stay to help with Christer. My lord can tell the Abbot you are here, that you assist me in nursing the sick, a work of charity."

Lord Ivar agreed. He had gone in to see Christer, but he was a man who bore with great equanimity the misfortunes of others. And he had much else on his mind. Yet he was pleased that Donna engaged herself in good works instead of gaiety. "My sweeting, the country life is doing you good." He wished me to improve the time by reading aloud to Donna and found for us a well-thumbed parchment, the precepts of Saint Birgitta, an instruction for women to help them attain humility. The book had belonged to my lord's mother, who had much admired that adamant saint.

When my lord had gone, we went in to sit with Christer. In

body he was much restored; maids had dressed him that morning, but he had walked to the close-stool alone, though his legs gave him pain. And his left hand was stiff, the fingers worked as if on puppet strings. The right had been gloved when we found him, but the left hand bare.

He sat in a high-backed chair before the fire; he looked up as we came in, and I thought again how noble his face was, the high forehead and deep-set eyes, and the rare, sweet smile with which he greeted Donna.

He would have risen when she came in, but she told him to sit; she went to him and took his hand. And then his eyes clouded. We saw that his mind was clouded, too. For he said, "My little Duchess, how can I work when you constantly leave me? Will you sit a while? And smile. Smile as if there were kisses to come. I will not trouble you long, I am nearly done. When I am done—a little time only—I will give you immortality."

He spoke in Italian. I understood much of what he said, though not all. Church Latin had not prepared me for that. Nor for words so strange.

Then Christer looked at me with sadness in his eyes. "Ah, Beppo, six feet do not make a man. You have much to learn. Why do you pant after my little Duchess? She will have you once and then cast you off like yesterday's gown. Why not take a sweet-sour maid in the ditch? When you have done, you will know all you need to know of women, then you can get back to work."

"Yes," I said, to humour him, though the words were nonsense. And Donna spoke softly in Italian. And Christer was calmer—until Dame Agnes came. Then he was in a rage, cold, pained, his lip twitching. It is fortunate that she understood no single word of what he said. "*Let* the Duke plead. No. I will not do it. Not if I am banished. You do not in the least resemble the Blessed Saint Anne. There is greed in your eyes, and no compassion."

"He is much disturbed," said Donna. "I beg you, Dame Agnes, leave the room. He is ill; do not mind that he frets."

Dame Agnes left us, but sent in warm wine with a little physic, and Christer was quieted. He sat and stared at his hands, and at the wall, as I have seen men do in the alms-house prison.

We sat with him and I was dutiful. Since my lord had ordered it, I began to read aloud a homily of Saint Birgitta's.

We had ten minutes of it. Then Donna said, "Jon."

"Yes, my lady."

"I wish Saint Birgitta were here. Here in this room. Do you know why? Because if she were, I would stand before her and stick out my tongue." She puffed out her cheeks and stuck out a small pink tongue. I thought she looked delightful.

"You read very well, Jon. So do I. If I wished, which I most certainly do not, I would read Saint Birgitta for myself. I will not hear another word. I am suffocating. Saint Birgitta was a prig. I expect she looked like Dame Agnes. Like a bale of starched laundry. With a wart like a blob of lard upon her chin."

I may say that I fully agreed with her.

"Jon," she said, and her eyes glowed. "I am not to be shut in on such a day. The sun shines, the snow is sparkling. I will order the sleigh."

"But my lord said——"

"I do not care. He wishes me to be pious. Like his mother. I will go to church. We will take Christer to church, and give thanks to God for Christer's deliverance. An hour's ride in the snow, in the sun . . ."

"I would not go against my lord's wishes," I said doubtfully.

"You would go against mine?"

She knew I could not withstand her. She was so pretty and pleading, her cheeks very pink. "Do not worry, Jon. It is perfectly safe. We will take *four* outriders. And I will tell my lord that Saint Birgitta so inspired me to piety that I had to go to church to ask for strength in my new resolve."

"Yes?"

"Oh, yes, Jon. I wish to be more constant in devotion, like my lord's mother." And she pulled a long face, tucking in the corners of her mouth in mockery, but then she was laughing.

We were laughing in the sleigh. The day was golden; we rode beneath a shining sky, pale and blue as porcelain. On the snowcrust the sun struck sparks—blue, topaz; shards of ice lay beside the road, like piles of shattered crystal. Twig and bough and red winter berry were coated with rime; and the horses' hooves struck the snow-packed road with sharp, singing sounds.

Christer said nothing at all, he sat huddled in furs like a man in a trance; but Kari sang and Donna was laughing.

Yet when we reached the village chapel, my lady was very sober. I was at first surprised. For at court they pay little heed to Church observance, though the Queen is said to be religious. Yet Donna knelt, absorbed in prayer. She was earnest and sweet, devout as a child. Her mother had so taught her. I think of this now, think of her deep, abiding faith; and how it came to be that she was accused of unnatural practice, of devotion to the Black Mass, and all abominations.

We were alone in the chapel. It was quiet and dim under the low stone arches. The chapel is old and small with wooden crossbeams and bare plaster walls stained with damp. From the wall a harsh stone Christ looked down upon us. And Christer went to stand before him; there was, I think, in the back of his mind a stirring of blurred memory. He cried aloud in a strong voice, "Ah, God who made us, why must it be so?" Then he held up his useless hand and made a fist; there were tears in his eyes.

Then he was beating the plaster wall with his fist; he looked up at the dark little window and said, "Let there be light." He became, in fact, so disturbed that we took him out of the chapel.

In the sleigh he was calmer; though he said again, in a voice of infinite sadness, "Ah, God who made us, why must it be so?"

We came to the crossroad; there is the wayside shrine. A wooden Saint Francis stands beneath a small sheltering roof and holds out his hands to all who pass by; at the foot of the statue there are small birds carved in wood. Few men stop at the shrine, but birds do; they flutter down to perch on the head and arms of the gentle saint. The shrine is open to all weathers; and now the roof was broken by the weight of winter snows; the figure was chipped and scarred by wind and storm.

Monks were at work repairing the shrine; they had colours and brushes and plaster. Poor Saint Francis, he has a hard time in winter. Ice breaks his nose, the paint melts and freezes on his robes, his gown is stained. He is patient, though boys throw snowballs at him. The niche behind him was painted with sky and stars and a barren hillside, and this was much defaced.

We stopped to speak with the monks, two of them from the monastery. And suddenly Christer was wild. He was muttering, clutching his head in his hands. We thought he needed to relieve himself, we helped him down from the sleigh. But he did not go to make water. He went to Saint Francis and took up a paintbrush, cast it away and took another, and a pot of azure.

He began to paint, with the most delicate strokes, very swift and sure, his hand moving as if it were not part of himself. We stared at him. He drew on the azure background a shower of radiant stars; and two small angels with sweet, chubby faces. Under his brush the hillside took form and distance; then it was wooded with trees, some dark and some of palest green. It was beautiful. And he turned to one of the

monks and said sternly, "Where is the gold? Where is Pietro
. . . Aldo . . . all of them? A pox on all apprentices! I keep a
sty of rutting pigs. The gold is not ground, the siena must be
crushed; who has mixed the sizing and the glair? Rutting
pigs, all of you, always off to carnival."

He gave a wild, guttural cry and sank to his knees in the
snow. His head dropped into his hands.

Donna went to him and took his hand with great gentleness. She spoke as a mother might speak to a child. He clung
to her as a child would and allowed her to lead him back to
the sleigh. He slept heavily in the sleigh and could scarcely
be roused when we reached the manor.

We helped him to bed; he slept for an hour. When he
woke, Donna was sitting close by. *"Molto bene,"* he said,
smiling. "You will sit now, my Duchess?" And now she knew
what he wanted.

He took from the hearth a piece of charred wood. The
parchment of Saint Birgitta lay on a chair; the cover page
was blank, and he ripped it off.

He arranged Donna, her hair falling as he would have it;
then he cupped her face in his hands, touching her gently,
the curve of her cheek and the brow, as if he felt through his
stroking fingers the shape of her face. We saw that he had
been a sculptor as well as a painter. Then he sketched my
lady with quick strokes. With a very few lines he caught her,
a magical likeness, all the sweetness and depth of her eyes
. . . and the question in them.

In the morning Donna sent to the monastery where there
is a workshop and men constantly labour to illuminate the
books which are the Abbot's joy. Pots of colour, brushes, palette knives, a smoothing tool of amber, linen and parchment
and ground glue were sent to us.

A small boy from the manor brought all this. His name was
Hans, but Christer said, frowning, "Guido, you are very
naughty. You have not sized the canvas, you have not ground

the umber; you have run all day in the orchard and eaten so many apples that now you groan with colic, grunting like a small pig. Yesterday when I called, you were climbing the bell tower. Today when you came at last with the almond cakes, as Madonna Ginevra sat for her portrait, you had a toad in your pocket. Ah, I despair of young apprentices."

Small Hans stared at him, mouth agape. The lad had never seen a bell tower or an almond cake. The orchard at the manor was drifted deep in snow.

Christer turned to me. "Beppo," he said sadly.

"No," said Donna, firmly. "Not Beppo. He is Jon."

"Ah, yes," said Christer. "Jon, the beloved disciple." And he looked upon me with affection. But then he said severely, "Beppo, you abuse your gift. Well, Madonna Beatrice is pleased, perhaps with the portrait, but most certainly with you. But, Beppo, the crimson is too deep. Madonna Beatrice is of Venice, in the red of Venice there is much gold. And the folds of the gown. You are painting stiff folds, but they must be all softness, like her body beneath them. *You* should know! Green for the background, dark for the cypresses, dark as sin. And a gold wash, for the golden mist of Venice. You paint the brow well. The mouth, a mouth pursed for songs and kisses, you surpass there. But the eyes, Madonna Beatrice has wide-set eyes, green as the waters of Venice, and they have evil in them, they breed lust in men as the waters of Venice breed fever. Do you see? Go now, my Beppo, off with the others to carnival and eat too many comfits and go a-whoring. Come tomorrow with a bellyache and empty pockets. Then you will start again with the eyes."

So we began to guess at his past, though he never told of it, except in this way. He did not remember it. If we questioned him directly, his eyes would cloud. It was only when he spoke as in a dream that we could picture the world he must have lived in—a great city, a great workshop, with many young painters apprenticed, and artisans working in marble and jewels and gold. A world of saints' days and royal processions; of mummery shows and feasts of the guilds. A world of much talk, in a ducal garden or in a wayside inn; great talk of war and politics; of art and poetry; and the passions and frailties of mankind.

Of the passions and frailties of mankind, I believe Christer knew much.

We learned where he had worked. For Christer spoke of Giotto. "It is a masterwork, the bell tower." He spoke of brown hillsides, misted with green and drifted with almond blossoms in spring; of iris, blue spears broken on the banks of a brown, swollen river. "The Arno rises, the square will be awash, for the great procession for the Cardinal. What of the fireworks, now that it eternally rains?"

Of companions in the workshop. A girl of the streets named Angelina. "That gutter slut *exists* because I have painted her. A lying, whoring wench, rotten with French pox. Let her lie with others. In scorning the portrait she has scorned all I know of truth and beauty. Let her wither. I have forbidden her the workshop."

Of other companions. "Arezzi will come to sing today, as the little Duchess sits. And I have bought a goldfinch. If he sits on her finger and sings, perhaps I will coax from her the ghost of a smile."

Of the Cardinal. "Tell His Eminence I am glad he likes the Madonna. He has sent me a wonderful jewel, yet the true joy lies in this, that for him I have done my best."

But Christer spoke most often of the Duke, his patron.

And we thought of the parchment, stained and water-torn, found on the ice of the inlet, where Christer himself was found. The great waxen seals stamped with a coronet.

And Donna repeated the words on the crumpled parchment: " 'Christer . . . Magister . . . Medici . . .' Now we know. Christer *is* a master. He has lived in Florence and worked for the Medici."

And even I had heard of them, the strong lords of Florence, of their power and their wealth beyond imagining.

It was decided that I should stay on at the manor, for so my lady would have it. Lord Ivar agreed. He was much abroad at this time; he would ride to Falun or Arboga, with the bailiff, on business for the King. It had surprised him that Donna did not long for Stockholm, for the gay life at court.

She said demurely, "I would grow in humility, my lord, as you would have me. Jon will instruct me."

"My lady," I said, "surely you have been instructed by wiser men than I. I am only a lay brother."

"I was instructed by a bishop. A wise man, but very worldly." And Donna gave to my lord a brilliant smile. "I have thought much of this since the night when we sat by Christer, when he lay as one dead. I am remiss, an undutiful wife. I am of stubborn temper and willful thought."

My lord looked fondly at her. And I said, "I cannot advise on women's behaviour, my lady. A beguiling subject, but I know little of women."

"Then, Jon, we will teach each other. Many things."

Yet it was Christer who taught us all, much of beauty and aspiration. Much of truth. His mind remained blurred; he did not recall why he had come back to Sweden. Or much of his past. But he spoke more often in Swedish now, and often words of the Church. He had worked much, I think, in cloisters and great churches; he had heard these words; they lay at the bottom of his mind like jewels at the bottom of a well. He must have spent hours on high scaffoldings, at work on a ceiling, perhaps modeling in gilt or gesso; or painting an altarpiece, while below him monks were chanting.

To each of us he gave words like firebrands, so that our hearts burned within us. To Donna, the strong message was of love, that this was the great star to be followed though it bring pain, though it lead at last into the valley of the shadow.

Once Christer said quietly, " 'I am come that they might have life, and that they might have it more abundantly.' "

And so it was for me. I saw what life could be outside the iron bonds of the Church as we knew it. And I too learned that love is the shining star, though I could not foresee where it would lead me at last, on what dark road I would travel.

For Kurt, the message was different. He learned how to hate.

Chapter 6

We had not seen Kurt since the night when the village men stood outside the manor in the snow, to cry their rage at the bailiff.

But my lady thought often of Kurt. I knew this, for her mouth would look, as Christer would say, "pursed for songs and kisses." And her eyes were soft then and very deep. When we rode abroad in the sleigh, then Donna seemed always to be listening. Listening for the sound of hoofbeats, the sound of a horseman on the road who might be Kurt.

And Kurt was in the neighbourhood . . . or some of his men. The bailiff was now abroad with Lord Ivar; they had ridden north to Falun. But three of the bailiff's men stayed on with us, though they did not come to the manor. In the upper pasture they were housed in the old summer kitchen, rough-built of pine logs but spacious and warm. There were small outbuildings, a larder and a buttery where the bailiff's men worked on tax accounts. And a stable for their horses. The bailiff and his men were always well mounted.

One cold morning we woke and saw on the white dawn sky the dark smudge of smoke. The strong smell of charred wood was in the air, the acrid smell of burning hay and manure. In the upper pasture the loghouse and the stable were afire.

My lady thought not of the bailiff's men but of the horses. Always she loved horses. "Come, Jon!" She was breathless, pulling the furred hood over her hair. She ran ahead of me down the trodden path in the snow and stopped at the pasture bars where drifted snow lay deep. The horses had been let out; they raced and reared in the pasture, snorting with fear.

"They are safe, the beauties," said Donna.

Since dawn men from the manor had laboured, piling snow against the walls of the loghouse. In the chill air they were sweating; their eyes streamed and their faces were black with smoke. The smoke was thick and odourous; drifts of it blew toward us in the sharp wind. And a wave of heat beat toward us from the loghouse; we could go no closer.

But two of the farm lads drenched their leather jackets with water; they pulled soaked hoods over their heads and crept into the buttery. This had not yet taken fire, though smoke curled beneath the doorsill. They forced the door; a rank cloud of smoke surged through it and settled, staining the snow with charred particles.

Within they found the bodies. All three of the bailiff's men were dead.

Smoke and flame had not killed them. They had been strangled. Around the neck of each was a noose, knotted of bridle straps.

And behind the buttery a stuffed image lay in the snow. The bailiff's velvet cloak had been packed with manure and straw and smeared with tar.

"It is horrible," said Donna; her mouth was trembling.

"Come away," I said. "There is nothing to be done."

And our men abandoned the loghouse. We heard a thud and crash within it as part of the roof fell, and part of the chimney breast. The men were seeking to round up the horses. They would bring sledges down and load the bodies and take them to the almshouse.

We climbed the snowy hill to the manor, to the morning meal.

Donna ate almost nothing, she drank a little wine. Her small face was much troubled.

And I was troubled, but kept it from her. I sought to distract her. I told her of the time at the monastery when two young lay brothers had been much plagued by an old monk who declared that devils would come in the night to claim their souls if they did not amend their slovenly ways and attend to piety.

"The old man slept in a small stone cell at the far end of the cloister. He would pore over parchments late into the night, bending over his book with a single rushlight. He would mouth aloud the words of Saint Jerome. As shadows moved on the walls of the cell, he would mutter and cross himself countless times. So the two young brothers——"

"You were one," said Donna, beginning to smile.

"I confess it. We set a brazier outside the cell beneath the small barred window. We packed the brazier with rank herbs, a witches' brew. And set it alight. Such smoke, such a stench. The old monk took fright and howled that Hell itself had opened, that devils were coming to claim him."

My lady looked at me. "For shame, Jon." But I saw the little dimple.

But then her sweet face grew sober. "A prankish trick, Jon. But this morning as the loghouse burned . . . The bodies in the snow . . . I have thought much of what Kurt told us, the night he came to sup with us. Of men in the mines beaten to labour and half starved. Of cruel want in the village. I think of the men I saw in the village inn. Brutish as beasts. That night as they stood in the snow outside the manor, they were patient as beasts. Until the bailiff showed himself. It puts me in mind of the King's chamberlain."

"I do not see——"

"At court he kept a great Welsh mastiff, huge, strong as a lion. But gentle. He would train it for the wolf hunt. Teach it to endure cruel hurt in the hunt, to hang from the wolf's neck, to cling even when clawed. I have seen him beat the dog with a barbed whip till its neck streamed with blood. And one day it turned upon him, savage as a lion. His men beat it off; it was destroyed. But he bears the scars on his arm; he will never regain the use of his hand."

"Yes. But men are not beasts, my lady."

"But men will turn against their masters. Even in Stockholm I have seen such anger. I rode out with the Queen one day, but a great crowd gathered. From shop and hovel and inn they streamed out upon the streets, like herrings poured from a barrel. Marching and shouting. They had Danish flags, they burned these in the square before the palace. The King sent armed men among them to ride them down, but many fought back with knives and clubs, even with cobblestones. Of course, they were dispersed. But the King forbade us to ride out for near a week."

Near sundown Lord Ivar rode into the manor courtyard. He had left the bailiff in Falun, and that was as well.

I will not forget his rage. A righteous wrath, I admit it. But I had not seen him before in one of his winter moods, silent, icy, bitter as winter chill.

He sent men to the village to make inquiry, but this was fruitless.

And I kept my counsel. Soon after noon I had gone down to the pasture. It was deserted, the fire in the loghouse had burnt out. But I could not enter the building; the heat was still in it.

Even in the buttery so strong was the stench of smoke and manure that my eyes burned. The small room looked as if a pack of hounds had raced through it. Oaken table overturned, stools smashed or tipping on splintered legs. And the floor littered with parchment, with tax rolls. These were ripped, defaced with ink, smeared with manure.

I found near the hearth a single gauntlet. Of rough black leather, the cuff worked with an inlay of calfskin. A small design of oak leaves.

The oak leaf was Kurt's badge. At Kurt's manor, most of his men wore it on breastplate, or cap or tunic.

Kurt's men had been here, but not Kurt. I thought not. The gauntlet was rough, the design in crude stitchery. Kurt's gauntlets were sewn with skill in Stockholm.

And he would countenance no violence. As yet.

But among his men there were rough men of the road. Men of the mines and the forest.

And others. I counted myself among them.

I took the glove and an iron poker from the hearth. A little stream runs through the pasture. It was hard frozen; I cracked the ice loose with the poker. In the frozen mud of the stream bed I left the gauntlet. And piled shards of ice upon it.

I said nothing of this to Donna. Or to my lord. He left us in the morning to join the bailiff in Falun, to be gone for some days. He commanded that Donna stay close within the manor; he forbade her to ride even to the Abbot.

.

Chapter 7

She was content, for now she was much occupied with Christer. He spent the day sketching and painting, and Donna would sit for him hour after hour until the light faded. The solar was his workroom; there he had the last, late rays of the sun.

He was still weak in body. The great dark eyes seemed sunken in the pale, gentle face. He would sit and move the stiffened fingers of his left hand; there was a sadness about him then, a stillness.

Yet when he was painting, power seemed to flow from him. An aura almost visible, like the radiance which flows from the halo of a saint.

My lord was ever uneasy with Christer, and at times out of patience with him. We sat with him at table one day and Dame Agnes came in to us in her square robes, her square headdress. It was as if a tombstone approached us.

Christer looked sourly at her and turned to my lord. "I cannot express my gratitude, Your Grace, at the suggestion. I am honoured. But I cannot wed her." He frowned at Dame Agnes. "I cannot wed her even if she is noble, greatly dowered, and your cousin. I have my work to do."

My lord stared at him.

"A further objection." Christer fingered his wine cup. "It is chiefly a matter of proportion. Her shoulders, her forehead, her chin. I would as soon bed with a gelded bull."

My lord found these lapses disturbing, but bore with them for he saw the wonder of Christer's work, the power of it. He decided to adorn the village chapel in memory of his mother. Christer would do a large altarpiece, a Crucifixion, and side panels with scenes from the life of the Blessed Virgin. Donna was posed as the Madonna.

Men were sent to scrape and smooth the chapel walls. These are of stained plaster heavy with whitewash, coated with it after the Black Death some years ago among us. Crude lime wash is thought to conquer the contagion.

Lord Ivar wished the paintings to be done "in richest colours." No expense would be spared. Hampers of materials were sent from Stockholm. But Christer liked to compound his own colours and I became his apprentice, though I never touched brush to canvas. But I was quick at grinding and mixing the pigments. And whipping white of egg to bind the colours, though Christer sometimes said to me, "Impossible. You whip the egg too thin. This is posset, pap for babes. This is not glair; a proper glair must be thick, or it will not fix the pigment."

We would work for hours undisturbed. The manor folk came into the solar seldom; they served Christer with ill grace. They were frightened of him, of his dark, disturbed moods. And his devil's tongue—they called it so when he muttered in Italian.

They need not have feared him. He was the most gentle of men, though he could be silent and scornful. When one of the lads at the manor aped him, his strange speech and his manner, Christer made of the child a large sketch, the fat face swinish and distorted, but very like; and the body was that of a suckling piglet, small hooves, fat haunches and belly, and curling tail.

So much that Christer said was strange. One day we sat in the solar with him; my lord came in to us, seeking my lady.

My lord had with him an Italian, a Papal emissary, with us for a few days to discuss the price of indulgences. As always the tithes to Rome would be increased. A further burden upon us.

The Italian was from Pisa; he spoke with oily courtesy to my lady, but he was chill of humour and scornful of those beneath him.

Christer was painting but put down his brush. He looked at the Pisan, at the sweep of his green robes faced with scarlet, the heaviness of his gold rings. And at the dour face; the man had a habit of sucking in his cheeks; his eyes were black and lusterless.

Something stirred in Christer's shadowed mind. He said, "It is a bitter face, Roberto, because of evil within you. Why do you keep such an inn? You snatch thrice the lawful wage from men who starve their children to buy the rancid vinegar you sell as wine. And your slattern daughters—you would sell them for an hour's service to a rutting goat, if men paid you to witness so foul an act. Why are you ever impelled to evil, does the blood of the basilisk run in your veins?"

My lord said angrily, "Come, Christer, no further word is necessary. Devote yourself to your work."

Christer picked up his brush. And that evening at table with my lord and the Pisan, he was rational as most men, talking of Holy Week in Rome and the great processional; of the gardens at Castle Sant' Angelo; and a dolphin fountain commissioned by His Holiness.

The Pisan made an effort at courtesy. He turned to Christer. "You were many years in Italy? And had the supreme honour to serve His Holiness? I marvel that you would relinquish a post of such esteem. What occasioned your return to Sweden?"

Christer's eyes grew dark. And beseeching. It was always so when he was questioned directly about his past. He stared into his wine cup as if he sought in it an answer. Then he brushed his hand across his eyes and began to mutter about "the powers and principalities of darkness."

Behind him two of the serving maids were whispering. Often the manor folk talked among themselves of Christer. When Christer spoke words of the Bible, often as in a trance, they said, "He is possessed. Even the Devil quotes Scripture." They thought his wonderful gift was of the Devil, so magical was his painting. And so they say too of men who make music, that only Satan can guide the nimble fingers of the fiddler. So grim is our life and so harsh our Church, we cannot imagine that beauty comes from God.

When Donna had sat for him some hours, Christer would release her, though he would work on. He scarcely knew of time passing.

And Donna and I would wrap ourselves warmly and run out into the snow. "Like children," said Donna, "though I am full-grown and married, and you are so tall and sober, Jon, in your monk's cloak."

I took joy from her joy. Always she loved the snow. She would shake a pine bough, heavily laden with snow, and watch the shower of bright crystals falling. She would stamp childishly where thin ice glazed the ruts in the road and laugh when the ice crackled. By the stream, still ice-bound, we found the first yellow tassels on the hazel, and Donna picked a handful for Christer. Laughing with her, watching her, I thought her face was like a Christmas rose.

We followed a frosty track out of the forest one evening as the sun was setting; there was red-gold light on the snow-crust, and there running beside us was a little fox. A little vixen, lifting her paws so lightly, her brush waving as if she were dancing. And her eyes were dark and aslant, like those of an Eastern mummer at the fair.

Donna was enchanted. "A fairy world, the winter forest. The little foxes are less than men, and more than human."

Then we heard a fox barking, a silver sound, fluting, yet mellow and wild. We saw the male on the hillside; the little vixen ran to join him.

"So quick, so free," said Donna, and her eyes were wistful.

"Yes," I said, "and once you have seen this, the little vixen passing close, paws so light upon the snow, you have always the mark of the country upon your heart."

"I have it now," said Donna. "I am grateful to you, Jon. My friend."

But I wondered if she were thinking of Kurt.

When we reached the manor, Kurt was there with Peter, his young squire. They stayed to sup, though Lord Ivar was absent. At the meal we were merry, though Peter did not play the fiddle; he had burnt his hand. A slight wound and healing, I looked at it. But I thought of the night of the burning, and the murder of the bailiff's men. The loghouse in the pasture was now a charred ruin in the trampled snow.

After the meal Peter went down to the kitchens with Kari, the little maid he loved. Hand in hand they left us, whispering together as young folk do.

In the solar Donna sat for Christer again; she was quiet, holding the pose. She sat before the fire in a high-backed chair, like a young saint in a carved wooden niche. Christer arranged her so that firelight would glow on the folds of her gown, and candle gleam gilded her dark hair. He wanted, he said, a radiance about her. And she *was* radiant, listening to Kurt.

We talked before Donna as if she were one of us.

Kurt said, "I have been to the Bishop of Lindhagen to see if sin could be made a little cheaper."

"What do you mean?" asked Donna, leaning forward.

"*Ma Donna,*" said Christer, "*per favore . . .*" And Donna sat back again in her pose.

And Kurt said, "My lady, men will sin, and I am first among them. We go to the Church for pardons, at a price. The price of remission of sin goes up. Though the sins remain the same, there are no new ones."

Christer said sadly, "Must God's love be bought? Ah, God who made us, why must it be so?" But then he seemed to forget us; he was touching the portrait of Donna with gold.

"The Church will squeeze out its share," I said, "though men starve."

And Kurt said, "If the money went to the poor box . . . But the money goes to Rome. Or into the Bishop's pockets. The bailiff howls for new taxes. To pad *his* pockets. Where will our men find the money?"

"Fat new wages," I said sourly, "for men who will work in Hell Gate mine."

"Not a man will work. I have talked to many."

"The mine can never be worked again," I said. And I felt so, for I had been down into the first chamber with Kurt, since the accident.

But Kurt said, "Perhaps, Jon. Not from the old shaft. But farther along in the vein. I have ridden on the surface, watching the way the rocks lie, the vein of iron in them, the stain of ore upon the earth crust. I followed the stream where it wells up from underground and the water runs red with rust. Beyond this, if we strike a shaft down . . . But it will take time. More time than the King allows. We may strike blind channels at first. And the men are fearful."

"If the mine is blessed . . ." I said doubtfully.

"That must be soon. A spring thaw will melt the ice in the old surface chambers. The mine will flood." Kurt got up to stride restlessly back and forth. "Ah, Jon, I agree. Hell Gate will not be opened again. Yet my lord, my cousin, will not agree. Unless he sees for himself how it is."

"He is due back within the week."

"Then God send winter weather until my lord comes. Strong winter cold, to bind the ice in the mine chambers. And we will take my lord down into Hell, with bell, book, and candle. Ah, God, does he know what he asks? Money spent on Hell Gate is lost. Let the King spend it on the other mines. New wheels, new ropes, new supports. The men work always in danger. 'If the men mutter, speak with them,' says my lord. I'd urge him to a little charity. Food for empty bellies, balm for winter sores."

Of a sudden Christer put down his brush. His eyes were remote. He said, as if in a dream, " 'Though I speak with the tongues of men and angels and have not charity, I am nothing worth.' " Then he took up his brush.

"I have small knowledge of Holy Writ," said Kurt, "yet this I know: there is 'a time for silence and a time for speech. A time for love, and a time to die.' I see men around me marked for death. In the mines, in the foreign war, by pestilence and starvation. It is past the time for silence. Past the time for speech. It is time to die—in our *own* cause. A man should have the right to choose what use is made of his body. A right to the death of his *own* choice."

"Ah, Kurt," I said, "what man can choose? A man can die in a great bed hung with velvet and fur, with a butt of malmsey and a haunch of venison beside him; and a soft little wife like a feather pillow to warm him. Yet he grows cold."

I poured more wine and Kurt took his goblet to sit by the fire. He was staring into the heart of the leaping flame. And now and then looking at my lady.

And at the portrait. Donna was shown as the young Virgin to whom the angel came at the time of the Blessed Annunciation. In the picture my lady looked up in wonder, her eyes dark and shining. In her sweet face there was stillness, too, as if she knew that such great joy would be hers . . . followed by such great sorrow. And there *was* a radiance about her—the sheen of light on her blue cloak, a misting of gold on her cheek and her hair. Her hands were clasped in her lap, loosely, holding a golden lily; Christer had brushed this in, and behind my lady a deep sky full of darkness . . . yet there were stars.

Peter came to tell us it was late. Did Kurt want the horses brought up?

Then Peter stood before the portrait. And sang the little verse we hear at Christmastide, of the Holy Birth:

> "Witte hath wonder that reason no telle can;
> How maiden is moder and God is man.
> Leave thy reason and believe in the wonder.
> For faith is aboven, and reason is under."

Then Christer smiled and said, "Believe in the wonder."

But Kurt said, "Reason. This above all. The depth, the truth, the power of a man's mind. I believe in this."

Donna said softly, "I believe in the wonder."

She rose to bid Kurt good night. "You will come again?"

He took both her hands in his. "Soon. I must come. To see your husband. And to look at you."

On the following day Christer worked on a new painting; he was sketching on parchment the grouping of figures for the Holy Birth. He did not require my lady to sit for him; and she was restless.

A day of leaden sky, but the wind was still. Snow fell softly, whispering against the casements. Toward sundown the sky cleared, but the cold seemed sharper than ever. We walked a way down the long drive; my eyes smarted with cold, but my lady seemed not to feel it.

Wading through fresh drifts, she held my arm. I felt my heart pound in my throat at her closeness. In the gathering dark, we made our way back to the manor. The deep sky seemed to tremble with light, so thick were the stars.

We had an hour before the evening meal. Donna ordered tawny port brought up from the cellars and a rare Burgundy. And she dressed herself with care; I knew she hoped that Kurt would come.

She stood before the casement in the great hall, a slight figure, full of grace in a sweeping gown of crimson samite, dark as my lord's rubies. But she did not wear them. She wore pearls which seemed to take faint colour from the firelight; and the sleeves of the gown were slashed with white and gold brocade.

Standing before the casement, she was thoughtful. She put her hand against the dark leaded panes, feeling the chill behind them. They were crusted with hoarfrost, thick and glistening.

For a moment the frost was rose and gold, like a shower of sparks, as below us in the snow my lord's men moved about with torches and light struck the glass.

"A winter garden, Jon. The heavy rime upon the window. Like a garden enchanted and turned to crystal. Crystal fronds of fern, bell flower, wind flower, tiny twig and branch, so delicate. Or like gardens under the sea—my mother told me of those. She had corals, many of them, from Italy; as a child I loved them. She told me of the Italian coast, of the slow blue wash of the waves and, beneath them, sunken gardens, with waving sea grass and branched corals. A menace, too, of strange fishes. Perhaps the mermaid swims through such a world, thrusting her tail, all shining scales, to ward off monstrous fishes."

She smiled at her own fancy, and I smiled with her.

But then she said, "Deep undersea, so many fathoms down, a strange cold world. Cruel as the cold is. And as my

lord at times. Well, no matter. So we live, in our world." Her
small face was wistful. "Heaven is kinder, so the priests say.
Do you say so, Jon?"

"Earth is beautiful." And so I felt with her beside me.

She stood quietly, with clasped hands. A gusty wind tore at
the tall oaks beyond the casement. Her eyes were very deep.

"Do you long for Stockholm, my lady?"

"No. No, Jon. I am thinking of . . . of many things."

"Of Kurt."

"Of what he says. 'It is time to die. In our own cause.' If he
makes it his cause to defend men of the mines, men in need
and misery who cannot speak for themselves, I see reason in
it."

"And I."

"My lord does not. Such men are no more than brutes, he
feels. God has ordained their station in life. They require no
voice in government. They are not fit to rule themselves;
their betters must rule them. So says my lord."

I felt anger rise in me like sudden flame. "Is a man to have
no voice when he lives in hunger and oppression? No right to
protest the cruel burden of taxes? No right to anger when
taken in chains and sent to fight a war to support the King's
pride and further his greed?" Then I checked myself; but my
hands were fists.

Donna put a hand upon my arm. "Jon, my world is chang-
ing. At court I thought little of such things. But now . . ."
Her smile was wistful. "Now I am like the mermaid, swim-
ming in strange waters. So much to doubt, to question.
When Kurt speaks, when you do, I think of much that did
not trouble me before."

She sat on the broad window seat, her crimson skirt
spreading around her. "My lord says such talk is trea-
sonous—when men of the mines, of forest and field, dare to
question the ordinance of the Council, the will of the King.
When men marched in the streets in Stockholm, protesting

the foreign war, burning the Danish flag, my lord was furious. It is treason, he said, against the divine right of monarchy. But I . . ."

"You did not feel so, my lady?"

"I have known no life but court life. There my allegiance should lie. With the King. Yet as we stood in the palace gallery, watching the mob in the courtyard, men trampled by the King's men-at-arms, men beaten and taken in chains, my heart was with them. I saw such faces . . . I felt such pity."

"A Christian virtue, my lady."

"My lord said it was weakness in me, to allow such thoughts. Recall, he said, your station in life; consider that these men rebel against your King. By ancient custom, by rightful law, it is the duty of men to honour the King, to abide by his ordinance, to serve him. I felt so before. Now . . ." Donna's hands were knotting in her lap. "I would not anger my husband; I would be obedient. But I cannot command my thoughts. To feel pity, to share the burden of others, to temper their misery and grief—is not this our Christian duty?"

"Yes, my lady."

"So it cannot be disloyal to my husband to feel . . . to feel that Kurt has reason in what he says."

She went to stand by the fire, lifting her hands toward it as if she were cold. "It seems so long ago, Jon, that I thought only of dancing, of dresses, and silken ribbons for my hair."

There was the sound of horsemen then in the courtyard; Kari came to tell us that the Abbot had come.

My lady smiled, though she had hoped to see Kurt. She was fond of the Abbot, and he of her. He came often to the manor to see her.

And to see Christer . . . in the beginning because in the village folk said that a man had died of exposure and cold, and now lived, returned from the dead.

But the Abbot said, "We will not see resurrection in our

time. Only crucifixion. Among us Christ is crucified anew every day."

The evening stays in my mind, for afterward there was no stopping the talk about Christer—that he leagued himself with the powers of darkness, that a devil dwelt within him.

Christer was still weak, and his mind forever shadowed. Yet with the Abbot he was often lucid, for they spoke of art.

The Abbot loved art above all things, perhaps even above the service of God. The monastery is famed for its manuscripts, some of great age, some the work of our own scriptorium. No other in Sweden produces such illuminations; the parchment pages glow with azure and dragonsblood, with verdigris and gold.

The Abbot had given of his own fortune to further the work. He was born to great wealth and privilege, though he chose to forsake worldly estate and serve the Church.

"I am happy," he said, "in the life of contemplation. I have seen the world. And seen little in it to console me as my books console me. Besides," and the small smile was gentle and ironic, "an Abbot is safe from the tribulation of marriage."

He came into the hall; Kari took his cloak; she knelt to brush the snow from the hem of his gown. He put a hand in blessing upon her head, upon the waves of sun-gold hair.

The Abbot was thin and grey and stooped; his eyes were weak from poring over parchments. He was careless of his monk's habit; it was often shabby. Yet in him there was a great power of intellectual faculty. And much compassion.

He stood before the fire, warming his withered hands and rubbing his cheeks; on them the faint tracery of veins was visible. "I am parched and near frozen. Ah, the frailty of mortal flesh. I have spent the day in Lindhagen enduring a very jeremiad of complaints from the Bishop. And would have spent the night if my reverend lord of Lindhagen had his will. But I would be back at the monastery before the hour of

Compline for the blessing of the sick. Many lie ill; not a cot remains empty in the infirmary. Two young monks, mendicants, stopped with us for the night not long ago. They bestowed upon us no coppers for the poor box. Only a plague of coughing and rheum of the nostrils. Ah, pestilence, like the poor, is always with us."

He turned to smile upon my lady; she urged him to stay and sup.

"I cannot. An Abbot must resist temptation be it ever so strong." But he stopped for an hour to sit before the fire; maids came in to us with spiced wine and yellow winter apples, though these were somewhat wrinkled and juiceless.

Christer came in to sit with us. In firelight his face was darkly shadowed; his eyes were remote. Absently he picked up his wine cup. And set it down. He was with us in body, but not in spirit.

Serving men built up the fire. And a maid threw upon it a handful of herbs of sweet savour—lavender, rosemary, fennel. Snow was falling again beyond the casement, and the wind mourned. But in the great hall there was the scent of summer, of hayfield and blossoming meadow.

The fire snapped and flared, taking a multitude of colours from the crisp, burning herbs.

Christer stared into the flames. In them he must have seen strange shapes. "I begged them to have no part in the venture. But you know what it is with young apprentices. In the end I went with them to see that they suffered no hurt. Well, I confess, I was curious. The Sicilian had a great reputation. There was much talk of him in Florence. It was said that he could call up such a multitude of demons, Lucifer and his dark minions, the citizens of Hell. The sorcerer could command these fiends to serve him; and one could ask of them to reveal the future, or the whereabouts of a missing goldpiece, or whether a lost love would be found."

My lady gazed at Christer; her eyes were enormous. The Abbot leaned foward with interest.

On the hearth the great fire crackled and sputtered; a streamer of glowing sparks arose from it; the scent of the burning herbs was strong and pungent.

Christer took up his wine cup. "It was close on to midnight; my boys and I were armed. I with a fine short blade of my own making, the boys each with stiletto. We went to the sandy stretch along the Arno below the Ponte Vecchio. The place was deserted at such an hour. The strong smell of the river came to us, fetid as the dark river which flows through Hell. A night of fitful moonlight, of scudding cloud, a whispering in the pines. Ah, to paint it . . . The wind bent the oaks and the leaves were dark, yet seemed to take flame from our torches; the boughs were tossing as if unearthly spirits rode them."

"The sorcerer was there?" My lady's hands were tightly clasped in her lap.

"The sorcerer was there, with two others. One dark of brow, a big man, grizzled and hairy. The other slight, wrapped in a dark cloak, the hood drawn closely about the face. And a young boy with them who served them. The sorcerer said the spell would not be productive unless he had with him a boy not yet beguiled by passion, a virgin boy still innocent. And I believe the lad was so—he had a small piping voice. But the Sicilian . . . in his face was a crafty evil. He built up a fire of olive wood; the wind whipped it to quick flame, and sparks rose in the smoke. I could see in the smoke . . ."

"Yes?" said my lady, breathless.

"In clouds, in moving water, in curling smoke, always I see . . ." Christer brushed a hand over his eyes. "The sorcerer spoke the incantation in Hebrew, in Latin, in strange tongues. Then he threw herbs upon the fire, assafetida, others, very rank; the stench of Hell arose. Suddenly one of my boys cried out, '*Aiuto!* I am attacked! They crawl upon me, dark winged things, monsters with scales!' 'It begins,' said the Sicilian. 'Be quiet,' he told us. But the boys were so affrighted that one of them shrieked and said that an army of demons approached. One of them cried out that the Arno was in flames. Can you credit it? One vowed that the Duomo had burst into flames, the bell tower was rocking as if the earth parted beneath it."

"You saw nothing?" The Abbot peered closely at Christer.

"I saw rising flame from the fire, I saw wind-tossed trees. In the fitful light, in the moving shadows, one could see . . . anything one expected to see."

One of the serving men was bending over Christer to fill his wine cup; I observed that a little of the wine spilled.

Christer did not notice it. "Men say they have seen in vision the Blessed Virgin, beatitude incarnate. Why not then the dark angel, Lucifer himself, the embodiment of evil? Evil is coexistent with good, both dwell within us, in the dark heart of man. Our cruelty to one another, our want of compassion. Anger uncurbed is a devil in the flesh. I have been so possessed at times."

Behind Christer, one of the serving maids crossed herself, and her lips were moving, but no sound came. Without leave she rushed from the room.

The Abbot got to his feet; he stood by the hearth. Over it, there was a tapestry, very large, worked in tawny browns and faint reds, and dim with age; the figures were indistinct, as if they stood in an autumn wood in hazy light. For a moment I had the fancy that the Abbot had stepped out of the tapestry and would soon return to it.

He smoothed the front of his worn brown cowl. "I must go," he said sighing. "But not till I hear the end of the venture."

"Of a sudden," said Christer, "we heard on the Ponte Vecchio above us the sharp sound of hoofbeats, a clatter on the cobbles, the jingle and clash of arms. The Duke's guard patrolling the bridge and the river bank. The Sicilian and his crew dashed to the river; they had a small boat tied up, hidden among the reeds. They slipped away like dark spirits themselves; we heard the splash of oars. We scrambled to hide ourselves among the rocks beneath the arch of the bridge, till the Duke's guard had passed. We doused our torches in the river and made our way by thin moonlight, in mortal danger of footpad and cutthroat, back to the studio. And two of my boys were ill, retching and feverish for some days. I believe that in the burning herbs there was a noxious substance to cause them to see visions. For a day I kept in my clothing the stench of that foul smoke."

"God watched you," said my lady, "that you should take no hurt."

"In Paris when I was young," said the Abbot, "a student at the great cloister of Cluny, there was talk of alchemists who could pass beyond the dark curtain of death when they so willed it and return to the world with uncanny knowledge. There are forbidden books . . ."

Of a sudden I knew that the Abbot had read such books, though these are works of heresy.

Yet he was of all men I knew the most apt candidate for sainthood.

He put a thin hand upon his heavy crucifix. "To know the unknowable," he said quietly, "to rouse the dead, to look beyond the veil of our mortality—men have always sought to do this. And some claim to have done it. But this is illusion. God will reveal His mysteries in His own time."

"Illusion . . ." Christer took up his cup, not to drink, but to examine the gold moulding upon the rim. "A wicked illusion of monsters and demons that my boys perceived in moving shadow and smoke. Yet from illusion can come a vision of truth. The puppets in our mummery shows—these are but

−73−

wood, jointed with strings and catgut, made by men to play and prance. Yet in the puppet show we see great mysteries made plain and truth illumined. As in the play of Christ's Passion. Or the pageant of Mary and Joseph. Or consider the painting—only a slab of wood or a linen backcloth. Earth pigment brushed upon it to mimic men in the posture of the living. Yet we see beauty made manifest. Is beauty illusion?"

"Ah, no," said the Abbot. "Beauty is the ultimate reality." He was knotting his frayed girdle.

Christer said softly, "The cathedral is more than its stones, more than the thrust of its arches, the tremour of light in the glass. The cathedral is a presence, a power, a way to aspiration."

The Abbot left us. Donna went to the casement, to watch as the Abbot's men were mounted. They rode off beneath the pines; in the sifting snow they were soon lost to sight.

"A bitter night," said Donna, though in truth the cold had somewhat moderated. She turned away from the casement. Her eyes were soft and very deep. "A cruel night to be riding out. Yet Kurt is ever abroad in such weather."

Christer went to put a hand upon her shoulder. "Love is more than touching, more than conscious thought." And then he said quietly, "Surely this is the greatest sin: the denial of love."

A gentle thought. Christer was ever gentle. On that evening, too, he had been clear in his mind for a little time; he had had a sharp remembrance of the night on the riverbank with the Sicilian sorcerer.

It is curious that when he was at his most lucid, the manor folk feared him most. From that evening on, they avoided him when they could. Increasingly they murmured among themselves: Christer had consorted with magicians; he had surely had traffic with the Devil.

Chapter 8

"The first sign of spring," said Kari with joy. "The *domherre,* the little lord of the manor!" The little bird perched on the casement ledge, feathers ruffled against the cold, its red breast glossy. My lady threw crumbs upon the snow for it.

She sat for Christer through the long, grey day. He had begun on a new panel, the Holy Birth.

At sundown Kurt came, with Peter.

Kurt had brought to my lady a little bear cub. Not more than two months old, I thought; its brown fur grew stiff with fear as my lady approached it. It shivered; its eyes were soft and deep, its small red snout moist and snuffling.

"Like a village child," said Kurt. "This little one is always hungry."

Donna was enchanted. "How can I feed it?"

"A sheep's bladder. Jon will show you." Kurt was looking at my lady fondly. "A sheep's bladder filled with thin milk gruel and honey. Make a small teat—Jon will do it—of sausage casing, sheep's gut. Jon and I have raised such little ones before."

"Where did you find him, Kurt?" I put a hand out to the small bear, to gentle him.

"In the rocky hollow near Lord Ivar's lake. Near the cave where once we hid a poacher's bag and arrows, one day long ago when my lord's men came upon us. Recall it, Jon? Peter and I rode that way a few days ago. The mother bear is still close by, I think; be wary of walking that way. There were tracks in the snow down to the edge of the lake. The shallow ice had been crushed, and the bear had cleared a little pool, in still water, clawing at the ice as we have done, Jon, to fish."

"Yes. Cold fishing, Kurt."

Donna was kneeling to the little bear. It stumbled and lumbered toward her, its small paws slipping a little on the oaken floor.

"Take care," said Kurt. "Until he knows you. His teeth are no danger yet. But his small claws are like needles. When you have fed him, he will come to know you."

"He shall sleep on the bearskin before the fire, in the great bedchamber," said Donna happily. And then her face grew shadowed. "When my lord is not with us . . ."

"No," said Kurt. "Give him a bearskin to nestle in but let it be below, in the manor kitchens. Or the buttery. Where my lord's dogs will not worry him. He cannot fend for himself yet. But the day will come. Jon will know when you must give him up and set him free in the forest."

"Ah," said Donna, her eyes shining. "He is so small. And comical. And sweet."

"Like a summer love," said Kurt, smiling at her. "Small. And a little comical at times. But sweet. Bittersweet, my lady. Young love grows old and sometimes bitter. The bear will grow savage and strong."

"Like love—in your experience, Sir Kurt?" Donna's face was elfin; I saw the little dimple.

"I am no expert, really." Kurt was laughing at her. But then his face grew hard. And closed.

Donna said, teasing, "I am not afraid of love. Though it be

wild and strong." Kurt looked at her then, a long, dark look. I saw that his hands were fists at his sides.

"I am not afraid," said Donna again. "Even of the bear. We had a man from Norrland at court at Christmastide. He brought a trained bear to His Majesty. Poor scruffy brute, chained and mangy. I felt sad for him. I would have given him meat to eat, he looked starved. But the King would not permit it; his trainer must feed the bear, he said. I believe he feared the poor beast, he sent it away. But the man from Norrland said that women had nothing to fear from a bear. There is a tale among them in the north, he said, that a bear will not attack a woman if she meets him on a forest path. If only he knows she is a woman. She has only to lift her skirts and show him . . ." And Donna's sweet face took on soft colour.

"And the beast is tamed by beauty," said Kurt.

"Among us," I said, "among men of the mountains, there is such a tale—that the bear will not molest a woman if she curtsies to him. Thus to do him homage, for he is king of the forest. But I would not put it to the test, my lady."

Kurt came with Peter on most nights thereafter. "To see the bear," he said, teasing my lady.

They would play with the little brute, laughing together, both on the floor before the fire in the great hall, kneeling, tossing a stitched pomander, a soft woolen ball for the bear. Or waving a silken scarf of my lady's, letting the small bear take it in his mouth, to tug at it.

"He grows strong," said Donna happily. But then her eyes were wistful. "I had in Stockholm a little dog of my own. So sweet. But my lord said he must not come with me because the hunting dogs here would tear him to pieces. Though I would have taken such care . . ."

It is well that my lord was not there with us, with Kurt and my lady; happy as children with a new puppy, laughing at the bear. Often their eyes met, and their hands touched.

One day shortly after the midday meal, Kurt came with Peter. Donna was standing at the casement; she saw them on the drive below us. The horses' flanks were wet; the armour of the men was powdered with snow, on leather helmet and shoulder. There had been a light snowfall that morning.

But at noon the sun broke through swollen banks of cloud. Clouds puffed with wind and edged with gold; on the snow-crust the light was dazzling. Beside the manor drive, the dark pines were bent with wind and dripping; the light was caught in them, and winking, as if melted gold dropped from the boughs. The still pools under the pines seemed to fill with liquid gold.

Kurt strode into the manor hall.

"Come," he said. "You have not seen it, my lady. A wonder you cannot see in Stockholm. The ice is breaking up. We rode by the inlet an hour ago; it is beginning. A long seam on the ice face. As we watched, a network of seams spreading. The ice clouded and grey and flooded with water. Come."

Donna looked up at him happily. "I will fetch a cloak. And order the sleigh."

"A warm cloak, yes. But not the sleigh. Old Matt is slow, the sleigh takes time. You must come at once. The ice goes out swiftly. Will you ride with me, my lady?"

He saw that she hesitated; two of my lord's men stood close by.

"Jon will bear us company," said Kurt. "Peter can wait upon his little maid in the kitchens. Jon will be well mounted on Peter's good roan mare. Come."

We rode hard. In the sharp light the horses cast thin shadows on the hard-packed snow, shadows fleeting as the wind. And the wind was strong in our faces. My lady's face was pink with cold; her eyes were shining; the furred hood was drawn close over her hair. Kurt held her strongly before him on the tall horse.

On the rocky crest above the inlet, we tethered the horses.

On the road I felt that we were soaring, as the eagle does, in wide, windy space. And here on the rocks the wind seemed likely to lift us off our feet. My lady's cloak was whipping behind her. Like wings, I thought. The blue silken wings of a spirit born of wind and water.

Kurt held her, close by his side; and I stood fast on the other. Her hand was tight in mine.

"It is . . . glorious," she said softly, on a little intake of breath.

Then we were silent. And strong against the wind.

Below us on the shore, great ice cakes were piled. Craggy shapes, blue-veined, and shining. Shards of ice glittered upon the rocks.

The ice face was grey and streaked with light.

And then there was a great rush of wind, sharp and gusty, like needles against the skin. The ice was hissing. Hissing and then singing. Like the wind in thin brittle reeds.

Of a sudden there was a long rumble of sound. My lady clasped my hand more tightly. A harsh rumble of sound, like a great fall of stone, a landfall of stone on a mountainside.

The ice split.

And then such a roar of sound. Ice cakes were flung up, masses of ice, churning and crashing together. And geysers of water, white water spurting. Ice masses rolling and turning and sinking. And at last below us, the rush of the strong spring tide. Blue water, a sweep of blue water, shining and free.

I have seen the ice break up many times. But never like this, with my lady beside me, her hand tight in mine.

Kurt stayed to sup with us that evening. After the meal, Donna sat again for Christer.

We had eaten lightly; but serving men brought the wine cups to us. Christer was draping the blue cloak about my lady. A blue as deep and soft as twilight. He arranged her dark, shining hair; and upon it, brushing her cheek, a veil of gossamer, golden as spun sunlight.

"Light and shade . . . sun and shadow . . . in the painting, as in life itself. The light must shine." Christer was brushing gold upon the painting. For a moment he put down his brush, and his eyes were remote. "There must always be more of the dark."

And so it was with him, I thought; he had his dark moods, his mind was shadowed; yet he could speak with clarity like sunlight, with reason sharper than most men.

It was often so when he spoke with Kurt.

Kurt and I would take our wine by the fire. And Peter would come with Kari, to sing for us. Alone of the maids at the manor Kari had no fear of Christer. She would sit on a wooden stool by the fire, her grey skirt spreading around her, her eyes upon Peter when he sang.

"I will paint you, little maid," said Christer. "Your golden wealth of hair. And on your face the look of loving. Of giving. The corn maiden, the nymph of the harvest field. You will stand with hands cupped under your breasts. In the background, the gold of autumn sun. And the rich gifts of the harvest, corn and mellow fruit."

"I am no one," said Kari, her cheeks taking colour. "How can you paint *me*?"

"The song of the urchin in the street, piping with joy, a notched reed in his hands . . . this is often as sweet as the music of men with viol and lute who attend at the Duke's table." Christer took up his brush and turned again to my lady.

"Music speaks to all men," said Donna. "And among us all, rich or poor, joy is the same. And loving."

"Loving, yes." Kurt was looking at my lady. But then he said with bitterness, "I see little joy as I ride along the roads. Or in Stockholm—there the complaint is the same. The harsh burden of taxes, the rule of the Danish bailiffs, our bondage to a Danish King. Women stand in the snow, in rags, before the palace gates, begging for bread. Hunger is not the same for common men; for the lord's hunger is filled."

"What man is common?" said Christer. "Each is unique. In each a solitude of thought, an aspiration all his own. No two faces are alike, even with twins. So small a line on the painter's canvas shapes the nose, the brow. But the line differs, if only by a hair's breadth, in each man. Among dogs, among sparrows, there are duplicates. But in man, each is a separate creation. Even the print of a man's thumb in the sculptor's clay is his alone."

Then Kurt spoke of the Hussite revolt in Bohemia, where common men had declared themselves the equal of all, even of great lords and bishops—"those men like iron chessmen," said Kurt, "with iron hearts. And power to move themselves and others to evil."

And Christer spoke of Italy, of a great wave of thought among men there called Humanism . . . of the right of each man, even those of lowly birth, to fullness of life and liberty of thought.

Words like firebrands . . .

And Peter sang the song from England, where men had risen with pick and ax and shovel against the hard rule of the barons, and even of the Church:

> "When Adam delved and Eve span,
> Who was then the gentleman?"

We felt a bond between us. We felt a stirring in our hearts. As if a clean strong wind swept through the firelit chamber.

"It begins," said Kurt. He stood before the fire, staring into the leaping flame. "Among us, as among others. We have been silent too long. Frozen in submission, without complaint. As the inlet is hard frozen in winter. Beneath the ice there is the strong surge of the tide, stilled by the iron grip of winter. And then the driving force of the spring wind, the rush of the spring tide, and the water is free."

We were silent a moment.

Then Kurt said, "There can be no stemming the strong tide of anger. Of man's will to freedom."

I saw that my lady was troubled. Her eyes were shadowed; she was twisting the silken knot of her girdle. Then of a sudden she lifted her face to Kurt. And smiled at him.

Peter had left us to bring up the horses. And now he came to say that a new colt had been born, in one of the barns. "Come and see, my lady."

And Christer said, "A birth and a beginning."

I stayed with him, and Donna and Kurt went out into the deep starry night. Starlight lay like a film of frost over the snow. In bare black branches the wind was still. Down by the barns there were men with torches. The mare had been eased; beside her in the stall was the colt.

"So weak," said Donna. "So vulnerable, with legs like little sticks. And its great soft eyes." She put out a hand to gentle it. But the mare whinnied; the stable boy told her to stay back. The straw was fouled with much blood.

"My beauty," said Donna softly to the mare. "Why must she have so hard a time? So much blood."

Kurt said, "It is always so, my lady. So much blood at a birth. A birth and a beginning."

They climbed the hillside together. At the manor door, Kurt thrust his torch into the snow. He held out his arms and Donna came to him, without a word. He held her strongly, but then he shook his head, as if to be rid of her. And he was all gentleness, as he kissed her. And put her away from him.

"My Donna, I cannot ask you to share it. The beginning for us . . . for men of the mountains. The blood. You are not one of us."

"Yes, Kurt!"

"No, my dear heart, my Donna. For you and me, there must be no beginning. Because if there were, there could never be an end to it. To my love for you."

He left her standing there, on the manor stoop. Beside her, stuck in the snow, the torch began to sputter and die.

And when she told me of this, her sweet face was so sad, I wanted to take her in my arms for comfort. To comfort her—or my own sore heart?

Chapter 9

We had some days of fog and thaw, and the piles of snow around the manor grew less. We were close within doors, for the wind was raw. And Kurt did not come. Donna was restless. She sat for Christer but could not hold the pose. At last he gave it up and set the new Madonna aside; he began to sketch on a large parchment the grouping of figures for his altarpiece.

I sat grinding colours; and Donna began listlessly to whip the glair we used to bind the pigments.

Toward noon, there was the sound of horsemen in the courtyard, the clatter of boots and spurs on the outer hall. Donna looked up; I saw the light in her eyes. And watched it die. It was not Kurt.

It was Lord Ivar, in an evil humour. And he felt that Donna was not happy to see him.

"Perhaps, my sweeting, you tire of country life?"

"Oh, no . . . no."

"I have ridden from Graneby to see you. Four hours in the saddle, in raw cold. The roads are a mix of mud and melting snow. I come home to a cold welcome. Perhaps you are tired of me?"

"Oh, my lord . . ."

"Then come and kiss me."

And she did, but he did not miss the little sigh which escaped her. He frowned at her.

"Forgive me, my lord, I . . . perhaps I am not well. It is nothing, it will pass."

And she exerted herself to please him.

But nothing would please him. He had determined that the blessing of Hell Gate mine would take place on the following morning; he dreaded it; and so he indulged his evil humour. I did not much blame him. My lord despised to admit weakness, though weakness is the common lot of mankind.

Word was sent to Kurt to make the necessary arrangements; we would meet at the mine pit at nine in the morning. I was bold to suggest that baskets of food be brought; folk from the village would come to watch the ceremony. Dame Agnes was sent to see to the loading of hams and cheeses in the large farm sledges.

And Lord Ivar settled down to his bitter mood and a great deal of wine. By evening he was much in his cups, and his voice was thick and harsh—the first time I saw him so.

And Christer was in one of his dark, disturbed moods. I will never know what prompted his outburst at table that evening. He took up his knife, but not to eat. He tested the heft of the knife in his hand. His eyes were dark with grief. He looked at Donna. "My Duchess, the Duke asks too much. I have made daggers for him, of fine goldwork; I make them well because I can use them well. The balance, the temper of the blade, that is first, though the goldwork be fashioned with art. I will make no more. No more daggers for brawling, no great cups for drinking. My Beppo has been killed in a tavern brawl. Beppo, my son . . . not of my blood . . . but like a son to me. I have many sons, though none are in truth of my flesh. Beppo was dearest to me."

And Christer would not eat but sat with his head in his hands. My lord left me to sit with him and urged my lady to bed.

But after this Christer called me rightly "Jon." He never called me Beppo again. And in time he learned that my lady was not his little Italian Duchess. And he would call her "Ma Donna"—"*my* Donna." I wished that I might call her that.

In the morning my lady was pale; there were shadows under her eyes, though she was no less lovely for that. But my lord looked at her sourly. I could guess that he had taken her roughly in bed and now regretted it. This, too, he regarded as weakness in himself—the obsession of his love for her, the need for her, which ruled him. For my lord was beginning to see that she could not love him.

We rode early to the mine, Lord Ivar on horseback, with twelve outriders, Donna and Christer and I in the sleigh. A grey day, heavy with weather. The air was raw; the road was rough. On either side, the dark pines were dripping; there would be a rush, a sighing of sound, as the branches released a fall of wet snow.

We took the road which skirts the iron mountain. Beneath the mountain, the mouth of the mine is a black gap in a snowfield; this is the entrance to Hell. There are rocks stained with rust and crusted with ice; and mist was rising like steam from the trodden snow.

A white field of mist, and rising in it, thin red flames. A crowd had gathered; they had built fires in iron kettles; they stood around the hissing fires to warm themselves and wait for my lord.

Such folk as Donna had not seen. Rough miners she had seen at the inn, but not such folk as their women. Troll women, in rags and shawls and skirts of sacking, in coats patched with fur. The fur of cat or rat or weasel . . . the skin of a dog. They bind themselves in these, like moths in a cocoon. They wrap their hands in strips of wool, but the raw red fingers stick out. They are always cold, but their children cling to them for warmth. The children whine and scratch, like small dogs with mange. On their faces is a red crust of sores; they never stop coughing.

We did not see Kurt at first, but then he emerged from the dark mouth of the mine with two foremen. They had rigged a windlass and been down to strengthen the ropes; they had taken a cage of sparrows down, to test for that evil breath of the mine which chokes and smothers.

Men say that giants sleep within the mountain; if men trouble their sleep with the noise of pick and shovel, these old ones will spew out the foul breath that kills.

And the thin flame of a candle can set it off, in the dark channels of the earth, a flash and roar of explosion—then God grant that a man dies quickly.

Kurt had lowered into the pit an iron cage with a meager fire built of sticks, to test for fire damp. He thought it safe to take candles down for the ceremony.

In the pit, some of the timbers had held, though much of the roof had fallen. Beneath split rock and frozen mud the dead bodies lay. The sleeping giants claim a sacrifice, in blood and bone, for the treasure men take from the mountain.

Kurt came toward us; my lord dismounted and shook his hand. I saw on my lord's lip a shine of sweat, though he was cool and courteous. He was, for the most part, a man of icy self-control.

Kurt came to the sleigh and gave us greeting. I saw the look that passed between him and Donna. I saw on their faces the sharpness and strength of their longing, and the pain of denial.

My lord did not see it. He was engaged with his own thoughts and did not see it as yet.

Kurt said that six men would go down into the pit. "No more. It is unwise."

"Surely," said my lord, "it is safe." He spoke so many could hear, but his mouth was tight.

"I am always aware, cousin, that a mine is never safe.

There is always risk," said Kurt calmly. "We will take two foremen to help you, my lord—to manage the ropes, as I think you have not the trick of that. And two priests to chant the blessing . . . softly."

I began to be uneasy. In many a mine, a footfall, a whisper, has brought down an avalanche of stone.

Yet I offered to go down. But my lord told me to stay with my lady. She was glad to have me; the crowd was pushing close to the sleigh for a glimpse of her. I hoped none would turn surly. But they would not dare—I thought not—with Lord Ivar's men on tall horses armed with pikes and axes.

Yet I saw on their faces the hard look of anger when the golden casket, the reliquary, was unveiled. We had brought it, wrapped in velvet, in the sleigh. It is a great wonder, such as we would never see in our poor village. But Lord Ivar's mother had commissioned it from Antwerp; it is brought out in the spring to bless the fields and then carried in procession.

It is more than a foot in height; it holds some bones of Saint Martin, his collarbone and his jawbone. These can be seen through a window of rock crystal. The casket is of heavy gold, with curious moulding, with round rubies and other stones. The spire is of twisted gold, delicate as lace, and set with a great sapphire.

A sapphire of such great price. Sold in Stockholm, it would bring a sum to feed our village folk for years.

There was a murmuring in the crowd.

Then they fell silent, for Christer rose in the sleigh—he was very tall—and stretched out his hands toward the golden casket. His eyes had that strange dark look. "A marvel. A master work!" he said, and many heard him. "Who is the master? Who is the master?"

My lord turned upon him and spoke in anger. But Christer looked at my lord and said in a strong voice, "*You* are not the master!"

My lady rose and took his hand. She spoke softly to him and begged him to sit down. Christer was quieted. He brushed a hand across his eyes and stared at the snow.

Lord Ivar said, "We will get on with the business of the day."

The golden casket was fixed in a cage of strong wicker canes, to be lowered into the mine.

And Kurt descended first, thrusting his legs into the rope slings, clinging with one hand to a loop in the rope and carrying a tin lantern. He dropped from sight, while men strained and jerked at the windlass.

And then my lord. My lord denied the need of help; he would not go down in a basket. He thrust his long legs into the slings, grabbing the ropes as Kurt had done; but his cape caught in a loop of rope and he made no move to free it, though it was wadded round his neck. He clung with both hands to the ropes, and I saw that the skin of his knuckles was white. And his face was grey—though I think few in the crowd saw that.

A fat priest went down in a basket of willow wand, with holy water and candles; and then a young one, his cape billowing as a small gust of wind caught it; then it dropped limply, as he was drawn down into the dead air of the pit.

The two foremen were last; one of them lifted an arm from the rope in a rude salute.

Donna took my hand. "Jon, it *is* safe?"

"I feel so," I said, to comfort her. "Kurt would not take my lord down. Ah, it is as Kurt says, there is always risk." Then I felt that this was a poor answer to give her, and I said, "Would you ask if the sea would never rise, when the wind rises? Ah, my lady, do not fret. They do not go deep. Only into the first chamber. I have been down with Kurt."

"You were not afraid?"

"I have been down in the mines often. I worked there. And my father was a miner. I've taken his black bread and pork rind to him many times, as a boy. I could crawl down the ropes like a rat. And then through the tunnels to find him. I would see his candle ahead. A little glow in a dark cloud of steam. He'd be lying on his back, in the mud, chipping at the rock with an iron mallet. I always found him. Or one of his fellows."

I had thought to distract her. But she bit her lip. "It is not such sport as my lord has ever known."

"He should have. Much of the mine revenue is his. A part belongs to the Crown. And a part is Kurt's, from his father. Only a fifth part. But Kurt's manor is large. Not like my lord's, of course; and my lord has such great estates in Skåne. But Kurt's manor is on the sea; there is rich pasture and much woodland."

I spoke so to pass the time; I thought the men could not be long underground. But we were feeling the chill, and the crowd was growing restless.

Then I saw the two midwives. Dame Barbro paid us no heed, as yet. And I was glad for that.

But the crazy old one, her companion, Mother Svenson, pushed her way through the crowd toward us. She had a red blowsy face and a scrap of dirty yellow wool on her head. Grey strings of hair fell over her face, and she wore the bottle-green cloak, patched and torn, which someone had once given her.

"Do not mind her," I said to Donna. "She will speak to you for a small coin. And go her way."

The old woman stretched out a dirty claw to Donna; she stroked Donna's beautiful fur cloak. "A pretty kitty," she said, in her daft voice. "Kitty . . . kitty . . ."

"Good day, mother." Donna gave her a small coin.

Mother Svenson nodded and cackled, and went her way.

"She is horrible," said Donna.

"She comes often to the mines, looking for her husband.

Old Svenson was crazed, too. He's dead now. Still she comes looking for him."

"Oh, Jon, I am sorry. But she *is* horrible. Was her husband killed in the mines?"

"He killed himself. He was no man for underground. He was a charcoal burner. But taken for the mines. He never feared the forest, though some do. God knows a man can wander there, with wolves at his back; or lost, under the dark trees, following witch lights. Svenson would go deep into the forest to gather acorns, bitter fare when boiled, but better than stones in the cookpot. He never feared the forest. But the mine . . . he thought he saw the Devil himself below ground. And the fires of Hell. The fires are built by the men to crack the rock; with fire and water they split it. There is dense steam. Old Svenson saw one of the men with a pick and thought the Devil was after him. He struck out with his mallet and killed the other man. Then he went into the forest and strung himself up with a rope. He'd not give the King's men the pleasure. But the old woman comes to the mine, looking and calling. One of the men will take her down."

"Into the mine?"

"She lifts her old green skirt, showing her buttocks and her crooked knees, puts her legs into the loops of the rope, and clings as if she were riding a broomstick."

"Why do the men let her down?"

"It's best not to cross her. They say she's a witch, that she can put a blight upon you. They say she can fly down, fly down backwards as the Devil descends into Hell, if she wants. But when she is let down into the mine, she just stands and calls for her old man. She comes with bread and cheese; she gives this up to the first man she sees, and says, 'Take it to my Svenson.' "

"I am ashamed," said Donna. "This woman is poor and old. Yet I feel small charity."

"Save your charity, my lady." For I saw with dismay that Dame Barbro was coming toward us.

Barbro approached. She was tall, with heavy shoulders; she walked like a man in her heavy shoes. But she was lean and spare in her movement. Her clothes were musty black, hanging upon her like webbed wings. On her head was a scrap of squirrel skin, yellow-grey and mangy; her hair hung in strands like limp feelers. Her face was pasty, but on her cheeks the veins were mottled red, for she was out in all weather.

My lady said softly, "This one is evil. I know not how I know. It is as if I stretched out my hand and she gave me a toad."

It is curious that Donna felt so from the beginning, as if she had a dark foreknowledge of the great harm Barbro would bring her.

"My lady, if she troubles you, send her away."

"No. If she is of the village, I must speak with her." And Donna tried to smile.

And Barbro smiled. Her lip drew back from her teeth. She was looking with bitter envy at Donna in her beautiful cloak. But she said in her deep, harsh voice, "It is luck I would wish my lord's lady."

"I have need of luck," said Donna quietly. She gazed at Barbro, and Barbro's eyes held hers. A kind of entrancement. Barbro's eyes were lashless and pale, with tiny pupils, the white, clouded eyes of one who sees into the future.

Suddenly Christer said, " 'Thou shalt not suffer a witch to live.' " He felt it, too, the aura of evil in Barbro. It was a power in her.

Donna said quickly, "He is ill, Dame Barbro." But then Christer was smiling. For Barbro's grandson pushed out of the crowd to find her.

This was little Anders; Christer reached out to put a hand upon his head. He was a most beautiful child; his eyes were deep and shining; his mouth was sweet, yet he had a firm chin. And a look about him of wonder; and yet of old wisdom and long patience, for he had endured much. His head was so beautiful that folk did not heed the crippled body, the stunted little legs.

And Barbro often beat him, yet now she took his hand and said, "It is hard for him. He cannot run like the others."

Donna reached for a coin. "Poor mite . . . so beautiful."

"The very model," said Christer. "Bring him to me tomorrow." Then he was silent and sunk in dream; I knew he thought of the painting to do, of Anders as the Blessed Child, the Christ.

"A copper for every day he comes," said Donna. "Christer would have him——"

"Ah," said Barbro, her face hard. "And why are you wanting him? He can't carry wood or water. He's slow, a burden to me. Is it sport you'd make of him? A toy? To dress in mummery clothes and give him to drink and watch him stumble on his poor legs? Fine sport . . . fine sport the rich have."

Folk were turning to us. Barbro's voice was loud. "Hush your noise," I said. "Bring the child to us. No harm will come to him. We want him only to sit."

"Sit? Who gets coppers only to *sit?*"

"Christer will paint him," said Donna. "No harm; I will be there."

And Barbro dragged the child away, for she saw that she could bait my lady no longer.

Donna sat quiet, her hands curled in her lap. She was gazing at the dark mouth of the mine. "The men are long underground," she said in a small voice. "The mist grows thicker."

It lay in white, cloudy pools in the hollows under the stunted pines; it curled like smoke from the mine pit and hung in the chill air. And the crowd no longer spoke or moved; the people stood huddled in their rags, in apathy, waiting.

Then in the stillness, we heard the thin chant of a priest. It rose like a breath of wind from the mine pit, a voice wailing in the mist, a voice without body. It died, and the stillness seemed more profound.

And suddenly there was a rush, a roar of sound from deep within the mine. Like a breaking wave beneath the earth crust. A long rumble of sound, as if within the mountain the sleeping giants were stirring, moving their long bones.

Folk drew back from the mouth of the mine. A woman's mouth opened to scream, but no sound came; and some of the women crossed themselves, but some made the witch sign with crossed fingers.

Donna clutched my hand. "God's help," she said softly.

"They will be coming up." I spoke with a faith I did not feel.

Men were sweating at the windlass, tugging at the ropes; the basket came up. And in it the golden reliquary, grimed with soot, all its brightness dulled, yet it had taken no harm. Folk muttered and hissed when they saw it—*men* were still below in the mine.

And we heard again a long rumble beneath the earth, distant now, like mountain thunder.

The basket came up with the broken body of a man. One of the foremen. He must have been looking up, at the beamed roof of the mine, or toward the pale light at the top of the shaft, when the rock fall came. His neck was broken, the head twisted strangely, and crushed so the jawbone was laid bare; a long splinter of bone hung from the bloody mess of his face. His jerkin was soaked with the thick bright blood.

Men lifted him from the basket; they laid him out upon the snow. I left my lady and went to help. But there was no help for him save God's, and I think he had never known much of that.

Then my lady was standing beside me. She took from her belt a cross of ivory and gold and laid it upon the covered body.

Out of the crowd a woman came running. A young one I did not know. She tore the scrap of woolsey from her head and laid it upon the body. She knelt beside it, her tawny hair loose upon her shoulders; she was sobbing without sound, her hands knotting together.

My lady knelt beside her in the snow.

She did not heed my lady, but then Dame Barbro came to us. Barbro said, in that harsh voice, like a man's, "Come. There is no help for it now. Come away."

The young one got to her feet; her tears stopped. She stood stiff as a wooden puppet, staring with dull eyes at the snow.

My lady took the cross from the dead man's body and would have given it to her.

But Barbro said, "She has no need of that. I will help her." And she gazed at my lady. There was hatred in those strange pale eyes. I felt again the power of evil in her. And Donna could not meet her gaze.

Barbro said again, "Come."

"I will look upon him," said the young one. "I will see the hurt they have done him. I will see his face!"

"No," said Barbro. "It is over. Over and done with." And she took the woman by the hand and led her away.

The priests were pulled out of the mine unharmed, though the fat old one was mumbling, in a broken voice. He was clutching the Holy Book with a fleshy hand; his chin was shaking, saliva dropped upon it. The pale young priest took charge of the body. I stood by my lady, watching the mouth of the mine.

The ropes were swaying like boughs bent beneath rain. Lord Ivar came up.

He stood as if dazed for a moment, as if he had risen like Lazarus from the dead. His face was ashen, his fine cloak covered with soot, but his hurt was slight, only a long gash across the back of his hand.

My lady ran to my lord; she took up his hand and kissed it; she took her linen neckcloth to bind the wound. And he looked at her fondly. He paid no heed to the wound. He looked once at the body upon the snow, a humped shape beneath a ragged cloak. "Let the body be disposed of. That is to say, let proper arrangements be made. Let a purse of coppers be taken to the widow."

He raised his hand for silence among the crowd. And all men turned to him, as he would speak.

And then I saw on his face a dark flush of anger. For he did not miss the look on my lady's face as Kurt came up out of the mine.

Kurt's clothes were fouled with soot, as much as any village sweep. Blood oozed from a gash on his cheek; he brushed at it with impatience. His mouth was tight with anger.

My lady gazed upon him with her soul in her eyes.

Lord Ivar said, in a choked voice, "A pity, Kurt. A man lies dead because of your misjudgment. You gave us no *clear* report of the wreckage in the mine. You vowed it was safe to descend. And now a man lies dead."

Kurt said roughly, "Now you believe! Yes, cousin, you see for yourself why no man will serve—no man will work in a mass grave. And who would serve a King to whom men are beasts, beasts to be whipped to labour until they drop. A King who——"

"Enough! You forget yourself. Before all men, you speak treason." But then my lord controlled himself. He was well aware that Kurt had the ear of our common folk, that Kurt was necessary to him. He said icily, "You will come to the manor this evening, Kurt. I will remind you of your duty. For the last time."

My lord mounted his horse then. He sat high above us and spoke in ringing tones to the crowd. He recalled them to *their* duty. Hell Gate could not be opened as yet. But the other mines—they must double the yield. They must serve the King's need, the needs of the war. They must take up the King's cause; they must give of themselves, in work, in sacrifice.

He spoke nobly, I am sure; but when he finished, the crowd stood dumb as beasts in a field.

He made a further effort. "Men of the mountains, rally yourselves! You do not bear the burden alone. All over Sweden men are marching. I am among them, *I* have served and suffered wounds in Holstein. We of the court, we give our lives, as much as you. All over Sweden men work in the fields, they work in the shipyards, they give of themselves, in work and war, for the King. They give their lives."

A muttering in the crowd. But no man stepped forward to stand by my lord.

At last my lord said coldly, *"Are* you men? Do you fear death?"

Then a man crept out of the crowd—old Jens, stooped from years in the tunnels and near blind from picking at the rock face in the dark. He stood before my lord; slow tears squeezed from beneath his swollen lids and streaked his cheek. His tears were black, in the furrows caked with soot.

"Ah, *we're* a-fearing? Fearing of the grave? We spend our lives buried alive. Dead, a man doesn't grub, and he's got the priest's blessing. And what's it for, the grubbing in the dark, the bloody sweat?"

"Kurt," said my lord sharply. "Speak to the men."

Kurt lifted his arm, with a clenched fist. His eyes were like coals, I thought, coals of fire. He was shouting. "Men of the mountains, rise to the cause!"

But old Jens said, "We've got no part in that. 'Tis not our

war—be the King so grand and our master, and begging pardon and mercy, my lord—'tis not our war. 'Tis the Danes' war. We work for bread and beer and our own need."

But a young miner stepped up to Kurt and clapped him on the shoulder. "Our need is more than that, more than bread and beer. We've a greater need."

"Yes," said Kurt. And he lifted both arms high, with the fists clenched and the wrists crossed. He stood so for a moment. And all men watched him.

Then the men were shouting with him and lifting their arms, with hard, tight fists. "For the cause!"

Lord Ivar was satisfied. "I will leave you now, Kurt. Distribute the food baskets."

We took the rutted road back to the manor. I was deeply troubled. My lord did not know that this was a sign among us, the sign of the raised arms and the crossed fists. He thought the men had rallied to the King's cause. He did not know that this was the first move to open rebellion.

Certainly I would not tell him. I have ever been Kurt's man, and one with them.

My lord rode ahead of us, now and again glancing back at us in the sleigh. When we reached the manor he said to my lady, "It will not be necessary, my Donna, for you to join us this evening when Kurt comes. You have had a day in the cold, and you look perishing from it. I bid you go up. I will send meat and wine to your chamber."

And he made no move to kiss her good night.

Chapter 10

Kurt did not come to the manor that evening. He sent Peter with word that he saw his duty clearly. He needed no further instruction from my lord.

And I felt my heart jump.

My lord said, with a slight smile, "So he sees his duty. Indeed it is time."

He finished his wine and went early to bed. And I thought of him there in the great bedchamber. Oak logs ablaze in the deep fireplace. Firelight glancing on dark walls and leaded casements. Carved on the high stone chimney breast, my lord's arms, the boar's head and crossed swords in gilt and plaster. My lord's shield on the wall, bosses gleaming in candlelight.

I thought of the alcove curtained in plum-red velvet, the massive bed with piled eiderdowns and furs. And my lady's head upon the pillows, the tumble of dark hair spreading.

Then I thought of my lady's face as she looked at Kurt, of the light in her eyes. And now this day my lord had seen it.

And now he was with her in bed. I thought of her whiteness and softness and how my lord might hurt her.

I swallowed my wine and went heavily to bed.

In the morning my lady was pale. But my lord's mood was lighter; I saw that she had been able to ease him. I knew how. And felt for the first time so fierce a thrust of jealousy that I was one with my lord.

And then was shamed. Carnal love is a bitter sin in a priest.

Over the morning meal, my lord awaited the Abbot.

The Abbot was in a sour mood. He had received the evening before a richly ornamented manuscript of the life of Saint Ursula and her retinue of virgins, ravished by Hungarians, martyred and slain, suffering man's lust. The Abbot had planned to spend his day perusing it. But the assaulted virgins must wait. And I think he had little interest in lost virginity; he treasured the book because it had come from the great monastery of Saint Gall and the illustrations were in ink wash and thick gold leaf.

And he knew why he was summoned to the manor. My lord would discuss with him some remission of the corporal works of mercy—the distribution of coppers among the poor. My lord proposed that the money be diverted to the King's fund. "Charity where it is most deserved," he said. "The King's fund is used for medical aid to men in the field in Holstein, wounded in service to their King. And thus better spent than in alms to men who will neither serve, nor labour for their bread."

The Abbot would never agree to this; and he could deliver some granite answers. My lord was in for an arduous morning.

The Abbot sat down with my lord. Beneath his cassock he was rubbing his buttocks. A balky horse had carried him here over roads rough with ice and frozen mud. And before the inn he had been offended by a brawling crowd.

"Fighting?" I said quickly.

"No. But surly. Calling to me as I rode past. Rough words,

an offense to the cloth. Some threw stones, my servant's horse shied cruelly. And I felt a frozen clod of mud against my cloak." The Abbot's fingers were tapping on the table. "Ah, there is always resentment against us in the village. Because we would give our lives to God in quietness, not to labour and sweat and the burden of living. And because when we hunger, we choose to do so; we elect our days of fasting. In the village men go hungry without choice." The Abbot looked at my lord with wise old eyes. "There is the same anger against men of solid estate as against men of the cloth."

My lord dismissed the incident at the inn; he was not concerned. "A crude defiance. As boys throw stones at a bull, and make much bluster. If the bull starts at them, they are quick to leap the fence to safety."

"My lord," said the Abbot firmly, "in the village there is bitter talk. Because a man was killed yesterday, one of the best, in Hell Gate mine. It might be politic to ride down to the village, show yourself, listen to grievance."

But my lord did not intend to let the Abbot off so easily. "We have much to discuss. We will attend to the duty at hand."

The Abbot sniffed. My lady came into the room; he greeted her with blessing; he remarked on her pallor.

"I slept poorly," said Donna. "I dreamt so cruel a dream. Of the woman whose husband was killed. I thought she waited below the casement, waited in the mist, crying and calling for him. In my dream I went to her, yet her face was blank . . . streaming hair . . . but no face at all . . . no eyes."

My lord looked at Donna severely. "You said no word of such a dream when you woke."

"I would not trouble you, my lord, you have much on your mind. Yet I am troubled by this woman. I would go to her, if it is your will. Take a purse and meat and wine. And offer some words of comfort."

"Yes, yes," said my lord with impatience. "Take Jon with you. Christer, if you like. And two outriders. Send my steward to me." He was bending over a sheaf of parchments heavy with royal seals and did not look at her. But I saw the little smile and the quick dimple. She had thought to be kept in the manor today.

But in the sleigh she said, "I do feel my heart turn to this poor woman."

"And to Kurt."

"Oh, yes, Jon. I confess it. Always my heart turns to Kurt." Then she was singing softly, but I caught the words. We all knew this song of Peter's.

"My love is strong as sea, and sure as sunrise, and deep as night."

Yes, I thought, that is how love is, but I could not say so.

And Christer said, " 'Love one another.' " But his thought was not on us, it was on the look of the sky, water-blue, with high scudding clouds; on thin sunlight bringing faint colour to bare branch and mossy tree trunk, on wet snow in the hedges and the first yellow-green of willow shrub, the flush of mauve, as pale as mist, in the thickets. The colours of spring in our northern woodlands, and these I saw later in his paintings.

The air was mild that day, yet fresh against our faces; my lady loosened the hood of her furred mantle. "Jon," she said, "I love you, too." And she patted my hand as she would pat a dog.

"We will take the back road to the village," I said, "though the ruts are cruel. We will go nowhere near the inn where——"

"Where I might see Kurt."

"Where you might see injury, my lady."

"Who would harm me? Or you, or Christer?"

Yet she had her way. The back road was impassable. An icy track running with water and blocked with snow, great grey drifts in thaw.

The road through the village was nearly as bad. At last we abandoned the sleigh. We left Christer in it, with one of my lord's men; the other tethered his horse and took up his pikestaff and went before us. We picked our way through mud and slush; in places the way was well-nigh blocked by branches splintered and brought down by winter storm and left to rot in the mire.

I heard the leper's bell and hoped my lady would not see him. He *was* faceless like the woman in her dream. But he crept from the road before my lord's man could strike at him. He crouched in a hollow in the rocks, hiding his death's head with the bandaged stumps of his arms.

We had seen no one near the inn, and at this time of day the village was empty. Men and most women were at work, in the mines, in the sodden fields or the forest.

Rats ran from a heap of refuse beside the road; a mongrel dog followed us; children clustered around us, whining for coppers. We saw by the road a man, a young one, stretched out dead drunk; horse flies were settling on his face.

I saw that Donna was dismayed; I begged her to go back to Christer, but she would not. We found the hut where the grieving woman lived. A hut of crude logs, the chinks plastered with mud, like all the others.

Dame Barbro was there.

Barbro blocked the door, with her height and her square shoulders; her black garment hung loosely over her scant breasts. It was said that she had two extra teats, which her witch-familiars, a cat and a hare, were allowed to suck. The cat was at her side now; it was tawny and wild; it brushed against her skirts and spit at us. I think it would have clawed us; but my lord's man said, "Take it away. And show courtesy to my lord's lady."

"So ye come with an armed man," said Barbro spitefully. "To do us further hurt? We have hurt enough."

"We come with blessing," said Donna.

She went to the woman who lay on a pile of rags and catskins by the hearth. A thin fire burnt on the turf hearth; the smoke in the hut was thick and acrid.

The stench of sweat and sour lard hung in the air.

The woman lay quiet, almost in stupor; my lady pulled up a wooden stool and sat beside her.

"May God ease you," said my lady and put out her hand. But the woman turned to her with blank eyes. I saw that Barbro had given her a potion, one of those bitter draughts of wild root and woodland berry which Barbro mixed with skill.

The woman said, in a thick voice, "It is nothing to you."

"Yes," said my lady gently, and then, "I have brought food."

"Take it back," the woman said roughly. "Can't I have my grief to myself? My own grieving . . . mine, the only thing I have. Will food ease it? I've no need to eat. *He* can't eat it now. And he'd no stomach for his food in this life. He'd be saving of it, the bit of salt herring, or the cabbage, for me."

My lady put the purse beside her; she made no move to take it. She turned on her bed of rags, clutching at the rags; she lay with her face turned to the thin fire, her mouth working; then she was still.

Dame Barbro took up the purse. "I'll be keeping it for her."

"You'll be giving it to her," I said.

"She'll have it, in great part. I'll take my mite. My wage, for tending her. I'll be spending another night."

A shadow moved behind the piled brushwood by the fire. A small humped thing. At first I thought it was a dog. It was little Anders, on hands and knees, playing with sticks. He dragged himself into the light, on thin stunted legs; he looked at the basket of food with round eyes but said not a word.

"I've no time to be bringing him to the manor," said Barbro, watching my lady. "A far way to go. For a poor wage."

"We will take him with us," said Donna. "He will stay at the manor for a few days, sparing you trouble. Come at the end of the week and collect his wage."

Barbro scowled at her; in truth she was glad to be rid of the boy.

I carried him, for he was slow on his pitiful little legs. When we came to the sleigh, Christer sat there, surrounded by children. Small ones with smudged faces, noses streaming, scratching their sores, and calling out names. They did not dare approach too close, with my lord's man there. Christer did not hear the foul names he was called. "The old crazy one . . . talking to himself . . . whoreson . . . the Devil's bastard."

To Christer, the thin little voices were like the chirping of sparrows in a hedge. He was lost in dream. " 'Suffer the little children to come unto me,' " he said.

I saw some of the faces later, in what I think was Christer's greatest work. And there as he painted them, the children's faces were clean and shining and full of light. And that is the way he always saw such little ones.

Anders was tucked in the sleigh, with his dead squirrel, a baby squirrel he had pulled from within his jacket to fondle; at first I thought it was a rat. It had been his pet; it had died that morning; he would not be parted from it. But he was quiet and very good; Donna said he should have sweetcakes when we reached the manor.

"What are they, lady?"

"You will like them. I promise you."

And I promised myself that we would soon bury the squirrel.

We stopped at the village chapel; Christer wanted to look at the wall space. He had finished the sketches for his panels, and some of the work would be directly upon the chapel walls. So my lord wished.

"After weeks of fog and damp, we will see," said Christer. "I cannot work on a wet wall. If dampness rises from the foundations, if water seeps through the plaster, nothing will hold. No matter how strong the gesso, no matter how many coats. Damp mortar, lime from a wall, will dissolve the colours . . . mould will grow . . ."

He spoke as if to himself; we went into the chapel, and there he was so bemused in the dim light that he did not see Kurt before the altar.

Kurt knelt, in black leather armour, before the iron altar rail. He was alone, absorbed in prayer, God's mendicant, as men are before battle, or a long Crusade. He did not hear or see us; his head was lifted to the harsh stone Christ.

I had never seen Kurt so. Nor ever will again.

My lady moved toward him as if in trance, her skirt whispering on the stone floor; without a word she went to Kurt and knelt beside him.

He looked down at her, and took her hand in his. They stayed so for a moment, in stillness, kneeling together, my lady in furred mantle and Kurt in his dark armour. From the narrow window there was a long shaft of light which touched their shoulders.

I left them there and went out into the churchyard.

And Kurt helped my lady to her feet and led her down the chapel aisle as if they walked from the bridal Mass.

In the chapel porch under the dark arches, they were alone; he took her into his arms. He kissed her hair gently, and then her sweet face; and then, strongly, her mouth— a deep kiss, the first.

But then he put her away from him, though she swayed against him; he was gripping her shoulders.

"Ah God, my Donna, God knows how I love you. There is no help for it. I want all of you. Forever."

"I am yours."

"No. Today I have asked God to help me hate. As He must

hate men of low birth, men who exist without hope. I asked for strength, to send many men to death. It must be so."

"It is the beginning? Of all you and Christer have talked about . . . against the King?"

"Yes. For us, the end."

"Kurt! Take me with you." She put her hand to his cheek.

He could not help himself; he kissed her. But then he said savagely, "I am undone by such love. I will nourish my hate. Against your world. Go back to my lord, my cousin. Let him hold you as I would hold you, in the still of night."

"Kurt. I would leave him and never look back."

"I cannot give you rubies. Only hard, cold nights on the road. Sleeping in field and cow byre. My lord's horses will have better stabling than my men. I will ride with death behind me. Blood on my hands always. No. Let it end now between us—the longing, the close bond, two as one." He closed his eyes, his mouth was tight with bitterness. "I have work to do. You have no part in it. Go back to court, my lady of the rubies."

There were tears in her eyes, but he did not see them. There were tears in her eyes when she told me later of this. And now she turned from him, lifting her head in pride, pulling her hood over her tumbled hair.

"God keep you, Kurt."

"Spare me your prayers. God keeps only the rich, my lady of the rubies."

So she left him. In the churchyard she walked past me without a word. But I saw her face, the hurt in it; I could guess what had passed between them.

When I went into the chapel to find Christer, I found Kurt, in the dark little porch. He sat on a stone bench, gripping the stone; he was staring at the wall like a man in gaol.

"Now . . . now, Jon, I have wounded her, my dearest heart, my Donna. And my hurt is worse than hers because I had to hurt her."

I put a hand on his shoulder. I could find no words.

"My good Jon. I wanted you by my side in what must come. But now, stay with my lady, watch over her. Get her back to Stockholm."

"I think she will not go."

"If there is time . . ." he said, as if I had not spoken. "I hoped the first strike would not come yet. June, perhaps. When the roads dry out and the spring crops are planted. We'll have need of those. I've urged the men to wait, to curb their anger. You know it. Now there is no stemming the tide—since yesterday in Hell Gate mine. Does it strike you, Jon, that the force of hate is so much stronger than the power of love? If we could have won by reason, in peace, in parley . . ."

"Perhaps there is still time."

"The iron men are marching. Peter brought word this morning. Men from our mountains. And men from Dalberg, from Kopparsten, from Tallbacken. A rabble army. No weapons but picks and knives. Some with no weapon but anger. But all have the will to die. And a rage to kill. Our men will join the others."

"Against my lord?"

"I think not yet. Why hunt the wolf when the bear is loose . . . the King. The men march to Stenborg; the King meets there with his Council, those who support the foreign war and the Danish rule. And the King's greed, and their own. Lord Ivar among them. Fawning nobles, trained to nod their heads at the King's will, like puppets at a fair. A puppet council. Some talk, much feasting and hunting."

"And they are the hunted. Yet our mountain men against the King's men? Knights mounted and armed, trained in the field, in Holstein . . ."

"Most are mercenaries. They fight for a measure of wine and a handful of silver. Our men fight for bread, for bare existence. We fight for our lives."

"We will be cut down like hay in a pasture."

"Some of us. We can die as well as the King's men. Better, perhaps. We've nothing to live for. Unless the King is at last persuaded to see reason."

"As well ask a mountain to move itself."

"Yes. So violence must come. I can no more stop it now than I can stop a great rockfall in a mine after the first small fall of stone, the stream of sand from the rafters. Our grievance is too deep. Yet there is time, I think, for my lady to leave, before the roads are blocked with marching men. The village is quiet now. But later . . . Ah, God grant a little time to my gentle lady. When you can, Jon, bring me news of her. I will be here at times. Or Peter will come."

"News of her, Kurt. And of all else you need to know, when I can. Often I act as my lord's scribe and copy his letters."

"Yes. You will know where to find me."

"Yes." Then of a sudden I said, "God's blood! My lady cannot leave. Unless my lord wills it. And he knows nothing now of men on the march, of full rebellion."

"God help us, my lord will know soon. But then . . ."

"It may be too late."

Chapter 11

Within the week my lord left us. A day of strong spring sun and fresh wind. He rode with a large party—stewards, squires, outriders, four of his prize hounds, with their handlers. Two falconers, with his favourite hawks. There would be rich hunting at Stenborg with the King.

He left my lady with reluctance. I thought he had forgotten his displeasure with her. He kissed her fondly. "My sweeting, while I am gone, do not fret."

"I will not fret." My lady was demure. But I saw the quick light in her eyes. "But I will count the days, my lord, till your return."

Indeed she would, I thought. She will count the days of freedom from his hard will against hers and his rough demand for her in bed.

"I would not leave you so often," said my lord. "The King's command . . . well, you must occupy the time. With Christer. And with Jon. I beg you to continue your instruction, to nourish piety and suppress frivolous thought as much as you are able. Set your mind to responsibility, to works of charity in the village. Yet I beg you to be prudent. The Abbot says that a sullen wind blows in the village. Take care, my dearest

Donna. And when the Abbot comes, the best malmsey. When the bailiff is here, the tawny port, and liquor of cloudberry. He is fond of both."

My lady was all sweet patience, though she had heard all this before; my lord repeated his instructions whenever he left us.

He kissed her again. And then his face grew hard. "One last admonishment, my Donna. I have ordered that Kurt, my cousin, will not be received at the manor while I am gone."

"I will not give him welcome." The soft colour came into her face.

We waved my lord off. We watched the brave company—men in polished armour, men in velvet and marten and multicolour; men in my lord's livery of azure and fawn. The beautiful horses, some with gold-mounted saddles, some with nodding plumes. My lord's blue cape billowed in the wind. They took the turn in the road and were gone.

My lady turned to me. "Truly, Jon, I will not give Kurt welcome. Because he will not come. So I will go to him."

"Early in the week, he left us. Riding north."

Her eyes were deep. "Does he ride to danger?"

"Often he has, my lady."

"Yes, I know," she said, sighing. "Oh, Jon, the long days ahead. And perhaps no news of him." Then her little chin lifted. "I am perishing! I will ride out. Fast and far. You shall ride with me. Christer is painting like an angel; he'll not miss us."

"The roads are mud tracks, my lady. The mood in the village . . ." It was no use, I knew it; when my lady was willful, an angelic choir could not persuade her from her will.

"No outriders, Jon. I feel like a nursling, always under guard."

My lady rode as if the Devil pursued her. I could not keep pace with her. Her own horse had been brought up from Stockholm, a black mare, Arab, a gift from the King himself.

She had ridden often with the King's hunt. I am born to horses, like most men of the country, yet she streaked past me, her furred hood flung back on her shoulders, her dark hair loose and streaming. At the turn of the road she checked the great horse and waited for me. She was laughing when I came up.

I reined in beside her and gentled my horse, one of Lord Ivar's best.

"Jon. Forgive me. It has passed now . . . the black mood which took me. Which way lies Kurt's manor?"

"I have told you he is not there."

"How do you know, Jon?"

"Because I am Kurt's man, and ever have been."

"Have you any doubt where my loyalty lies?"

"None, my lady."

"What possible harm in taking the road past Kurt's manor?"

"Nothing of it can be seen from the road."

She bit her lip. "You are without mercy, Jon. Mercy is most becoming in a priest."

"Recall, my lady, that I am only a lay brother. Ah, well . . . we'll ride that way. But I am no centaur. We'll not outrace the wind."

So she kept her horse to an easy pace. The sun beat down on our shoulders . . . the miracle of sun, after weeks of fog and raw weather. In a wide blue sky, the clouds were racing, white and swollen and full of wind. I shall not forget it. Patches of snow on the red-brown furrows in the fields. Wet snow still in thaw under the dark pines near the road, yet the pines were taking colour—green, plumy, the needles shining with sun. Christer had taught me to see these things. The ditches were running with swift brown water; by the road we saw the first of those small ragged flowers which we call fool's gold. The first brave bloom of spring.

And I felt that my lady was happy, riding beside me. A fool's dreaming, perhaps.

Until we reached Kurt's manor, we saw no one but old Mother Svenson, the midwife, crouching beside the road. She had her bag of herbs and simples; she was stooped, looking for fern, I suppose—the tiny curled tips pushing through wet brown leaves—or some such plant for physic, for making an herb tea to ease ague or fever. We stopped to greet her. She squinted up at us, puffing her cheeks and pursing her lips.

"Jon, is it, from the monastery? Riding out with a fine lady. A fine life the monks have. And wine with their meals. Have ye seen my Svenson?" Her voice was shrill.

We rode on, taking the forest road. Where the road turns into Kurt's land, there is a grove of great oaks, the bare branches arching overhead. Branches like iron lace, with a glimpse of blue sky between them. Ekholm, Kurt's manor, takes its name from the oaks. Nothing of the manor could be seen through the thick forest growth.

But beside the road there are stone gate posts, weathered and overgrown with moss; a high iron gate, spiked and scrolled with copper now green with age, though much of Kurt's land was not fenced.

We dismounted and tethered the horses. I spread my cloak on a mossy boulder; we sat close and I could scarce catch my breath for happiness. And here again was a patch of *tussilagor,* fool's gold, the stems stunted and branched, the tiny flowers shaggy, no bigger than copper coins. My lady leaned over me to pick them; the wind lifted her hair; strands of it blew across my face. Silken strands and scented. My lady's scent was of dark violets and white; and something else, a green scent of the woods, of fern. My lady's pomades were compounded in Stockholm and certainly costly.

And there was another scent about her. The warm, honey

scent of womanhood. I could not bear it. I got to my feet and led her across the road to Kurt's gate. The family arms were carved on the old stone, but the stonework was crumbling and streaked with wet green mould.

"Three stars . . . three of Kurt's forebears journeyed on Crusade. The falcon, now so furred with moss; oak leaves surrounding. The motto: 'The oak withstands the winter, though the storm wind shakes it.' " I knew she wanted to hear these things.

She touched the carvings and her face was wistful.

"The manor is large," I said, "but not kept now as it was when the lady Margit lived. That was Kurt's mother. A lady of learning and strong will. Yet a gentle heart."

"I wish I might have known her."

"I knew her well. I owe my life to her."

"To Kurt's mother? Tell me, Jon."

We crossed the road and sat again upon the mossy rock, the spring sun warm upon our faces.

"It was because . . . well, I was born on a small croft. I slept as a boy in the dark loft over the barn, on piled hay, in summer. In winter I slept with my parents by the turf hearth in the hut; we had sacks stuffed with straw; we rolled ourselves in these, and in wolfskin. Yet I remember the wind and snow sifting through the chinks in the log walls. My father's wage was two coppers a day. Though he worked hard. Nights in the mines . . . ah, night and day are alike underground. By day, like most of us, he was a poacher. He was caught with two partridges. So small a bag to cost his life."

"His life, Jon?"

"He was caught on Lord Ivar's land. Lord Ivar's mother gave him the usual judgment. His hands were cut off. So what is a miner to do—gnaw out the ore with his teeth? And the stumps of his arms festered. He drowned himself; he would not be a burden. I found him where the mill race rushes out beneath the wheel. I was eight then."

"Oh, Jon!" My lady's eyes were soft with pity. "And you so small."

"Old enough to work in the mines. Many begin then. A boy can crawl along ledges, into clefts in the rock where a man cannot go. A strong boy is harnessed to the windlass."

"It is horrible." Donna was crumpling the small flowers in her lap, not heeding what she did. "Children harnessed like beasts."

"Small wonder we grow to act like beasts, some of us. I saw much of brutishness as a child. The big boys put us to the test. Cruel they can be, when a young one begins."

"Tell me. Though I would not hear it."

"I would not tell you some things, my lady. But others . . . a new boy hung in the ropes of the windlass. And there he would swing over the pit all night. And at last be let down. A child penned in a cave in the rocks, far below ground. And left for a day. I was that child."

"Yet you are not afraid. And not bitter."

"The men would harden us. A man below ground must know that his fellows can bear all things that he might bear. So in strong need when all are in danger, no man will take fright. It is the same when men go to war. I saw ugly things. And other things. Men are comrades in the dark tunnels, as men above ground can never be, men who have not shared a common misery, a common danger. Kurt's men now, who march with him—there is a bond between them strong as the iron they dig from the rock."

"Tell me more of Kurt. Of how you were friends."

"We met when I was ten. And Kurt four years older. On a child's wage I could not feed my mother. I poached like my father before me, setting snares at night. And I was caught. On the lady Margit's land. And she had pity. She took my mother to serve her at the manor, in the kitchens. And I would have served her. But my lady said I was wild as a weasel in the field. She sent me to the monastery to haul wood and carry slops, and receive instruction. And saved my life. For I would have grown wild as a wolf, in time."

"I cannot think it, Jon."

"Yes. I gave the monks much trouble. The work was nothing, after the mines. But the long hours on my knees, the monks droning plainsong at table, the hours when speech was forbidden—I was not tamed to that. I would run off, like a forest creature, into the woods. Or to the manor to see my mother. I was there one day and Kurt came to her. It was the first time I saw him. He had hurt his hand, setting a wolf trap. His hand was ragged flesh laid back to the bone, blood soaked his sleeve. And he was angry. White with anger that he had been so clumsy, and white with pain. He said through his teeth—I can hear him now—'Fix it, goodwife Gert. So I can ride tomorrow.' "

"Did he? Ride so soon again?"

"Not for some days, though my mother bound the wound well and gave him ale and physic. Kurt loved her, as I did. His parents were often at court; he spent long hours with a tutor. And Kurt became my tutor, in much. But I showed him forest ways. Where to take crayfish on still summer evenings, at the edge of the lake on Lord Ivar's land. There in the crannies of the rocks we found the best. We'd take torches to shine on the shallow water; the light would draw the crayfish from their holes. I showed Kurt how to find a honey tree. The track of the bear will lead you to it, and then you hear over your head the humming of the bees. And I taught Kurt to set a proper trap. A poacher's ways."

My lady smiled at me. "I would have known you then. And Kurt."

"He was wild as I."

"I can believe it."

"As we grew older, we played rough tricks at times. I had gone back to the mines; the monks had given me up. And Kurt was much with me, and lads of the mines. I was the first to take him down in the tunnels. And he seemed one of us, though born to gentle estate. We'd go to Granholm to learn what we could of life, drinking and whoring. There was an inn. My lady, I'd not meant to speak of that."

"Men must prove themselves," she said, and I watched the little dimple.

"The Abbot is right, perhaps, to say that Satan occupies half our hearts. Often in Granholm there were fights. Lads from the mines against men of the King's garrison. And one night Kurt would try his luck with a blowsy girl; she belonged to the Bishop's squire. She was only a piece of panting flesh, but Kurt had a score to settle with the Bishop's man. I found him outside the inn, bloody and beaten. He'd been set upon by four of the Bishop's guard. A little rain was falling; he lay with his head on the wet cobbles."

"You cared for him."

"As he would have done for me. It was often my turn. Yet that night was the end for us. The Bishop came to the manor, full of complaint. My lady Margit was there then. Kurt's father had died. She heard the Bishop out. And Kurt was sent off to Stockholm to a kinsman at court, to learn courtly ways. I did not see him again for three years. I remember well the night I bid him good-bye. We walked beside the inlet, watching the waves crest and sink on the rocks. A heavy grey day. And my heart was heavy. I knew it could not be the same for us again."

"Was Kurt sorry to go?"

"He knew he must one day go. He must study and learn the ways of the gentry. 'But I'll come back,' he said. 'As manor lord,' I said with bitterness. But he said then, 'I'll come back your friend, Jon. If you will have it so.' "

My lady's eyes were soft as I told her this. "Then, Jon, you went back to the mine?"

"For a time. One day there was a fall of rock. Not large, but a long seam opened in the rock face; we'd worked too deep there. Foul water rushed into the black chamber where I was. Muddy water, knee-high and swift, pulling and curling round my legs. Afloat in it were many rats. Dead rats . . . the wet rigid bodies tumbled in black water. Yet clear to see, in torchlight."

"I cannot bear to think of rats."

"There are always rats in a mine. Alive . . . well, a miner uses his pick for more than hacking at rock. Dead rats are no danger. Though the stench—— Forgive me, my lady. That night I took the forest path, walking to clear the stench, the thick foul air from my lungs. In the dark heart of the woods I came to a still green pool. There were water lilies, closing at day's end, afloat like small stars, on dark shining water. I sat on a rock and thought of Kurt. Our life had not been all roistering. We talked much, as the young do, of life and love and aspiration. And Kurt would say, 'Would you spend your life below ground, Jon?' And often, 'You must learn your letters.' My lady, I could not write my name then. I am shamed to think it."

"But you had small chance of learning."

"No chance, but for Kurt. He would teach me to read. But I was stubborn."

My lady was watching an ant on the rock beside us. It tried to make its way from a mossy crevice. But it was trapped by the tiny spears of lichen, green and grey on the rock. "To the little creature," said Donna, "moss is as tall as a forest, and as trackless." She took up a twig and brushed the ant out of the crack, but it ran in circles and scurried again into the crack.

"So it was with me, my lady. Aimless as the ant, and trapped. Living my life in the mine . . . somehow that cool green evening I knew it was not enough. I know not what turned my thoughts that evening. But I did not choose to go to Granholm with the others. That was as well for me. A great brawl there was, between miners and Bishop's men.

The Bishop was hot with wrath. An offense to the holy office, he said; and worse, a gold ring had been stolen. The guard was called from the garrison; two miners were taken. One had both legs broken on the rack; one was put to the iron torture . . . the spiked boots."

My lady's sweet face was troubled. "What are these? The boots."

"Boots of iron lined with sharp spikes. Forced on a man's feet and the straps tightened. Then he is made to run, with men and dogs behind him. We will speak no more of this, my lady. I would not distress you."

"I must know these things. It is for such things that Kurt's men march in wrath against the court."

"Yes."

My lady said sadly, "That men can be so cruel to one another—is there no defense against such judgment?"

"In a King's court, or judged by a great lord, none. Men are blinded or lamed, or put to the rack. Often for slight offense. I earned such judgment often. With luck, I was not caught. How long, I thought, can my luck hold? And Kurt had told me often, 'You'll be a fighter all your life, Jon. God forbid that one day the King's men take you. Learn to read. If a man can read a page of Scripture, he can claim benefit of clergy.' So a man is tried in Church court and the Church forbids bloodshed, except in war. The Church gives no judgment that maims. It exacts fines if a man can pay. If not—months in irons, in a cell. Or scourging with a whip. But a strong man can suffer these without injury. My lady, I fear I weary you."

"No, no. I would know all that troubles Kurt, all that brings men to his side in anger." In her lap, the small flowers were wilting; she brushed them from her blue skirt. "So you learned to read, good Jon?"

"I took the only way; I went back to the monastery. Kurt's mother persuaded the Abbot to take me. The Abbot knew I had no vocation. Only a strong back. I could tend horses. The cloister was being rebuilt; I could haul and set the heavy stones. Ah, I was often rebellious still."

"At the discipline? The long hours of silence?"

"Yes. I felt caged. As a bear is caged and hauled on a wagon to the fair, where men poke sticks at him through the bars and make mock of him. For some of the monks did not welcome a brute miner as one of them. But the Abbot said, 'There is more joy in heaven over one black sheep that is found . . .' I owe much to the Abbot."

"He is very wise," said Donna. "And not as most monks are. Not dour and solemn."

"In time I saw that. Once when I served him as acolyte we took the Mass to an old miner in the village. The man lay dying of black lung; great spasms of coughing shook him; his eyes were dim, and in the hut there was the smell of death, though he still breathed. The Abbot left open the door of the hut. A thin bar of sunlight lay upon the turf floor; and yet the smell was suffocating. The old man lifted a palsied hand to take the wafer, but could not hold it. Crumbs fell upon the floor. And a sparrow flew into the hut and alighted upon the floor. It was pecking at the crumbs, crumbs of the sacred wafer. I thought the Abbot would be offended. But he said later, 'These little creatures are God's own. His eye is on the sparrow, as Brother Francis knew when he preached to the birds.' "

My lady said softly, "The Abbot is gentle as Saint Francis. Yet of certain strength."

"Yes. He set me to learning my letters. In time . . . you see me now, in monk's clothing. A lay brother only. But with some small learning."

"And a great heart, Jon. And devout. In the Church you found what you were reaching for, that night in the forest by the water-lily pool."

"Not really, my lady. I never found what I sought—an answer to my questions."

"Nor I," she said quietly, "though once I thought so. With you . . . with Kurt . . . I have seen the misery that men are condemned to only by their birth. 'Ah, God who made us, why must it be so?' So Christer says. With him, I begin to ask new questions."

She sat with her chin in her hands, deeply thoughtful. Sunlight had left the rock where we sat; the wind had dropped, there was only the whisper of leaves in the thicket behind us. The grey light deepened beneath the trees. The horses were stamping and neighing.

"It grows late, my lady. Come." I got to my feet.

She stood facing me. "I am grateful for you, Jon. And glad that I came away from Stockholm."

"You must go back."

"I will not do it. I belong here now. I belong where Kurt is . . . though he will not have me."

"He would have you safe in Stockholm."

"No."

And then we heard the sound of the cart. The creak of wooden wheels, the slow slap of leather reins, an old horse snorting and blowing.

Beside us on the road, the cart came to a halt. It was piled with rough-cut logs; on these, his shoulders hunched, sat Sven, wild young Sven who had found Christer that bitter day on the ice. Sven's hands were heavy on the reins; his thatch of iron-red hair was unruly; his face was flushed, as always, with drink.

With him was Fale, his brother, his strawy hair matted, his blotched face creased in a grin. Fale was somewhat slow of wit and always grinning.

I gave them greeting.

But Sven scowled at us. He would never forgive us for saving Christer. "I'll not give you goodday. Ye've had a good day, I can see that. When my lord's away, my lady will play."

I was hot with anger. Yet I wanted no trouble, with my lady there; and what could I say to men so besotted?

I took my lady's hand. "Come away."

"See," said Sven, "he takes her hand. He can't take any other part of her—he can't get his manhood up, under a monk's gown."

"By Christ!" I said savagely, and would have seized the bridle then and forced Sven down from the cart. But he whipped the horse and they were off, jolting down the road.

"Ah, my lady, that you should hear such rough talk!"

"I have heard worse in Stockholm," she said quietly, but her eyes were dark with anger.

"They were drunk, but that does not excuse such offense. My lord must be told."

"No. It would only make trouble. My lord would be wroth that we rode out alone and were seen at the gates of Kurt's manor. Ah, there is no argument with men so stupid." Her little hands were fists. "I hate them because they would wound you, Jon. And why are they not with Kurt? With braver men than they, in time of need!"

"There are always men like Sven, who take without giving, who will not put themselves to risk. Yet if there is profit, they demand a giant's share."

I gave her a hand up; she leaned to stroke the neck of the great black horse. Her dark hair fell about her shoulders. "Will we pass the cart on the road?"

"We'll take the long way round. Past the iron mountain."

We rode slowly; the way was stony. The dark pines seemed to crowd us off the narrow track, so thick was the growth on either side.

Then we rode into the clearing. This was Helge's pasture, but he had abandoned it long ago. For this is a haunted place—or so men say. Slow streamers of mist were drifting in the pasture, curling among the rocks. It was not long till dusk. And before us was the great granite mass of the mountain. The lower slopes were lost in shadow; but on the sheer rock face, the long, late rays of the sun lingered.

We reined in our horses, side by side; we were silent together, our faces lifted toward the mountain. I saw in her eyes a kind of dread; she drew her cloak around her as if to shield herself from chill.

There is a power here, a presence hostile to man. I cannot say what it is. But all men feel it, and look upon the mountain with awe.

They say there are giants still within the mountain. These are the old ones, the frost giants, born to earth before man. They have beards like frozen waterfalls, and teeth like rocks; their eyes are like ravines, like dark pits in the mountainside. They are blind in daylight, yet crouching underground they see through earth and rock and the roots of the oak tree.

But their sign is on the mountainside, cut into the rock face. Huge figures, sometimes lost in fog. And sometimes the clefts are filled with blowing snow. But on days of sharp sun the figures can be seen. Some have the shape of man, with long thighs, and between them the stiff potent organ of man. One is of a woman, with full breasts and belly great with child. There are figures of horses running, of reindeer with locked horns. And of the sun, like a wheel, with long rays. The rays are gashed in the rock face and filled with earth stained with ore, so that they glow red in the strong light. Wind has torn much earth from the carvings; now, in our time, it is as if the sun were banked in cloud.

I felt my lady's fear and wanted to ease her. Yet I felt that my voice broke into a silence as old as stars, as old as stone. "Kurt and I tried to climb the cliff when we were boys. We had to turn back. A strange wind came up, so sharp and sudden. The air was full of sound, of sand and blowing scree, as if the mountain itself attacked us. We never tried again."

"There is an old evil here. I feel it," my lady said softly. "The figures are of another world, a world of darkness."

"They have been here since time began. So men say."

"As if cut in the rock face by lightning. Or carved by gods of storm. Ah, this land is so old; the mountains are stronger than men. I feel of a sudden that evil is stronger than men . . . here, I feel it."

"In the old time, men made sacrifices here, in the oak grove at the foot of the cliff. Great fires were built in potholes in the rocks, and children were roasted alive in iron kettles."

She crossed herself. "In heathen times, surely."

"Even in our time. During the years of the Black Death among us. Folk said the powers of darkness walked the earth spreading the plague . . . craving blood. Four young children were sacrificed, the Abbot remembers."

Of a sudden my lady's horse shied. A grey hare, flashing across the pasture . . . a shadow we could not see?

We were silent, riding homeward. The slow twilight crept ahead of us on the lonely road. Once my lady reined in her horse and was still, as if she were listening. As if she heard on the stony road behind her the hoofbeat of horses. But the road was empty of all but shadow.

Chapter 12

The sense of dread stayed with me. Yet at the manor we were quiet. For a time. Rumour reached us—rumour of men marching toward Stenborg where the King met with his Council. Small troops of men from the mines, from the forest. Cutters of wood and charcoal burners. Shepherds and men of the farms. Men in sheepskin, or rough blue wadmal, in jerkins of worn cowhide. Armed with picks or the iron mattocks with which they scratched at the hard, rocky soil. With wolf knives, with clubs of gnarled oak, with scythes of beaten iron. But there was order among them. As yet.

We had no word from Lord Ivar. Nor did we expect it.

It was past Whitsuntide. As Peter would say, pipes of spring were sounding everywhere. Peter had made a song about this, about the small birds piping in the hedgerows, the rush of swollen brooks. And those small flowers of spring, in thousands, like a torrent down the hillsides, foaming white between the rocks, lying in still blue pools in the meadow. The little wood anemone, or so the Abbot called them; he was often with us.

When the strong winter is over, the months of winter dark, it is for us like a resurrection when spring comes again. Even the ruts in the brown road are beautiful, holding in still water the image of moving cloud, the blue of the sky.

We would walk in the spring meadow, or by the stream, to cut the yellow catkin; my lady would boil the bark, to give a yellow pigment like spring sun. Mushrooms and new green birch, even our iron-red earth—from these, Christer would compound his colours.

Christer was painting as never before. "Like a saint," said Donna.

Or like a madman, I thought, like one possessed. He seemed to have a dark foreknowledge that his time with us would be short.

He moved his paints and panels from the solar; there the winter darkness seemed to linger; the light was clouded by thick-paned casements. But in the meadow there was a barn, used no longer though the wry odour of horses was there still, and the manger was piled with hay. Even now the grassy scent of hay brings back to me this time with Christer.

And the sunny afternoon when Lord Ivar came in to us in the barn.

I cannot forget that day for then we had an intimation of why Christer had at last left Italy.

My lord had ridden down from Stenborg to see my lady, for two days only; he spent his time with her.

And at the kennels for which the manor was famed. My lord loved hunting dogs with a passion—indeed with a kinship he did not feel for most men. He proposed to take back to the King the pick of the new litters. Wolfhounds, boarhounds, highly bred and trained by my lord's master handler, Sverker, the dwarf, a man I could not like.

Nor could my lady. "Though I am shamed, Jon. I should feel pity for him, for his deformity. But his face, the ragged thatch of black hair, the small cruel eyes. He seems of the darker world, as if he has clawed his way through earth's crust, stumbling and blinking in daylight. And at night crawls back into a troll's burrow to sleep."

He slept in fact with the dogs; perhaps he had taken on from them his air of brutishness. He was swarthy and squat, no higher than my armpits; but his shoulders were thick and powerful. He was not born a dwarf but had been maimed as many had, his legs broken upon the rack, long ago, before he entered my lord's service. He had earned torture for thievery; and he was thieving still, and sly, and foul of speech. But my lord would hear no word against him.

We sat in the barn with Christer; my lord came into the meadow with Sverker and two Irish hounds.

The hounds raced off, following a scent along the stream, but my lord came into the barn where Christer was at work. I was pounding lapis lazuli in a bronze mortar; my lady was mixing gold dust with orpiment.

"It is very poisonous, ma Donna," said Christer, "take care. Ah, I would set you to trimming brushes instead." He was near done with a portrait of my lady as the Virgin Mother; he was burnishing the golden halo with a wolf's tooth. "Though a dog's tooth is also good, a cat's tooth will do—'in general that of any animal which feeds decently upon flesh,' so Cennini tells us."

My lord came to stand over him. "The portrait is of great excellence," he said cordially.

Christer smiled at my lord.

And then of a sudden Christer was in a rage, his face waxen, his mouth tight, his eyes burning.

The dwarf had come into the barn. He waddled on bandy legs to the painting and pushed out a stubby forefinger, touching the blue folds of the Madonna's cloak.

Christer struck his hand away.

"*Dio, dio,* the paint is not dry. *Non toccare!*"

The dwarf squinted up at Christer. In his eyes there was

an ancient evil. He muttered an ancient curse and ambled out of the barn in search of the hounds.

"Son of wolves . . . spawn of monsters!" Christer turned in fierce anger to my lord. "Have I not served you well, Your Grace, since I came to Florence? These many years . . . but this I will not endure, *non e possibile*. As you are master of Florence, I am your servant. But I am master in my studio. I will not have it, the dwarf is thieving—six ounces of gold dust the last time, before that, a fine cameo that I would set in a saint's diadem. Ah, he knew you would defend him!"

My lord was staring at Christer. The dwarf Sverker had never come into the barn before; this was indeed the only time.

"Here in the studio . . ." Christer's voice was harsh. "A perversion among my boys. Two of them, perhaps three, are still virgin. Ah, I know well you are amused by his antic tricks. But, Your Grace, it is insupportable. You found him under a table in Pietro's vile tavern, that sinkhole of corruption. Found him lying in his own filth, and now he wears crimson, fine as any cardinal. I am shamed for you, shamed, Your Grace. The night of the wedding feast for Madonna Clara . . . the dwarf drunk and capering upon the table, a leopard pelt about his twisted loins. Upon this thumb the great signet I made for you, the emerald! And the ladies laughing when he pulled down his breeks and emptied himself into the golden goblet I fashioned—the great flagon, gold florins melted down to make it, Neptune upon the rim, with the little mermaid, rock crystal, turquoise, and ruby. The little monster fouling my great cup, and the ladies laughing." Christer's head sank into his hands. "And Madonna Ginevra fondling him in her lap, in his hairiness, his nakedness, as if he were a pet monkey."

My lord said in astonishment, "You are surely mad."

"A madness . . . *si*. A madness that you would have me paint him. Madonna Ginevra . . . *si*. She is the most beautiful of all your mistresses." Christer looked at my lord; his eyes were dark and beseeching. "There is no need to show her with the monster. For contrast! Her beauty needs no foil. I will paint her, her red-gold hair loose upon her shoulders, with her white cat, or with her small son. But not the dwarf." Then Christer's face grew proud and still. "*Mi scusi,* Your Grace. I would not anger you. But I will not paint the dwarf."

My lord turned on his heel and left us.

My lady could not console Christer. He was silent, staring at the wall.

Though my lord rode off the next morning to be with the King, Christer did not paint again for several days.

He was much disturbed. He said to me, "I dare not go back to Rome. I cannot stay longer here in Milano. The Duke's agents are everywhere. Is there no city in Europe where he has not established his great banking business? In business, his word is beyond reproach. But I cannot trust him in other matters. I cannot accept his apology . . . sweet as Tuscan wine, but often there is poison in that. He was so wroth with me . . . and I with him. So many cruel words. You say he would have me back. Ah. The Duke has power of life and death in Florence. At his word men are removed from posts where they have served with honour, and bodies are found, stuffed into sacks, caught in the rocks in the swift race of the river below the Ponte Romano. No, no," said Christer sadly. "A pity. I had affection for him once. A man given to vice, to cruelty . . . yet with such force of mind, such clarity. I cannot trust him. I will never go back to Florence."

"Where will you go?" I asked him.

But Christer made no answer. His eyes were remote.

At last Christer was painting again. He did not seem to recall anything he had said to us of his past.

In the barn, the spring sun poured in like a golden tide through the open doorway; it lay in golden pools on the earthen floor. Shafts of sunlight streamed from the raftered roof, sunlight full of dancing motes of dust. In his dark linen smock, Christer bent over the easel, intent on his work. He posed Kari as the penitent Magdalene woman, but she found it hard to sit quietly; she was large now with the burden of Peter's child.

She had the look he wanted: the corn-gold hair, the fresh skin with the bloom of sun upon it, the full breasts—a woman ripe with love. Yet in her eyes there was regret. Or was it only longing, longing for Peter? Once as Christer paused to trim his brushes, Kari put her hands to her swollen breasts and began to sing softly, a little song of Peter's.

"O spring, do not touch my heart.

I will not heed the small green leaves of springtime,
Tiny, tender, unfolding
Buds on a branch, small flowers like sun in the meadow.
I know when the leaves are full
Then summer is come with its fullness . . .
Blossom and fruit . . .
But when summer comes, my love will be far away."

And my lady's face was wistful, hearing this. She longed for Kurt; there had been no word of him. She sighed a little, pushing the dark, shining hair back from her forehead.

Christer looked up from his work; he felt her mood. There was between them always a deep bond of love. Not the love of man for maid, the strong surge of the senses. A bond of spirit and something more—the tenderness of mother for son, or father for daughter.

Christer said, "Ma Donna, do not be sorrowful. Though you have cause when Kurt is far way. Near or far, you love him . . . thank God for loving. This is the first and great commandment: love one another." Then to coax a smile from her he began to talk of the great fete when the Duchess of

Milano had married, and how in his workshop they had painted the banners to be borne in the great processional; how dozens of white doves had been released over the wedding canopy; and how he had made for Visconti, Lord of Milano, a wonderful chalice of rock crystal and gold, set with emeralds and small enamels.

My lady looked up at Christer with tenderness.

"And," he said, "there was the day when the Cardinal first came to sit for his portrait. I had longed to paint that face. Like a satyr's face, in it great strength, and yet such cunning, such cruelty. He was wearing the robes of office—the crimson, the folds shot with gold and shining. It required ten ounces of gold to paint the cope. To paint the laces, the finest brushes of camel's hair, as if one stroked the panel with cobwebs. But His Eminence must take off the cap, the cardinal's cap. I would see the shape of his head and feel the strong line of bone under the high forehead. The cap lay on a chair and one of my boys—Aldo, the youngest, so naughty always—filled the cap with plums bursting with juice. The Cardinal, unthinking, sat upon it."

Then Donna urged him to tell us more of how he had left Milano, but he gazed at her with vacant eyes. We did not question him again.

For Christer's sake, Donna tried to be gay. She was apt at mimicry; she would speak of the Swedish court and ape the Queen's ladies. "Two old ones, who had served the Queen's mother—the Countess of Bedford and my lady Somerset. Bedford is fat, ah, who could count those chins? She has a mountainous front; in the folds of her neck are pearls, and then cascading ropes of pearls plunge over her great bosom like a waterfall over a rock. She nibbles sweetmeats; her soft little nose, like a putty nose, wiggles as she eats. Like a rabbit chewing in little bites, the nose wiggling."

And Donna was suddenly the Countess, her chin quivering

as she sucked a grass blade. Though how so delicate a face as my lady's could become the very likeness—we knew it was so—of the fat Countess . . . Donna ambled before us, puffing a little. "When the Countess walks, she rolls, and her furs shudder, her laces trail and flutter.

"And the ancient Somerset. She smells musty, like old flannel. She is a little addled. But mostly she is asleep. Sitting by the Queen, her tapestry work in her lap. Or in church, she purrs and snuffles in sleep. Once at table, her arm rested near her plate; her wide sleeve fell back from her wrinkled arm; from the sleeve a little mouse wandered out, to sniff at her loaded plate. The old Somerset was awake . . . a wonder. She scooped up the mouse and stuffed it into her purse for privy monies and pulled the drawstring tight. 'The little one shall feed later,' she said." And Donna's face was full of mischief. "I asked her how many babies she had. She said two, but only one was tamed. Think, Jon, what it must be to share her bed. The babies must surely sleep with her."

I smiled at my Donna. "A trial, to be attended by such ladies."

"Ah, yes. But the Queen is always kind. Though the King will not suffer these two near him. When he is at court they must stay in the Queen's gallery. The King will have only young and lovely girls. Laughing girls. Most of the Queen's women are so."

"You, my lady." I dared to say it.

Her face clouded. "Young, certainly. But not always gay. The King lives for flattery. And I have sometimes been . . . tart of tongue."

"The King must live for more than flattery now. Or drinking and wenching and the chase. The huntsman is now the hunted."

"Yes," said my lady soberly. "Jon, will it come to open fighting? Kurt's men against the King?"

I was sorry I had spoken so, bringing her thoughts back to

Kurt. "Kurt has hope of keeping his men in check, of trying again to settle our fate with reason."

These were idle words, and I knew it.

Donna knew it too. Soon the first violence must come to the village.

How soon?

The Abbot had said that in the village a bitter wind was blowing. The manor folk were saying it, too. Most had kinsfolk in the village. "Hunger and want there. Most of them be eating willow shoot and acorns. Now and then a sparrow in the cookpot. Or rabbit. If the boys can net them."

I knew that most of the men were apt at poaching; they would bring back partridge or hare or a catch of fish. But most of the men were marching with Kurt to see the King.

"What be the good of that?" said the manor folk. "The King has a deaf ear for poor men who labour."

My lady sent men with baskets of food from the manor. Women would cluster round the village well. They were huddled in ragged shawls; their faces were grimy and worn; their eyes were dull with hunger. Children clung to their mud-spattered skirts.

I rode down to the village with my lord's men. I thought to give the children blessing, if any would receive it. And seeing them in their filth and their apathy, I thought of a sudden that if man is made in God's image, then God has a poor, swarthy, brutish image.

Small wonder there was bitterness among them. Even against me, though I was one of them. Born in a poor croft like them, a man who has known cold and hunger.

But I knew it no longer. I was housed and fed at the manor. The women muttered against me. They hissed like angry cats at my lord's men. But they snatched at the food baskets.

I had no blame for them, only pity. What chance had they to be other than what they were? The harsh ugliness of their lives brought ugliness to their faces.

And my lady pitied them. She would ride to the village. "If I can help . . . listen to grievance . . ."

"No," I said. "You would only provoke anger, my lady of the manor. In cloak of velvet and gloves of soft fawn."

"I know," she said sadly.

But we rode out sometimes with Christer. Near the inn there is a swift, brown stream and a rude bridge over it of pine timbers. Christer liked to stand there, leaning on the scarred rail, watching the rush of the stream beneath the bridge, the glassy flow of light on tumbled water. Below the bridge my lady would climb among the mossy stones, seeking violets and fern.

I cannot know what Christer saw in moving water. Faces from the past perhaps.

One day he stood bemused, gazing into the water. I was beside him. Two of the village women approached us from the road, barefoot, their brown skirts bedraggled; leaf and twig clung to their skirts. One had a willow basket with mushrooms, a scanty picking. With them was a lad, tow-headed; he had two small, silvery fish on a string.

And a girl in rough grey linsey, her tawny hair tangled on her shoulders. The girl's face was smudged, but it was sweet with the freshness of youth. Her skirt was gathered above her knees, a rude sacking to hold the fresh green shoots of nettles for soup.

Christer suddenly stood before her; he took her by the shoulder, but his touch was gentle. "The bone beneath the flesh." He turned to the lad. "Do you see, Carlo? You must seek the bone, and know it. Feel the cheek bone, line it in with charcoal first, before you would fill out the face with flesh. I was a long time learning. Dead bodies are hard to come by. Those dark nights with Alberti, when we went to the hanging hill beyond the city wall and cut down the bodies from the gibbet. I dream of it still, dream of those black nights. The poor men hanging . . . ah, crows would have taken them, in time. We would say a Pater Noster; and then we cut the bodies down and dragged them back to the studio, wrapped in heavy sacking. We would lay them out on the stone bench in the *loggia*. Even there, in the clear air of dawn, the smell was often . . . Alberti would swab the bodies with strong white brandy. And we sought with the surgeon's knife to trace the course of muscle and vein."

The girl wrenched loose from him; her eyes were wide with horror. The women were staring, as if in trance; at last one of them shrieked. The lad spat at Christer. And all of them ran from us, like foxes, into the forest.

Christer turned to me. "That night when we were set upon by the city guard . . . a gusty night, the dark of the moon. We thought we were safe. We were not far from the studio, hauling the wrapped body between us. I owe my life to the Duke. He vouched for us; he paid off the city guard. If not—we would have hung with those others, outside the wall. But the Duke loved sculpture above all things; he knew we must study, we must learn from life. And death. And he knew we had *caused* no deaths, as he had often, in war. Ah, that night he saved us. But God watched us."

My lady was climbing toward us from the bank of the stream, her hands full of flowers. She had seen or heard nothing of all this. She was sad to find Christer leaning on the bridge rail, slumped over it, his head in his hands.

There were tears in his eyes. "The sculptor must learn. As the surgeon learns. Was it wrong? Was it *wrong!*"

We rode often to the little chapel, where Christer worked on the altarpiece. He was finishing the central panel.

And this was the great work.

There was a mistiness about the painting, as though the panel were bathed in golden light. A tall, young Christ stood in a sunny meadow, surrounded by small children. The still, green meadow was full of sunlight, the grass was starred with small flowers. Warm light touched the faces of the children, uplifted to the Christ; their eyes were deep with wonder, and with love. Christ's arm was raised in blessing over the children, the little cripple, Anders, among them.

The hand of the Christ was Christer's own, that strong hand which could evoke such beauty. The eyes of the Christ were dark and shining. There was in them a depth of infinite love, and yet a strange compulsion. The gaze seemed to follow me. The face was strong, and sad—yet tender. A face I could never forget. It was like no face I had ever known.

"Ah," said Christer, "we can never know Him fully."

I stood watching him; he was brushing in the background of the painting. A soft blue sky and a little copse of birches, feathery in their spring green. The old iron bell of the chapel began to toll, I know not why. And Christer was murmuring about the bells of Florence. Yet I think he had no true religion as we think of it. His worship was not of the Church, it was of life in its abundance. He wore his great gold crucifix because he liked the fashioning of it, the workmanship, and not because he was devout.

He loved and worshipped life. "God so loved the world," he would say, his face alight; he would be smoothing the silken petals of a flower in his hand, or watching a dragon fly poised on a leaf, the green-gold wings like gauze and trembling. He saw so much that others missed: every vein in the leaf, every tint in the flower, the dewdrop on the stone, and all the colours in it. Crystals of hoarfrost on a winter branch. And clouds and stars.

Christer stretched out his hand, moving the cramped fingers. He had worked for hours on the altarpiece. Though in truth, he did not seem to labour, only to be captured by the work.

I left him; I went out into the churchyard to be with Donna. She sat on the grass, her blue skirt spreading around her; she was weaving a chain of buttercups for little Anders. He was making a chain, too, for my lady, his sweet face intent, his small, stubby fingers busy. Much of the time the little boy was with us; Donna loved him dearly.

Then on the road we saw Dame Barbro, his granny, swinging along with her long stride, her black cloak billowing behind her. She was carrying her bag of herbs and simples and the birthing stool. Some poor lass in the village had brought a babe to birth.

She saw us, she came toward us; she would collect Anders' wage. My lady gave her greeting, but Anders said not a word.

Barbro stood over my lady. Her strange, pale eyes were full of malice, the thin mouth was tight. "So Anders has no greeting for his granny?"

The child looked up at her. His little face seemed pinched, his eyes were wide and fearful. He pointed to his granny. " 'Thou shalt not suffer a witch to live.' "

Christer had said it often. When Barbro came to the manor to fetch the child, he would not permit her in the meadow barn. Watching her cross the meadow, he would say, "The Devil casts a long shadow."

Now Barbro stooped to Anders; she gave him a sharp cuff on the cheek. He cowered; he sat humped over his stunted little legs; his crumpled flowers lay on the grass. But he said again, " 'Thou shalt not suffer a witch . . .' "

I think he felt in my lady a strangeness, a kind of dread.

Barbro looked long and hard at my lady. "So you teach him . . . to scorn his granny, that's fed and fostered him."

Donna said quickly, "Anders, such naughty speech. Beg pardon of your granny."

But Anders hid his head in Donna's skirt.

"Oh, Dame Barbro, he has heard talk he does not understand. I am sorry."

"And will be sorrier soon." Barbro seemed to tower over my

lady. Her height seemed to swell, her eyes burned. "Evil words bring an evil return."

She seized Anders' arm and dragged him away. Big tears stood in his eyes, but now he said no word; he knew better.

Within the week he was back at the manor. Dame Barbro had no time for him and wanted his wage.

The child had a bruise on his arm and another on his forehead; he was listless. Donna cradled him in her lap; she sang to him and walked with him in the meadow. They brought back chanterelles in a basket. Anders was happy; he had found the mushrooms growing in the mossy turf beneath the birches.

Donna brought them to us in the barn. "No, Christer," she said gaily. "These will not be dried and ground to dust to make your colours. Though they are yellow as apricots. These are to eat, delicious, and fluted like coral. With such a delicate scent."

I took Anders on my shoulders; his little legs were weary, though it seemed to us that he walked more easily these days, not humping and crawling like an animal, as he had in Barbro's hut. I would carry him up to the manor to rest.

"A moment," said Christer. I stood with Anders on my shoulder; with one small hand he touched my hair.

"I will put you by the stream." Christer was choosing colours. "It is good that your shoulders are broad and strong, Jon. For an hour at a time, will you hold him so? Saint Christopher fording the stream, with the small lost Christ Child."

Though so much of Christer's work was destroyed, I have heard that this painting still exists, in the cloister at Lindhagen. But I cannot now endure to go back and see it.

I slept fitfully that night; the wind mourned in the great oaks around the manor; an owl kept calling. I watched the early grey light at the shuttered casement. At last I rose and said my devotions, though these seemed to me now to be mockery. The sweet face of my lady came between me and the Sacred Book. Ah, God, how could I say the words of grace, when I adored the wife of another man and lived on his bounty, ate his bread, and betrayed him in every thought?

I went out into the morning pasture. So early was it, the sky was pale; mist lay over the pasture, broken by thin bars of watery sunlight. The grass was wet with dew. And walking toward me, lifting her skirts a little from the shining grass, there was my lady. My heart beat strongly, as always, at the sight of her.

"You could not sleep either, Jon?" She smiled at me, but her eyes were darkly shadowed. "Ah, I dreamed . . . no, not of Kurt. Of Dame Barbro. I walked on a lonely road. A road that wound deeper and deeper into the forest. I was lost in the gloom of the great trees; there was no one to call. And then I knew there was someone who followed. Someone sly and evil and strong. Dame Barbro. Then she was suddenly ahead, her black cloak flapping like bat wings . . . great webbed wings . . . her pale eyes shining. She was waiting. She was there wherever I turned. Suddenly in the copse ahead, or just behind a rock——" She brushed the soft hair from her forehead, shaking her head as if to rid herself of the dream. "It is silly, I know. What can Dame Barbro do to harm me?"

"Nothing," I said strongly, and took her hand to lead her back to the manor, to the morning meal. And indeed at that time I could see no way that Barbro could bring us harm.

Yet I thought of the iron mountain, of the drifting mist at the foot of it, and the strong thrust of the cliff, the blood-red figures gashed in the rock in the earliest time of man. No man can conquer that cliff.

At dusk, the little iron bells of the chapel toll. Yet their small clamour is lost in the grey gloaming. The sound scarcely carries across the meadow. In the chapel yard at dusk the priest walks among the old graves; the stones are crumbling now, eaten with moss. The priest swings his censer, and shelters his candle. Yet his small light is lost in a black wind.

The old gods are here still among us; they wait, men say, in the dark heart of the forest; they wait, in the hidden caves in the mountains. They wait, those powers and principalities of darkness, until their time is come again.

I said nothing of this to my sweet lady; I tried to push such thoughts from my mind. In the still evenings the thoughts returned; I would walk at twilight in the pasture and see in the thick forest growth below the manor, a glimmer of light beneath the trees. Small lights bobbing like marsh lights, thin green flares in the thickets. And twice a little rush of wind brought the sound of chanting. The strange shrill chanting of the witches.

Sometimes close to the road I saw them, the hobbling old women, their rusty cloaks wrapped close about them, some so bent they were like a company of moles moving along the road. To the mangy strips of fur upon their heads some had fastened twigs of hazel tree; some had bits of yellowed bone. They were clutching their bags of herbs or bunches of sticks. It was not long till Midsummer—a witching night among them; and so they met, in the forest grove below the manor. And elsewhere as well.

I believe most were harmless. Most were from the village: Mother Svenson, old Marta, others. They gathered roots and nettles for soup; they gathered herbs from forest and hedgerow. If they called, in the dark of the moon, upon a power of darkness, if some would league themselves with the Devil . . . I cannot say.

Yet twice I had seen among the witches, a tall one, in a

black cloak, shoulders squared like a man's, striding ahead of the others. She carried a staff of gnarled thorn; on her head she wore the bleached and pitted antlers of a stag.

Dame Barbro . . . she was the leader.

Chapter 13

On a grey spring evening Lord Ivar returned to the manor. It was near dusk; a slow rain was falling; my lord and his company rode into the muddy courtyard, a sodden company, with dragging plumes and drenched cloaks. They had been on the road for hours; they were soaked and saddle-weary. Grooms splashed through the mud to take the horses.

My lady was heedless of the rain; she pulled a cloak over her hair and ran to greet my lord.

He dismounted; he patted the steaming flank of his horse. I saw that a little rivulet of water ran down the back of my lord's neck; his fine blue cloak was stiff with mud. He kissed my lady fondly, but his face was grey with strain.

"It has come," he said. "Come to the village." And I had no doubt of his meaning.

My lord sat down before the fire in the great hall. My lady insisted on drawing off his wet boots. Dame Agnes was sent for meat and wine, but my lord ate little. I poured his wine; his hand, gripping the goblet, was stiff, and the knuckles were white.

"Today, good Jon. In the village. Before the inn, the body of the bailiff. Sprawled in the mud, the veins in his neck slit.

The heart cut out of his body. Yes, by God's blood! The heart cut out."

I poured more wine for my lord.

He drank and loosened the wet neckcloth at his throat. "In war I have seen much. But this . . ."

I felt that I stood and looked down upon the body. That gross bulk that was the King's bailiff, lying like a slaughtered hog in the mud, and the tow-white hair with dried blood upon it.

My lord said heavily, "Tied to the body was a sign in rough letters. A chunk of scraped pinewood, the letters hewn upon it with a blunt knife. 'The bailiff has paid his taxes.' "

My heart jumped. Did this point to Kurt? I thought of the night when Kurt had faced the bailiff across my lord's table and said, his mouth tight with anger, "Bread from our mouths we give, blood from our veins. But we cannot cut the hearts from our bodies."

No. I could not believe such butchery of Kurt. But my heart was troubled for one thing. Kurt had in his company men he could not control.

"A sorry deed," I said quickly, for my lord was looking upon me with cold grey eyes.

"A wanton evil," said my lord. "And further, a vile insult to the Crown. You have worked much with the miners, Jon. Do you know of a man among them who could do so foul a deed?"

"No, my lord." And I said it strongly, though it was far from the truth.

"I have questioned the man who keeps the inn. Tomas, by name. A sullen lout. He denied any knowledge, of course, of the murder. He had been away from the inn during the day, when trade, he said, was small. He had gone into the forest. I have no doubt he had gone to poach hare. I got little from him. He said only that men of the mines spoke much of the bailiff. The usual complaint. And some had said of the bailiff in death that so much fat flesh might as well go into the cookpot. He had taken food from the mouths of others, and now he might as well supply a meal. But others said no—an old porker, gamey and rotten." My lord drank deeply. "By the wrath of God!"

I looked at my lady. She sat on a low stool before the fire; she was knotting her hands in distress; her small face was white. I knew she was thinking, as I was, of Kurt.

"Oh, my Donna . . ." I said, and checked myself; I had called her by her given name. But she gave me a wan smile, and my lord did not notice. And I thanked God for that.

I said, to distract my lord, "What of the Council meeting? Is His Majesty the King in health? And yourself, my lord, did you enjoy good hunting?"

Lord Ivar got to his feet, goblet in hand. He stood before the fire. His face seemed to swell; the veins on his forehead stood out. In those ice-grey eyes there were pinpoints of flame. "We rode out—the King and others, I among them—to hunt boar. In the forest, the royal forest of Stenborg, without leave or right, suddenly, swarming from the rocks, dropping from trees, there was a troop of men. Thirty or more. Men of the forest, or of the mines. Swarthy brutes. As if Hell had opened of a sudden and the Devil's beasts converged upon us. They attacked with pike and mallet; two seized the bridle of the King's horse."

"Oh, my lord!" said Donna, biting her lip.

He put a hand on her shoulder as if to ease her; yet I observed that the hand was shaking. "The King's men rallied, my sweeting. It was of course an incident of small moment to men trained in war. We left no man alive. One perhaps—I saw him on the ground, body broken, trampled by the King's great charger."

Donna got to her feet, moving away from him, from the weight of his hand on her shoulder. She said, in a small voice, "But you were not harmed, my lord . . . by God's mercy."

"I have suffered no bodily harm, my Donna. Though I consider it honour to bear a wound for my King. I have suffered a vital wound. A wound of spirit. I have relied upon a faithless man. I have offered counsel and kindness; I have tolerated too much. And now . . . ! While we rode out to hunt, five of the Royal Council sat in the Royal Chamber. The Bishop of Ulm, the Royal Comptroller, three others. All of ripe years, and not inclined to hunt. They were going over the tax rolls, a thankless task. And into the Chamber came, with iron arrogance, Kurt, my cousin."

"Kurt!" My lady turned quickly to me, so that my lord should not see her face.

"Kurt," said my lord with cold fury. "Into the Council Chamber . . . as he has come before, with mock courtesy. And treason in his heart. He presented a large parchment, a petition addressed to the King and signed by many. Many indeed were not able to sign but had marked the parchment . . . blots and crosses. But some of the signatures were of men of consequence. The Bishop of Vestvik. My lords of Holmen and of Tallbacken. Others. The petition was of grievance. Grievance at high taxes, of men conscripted for war, much else. It is not difficult for men in time of war to seek and find cause for grievance."

My lady and I were silent, yet if we had spoken, I think my lord would have paid us no heed.

"The final arrogance," he said, draining his goblet, "the petition stated in clear terms that at his accession the King had made to the people promises that he would hold their welfare in sacred trust. That His Majesty had not done so, but had broken faith. That the people—such as Kurt could muster—will now withhold their obedience to a King who has violated his oath to them. His vow to respect their liberties."

I felt my heart beat strongly. "Was Kurt seized?"

"He was not seized, but permitted to go in peace. And with him went the Bishop of Ulm and the Royal Comptroller. I believe they had no choice. Waiting for Kurt on the slope below the castle, armed with crude weapons, were a hundred or more men. With Kurt in spirit, shouting his name. And eager for a brawl."

"There was fighting?"

"No, no. Kurt entered the Royal Chamber alone; he spoke quietly. God's blood!" And my lord spat into the fire. "It is true that Kurt was accustomed to enter the Chamber on government business. I do not hold the King's Guard at fault, or the House Guard, which gave him safe conduct. I hold the King's men-at-arms at fault, in the castle courtyard, to see and permit so large a rabble army to gather on the castle slope."

My lord called loudly for a serving man to bring more wine. "Cowards," he said. "Mercenaries. Though they were much outnumbered. At last the mob dispersed into the forest. At Kurt's command!" My lord looked into his goblet and said wearily, "I have seen madness. A bitter malady, deserving of some pity. I have seen it in old prisoners of war, silent and staring for hours, sitting like spiders in webs of their own rags. I recall an old baron at court who went like a dog on hands and knees, with spittle dropping from his chin. At last he was confined. Yet he would harm no man. Kurt's is a dangerous madness. Infectious madness, leading others to treason. Large mobs move along the roads. A rabble army," said my lord in scorn. "Punitive measures will be taken."

My lord turned to my lady; his eyes were tender, for her. "My sweeting, you will go back to Stockholm. To safety."

"No! Oh, my lord . . . no."

"You will go without delay."

"I would stay here . . . by you."

"That is not possible. I will gather such force as I can. A

considerable force. From here, from Stockholm, from Skåne. I will be at the side of my King. Ah, my sweet Donna, do not distress yourself. For me, there is small danger."

For my lady was weeping softly. Her little face was streaked with tears, and I wanted to take her in my arms.

But my lord said with severity, "I have a bitter task before me. Do not add to my burden, my Donna, by such display of childishness. I thought you would welcome it, to be back at court. The life there, the dancing and mummery. All that you used to love."

"I love it no longer," said Donna, proud and composed; her tears had stopped. "Life is false at court. All dalliance and games. Now that I know Christer, I know there are other things. I would not leave Christer."

"Christer can go with you."

"And leave his work? No!"

This gave my lord pause. "I *would* have him finish the work in the chapel. Naturally. The memorial to my mother. It is fine work, I grant that." He looked up with impatience; a serving man was filling his goblet. "When the work in the chapel is done—a matter of weeks, I assume—Christer can join you in Stockholm."

"Left here alone," said Donna, "Christer would be distracted. He is not well. Though he paints like an angel, a devil is in him, a sickness."

At these words, "a devil is in him," I observed on the face of the serving man a look of dark misgiving.

Donna did not notice it. "It is best for Christer to work here alone, in quietness. Oh, my lord, from the village folk Christer has painted such faces. From forest and meadow he has drawn his backgrounds. Such power, such beauty in the work. I cannot leave him."

"You will go," said my lord testily. "Christer can join you later. He will paint as well in Stockholm. Would you deny him the chance to be at court, where with his gift he will be given work for eternity? At prices even I cannot pay. What of the Queen? She can do much for Christer. Few will see and remark his art in our small village. In Stockholm the world will welcome him."

My Donna was quiet, clasping her hands before her; she gazed into the fire, as if she sought in the leaping flame an augury . . . or an answer.

Then she said quietly, "I would not be disobedient. But I must stay here. I will tell you what I had hoped to keep to myself until more weeks have passed. I have reason to think . . . oh, my lord, I have greatly wished to bear a child. A son for you."

My lord let his goblet crash upon the hearth. He seized my lady's hands and held her to him strongly.

"My little Donna! My own sweet wife!"

Donna drew away from him. She said earnestly, "The trip to Stockholm now, on rutted roads, by coach or horseback . . . I would not endanger the babe. And you have said that the roads are crowded with marching men."

So of course my lady stayed on at the manor.

Chapter 14

I have not seen in any man such joy as was my lord's at news of the coming child. Indeed in our poor village a child is a burden, another mouth to feed, until it grows old enough to labour, or to fend for itself.

A lusty man was my lord; at his time of life it would be expected that in the village there would be some who bore his look upon them; yet so far as I know he had no issue out of wedlock, in the village or elsewhere. Most men assumed that it was not in him to sire a child. Late in life he had married my lady because her sweetness and grace obsessed him; she was his toy and his proud possession. I believe he had given no thought to the possibility that God might bless the union with an heir.

Now he made magnificent plans for his son. It did not occur to him that the child might be a daughter.

He spread the news of his expectations; he pressed gold *riksdaler* into the hands of his men-at-arms; he lifted brawny beakers of ale with the men of the manor farms; he rode to see the Abbot and desired that special prayers be offered for the welfare of my lady.

My lord sent Dame Agnes into the storerooms; his own

gold christening cup had been laid away, and the gold cross set with rubies, a gift on his naming day. These were brought out and burnished. His own christening gown of rich brocade with gold laces; the tiny cap of green velvet banded with miniver; a cluster of golden bells which his nurses had dangled before him as a babe to amuse him. These were brought out and displayed.

And it seemed that he was ever in attendance on my lady. He pressed her to eat until she said she felt like a stuffed goose. He took her hand to lead her down the great staircase, though she was accustomed to flying down, fleet as a bird, her little feet scarcely touching the steps.

My lord exhorted my lady to take every care of herself; and when he had to go, for a week, to Stockholm, he returned with baskets and hampers of gifts. Paints for Christer; gingered fruits for my lady and candied violets with angelica; her favourite pomades; a new furred mantle and a sapphire ring. He sensed that these gifts gave my lady small pleasure though she was quick and lively in praising them.

"Ah, my little Donna." He was tender and supplicant, a mood I had not seen in him before. "Haven't I tried always to please you? What is it, my sweeting, the babe within you, to make you melancholy? Are you not well? Or are you fearful? Do you guard yourself properly?" And I could feel a small sympathy for him who loved her so well and could not be loved in return.

We had word that the King was in residence at Stenborg; he summoned my lord to join him. My lord left us with great reluctance and with many fond instructions. My lady was on no account to ride her great horse. She must eat boiled leeks to strengthen the blood and swallow a daily measure of ale, which she hated. She must be constant in devotion to Saint Margaret, benign patron of childbirth, and to the Blessed Virgin.

My lady waved my lord off with thankfulness and proceeded to ignore most of his instruction.

I pleaded with her. And she laughed at me.

And the worthy Dame Agnes bristled with advice and admonition. As we sat at table, she approached my lady; the square starched headdress seemed hewn from granite. She leaned over us, her large rigid front pushing almost into my lady's face.

"Dame Agnes," said Donna, "must you tower over me like a monument?"

Dame Agnes was pained but persistent, offering yet another dish of leeks.

Donna wrinkled her nose. "Take it away. I would sooner eat straw."

"But I am instructed by my lord——"

"Since he is not here," said Donna coolly, "I will instruct you. Take it away."

The iron-grey hairs on Dame Agnes' chin quivered with indignation.

And I said mildly, "My lady, you must eat for the sake of the babe."

"I am well and strong; I shall fare as well as any woman, and the babe shall be born lusty. But if I swallow leeks and ale, I shall be ill. And then I shall be fretful, and that can do the babe no benefit. Oh, Jon, Kari is more in need than I of cosseting."

And this was true. Kari's time was not far off; the sweet bloom of womanhood was gone. Her face seemed pinched, and yet puffed. She walked with heaviness and could not sleep.

Kari was anxious because for some days she had not felt the child move within her. "I am afraid," she said. And I thought that her voice was like the small plaintive note of a bird in a winter hedge. "The child moves in me no longer. Is this a penance? Because the little one was fathered, as they say, in sin? There was no sin between Peter and me; our loving was blessing. So Christer said. Yet I am afraid. I would give Peter a fine strapping son. Not a dead thing like a log."

There were tears in her eyes, and my lady took her hand. Between these two there was strong affection. They were like sisters, not like mistress and maid.

Each evening before sunset we would walk—Kari and my lady and I—a little way into the forest, under the arching oaks, to the Virgin Spring. There is a sunlit glade in the forest; the place is full of the whispering of leaves. And the splash and murmur of water falling over moss-grown stones. Bright drops glitter on the moss.

Brown and sparkling as ale, the little stream runs between banks of fern and spreads itself in a still green pool. And here grow lily of the valley in abundance; these are the flowers of the Blessed Mary; so the shallow pool is called the Virgin Spring.

And called so for another reason: there is a tale among us that a nun walked here once, and a lady of surpassing fairness appeared and spoke to her. She spoke only a word of blessing and then she vanished, in a cloud, a golden radiance. This was long ago before our time, and I know not if it is true. It is true that at sunset there is a golden haze over the moss; in the green shadow beneath the trees there is a stillness, a peace. Perhaps there has been a blessed Presence here.

Our women folk go to the spring; they cup the clear water in their hands, clasping their breasts, that they may have milk to suckle a child; they bathe in the spring, to ease a troubled birth.

We smelled the lilies before we saw them. The leaf of the lily is a physic for a failing heart. But I thought that no physic could help Donna, so sore was her heart for Kurt.

Yet she was happy picking the lilies; they gave her more

pleasure, I thought, than any of Lord Ivar's gifts. "So lovely," she said, her hands full of flowers. "The scent. And the small bells set on the stem like pearls. What goldsmith could fashion anything so lovely?"

But Kari said, "With us, the flower is called 'the Mother Mary's tears.' " And her small face was wistful.

Then Kari walked ahead of us, climbing to where the flower grew thickest, and of a sudden slipped on the wet, shining moss. She fell heavily and could not rise. Her hands were clasped over her swollen belly. "A twisting . . . a tearing . . ." She was biting her lip; her face was wet with tears.

I carried her back to the manor; in my arms, I felt her grow stiff with pain, her hands clutching my sleeve.

At the manor Kari was put to bed in the large chamber off the solar; my lady tucked the blue eiderdown around her, for Kari shivered though the room was warm. Her teeth were clenched; her hands clawed at the quilt. She was lost in a dark tide of pain.

And this would pass, and she would lie back gasping against the pillows, her face grey with weariness. "The pain. Like a fiery sword. I fear that . . . the child will be born too soon. Too soon."

Two of the manor women came into the chamber. Good women and wise, who had seen much of birthing. One of them put a workworn hand on Kari's belly. "A hard birthing. If the pains can be stopped . . . but my lady, that is beyond our knowing."

"Where is Peter? Peter!" cried Kari suddenly. Her voice was strange and shrill. "Mother Mary . . . help me."

"Send to the Abbot, Jon," said Donna. "The Abbot must come."

He would come, we knew, if my lady called. "But he knows little of women's travail," I said. "No more do I. But there is one at the monastery, the old one, Lavrans, who is skilled in healing. Perhaps juice of poppy . . ."

This was used at the monastery, for the aged, the infirm. A potion of poppy is of benefit if a monk suffers from ague, in the strong winter cold.

Old Lavrans came at last; he had been roused from sleep and the evening chill was in his bones, he said; and further, he knew nothing of women's pain in labour—the curse of Eve, he said, and women were fated to bear it. He said a Pater Noster; he begged Kari to consider her state of mortal sin and to bear God's penance with fortitude. And then he stumped from the room. But he left with us powdered poppy.

The drug worked strongly in Kari. The pains were eased. She lay staring at the casement, where now the first light of dawning showed. But her eyes, we thought, were unseeing; her face was pale as wax.

"Peter . . ." she said, so low we could scarce catch the words. And then in a strange, high voice she began to sing. Some verses of Peter's. The words were blurred. Like the whisper of falling snow.

But we knew the words.

My lady bent over Kari. "We will send for Peter."

Kari smiled a little and seemed to sleep.

My lady stood by the casement, hands clasped, her sweet face much troubled. It is beyond my understanding that her compassion for Kari should bring upon my Donna a malignant evil. As Christer would say, "Ah, God who made us, why must it be so?"

I took the sea road—the short way—to Kurt's manor because my lady asked it, though I had no hope of finding Peter there. Where Kurt was, there was Peter.

The road skirts the inlet. At this hour the early light silvered the water; the fresh wind sent small waves curling among the rocks. In clefts of the rock, patches of heather took colour. The dune-grass was sun-struck, sun-gold, waving like wheat.

At this hour Kurt and Peter waked. Perhaps in a forest grove near Stenborg where the King held council. Or perhaps they had slept in wet meadow grass under a heavy sky and now waked, stiff and saddle-sore, to take council themselves with their ragged army of men.

At Kurt's manor, his men might know where he camped. A boy could be sent to find Peter. The tall grey horse had an easy gait. As I rode, I thought of Kari. Of her voice, a sad little echo of Peter's singing.

It was the ballad of little Karin; Peter sang it often, his hands quick and light on the fiddle, his head thrown back, laughing and teasing.

> Little Karin served
> At the manor of the King.
> All the young maidens
> Danced in a ring.
>
> Among the young maidens
> None was so fair.
> She shone like a star
> With her fine gold hair.
>
> The King saw her dancing,
> Lightsome and free.
> The King took her hand
> And went on his knee.
>
> Karin, little Karin,
> Will you be mine?
> A tall crown of red gold,
> This shall be thine.
>
> A tall crown of red gold,
> I will not have.
> Give it to your young Queen,
> And my honour save.

God's blood, Karin,
If you won't be mine,
I'll put you in the barrel
With sharp nails within.

They put her in the barrel
With nails strong and stout.
The King's men then
Rolled the barrel about.

Down from blue heaven
Two white doves came.
They took little Karin's soul
To save her from shame.

This, before Mary, I'll swear to thee.
Soon there were white doves three.

Up from the heart of hell
Two devils came.
They took the young King
Of evil fame.

This, before Satan, I'll swear to thee.
Soon there were black devils three.

I tried to put the tune from my mind. It must have seemed to Kari in her travail that she was trapped in a barrel lined with cruel spikes. An agony from which there could be but one escape.

I spurred the grey horse on toward Kurt's manor. From the inlet the road climbed and then dipped into the forest. And here a troop of my lord's horsemen passed me. I knew they patrolled the roads for hope of surprising Kurt. If they could take him alive, their reward would be royal. But they had orders to take him, dead or alive.

Kurt's manor was deserted. Or so it seemed. As desolate as if the Black Plague had tarried here and left no soul alive.

Then on the grassy slope below the manor, I saw two horses grazing. Two stablehands came to meet me, men long in Kurt's service, who had known me in boyhood. Old Jens put up a gnarled hand to take the reins of the grey horse.

"If ye're seeking Kurt——"

"Peter."

"Where they can be, we've no way of knowing. We two are left alone here. The women safe at the island. A pair of strong lads with them." Old Jens chewed a grass blade and scratched his chin. "We had word. Kurt and Peter be coming. Tomorrow or next day, God willing."

"Not here? Lord Ivar's men watch the roads."

"Aye, young Jon. So Kurt be coming by sea. Not here. To the island. Is there aught to tell him?"

"That my lord is at Stenborg with the King. That my lord has sent to Skåne for men-at-arms, and to Stockholm. The Bishop of Stockholm has promised a large company of men. I act as my lord's scribe often. I have copied his letters for Kurt. I will bring them when I can."

Old Jens' face crinkled; his lips spread in a wide, toothless grin. "Aye. Always the fox you were. Like Kurt himself. Bring the parchments. I'll be getting them to the island."

"One thing more, Jens. Peter must be told that Kari, his handfast love, lies ill at my lord's manor. Her time of travail is upon her. She longs for Peter. If he can come, saving himself, to the Virgin Spring, I am there each day near sundown with my lord's lady. But Peter must take no risk."

Throughout the day Kari slept, the strong hold of the drug still upon her. A shaft of sunlight struck through the casement upon the dark oaken floor—a long bar of gold, moving through the slow hours to rest upon the wooden stool, the settle, the wooden chest, and then upon the high carved headboard of the great bed where Kari lay. At last the light faded.

And still Kari lay as if in trance, an ice maiden under a spell. I put my hand to her throat and felt so faint a flutter of pulse that my heart was leaden in my chest. Had we given too heavy a dose of the deadly poppy, white and cloudy as milk, but a silken killer? A silent killer, and strong.

My lady was pale and shaken with weariness; I begged her to go to her chamber and rest.

And I sat, with one of the manor women, to watch over Kari. Old Marta sat stiff-kneed upon the wooden stool; her hands were knotted in her lap over the woolen apron. Thin old hands, the veins like cords upon them. Her lips moved but I caught no words. Perhaps she murmered a prayer.

Or perhaps an incantation. The ancient magical words of healing, rhyming words for aid in sore pain and trouble.

Many among the priests forbid these verses; they rank them with dark enchantment. But perhaps the verses have power. For at last Kari murmured and sighed, stirring in sleep, and opened her eyes and gazed at us, weeping a little.

My lady came into the chamber with candles, though we had no need of them yet. The white twilight of summer lingered in the room. On the stone ledge of the casement a small bird alighted and chirped; Kari turned her head to it as if it called to her. And then the strong pain gripped her. Her hands were tight upon the quilts.

Old Marta went to stand beside the bed. "Poor young one. Christ's pity upon her, to have it so hard. Christ's pity on the babe, to enter the world too soon. It cannot live."

"Jon," said my lady fearfully. "More of the poppy juice?"

"Poppy be evil," said old Marta. "Though the priests give it. One other we know, to slow the pains. Or if that cannot be, to ease the birthing. *Dvale,* the Devil's berry. A weed of the Devil's sowing." She crossed herself. " 'Tis wickedness to speak of *dvale*. Yet if ye've a mind to be using it . . . there be some at the manor can mix it."

"You, good mother?"

She shook her head. "Never, my lady." But her eyes clouded, those shrewd old eyes. I saw that she was lying.

"Bring it," said Donna. "I care not who will mix it, bring it."

The old woman was clutching her apron. "The Devil's herb. To some it will bring easing . . . a dark sleep. To some it brings nightmare . . . hag-ridden. A wickedness comes up on them, they be shrieking and screaming. But that be seldom. To most, 'tis a boon."

Then Kari screamed as the pain took her.

"I cannot bear it," said Donna; her little hands were fists. "That Kari should suffer so. And the babe be born to die. We will give the herb. Only a little of it. To quiet the pain, and stop the birth, if God wills it. I will bear the blame."

The bitter wine of forgetfulness, the Devil's brew, the nightshade. In the cup it was dark, with a whitish froth upon it. My lady gazed into the cup; her eyes were wide and fearful. "The smell of it. Jon, do we dare?"

And Kari moaned, turning upon the bed. "The babe will . . . will come. Oh, Mother Mary . . ."

Between us, we gave the wine. I held Kari strongly; my lady held the cup. But Kari turned from it, from the smell of it. A smoky smell, like rotting fungus.

"Kari," said my lady, pleading. "Only a little . . ."

Of a sudden Kari took the cup and drank deep; gasping, she drank till I seized the cup to take it from her; on the blue eiderdown, the dark wine spilled, a spreading stain.

Still I held Kari. I felt her in my arms, her heat and her sweating. I felt a shudder go through her. The gold hair fell upon my shoulders. I put her down gently, gently, though she did not feel it. Donna brought up a candle to set beside the bed. Kari gazed up at us, and her eyes were strange, the pupils large and dark, as if she looked beyond us into a darker world.

"It be easing her," said old Marta. "It may be she will sleep.

It may be she will dream, and be distracted. Or weep. And walk and wander. If she will walk, 'tis best to humour her. Be watching her, that she does herself no hurt."

Yet for a while, Kari lay quietly. The slow twilight deepened in the room. But on the grassy slope below the casement, the light lingered. I went to the casement and looked out. A little wind stirred in the trees. And I saw in the shadows beneath the oaks two figures, humped and hobbling, in ragged cloaks. And beyond them, a little cluster of witch lights bobbing. A green glow in the bracken, a pale flame under the trees.

Of a sudden Kari lifted her head from the pillows. "I will go now," she said clearly. But her voice was strange and shrill. "To the Virgin Spring. I will thank the Virgin Mother for deliverance." She was pulling the quilt around her shoulders.

My lady turned to old Marta in alarm.

"Let her have her way, my lady. Go with her. She'll not be going far. The pains be stopped; she'll be wanting soon to sleep."

Kari walked between us. Barefoot, in her white night shift, the long gold hair streaming on her shoulders. She was clutching the blue quilt; it dragged behind her. I wanted to take it from her, for fear she would stumble.

But she walked quietly.

In the meadow, the grass was wet with dew. There was still light in the pale sky; and there was the night scent of summer.

Kari walked slowly, lifting her feet as if she waded though shallow water.

From the meadow the path leads into the forest. There was a green darkness beneath the trees. The wind mourned in the bracken. There were forest murmurs . . . a whispering of leaves.

"Kari, Kari," said my lady in despair. "Turn back, you will take harm."

Kari seemed not to hear.

"It is not far," she said, in that strange slow voice. "To the spring . . . She will be there . . . the Virgin Mother. The water is cool and deep. I am burning, burning . . ."

"Kari!" I said sharply. I took her arm roughly, to shake her, to wake her from her trance.

But she pulled loose, in a kind of fury, and turned upon me and screamed. And then she was running. Running in the dusk, up the forest path, stumbling on root and stone. Branches whipped at the white night shift; briars clutched at her. Yet she was fleet, fleet as a fox, and as wild.

Then she sank to her knees, beside a mossy stone. Her head dropped on the moss.

She was not far from us; the white shift was a pale blur in the dusk. I would have run to her, but Donna seized my hand. "Jon, Jon! Go softly. She will take fright and run from us into the forest."

Kari was sobbing; the sound came to us faintly, like the murmur of water on stone.

Of a sudden there was a sound behind us, a sound to chill the blood. A rustling of wind in the thickets, the crack of twig and bracken. Then from the green gloom beneath the trees, from the leafy brush around us—swarming up the path like a cloud of hornets—howling and shrieking—there were the witches, their tarred torches flaming in the dusk. And around them a scattering of sparks, as if Hell opened and the Devil's creatures swarmed upon the path behind us.

I seized Donna strongly and pushed her to the shelter of a great boulder close beside the path. And I held her closely; her hands were tight in mine. I looked down at her, at that small white face in the grey light, and felt my heart pound.

For a moment her head was on my shoulder; I felt her softness in my arms and caught the scent of her hair.

"Jon . . . oh, God, what of Kari?"

Donna lifted her head. The witches were passing. In red

torchlight we saw their faces, among them, some from the manor. Two young maids, their hair loose and tangled. On their heads were ragged garlands of leaves. Their dark cloaks streamed behind them.

The others were old, in tattered cloaks of dun and black and grey; their hair fell in grey wisps upon their shoulders. Each wore tied in her hair a strand of scarlet wool, like a thin trickle of blood upon the scalp; knotted with the wool were bones, the small dry bones of ferret or weasel. In the smoky glow of the torches, these old ones were the shapes of nightmare.

And one stopped on the path beside us. We saw her face clearly. She stopped, jerking her head, peering around her as if distracted. Her grey shift was ragged and torn so that her breasts were hanging loose. Old breasts, sagging and thin. Between her knees she held a bunch of hazel sticks. The old face was strange and wild; the lips were drawn back from the teeth, and the eyes staring, red as flame in the strange red light. She was wailing, and then mumbling.

And I knew that she, and those others, had taken a draught of some noxious brew. The Devil's berry, or mushroom cap. Or other herbs to bemuse the senses. And now they believed themselves to be flying. Or captured by their horned god, and soon to suffer his embrace.

Beside me I heard Donna, her little intake of breath.

And then the old woman raced off, as if riding a lame mare, the sticks held tight between her knees.

And I stepped out upon the path. The witches were beyond us, rushing toward Kari. I saw that she lifted her head from the stone, and put her hand to her mouth. She was frozen in fright.

Then I lost sight of her, as the witches swarmed around her, hobbling and shrieking, circling her, waving their torches.

I saw only the dark shapes, jerking and bobbing in a cloud of smoke and sparks.

Then the witches rushed on, up the forest path.

I ran to Kari, calling her name. She made no answer; her head lay against the stone. She had fainted in fright.

I took her up in my arms, to carry her back to the manor. As we came out into the meadow, faint stars were showing in the sky. My little lady walked beside me, holding tight to the sleeve of my priest's gown.

At the manor I laid Kari down upon the bed. Her night shift was torn and stained. The green stain of moss, the brown of earth. And at the hem a blood stain; she had cut her foot, but the cut had closed. In her hair there were twigs and wisps of leaf; my lady took her own ivory comb to smooth it.

I bathed Kari's face with cool water. She opened her eyes then and looked up at me. So piteous a look. With eyes like the soft eyes of a young doe when the huntsmen surround it and the dogs go for its throat.

Old Marta stood by the bed, sucking her lip, and muttering. "The Devil's berry. So great a wickedness be in it. Give her wine."

But Kari could not lift her head to drink. We gave the warmed wine in spoonfuls; she would take only a little, then she turned her head away. "I could not . . . find her. The Virgin Lady. Gone . . . set upon by . . . the Devil's imps. I could not help."

"Sleep now," said Donna gently. "You have been dreaming, my Kari. An evil dream. Sleep. We are here, we will not leave you."

But Kari was moaning, her hands to her swollen breasts. She spoke through dry lips; we leaned close to catch the words. "It begins again. The pain, the pain. God's penance upon me. I . . . I cannot save the babe."

"Help her, help her," cried Donna, turning to old Marta.

But Marta said, " 'Tis past my helping. A hard birthing, my lady. There be one can help. Dame Barbro."

"No, no!"

"She be the one, my lady. In such a birthing."

Kari screamed; we bent over her; Marta drew back the eiderdown. We saw that the linen sheet was soaked with blood.

"The blood," said Marta. "It be time. Let Barbro come."

Kari lay limp against the pillows, gasping as a wave of pain left her. "Yes." Her voice was no more than a sigh. "Let . . . Barbro . . . come. It may be . . . she can . . . save the babe."

Within the hour Dame Barbro was with us. We had not heard her come; she was of a sudden in the doorway, her black cloak hanging around her and upon the hem of it a litter of leaves. Her hood was flung back; her iron-grey hair lay loose, like carded wool, upon her shoulders. And I saw that caught in the hood was a long strand of scarlet wool. And I knew she had been with the witches.

And Donna knew. I saw in her eyes the dark look of dread.

Dame Barbro gave us no word of greeting. She walked to the bed, her heavy shoes striking hard upon the oaken floor; she lifted the eiderdown and put a hand upon Kari's belly. She bent and sniffed the blood upon the sheet. "The water and the blood." She turned upon my lady; the pale eyes blazed. "So ye call me now in the dark of night, when it may be Kari is past helping?"

"No! Do not . . . do not say that. You must help, Dame Barbro, I beg you . . ." And Donna was weeping softly.

"When did she last feel the babe to move within her?" And Barbro's voice was harsh as the cracked note of a crow.

"Perhaps a week since."

"It may be the babe is dead," said Barbro. "And I'd not bear the blame for that, my lady."

"There will be no blame. Only help her."

Barbro took off her cloak and put it down upon the settle. She wore rusty black, as always; the gown was girdled with worn leather, strips of it knotted and plaited, and hanging from this—my heart leapt at the sight of it—was a slaughtered chicken. A cockerel, its crest pale and limp, its breast black and speckled, a dark splotch of blood upon its throat.

Barbro loosened the girdle, with the chicken. Heedless of the blood upon it, she put it down upon her cloak. It was as if she had set a trencher upon the table.

She went to Kari and put a hand upon Kari's arm. The hand was strong and square as a man's, with blunt fingers.

"Ye must be rid of the babe."

Kari looked up, her eyes dark with tears. "I . . . would save . . . it."

" 'Tis a dead thing ye carry within you, surely. It will bring your death. Unless ye are rid of it. I will give ergot, the spotted mould, the rot on the rye. To bring on strong pains, and loose the child from the womb, to stop the issue of blood. Life is in the blood; 'tis lost in the flow of blood from the body."

Kari said no word; her face was pale as bleached linen; tears streamed upon her cheeks.

Dame Barbro asked for wine. She delved in her ragged sack of herbs and simples and took out a leather pouch full of the mould, the ergot, an iron knife and an iron spoon. Carefully she mixed the potion, shaking the dusty grains of the rye into the wine and stirring it slowly.

She took the knife and went to the slaughtered cockerel and cut a thin slit in the limp neck. She let a little of the dark blood flow into the iron cup. "For strength."

She held the cup to Kari's lips. But Kari turned aside.

"Drink." And Barbro's face was harsh, the strong lines on it etched in black. In the thin light of the candles her pale eyes were gleaming. "Drink."

And Kari took the cup.

Then Barbro sent us from the room. "I'll not be wanting

you here. I'm not needing you. Old Marta will help, when the pains come on."

We went into the great hall. We stood before the casement and looked out at the night sky. So deep and remote, but full of stars. Moonlight lay over the summer meadow, a flood of silver. Rippling silver, where the wind stirred in the long grass. I caught the scent of clover.

So often Kari had run through the summer meadow, singing, her hair shining and loose, the grey cloak flying behind her . . . run to meet Peter by the barn.

So still was the summer night. And then we heard the cries, the harsh terrible cries of Kari in the agony of birth.

And I looked down at my little lady, my dear love, and thought in anguish that soon her own time would come.

She seemed to give no thought to that. I believe that she thought in those moments only of Kari.

It was soon over. Marta came to tell us that Kari and the child lay dead.

I begged my lady not to look upon the babe, but she would do it. A little girl with pale eyes, blank eyes, but blue as Kari's. And flaxen hair, like down upon her forehead. The babe lay beside Kari on the blue eiderdown.

And Donna sank to her knees beside the bed and took Kari's cold hand in hers. She was sobbing wildly.

Old Marta was mumbling. "The Lord gives. The Lord takes away."

But Barbro looked down at Donna in her grief; her lip curled in scorn. "A fatherless babe. Born to travail and trouble, to sour black bread in the mouth. If it lived to see harvest month. 'Tis better so, to lie in peace and feel no hurt." She took a wisp of rag from her knapsack, spit upon it, and wiped the rim of the iron cup.

Of a sudden Donna was on her feet, facing Barbro, screaming at her. "You killed her . . . killed my sweet Kari, with your witches' broth, and the hard pains upon her . . . killed her!" And Donna stopped, in a flood of tears; I went to her to take her hand.

Barbro said roughly, "Be not blaming me. 'Twas your own word there'd be no blaming. Ah, I've no trust in a lady's promise, be she so great a lady. Or a lord's promise, or the King's." She spat out the words; her pale eyes shone with hate. "Call me, ye will, in dead of night, too late. Too late to stop the flow of water and blood. Lord Jesus Himself could not stop the flow . . . the water and blood . . . from His own side, when He hung upon the tree!"

"Barbro!" I said sharply. "Say no more. My lady is distracted."

"Ah," she said then, turning upon me. "Distracted, is she? A poor weak creature—'tis so they're bred at court."

Donna bit back her tears. "Have you no mercy in you? No pity for Kari who lies dead?"

Barbro said coldly, " 'Tis not my doing she's dead. Be blaming the man who took in lust her maidenhead. Or the priests' God who orders women's pain at birthing." She knotted the girdle of her gown and wrapped herself in her mangy black cloak. "Four *riksdaler*, my lady. Four gold *riksdaler*, this night's work will cost you."

My lady faced her proudly. "Yes. Yes, Dame Barbro. You did what you could. I have said in sorrow words I did not mean. Bitter words. Forgive me."

"Four gold *riksdaler*." Barbro was stuffing the dead chicken down into her sack.

"You will have your payment," said Donna quietly. "To-morrow. Jon will see to it."

"Aye," said Barbro. "Be not forgetting it." Then she thrust her face close to my lady's; the pale eyes were glistening with malice. "And I'll not be forgetting the evil words you said."

She left us then; we heard the sound of her shoes, striking on stone in the great hall.

I could not forget the look in her eyes. I believe it was in her heart then to destroy, if she could, anyone Donna loved. And Donna herself, if she could find a way.

Truly she was of the Devil's begetting, one of his own.

Chapter 15

A still bright morning, the air full of birdsong. We rode, a sorry little party, along the road to the chapel. In the hedgerows wild roses were blooming; the fields were sweet with clover. So light was the wind, the green plumes of the pines were still, as if the great branches were weighted with sorrow as sharp as our own.

The Abbot was with us. And four of his men, hooded and gowned, and bearing no arms. And that was as well. We had two outriders only, but Lord Ivar's men go always armed, even to chapel. Women were with us from the manor, and four men to bear the small black box where Kari lay, in peace, with the dead child. I had closed the lid; my lady had covered it with flowers of the meadow.

Christer was with us. But I believe that Christer did not really comprehend that Kari was dead. His life had been thronged with people. Many, like those he had known in Florence, existed for him only in dreams now, or faces in his paintings, or shadows passing in his mind. I had gone to him in the meadow barn; he was grinding gold and mixing it with glair. I told him of Kari's death. "Kari is gone from us, Christer."

But Christer went to stand before his painting of Kari as the penitent Magdalene, and said, "No, no, she is here."

Though he seemed unaware that Kari was dead, he was disturbed by my lady's sorrow. In the chapel, I stood by my lady, and Christer on her other side. He took her hand in his. He was very tall and straight in his dark mantle; I felt in him an inner quietude, a depth of strength.

Yet when the black box was borne in, and set upon the rough stone flooring before the iron altar rail, Christer said loudly, " 'He that believeth in me shall never die.' "

The manor folk turned to look at him; the women whispered among themselves.

But he said nothing more, though his eyes held that strange, dark look.

My lady was composed during the burial Mass. She had done with weeping—though not with grief. Her sweet face was pale and her eyes were darkly shadowed. To the girdle of her black gown she had knotted the crucifix of ivory and gold which had been her mother's.

The priest's voice droned on, like the sound of a wasp against the leaded casement. The candles burned, with pale, steady flames. And at last one of the monks sang, as my lady had asked, a psalm which Kari loved:

Fairest Lord Jesu,
Ruler of all nature . . .

But could He rule the passions of our hearts?

The manor men took up the black box on their shoulders. We followed it into the churchyard. Some of the old gravestones were tumbled in the long grass; moss covered them, and wild flowers grew in the grass, such small flowers as Kari loved. It was still and sunny here, a place of peace, within the walls of the churchyard.

But Kari could not lie here, in hallowed ground. For the babe had died unchristened, and both of them unshriven.

Close by, within sound of the tolling church bell, there is a little copse of birches. And I thought of one of Peter's songs, looking at the slender white trunks, the little wind moving in the frail green leaves to set them a-tremble. "My love is shining and white as birches . . . the little brides of the meadow."

The grave had been dug beneath the birches. Beyond lay the forest. Oak and pine and hazel thicket, close-grown so that sunlight barely reached the ground beneath the trees.

I saw a green and brown shadow in the thicket. A flickering of light in the leaves . . . a little tremour of movement in the bracken. I saw it and wondered, for there the wind was still. Something moved in the thicket. A fox perhaps, alert and running for cover?

The black box was beside the shallow grave. My lady knelt and laid a fresh handful of field daisies upon it.

And then of a sudden we heard a cry, sharp, broken, shrill, like the cry of a fox in a trap. And from the thicket Peter came running.

He ran to us; he flung himself on the ground beside the black box. He clawed at it. "Open it! Oh, God, my Kari! Open it, she cannot breathe . . ."

For a moment, so sudden was it, no man of us moved.

My lady put out a hand to Peter; he stared at her with wild eyes. And I pulled her to her feet, pulled her away, for now my lord's men were upon Peter to seize him. They dragged him to his feet, but he wrenched loose; I saw in the sunlight the quick flash of his knife.

Then from the thicket, Kurt ran to us.

My lady's hand went to her throat. "Kurt!"

It was quick and violent. Kurt struck one of my lord's men to the ground; he lay there beside the black box, lay on his back, his mouth streaming with blood. And one of my lord's men was grappling with Kurt.

Peter was flailing about with his arms, kicking, fighting off two of the Abbot's men.

And then Kurt and Peter were running. Into the thicket, with four men after them. We heard cries, we heard the sharp crack of branch and bracken, horses neighing and snorting . . .

The old priest stood with us, by the open grave. He was mumbling and grey with shock. The Abbot stepped up to say the final words of the office.

One of the manor men was left to us. I helped him; we lowered the black box into the grave; slowly we began to fill in the grave with earth.

And our men came out of the thicket. One was stumbling, helped by his fellows. One of the Abbot's men had a long gash on his cheek.

"Away, clean away," he said. "They'd two men with them. And arms. And horses."

Our own horses were tethered near the churchyard gate. There was no hope of pursuit. By now Kurt and Peter were deep in the forest, following paths we could not know.

So it was, at Kari's burying. The last shovelful of earth was sifted over the black box. And Christer was muttering in Italian now, the words low and strange.

We rode slowly back to the manor.

And I thought of Kari, settled in stony earth, closed in from the sun. And of Peter's anguish.

I thought too of a night when I had seen her in the manor kitchen, dancing, a small dance of happiness because Peter was coming.

A winter's night, that was. I had gone to the casement to watch for Peter and had seen a field mouse, a tiny creature, a grey ball of fur, emerge from its hole in a snowdrift; saw it dancing, in a flurry, a small whirlwind of snow; then, shivering, it crept back into its burrow, so dark, so narrow and cold.

Day after day we woke to the sound of rain, dripping from the casements, streaming from the leaden gutters, splashing on the stones in the courtyard. For a week we were close-confined within the manor. My little lady would look up at the heavy sky, at the grey racing clouds, and, sighing, would say, "Ah, Jon, so sad a time is upon us. Kari . . . it is as if sunlight left us when Kari died. Even the wind mourns."

And I could not bear the look in her eyes, so full of hurt.

Christer made a sketch of her at this time, of Donna as the sorrowing Madonna. It was too wet to work in the meadow barn; he set up an easel in the solar. But Donna found it hard to sit quietly.

"Kurt," she said softly. "What if Kurt was wounded in the fight in the forest? I dream of it . . . the sound of it . . . the cries of the men . . . the horses screaming."

"Ma Donna," said Christer. He went to her, laying a gentle hand upon her hair. "The sun will shine again."

At last we woke to a bright June day. The meadow was flooded with sunlight; small flowers nodded in the grass. The sky was blue and shining; heaven had never seemed so high.

"We will go to the Virgin Spring," said Donna. And I was happy to see the light in her eyes again.

We climbed the forest path. Beneath the trees, the light was flickering, green and golden; golden light spilled upon the moss. The trunks of the pines were red in the shimmer of sun.

We came to the green glade in the forest close by the Virgin Spring. The valley lilies were blooming no longer. But Donna stooped to pick a handful of fern, the maidenhair. "Like green lace," she said. Then she looked up at me, her face troubled. "Do you hear it, Jon?"

I heard it, the sound of horses moving in the bracken, the creak of saddle straps. Of a sudden the horsemen rode out of the leafy shadow beneath the oaks.

Five of them, bearded men, rough and hairy as trolls, heavy-shouldered in leather armour. Upon his iron breastplate, one wore a blazon I did not know. All wore leather guards upon their faces.

We were surrounded. I felt my heart pound. But I took my lady's hand and told her, "Do not fear. God's help, perhaps they mean no harm to a gentle lady and a priest."

The leader dismounted. He walked to us, a tall man, and faceless in the black leather hood. We saw only the gleam of dark eyes through slits in the worn leather. And then he stripped the guard from his face.

It was Kurt.

He stood looking at my lady as if he would fill his eyes, fill his mind, with the sight of her, to nourish him in the weeks to come.

"My Donna. I have proof now that God at times sends an answer to prayer."

She put both her hands in his; they stood so, looking at one another. So strong was the bond between them, so sharp their love, that I felt they stood there, ringed by flame.

Then Kurt said, "The others will watch. If my lord's men think to ride this way. Come, my dearest Donna. I have an hour only. An hour to look at you. Then we are off to Arboga."

So we stood guard by the forest path, Kurt's men and I. And Donna led Kurt away into the forest, to the mossy bank beside the Virgin Spring. We heard only a murmur of voices, soon lost in the murmur of leaves. And then nothing. Only the wind in the trees, a note of birdsong.

And I felt a fierce pang of jealousy. She had gone with Kurt without a glance at me. Yet when she told me later of what befell them, I could feel in my heart a thrust of pain for Kurt, and Kurt's pain . . . and hers.

Beside the Virgin Spring, in the green shadow beneath the trees, Kurt took my lady in his arms and kissed her, a deep kiss.

And released her. His mouth was tight with bitterness. "Ah, God, it's torment. To kiss you so, when I want you so, all of you. But God forbid that I should bring you hurt."

"Kurt! Come to me, hold me. Take me!" And she spread her cloak upon the moss, and sat there, stretching out her arms to him.

"I'll not tumble you so, as kitchen girls are tumbled in a ditch." But he knelt beside her and took her hands. And then on her hand she felt the warm wetness oozing from his sleeve, the stickiness of blood. Her silken girdle was stained with it.

"Ah, Donna, my sweet," he said in dismay.

"You are hurt!"

"A flesh wound only. Almost healed. It opens a little when I ride."

But she saw that he was grey with weariness, and with loss of blood.

"Who has tended you, my Kurt?"

"A barber in Granholm. Bathed the wound and bound it. It is nothing. My sweet, I have soiled you." He took the stained fringe of her girdle in his hands.

"I am proud for it. Now we share it, the blood. I am proud." And Donna made him strip off the leather jerkin and looked at the wound. A flesh wound only, but deep. A trickle of blood still oozed from it; the binding upon it was brown and stiff with clotted blood.

Donna kissed the wound with tenderness; and then she knelt beside the Virgin Spring and cupped clear water in her hands; she bathed Kurt's arm. And took the linen kerchief from her breasts, ripped it loose from her bodice, and bound the wound.

"Kurt, my very dear."

"Two days, two nights of riding. A skirmish near Lindfors. We lost twelve men. Ah, God . . . I have bidden many men to death. I welcome death for myself, if in the end, our cause is won. But to ask my men to give their lives . . . Each man is solitary, sealed in his own skin, unique, a man like no other. As Christer said once. After the fight at Lindfors there was old Nilsson, born to insult, to bitter poverty. He fought like a bear; he lost a leg. There was filthy linen binding the stump of his leg, but we had a little wine for him; he was somewhat eased. He took out his reed pipe and piped the old songs of love and comradeship. Then . . . near dawn he died. I asked him to give his one life to a cause he could never understand."

"A cause for others, that they will not suffer the same . . . the hunger, the oppression. To die for others, this is true virtue. For this we honour Our Lord Christ. Kurt, my true love . . ." And Donna put her hand to his cheek, "Sleep now, sleep a little."

She drew his head down upon her lap.

Almost at once he slept, in deep weariness.

And when she told me of this, I thought of a book of the Abbot's, the tale of the mystical unicorn. Men hunt the unicorn, the beast unique, his single ivory horn spiral, his coat with the sheen of winter frost, and in his eyes, power, and a vision of distance, so fleet is he, on silver hoofs. Many join in the chase—men, dogs, horses, a bear, leashed and lunging and clumsy and trained to kill. But the unicorn can only be taken if a pure maiden can coax him to put his head, trusting, in her lap. She strokes the proud mane; he is made humble by beauty; at last he wears a jeweled collar. Then men and dogs can come upon him to capture him; and he will go with them gladly.

So Kurt lay quietly, his head in my lady's lap, sleeping, while she looked down at him, holding him, touching his face lightly. And the grey lines in his face eased.

I have given him peace, she thought, and her heart was warm with happiness. A little peace, for a little time.

A little time only. He was suddenly alert, as a soldier is. He had sensed in sleep a danger. And my lady heard the rustling of leaves, the snap of twig and bracken.

And Mother Svenson the midwife was shuffling toward them. She was clutching her old green cloak around her; her ragged cap was askew; there were shreds of leaves in the grey stringy hair. She waggled a stubby finger.

"Man and maid," she said in her daft voice. "Man and maid. So it was with my Svenson and me. On a bed of leaves. No cover but himself as he covered me. A cozy bedding that was. So 'tis Kurt's, my lady . . . the bairn ye bear within ye. The child is Kurt's getting—not my lord's, as they be saying in the village. Ah, my lord's past the prime of lusty wenching."

And Kurt would have sprung upon her and throttled her, so fierce was his anger. But she slipped away, like a shadow, between the trees.

He turned upon Donna. His eyes blazed.

"Is it true? You will bear his child? My lord, my enemy . . . now until death my enemy . . . you will bear his child!"

She put a hand to her throat; she felt her pulse flutter. "Kurt . . ."

"Ah, I know," he said roughly. "The rubies . . . a body in exchange . . ."

"Kurt, no!"

She was on her feet, facing him; she put a hand on his arm, but he shook it off.

"A fair bargain," he said in scorn. "A child to seal the bargain. From my lord, pride of wealth; from you, his child in payment."

"Kurt . . . no! That is not true. You are cruel . . ."

"The rubies become you, my lady. Though you pay so high a price." He spat upon the ground; and then he turned on his heel and left her. Left her weeping, by the Virgin Spring.

It was there that I found her.

She was close in her room for three days. She lay white and listless upon the great carved bed she shared with my lord. A bed shared with bitterness.

Dame Agnes coaxed her to eat; and I, to take a little wine.

She scarcely touched wine or meat and sent us from the room.

Often I went back to the shadowed room, close-curtained. I would kneel beside the bed and speak to my lady. Her eyes were closed, the dark lashes a shadow on the white cheek. I had no answer. But I do not think she was sleeping.

And I was deeply troubled. For Donna, for the babe she carried. And for old Mother Svenson. What if she spread tales of my lady—that the child was not my lord's but Kurt's? Would my lord give credit to the tale, though it could not be true?

Ah, God . . . the old woman was dim of wit; perhaps she did not recall that she had seen Kurt and my lady in the forest. I prayed that this might be so.

On the third day Donna joined us at the midday meal. She was quiet and pale; she pushed the wine glass aside.

And she would go again to the Virgin Spring. In hope, I thought in anger, of seeing Kurt. It was in her heart to forgive him, though not in mine. I could not forgive him his rage at being forcibly reminded that my lady shared my lord's bed. I must live with the sorry knowledge every day. Often she came to the morning meal, her sweet face wistful, shadows beneath her eyes. Once I had seen a dark bruise upon the curve of her shoulder.

We climbed the forest path. In sunny patches under the trees, wild bluebells were growing, the blossoms nodding in the little wind. But Donna did not stop to pick them.

We sat on the mossy bank beside the Virgin Spring. Over the feathery plumes of the ferns, a dragonfly was poised, a green shimmering of wings. The pool was green and gold and still in the late sun.

Donna gazed into the water. "Ah, Mary, Holy Mother, forgive me. I have always known why women pray to the

Virgin . . . the Mother who knew a woman's pain and travail to bring a babe to birth. Yet now I know why a woman seeks the solace of the witches, their potions to ease sorrow. They know the pain of earthly love, the dark side of passion, as the Most Chaste Queen of Heaven cannot."

She took up a stick and was scratching at the moss. I saw that she scratched the name, in ragged letters: Kurt. Shreds of moss clung to the stick.

"My lady, do not distress yourself so."

She tossed the stick into the pool. On the shining water there were ripples.

"Ah, Jon, I confess. I am distraught." Her eyes were dark with sorrow. "I am guilty of great sin."

"My sweet lady . . . never."

"Yes. My lord's gifts are a burden. A mockery. Because I am false to him. I confess that . . . that I will not bear a child."

"You have lost the babe?" I felt my heart leap.

"I have never been with child. Not for an instant. I have lied . . . a most grievous lie. It was the only way, the only course, to keep me here. Near Kurt if he should come."

I could say no word.

"I have done a great wrong. Oh, Mary, Holy Mother, have pity. I never wanted to love Kurt. I did not ask for this . . . this anguish, this pain of loving. Love should be joy, as Christer says."

"Yes."

"I did not ask for this. Nor did Kurt. A bitter destiny . . . it came upon us, strong and sudden as storm. A great wave to engulf us. I would not have had it so. Yet, Jon, I am happy for it. With Kurt I have known such pain. And yet . . . the world is new and Heaven is close. I see stars I never saw before."

"Yes," I said, from the depths of my own sore heart.

I took up a stone, flat and grey and smooth in my hand;

bits of mica winked in it. I sent it skipping across the shining surface of the little pool. And the green pool was clouded for a moment; a little streamer of brown mud came twisting up from the bottom. I thought the pool had never seemed so deep.

I said then, "What will you tell my lord? You must soon tell him of the child."

"Not the whole truth. I will not, I cannot say I have so deceived him. No, though Hell awaits, and Satan mocks. I will not say I have never conceived a child. Only that I have lost it. I must tell him soon." Her eyes were bright with tears. "He will be horribly angry."

"He cannot be. Others have suffered this, have not been able to bring a child to term."

She said sadly, "My lord tries . . . tries to be kind. But now I fear he will find me at fault. He will say I have not taken care. Dame Agnes will say I have not been dutiful, I have not swallowed leeks and ale. I have ridden out, hard and fast, on Arab. The stablemen know."

"How can he blame you, my lady? He loves you."

But she would not be comforted. "Our loving is like flame and frost—one destroys the other. Oh, Jon, my lord will send me away to Stockholm, I know it. How can I bear that? Not to see Kurt again . . . can you find him, Jon? If not Kurt, Peter . . . someone to take word to Kurt that my heart is his alone, that I will not bear my lord's child."

Chapter 16

It was useless to ride to Kurt's manor; it was deserted. Two of my lord's men had been wounded in the fight at Kari's grave; in reprisal my lord's captain had sent men to Kurt's manor to burn barns and stables, to set fires in the forest. The manor house was of stone; it still stood, but my lord's men had hacked to pieces the great door of heavy oak. Within, with pike and lance, they had smashed the casements and much else. But they had surprised none of Kurt's folk; all had gone.

I saddled the grey mare. I took the sea road, but not for long. I was wary of meeting a troop of my lord's men; they would offer me escort.

So I left the road; I cantered along the shingle beach. In early sunlight the sea was sharply blue and glittering, ruffled by gathering wind.

Soon the beach was broken by rock outcropping. We picked our way among the tidal pools, the mare slipping a little on wet moss and shale. At last I dismounted and tethered her, the good grey, in a grove of stunted pines.

And here a great buttress of rock breaks into the sea, a high, rocky ridge. I climbed the stony track up the ridge. Lichen spreads over the rock, a carpeting of grey and yellow and green. Scrub pine grows in the deep clefts, pines bent and twisted by the strong sea wind. Gorse clawed at the skirt of my monk's gown; at last, with my knotted girdle, I tied it up high above my knees.

On the crest of the rock, gulls screamed and wheeled over my head, and the wind was strong. I stood looking down upon Kurt's island, not far off shore, craggy and clad with pine. There are other islands, but these are small and visited only by seabirds which nest in great colonies among the rocks.

I thought of the day when Kurt and I discovered the island, long abandoned by men. Folk said the place was haunted. Even the fisherfolk would not go there. Borne on the sea wind, there was the sound of bells from the island. A deep booming, tolling as if for the souls of men drowned.

Small waves were cresting at the foot of the granite ridge where I stood. But the channel here is narrow; a strong swimmer can reach the island.

I made my way down the rock ledges. Here wind and storm had cut a deep gash in the rock face, where dwarf rowan clung. The berries were yellow now and crusted with salt spray.

The way down is perilous. Surely the climb was easier when Kurt and I were boys.

And there are other ways to reach the beach below. There is the forest track but I dared not follow that and chance meeting my lord's men.

And the long way by sea, from the wild coast north of the island. In hard weather no boat can butt its way through those crashing seas to the hidden haven on the windward side of the island. Even in mild weather, this way is full of risk; a strong riptide runs over sunken rocks and a boat must take the sea on its beam.

This was the way Kurt used now to the island haven; and he was a good seaman. We have made the run by night with lanthorns lashed to the bow and mast, the faint beams of light picking up rock and crag out of the dark, and a stinging shower of spray over us.

I was sweating when I reached the foot of the cliff. There thrusting from the rocks is a giant pine, like a sentinel. And just beyond it, hidden by gorse and thorn, is the mouth of the cave, a black gash in the rocks.

And within, I knew, a small open boat, kept there by Kurt for many years.

And I thought of the day when Kurt and I had pushed aside the thorny growth and looked into the cave and had seen within—in shadow—a movement. And two burning eyes . . . eyes like sunken coals.

And Kurt had flung stones, and then we scrambled for the ledge above the cave, and watched as the lynx came out, wary, arching his back, spitting, the tawny fur on his neck bristling like needles.

We had arrows and knives.

We skinned the lynx on the beach. For years Kurt had the skin.

Now I stooped to pick up a handful of stones. Of a sudden from the ledge behind me there was a rush of arrows. Three of them, swift, over my bent head. Two struck sharply among the rocks; one struck the water, sending up a little spurt of spray.

God was with me. If I had not been stooping . . .

I clutched the hilt of my knife and crept into the shelter of the cave.

I waited and said a Pater Noster.

Who had sent those arrows winging over my head? A poacher perhaps. Had he seen me crouched on the beach? Was he somewhere above me on the rocks? Or had the arrows come from deep within the forest?

I waited. There were no more arrows. In a while I dared to come out of the cave, dragging the boat with me.

The sea was choppy. I rowed against it; as I neared the island, I heard the booming . . . the iron crash of the bells.

We had been fearful, Kurt and I, that first day on the island. Climbing the rocks, pushing through the pines, our ears were full of the sound of the bells.

And then on the far side of the island, we came upon the chapel. Small, old, falling in ruin, the broken paving veined with moss. Before the rood screen, a dwarf rowan thrusting up from the stones, and bright with berries, the leaves like flame, like votive lights before the altar.

Swinging from an arch of broken stone were the bells. Old iron bells. The ropes were frayed as if rats had chewed them. But the bells were swaying in the strong sea wind; the sound of them was loud over our heads.

Close by the little chapel we found, in a hollow in the rocks, the broken skeleton of a man. The deep eye sockets were clogged with moss. A man in monk's gown like my own.

Under the pines we found two others. The bones were dry and yellow, wrapped in remnants of monk's cloth; stones had been heaped over them, and boughs of pine, now brittle and bare. But the shallow graves had been disturbed—by fox or marten perhaps. Nearby we found a small crucifix of walrus ivory, but cracked and yellow as those old bones.

How many brothers had been here? Ten, perhaps. Brothers of charity and certainly poor. A low stone building had housed them. But the roof had fallen, the stones were crumbling, the rubble overgrown with thorn. We found in the rubble iron pots and ladles, bits of potter's ware; a pile of heaped sheepskins, worn to leather and chewed by rats. Kurt lifted one; grey tufts of wool were left in his hand.

And in a small iron coffer we found the parchment.

A rough parchment, horny and brown, the letters fading. Kurt read some of it aloud.

"Winter is soon upon us. Yet we fear to go to the mainland. There the Death rages mightily.

"Today a fast day. We cannot fish. The sea is high and mighty, after three days of storm. Brother Anselm is weak; I gave him a broth of wild garlic; but he will not last the night.

"Dissension among the brothers. Most will go to the mainland, for fear of the hard winter.

"We starve. Brother Magnus netted this day a fox. We ate it.

"This day Brother Martin went to the spring for water. He fell on his knees beside the spring and could not rise. Mortal illness is upon him."

And at last the scribe had written in a faltering hand:

"We are two left to say the Matins, to toll the bells, to serve God as long as He wills it, though He has visited upon us, in our infirmity, in the frailty of our mortal flesh, in the grievous state of our sin . . . the Black Death."

That was long ago, when Kurt and I first came to the island. We came back often to fish; and through the years Kurt's men rebuilt the stone shelter where the monks had lived and the little chapel, in memory of his mother. The old bones were given proper burial.

And now I pulled the boat in on the narrow strip of beach and tied it up, looping the rope around a stone.

On the rocks above me there was a watchman. He knew me, in my monk's gown; he hailed me, raising an arm. It was old Jens, from Kurt's manor

"Kurt be gone. And Peter," he told me, scratching the stiff bristle of white hair on his chin.

And he told me that few of Kurt's household were on the island. "Most be gone. North to the mainland to Kurt's big farm. Saving the fighting men. They be following Kurt, to strike against the King."

"The strike will be soon?"

But he shook his head. "No way of knowing."

I gave him my lady's message for Kurt. She had written it

herself on stiff parchment; but the seal was my own, small and plain, with a cross upon it. Jens could not know that the letter was from my lady.

He took it, in stubby fingers. I knew he was curious.

But I said only, "It is urgent. And it must fall into no hands but Kurt's. Or Peter's."

He nodded, chewing his lip.

I rowed back, in a strong sea, to the mainland. And I took the forest path, to save the trouble of climbing the sheer reach of the cliff again.

And close by the path, in a leafy hollow beneath an oak, I came upon a man, flat on his back, his mouth agape, sleeping.

It was Sven, wild, young Sven who had found Christer upon the ice. He was snorting in sleep; his face was ruddy from drink, and the reek of drink was all about him. His leather flask lay beside him on the moss, and his poacher's bag, his beechen bow and arrows. And the stiffening bodies of three hares; on haunch and belly, the soft brown fur was matted with blood.

Was it Sven who had sent those arrows winging over my head? Had he seen me on the beach, seen me drag the boat from the cave and row out to the island?

God forbid . . .

When I reached the manor, my lord Ivar was there. He had ridden in with a small company, an hour before; and his mood was bitter. He sat before the fire in the great hall, drinking Rhenish wine from a goblet of chased crystal; standing before the casement, her hands clasped as if in supplication, was my lady. Her face was pale but composed; I saw at once that she had told him about the child. There was silence between them.

He nodded to me, scowling. "Come in, Jon. I suppose you

know the sorry news . . . of the child . . . the son of my old age, my heart's desire."

"Yes. Believe me, my lord, it has much saddened my lady to lose the babe. She has wanted to give you a son. She has guarded herself with care. Though sometimes willful about the leeks and ale. We must bow to God's will."

And so I lied, and convinced my lord that my lady was grieving over the loss of the child. I would have lied to save her pain, until my tongue turned black and dropped from my mouth.

Upon me, and upon my lady, for this lie, God visited a terrible penance.

Chapter 17

My lord had but three days with us. He was courteous to my lady; but I saw a change in his feeling toward her. He could not suppress his need of her, the strong surge of passion. Yet she had wounded him deeply. A bitter wound to his pride, to his manhood—the loss of the child.

At table he turned to me and said sadly, "I am glad of God's providence, that my mother did not live to see this day. To think that my Donna, my wedded wife, could bring such sorrow upon me." He stared moodily into his wine.

And I said strongly, "Her sorrow is as yours, my lord."

"No doubt," he said, frowning. But he turned to the Bishop of Lindhagen, who was with us. A powerful lord with vast estates and dedicated to the King's cause.

They spoke of the numbers of men deserting from the King's service and turning to Kurt.

"Many desert from Kurt's forces as well," said the Bishop. A paunchy man with jowls like a chipmunk and small eyes sunk in fat. There was greed in those eyes, and a certain oiliness as he looked upon my lady. His lips were red and wet and pouting as a child's though he was past seventy. He relished his wine. "Perhaps Kurt's movement will die a-borning.

Many lose faith in him. So my marshal tells me. Men say they will not fight a war of stalemate. All parley and argument. No action. Skirmishes on the roads, but nothing decisive."

My lord said thoughtfully, "Men slip back to the villages. Men from both sides, in large numbers."

And I ventured to say, "Harvest time is soon upon us. A long winter to come. Unless the men come back to till the fields and bring in the harvest, there will be much suffering in the months of darkness and strong cold."

The Bishop gave me a sour look. In his eyes I am sure I was of such lowly estate that I should not have spoken.

But my lord said, "No army can move, or fight, without provisioning. If men desert from Kurt's side to bring in the harvest—miners or brute labourers—what matter? The crops can be impounded to feed the King's men. And hunger is a powerful inducement. Men who labour in field or forest can be persuaded to join the King's forces. Even though most are in sympathy with Kurt. I am not concerned with such men. I am concerned because men of nobility, of honourable estate, desert their King to join with Kurt."

I saw then that small points of flame burned in those ice-grey eyes; my lord was of a sudden very angry. His long fingers tapped the table sharply, a sound like the scattering of stones upon the polished wood. A serving man hurried to bring more wine.

My lord said through tight lips, "Kurt, my cousin! I curse the kinship between us. Traitor to his King, and to his own blood, his gentle birth. And now winning others to his side, men as nobly born as he. With talk of the Kalmar Union, of breaking the bond with Denmark. Sweden for the Swedes! So says Kurt. So narrow, so insular is his vision. He would corrode and finally destroy a noble alliance, the bond between the northern countries decreed in good Queen Margaret's time. Norway, Denmark, and Sweden united as brother nations. United in mutual defense, in time of war. Reciprocal trade and customs immunity, in time of peace. The pact binding our countries is sacred, and so confirmed at Kalmar, in amity. And in our mutual interest. Sweden alone can never defend itself against the Hansa towns."

Of a sudden my lord's hands on the table were still. The pale lace on his long cuffs dropped over his clenched fists. I had learned to fear my lord when he was frozen in stillness; and his face grew white and hard.

The Bishop sipped his wine; he passed a wet, red tongue over his lips. "A matter of urgent concern. A devilish evil. Even in Uppsala, the Rector tells me that the university is like a besieged town. Students—men of probity and good birth—swarming in the square, setting up barricades, lighting enormous fires. And assailing all who pass by, fighting off the Rector's men. Hurling cobblestones! And shouting, 'Sweden for the Swedes!' "

I said no word. I had heard Kurt's view of the Kalmar Union. Outmoded, he said; a bondage like a noose. We are committed to fight a war in the Danish interest; we are crushed by taxes to support the Danes' pride; we are ruled by Danish bailiffs and a Danish King. A petty princeling, it is true; Eric was born in Pomerania. But his breeding is Danish; his allegiance is to Denmark. If the three northern countries are brothers, then Sweden is stepbrother.

I glanced at my lady. Her small face was very sober; she was biting her lip.

The Bishop was picking at the great seal ring upon his finger. I doubt that he could remove the ring, so embedded was it in fat, like a currant in dough. He reached out and put a hand—white and flabby—upon my lady's. She drew her hand away, looking upon the Bishop with distaste. There was something dark in her gaze, as if she feared him.

"My lady," he said, in his breathy voice—he spoke in little

gasps of breath, and spittle lingered in the corners of his mouth. "A dark time is upon us. A time of anarchy, of brother against brother. It were wise, my lady, if you returned to Stockholm."

"No." Donna turned to my lord. "I beg you to excuse me. You have much to discuss." She rose, with no further word to the Bishop; his gaze was upon her as she left the room. There was lust in those small, pale eyes; I could have sworn it. A pity she could not dissemble and show a gracious face to His Holiness. He was soon aware that she disliked him; in the end he brought upon her deep injury.

I stayed on at table, parchments and pens before me; the Bishop dictated a letter to his marshal. A small company of mounted men were to be marched to Stenborg, and from there, offer the King escort. His Majesty wished to remove to the fortress at Vestvik, and from there take ship to Denmark. The move was to be accomplished with utmost secrecy. The armed men would wear the Bishop's livery; the King would travel in monk's clothing.

My hand shook a little as I plied the pen. This was news of such moment I must get word to Kurt without delay. My heart pounded in my throat, but my lord could not know that, and the Bishop gazed into his wine glass, and then into the fire.

"So," said His Holiness, putting the tips of his fat fingers together. "His Majesty's person will be secure. And Kurt's men will fight sham battles. If it comes to battle. They will be ably opposed by the strong lords who declare for the King. His Majesty will return when punitive measures have been taken."

When the letter was done, I read it aloud. "I think, my lords, that I have omitted no word."

"You are a ready scribe, Jon," said Lord Ivar. "Bring wax and flame and my seal."

I had hoped to learn when the King planned to leave Sweden but could push the subject no further.

In the morning, my lord left us, with the Bishop. And my sweet lady was smiling again.

And I went to Kurt's island . . . I must get news to him of the King. Yet there they had no word of Kurt.

So I rode to the old inn in Granholm, the market town, and there learned that Kurt had passed through the town not long since with a small troop of men.

A black-eyed maid served me. A minx with shining cheeks and bouncing bosom. "Three days since. Sir Kurt were here, with two knights. In dark armour, all were. And sitting long over the wine cups, heads together, in heavy talk. No time for me, or Lena in the buttery. How's a girl to keep herself, if a man doesn't help now and then? With bidding to bed, and a good bawdy time. And a coin after, to ease the parting."

She gave me a saucy look. "Monks be the worst. Never a spare coin about them. Though a girl be bending double to please."

I put a coin on the scarred table. "Which way did Kurt's men ride?"

She could not tell me. She could tell me only that folk in the market town were wary. "Thieving, there be much of that, with armed men ever riding through. Ah, Kurt's men or King's men, they're all the same. All the same when their breeks are down."

I smiled at her. "Has there been fighting?"

"Brawling, aye. Men be ever ready for that. But most of the village men be gone. And the women grieving, and fearing."

For a great shower of falling stars had been observed in the night sky over Granholm. And some said that this foretold that a powerful man would fall from power.

Kurt? Would his hopes be shattered, his men beaten to despair, his movement die a-borning, as the Bishop had said?

A shower of burning stars . . .

And in Sundby the moon was seen to rise from a bank of cloud as black as the cloak of death. A blood-red moon, ringed with flame.

Men said that this foretold a time of blood.

Other portents followed. It was said that a child had been born in Granholm with but a single eye, and that in the middle of its forehead. The Abbot brought word of this to the manor. "I cannot think it possible," he said. "If only the word of God spread as fast as false rumour . . ."

But folk in the village said, "Odin's time is come again. Odin of the one baleful eye. The dark time of the old gods is upon us. It was so in the days of the Black Death. The days of pestilence."

And others said, "Days of famine."

For in July the rains began, relentless as in September.

Chapter 18

In the sodden fields, under the heavy sky, the women worked as beasts do. There were few beasts left to harness to the iron ploughs, to drag the farm carts; horses and cattle had been herded and driven north by my lord's men to be slaughtered to serve the hunger of armed men. Such beasts as were left in the village had been driven into the forest, or into upland pasture, to forage where my lord's men would not find them.

So the women harnessed themselves to the ploughs and dragged the farm carts piled with stones; the children dug with wooden forks to drain the standing water from the fields and shored up the channels with stones.

And a night of terrible storm tore loose the stones and scattered them. The fields were in muddy flood.

At last the torrent of rain abated; but the sun did not shine. "God has hidden His face from us," said the devout.

And others said in despair, "What of the harvest?"

My lady and I rode out in the grey weather, muffled and hooded against the chill, our faces often wet with the thin, spitting drizzle. The horses splashed through the streams of muddy water on the roads. My lord was not with us at this time to forbid my lady to ride out. And she was restless and would not be confined to the manor.

We rode one evening to the monastery to sup with the Abbot. In his bare, vaulted chamber, the walls were veined with damp; rain streaked the casements; chill rose from the stone floor. Yet on the hearth a bright fire burned; there was in the small chamber a sense of warmth and peace.

The meal was spare—a poached fish in a thin butter sauce with chopped fennel. Flat wheaten bread from the monastery bake-house, a cheese with caraway, and a sour gooseberry tart.

And a thin wine, pale as honey, in silver goblets. Beautiful goblets, wrought with a shell border and small dolphins supporting the stem. Part of the Abbot's treasure from his family estate.

"Brought out to honour you, my lady," he said, smiling at Donna. His thin hands upon his goblet were reverent, as if he lifted the sacred chalice. "I cannot give you much as meat. Only beauty to nourish you."

He showed Donna other treasures: books beautifully coloured, clasped with jeweled hinges, parchments scrolled with inkwork delicate as lace.

"And the world's wisdom in them," he said. "Yet small solace when we observe the evil that men do to one another. Or the evil wrought by dark mischance. Is it heresy to think that God has imperfect days? When He visits upon man a rage of storms and pestilence?" The wise old eyes were sorrowful. "I have been today to the village and seen such misery."

From the refectory below us, the sound of plainsong reached us. A thin sound, full of melancholy, yet touching the heart.

"Those who travail and labour, in sore need—what does the Church give them?" The Abbot gazed into his goblet, as if he sought an answer there. "They say the Church takes from them . . . the widow's mite, the child's sustenance. Small wonder they turn to witchcraft, thus to appease a merciless fate."

The talk turned on other things. Of the Abbot's years in Paris as a young scholar, reading philosophy and law.

But his words stayed in my mind. For as we rode homeward we passed the little chapel. The old iron bells were tolling, tolling as if for the dead.

And then in the churchyard we saw a slow processional . . . it seemed of the walking dead. The shapes were shrouded against the damp; they moved like phantoms in moving mist. Among the old graves, the mist rose and curled; it seemed that the scarred headstones moved and swayed with it. We saw the priest, holding before him the iron cross from the chapel altar; boys stood about him with candles, the small flames all but lost in the gathering dusk.

The hooded shapes filed into the chapel; we heard the sound of chanting, faint as the murmur of wind in the black, dripping pines.

A sorry little procession. A few of the village women had followed the priest through the ruined fields, praying without hope that the shadow of the cross would fall upon the fields, that the harvest might be saved.

My lady reined in her horse; her eyes were dark with pity. "Is it true, Jon, that if the rye is ruined . . . that folk will have no food in the dark months to come?"

I gave her no answer.

"They say so at the manor. Tell me, Jon. Tell me the truth."

"It is grim truth, my lady. Now in July, if the men were left in the village, they could not save the harvest either. But they would poach and lay in stores of hare and venison, though they be hanged for it. They would fish . . . ."

"Can nothing be done?"

"I think not, my lady."

We rode slowly homeward. It was near dark; yet we passed two women crouching in the ditch beside the road. They were gathering the wild rose hips for soup; yet I knew that the rose pods were covered with mould, a grey scale like frost, because of the damp weather.

And the rye . . . stunted stalks, broken by wind and rain, in the sodden fields. The rye grains were spotted with mould, black and furry with it.

Yet man must have bread.

Soon after this, we had a visit from the Abbot.

"My lady," he said, "to see you gives me pleasure. Ah, you know it well."

But then he said, frowning, "You must pay me no more visits. For a while. Today at the monastery gate, a man lay dying. We could do nothing for him. He could not take the Sacrament, he could not speak his name. I know not how he found the strength to crawl to the monastery, on the stumps of black and shriveled legs. God in His mercy released him from this life. We buried him." The Abbot sighed. "There will be others. My lady, I beg you, as I am your spiritual guide and your friend—do not leave the manor."

And so it began, the terror of St. Anthony's fire. I believe that the Black Plague is kinder; it kills in a few hours, or days. Those who suffer from St. Anthony's fire are doomed to weeks of misery; the lips, the hands, the fingers are blue as if from winter cold. Many lie faint; but many run screaming, pursued by nameless terror, seeing in simple things a shape of dread. A stone becomes a toad; a fish, a twisting serpent. A friend becomes a fiend, a devil in the flesh.

And the dread fire itself: the limbs burn as if the sufferer were in Hell's torment. And at last the limbs turn black and wither and drop off. We heard that in Sundby one such sufferer survived—arms and legs had separated from the maimed body. He was left with but a trunk and a head.

He survived. But many in the village did not.

The scourge spread. To Granholm, to Reyborg . . . and there, at the monastery of Saint Anthony, the afflicted came in numbers. Like rats crawling along the roads. These poor ones had been cast out of their huts and hovels. A child will be abandoned by its mother, and mother by son, so fearful are folk of the terror of the fire. But the monks of Saint Anthony will care for such as these, who carry with them the dread infection.

I know not what causes this plague. But I have seen cases of something very like it, when a maid has used the rotted rye to abort her child. Such a potion as the witchwives brew—such as was used with Kari.

The Abbot maintained that this was so, that the blighted rye brought about the disease. And yet, would God strike down His children through their daily bread, so hard to come by? If that is true—then, as Christer would say, "Ah, God who made us, why must it be so?"

And so I told the Abbot. I told him also that my lady did not fear the disease, that she rode into the village with hampers of food and physic, and I could do nothing to dissuade her.

"She is," said the Abbot, "in less danger from the disease than from folk in the village, folk upon the roads, who are bitter at my lord's wealth, his larders full of hams and wheaten bread. Have you observed, Jon, that the very poor, those who eat the bark bread, pounded from the bark of birch and pine—these are not afflicted? But God may feel that these, the destitute, have misery enough to teach them humility."

"Yes," I said. "I have also observed that the rich, who eat wheaten loaf, are not affected. But perhaps they are not expected to learn humility."

My lord visited us at this time, for two days only. It was in his mind to send my lady back to Stockholm; he spoke of it.

Yet he feared to let her travel on the roads and could not offer her escort. He was occupied with the King. And I learned that His Majesty was still in residence at Stenborg, he had not yet gone to Vestvik, to take ship for Denmark. His Majesty was fearful.

The Bishop had urged him, my lord had urged him, to take upon him monk's clothing, to travel with the Bishop's men as one of them, to ride with all haste to Vestvik where a stout ship was waiting.

But the King delayed. To travel on country roads, to stop at humble inns, to sup and drink with common men—so, he thought, he would be exposed to the dread contagion.

Against the contagion, my lord ordered that the wonderful reliquary be brought out, the golden shrine of Saint Martin, the pride of the manor. This was carried through the village, and through the fields. And he ordered that penitent Masses be said each day in the village chapel.

And that my lady keep close to the manor, until he could spare the time and the men to escort her back to Stockholm.

Chapter 19

Among the manor folk there were no cases of the disease, as yet. But there was a contagion as deadly—a contagion of fear.

They went to the chapel Masses because my lord had ordered it. But they were fearful of infection, suspicious of others, even of the village priest. And some among them murmured that God had forsaken men, that prayer and chanting brought small result. God had turned His face from men; but there were other powers to hear men's cry—the powers and principalities of darkness, to turn the tide of dark fortune.

It was the women who spoke so. I saw on many evenings the green flame of witch lights beneath the trees, the little tongues of light in the forest beyond the barn, where Christer was painting.

It was damp and chill in the barn, but Christer would not be moved. There he had light—a grey light, but clearer, more true, than that in the solar. My lady and I would sit with him in the barn. He would say, in his deep voice, "I cannot think where summer is gone. Already so chill here in Florence. Upon the Arno a thin glaze of ice. A soft snowfall in the mountains. Tell Aldo to come with braziers and coals, to keep the fires burning. My little Duchess sits, and her hands are cold."

So he spoke, lost in his past life. He was remote from us, rapt in dream . . . I think because of the painting.

He was painting "a miracle." So said my lady. This was the great Crucifixion which my lord had ordered. The panels would soon be mounted in the village chapel. The work was almost done.

I have never seen such work. Christer surpassed himself. In the face of the Christ upon the cross, in that sublime face, there was agony, an infinity of sorrow. And yet such light . . . truly, I thought, this is the light of the world.

And light fell upon the faces of the crowd at the foot of the cross. Faces from the village, or the manor. The two thieves hung beside the Christ and one bore the face of the King's bailiff. And one—I saw it with dismay—the face of Fat Tomas at the inn.

Sven the poacher was there, his thatch of iron-red hair unruly, his face flushed and sullen as in life. He knelt beside the cross, but not in prayer. He wore a soldier's tunic; he knelt with others, casting lots for the robe of Christ.

Dame Barbro was there, pale eyes blazing, lip curled in scorn, fist raised like a claw, reviling the Master.

Many others, painted from memory. The faces were fixed in Christer's mind as if graven upon stone. Truly he had no need of living models, though two of the manor folk had posed for him.

But most would not; they feared him. One day in the meadow he saw two of the young maids from the manor. A rare day of sun; the maids were spreading new-washed linens upon the grass to dry. Christer went to the youngest, a girl of modest face and soft, dark eyes. He wanted her to sit for "the other Mary." "She has in her face the shining of a soul," he said. He approached her and laid a gentle hand upon her arm. She ran from him, screaming.

Still, at times, he muttered in his Devil's tongue—they called it so, when he spoke in Italian. At times he spoke clearly in Swedish . . . of strange things.

The little cripple, Anders, was often with us; I made for him one day a small bird of folded parchment. He delighted in "flying" his bird in the meadow. He would not be parted from it; he fondled it, as he sat with us at table. And then—he could not help himself—he sent it flying about the room; it darted and swooped over the heads of three men who served us.

"Anders, no," said my lady, but she was laughing.

The Abbot was with us, and Christer turned to him. "Master Leonardo, I think as you do. Certainly man can fly. Not as in witchcraft, though you admit that. In witchcraft we have a levitation of the body, you say, as possible as the inspiration of the soul. Body is inseparable from soul; if one can rise, why not the other?"

One of the serving men dropped a silver platter.

Christer continued, "I have examined the drawings. The machines for flying are ingenious, Leonardo. But if you will try them out, may God receive your soul." And he lapsed into Italian.

Behind me, one of the maids was whispering. "He calls upon his devils."

In the village they said that he was skilled in sorcery. Often near the barn there was the rank odour of sulphur and of brimstone. The smell of burning Hell. For on flat stones near the barn there were small fires burning in iron braziers; iron pots were suspended over the fires, and Christer could be seen, stirring his boiling messes. From these, a thick, acrid smoke would curl. Did his private demons appear in the smoke to instruct him?

Often he asked for rag and bone and scraped sheepskin;

for the hooves or hide of a slaughtered pig—these went into the boiling pots.

Christer would stand bemused. Stirring, lifting the stinking mess with an iron fork. So it was that he compounded his glue, his gesso. Of burnt sulphur and earth pigment he often mixed his paints.

Folk muttered. And stayed far from the barn. And for that we were grateful.

Of Kurt there was no word. Of Kurt's men—some from the village—there was dread news. We had now a new bailiff. Danish, as the old one had been. A tall, sallow man, with huge shoulders. And large square hands with flat thumbs. Ah, I remember his hands. I thought he might strangle a strong man with ease. He always rode fully armed, with a company of armed men.

He came one evening upon a little company of Kurt's men, meeting in the barn behind the inn. I suppose he had his informers. The bailiff's men surrounded the barn. They strung up the village men—alive—on the rafters. Straw fires were built beneath the dangling bodies. The men were not hanged, nor burnt. They were smoked. All choked to death in the thick, surging smoke. The bodies were blackened and cured, like hams hanging in a shed.

There were other disasters. An early frost in the upland pastures. The grass lay beaten and brown. Cattle would starve this winter, as well as men.

And new cases of the terrible fire of Saint Anthony were reported.

The chapel bells tolled without cease. "So mournful a sound," said my lady. The Abbot sent his men through the fields; he went himself through the village, urging all who could walk to the penitent Masses.

Many came. Even such as Dame Barbro—though folk

swore that as she entered the chapel there was a noise of rushing wind over her head; and some said that they had seen behind her a shape, a dark shape, with beating wings.

On a grey evening, Christer and I went to the chapel. He would look at the wall space for the great Crucifixion; he would test the walls for damp; the great painting was near done.

Beneath the low stone arches darkness gathered. We walked in a grey gloaming. Boys came with pine-knot torches to set in the iron brackets; they tended the hissing candles on the altar; the old stone walls were streaked with thin fingers of light.

Of a sudden beside me, Christer moaned. And then he uttered a cry—low, harsh, terrible.

I felt my heart leap in my throat.

And Christer pushed past me; he stumbled to the altar. He pounded with hard fists upon the altar, and on the blank wall above it.

There on the wall his gentle Christ had lifted a hand in blessing and smiled upon humble folk in the chapel pews. The painting I had loved above all.

Now there was nothing. Nothing but a blank white wall. The gentle Christ had been coated with thick lime wash, effaced, destroyed for all time.

I know not who ordered the lime wash to be done. But so it was done at the time of the Black Death, to conquer infection.

The chapel walls, the stone flooring, even the leaded panes in the small windows, all were coated with lime, thick, rough, white as bone. Of Kari as the Magdalene, of my lady as the sorrowing Madonna, there was no trace.

Of a sudden the bells were tolling. Behind us, folk were

crowding into the chapel. Hooded, shawled against the chill, creeping like moles into the little space beneath the dark arches.

And Christer turned then, at the sound of shuffling feet; he stood before the altar, very tall and still, for a moment, looking down upon the village folk with burning eyes. And he raised his fist again; and then he was railing and cursing, his voice like the cry of a man chained to the stake.

Then he sank to his knees, his head in his hands. He was weeping like a child. " 'Father . . .' " he said faintly. " 'Father, forgive them, for they know not what they do.' "

I went to him, I took his hand. I led him out of the chapel, as if I led a child.

At the manor, Christer sat staring at the wall. I saw in his face, in the agony there, the sorrowing face of the Christ. Or perhaps that was only my fancy.

And my lady could do nothing. For two days Christer would not eat, until she dipped bread sops in wine and coaxed him to take a little. As she would coax an ailing child.

He looked up then at one of the serving maids and said, in a strange, still voice, " 'Is it nothing to you, all ye who pass by?' "

He was destroyed, in the destruction of his paintings. So much of himself was in them; they were illumined by the strength of his mind, his rare vision, his aspiration, even his tenderness, in the swift, delicate strokes with which he had painted the small animals of the forest or the flowers of the field.

It had been a grey morning, but soon after the midday meal, the sun broke through a bank of watery cloud. The meadow grass was shining; long bars of light lay across it.

"Come, Christer," said my lady gently. "It is a painter's light. See it! Come."

She took his hand; I helped him to his feet. The little

cripple, Anders, was with us; he tugged at the hem of Christer's dark mantle. And so we coaxed Christer to the meadow barn.

We hoped he would take brush in hand and lose himself in work upon the panel of the great Crucifixion.

But he stood before it, staring at it with vacant eyes . . . And turned his back upon it.

"He must work again," said Donna. "In a while, perhaps . . ."

We sat with him, on a low wooden bench before an iron brazier where a small fire burnt. Anders played at our feet. Christer had made for him a little puppet, a wooden soldier with a stout sword, most carefully carved, with arms and legs so cunningly jointed they moved almost of themselves. Anders marched his soldier across the plank flooring, then up upon the bench and into Christer's lap.

"See, Christer," said Anders. "He salutes you, my soldier salutes you. Why are you sad?"

Christer put a hand on the child's head and took up the puppet and made it dance but said no word.

"Perhaps if we leave him . . ." said Donna.

But she would not leave him alone, so I was sent to the manor for one of the maids—Anna, a good woman, old but plump and sound as an apple. With the gift of stillness in her.

And Donna and I set out upon the path to the Virgin Spring.

So it was from Anna, and two men of the manor, that we learned of what befell Christer. And I have done penance, with a sorry heart, because I was not there.

There was, Anna said, of a sudden, the sound of boots thrashing through the meadow grass. There was the sound of voices, harsh, menacing. A long shadow fell across the wide doorway of the barn . . . another and another . . . blocking the sunlight. And men were crowding into the barn, blocking the door. Twelve or more—miners, with blackened faces, lifting their fists and shouting. Men of the farms in rough sheepskin, with straw in their matted hair. And Tomas of the inn and Sven the poacher. Three women—Dame Barbro among them.

They stood over Christer, shouting at him. "He works evil. We lived in peace till he came. He works sorcery, he has brought darkness upon us! Blight upon the fields, and plague among us."

Then one caught sight of the painting, the Crucifixion. They all crowded around it, and saw there their own faces, their own ugliness, their greed, their stupidity, their faces, painted with utmost truth.

They turned upon Christer like snarling animals. And the strange, wild look came into his eyes.

"A sorcerer!" said Tomas of the inn; he spat upon Christer. "He lay dead in the inn the night he came to the village. I saw him. And yet he returned to life!"

Christer began muttering in Italian.

"He came to Mass," said one of the women. "Before the holy altar, cursing in his Devil tongue, as we came to pray, 'Give us this day our daily bread!' He cursed us all, before the altar. And he has meat and wine, and a fine gold chain of my lady. We starve!"

Her voice was shrill and wild; and little Anders was frightened; he crouched beside Christer, trembling; he put his head in Christer's lap. He was whimpering like a puppy.

Dame Barbro pushed forward; she seized Anders by the arm and tried to drag him away; but Christer held him strongly.

"See," said Barbro. "He is bewitched. The child is bewitched and will not come to his own granddam. What evil do you work with this child?" She took Christer by the shoulder; her pale eyes blazed. "You have defiled the child! You have used him in lust . . . no woman would have you, you have used the child!"

Then Christer put Anders behind him and stood very tall, facing the mob. His face was still, his eyes were remote; he spoke quietly in Italian. But if he spoke curse or prayer—we can never know.

"So it were," said one of the miners. "At Hell Gate mine. When the priests would bless the mine, after the rockfall. When we came, and my lord with the shrine of gold, to bless the mine. Christer were there in the sleigh. He rose up tall in the sleigh, speaking words of sorcery. And then were the fall of timbers in the mine, and one of the men killed . . . the best of us killed . . ."

And they howled like wolves, in lust to kill; they shouted, "Let it be there—at Hell Gate!"

They seized upon Christer and dragged him away.

He went with them quietly, walking like a man struck blind, forever lost in a dark world of dream.

They had horses tethered in the forest near the manor gate; and a farm cart piled with stable straw and stripped pine logs. Christer was pushed into the cart with the women. And these spat upon him and shouted abuse.

Two of the men bound Christer strongly, his arms and his legs, with stout leather thongs.

They were mounting the big farm horses, when two of my lord's men came out upon the road from the forest—two ploughmen. And these were made to go with the mob, for fear, I suppose, that they would run back to the manor and alarm the manor folk.

These two could do nothing; they could not help Christer, "though it were grievous to see him," said one of them later. "His cloak foul with straw and spittle."

"We'd have helped him," said the other. "Be it we had weapons. We had naught but a hay fork. And the mob was ugly. Many against us."

At the mouth of Hell Gate mine, Christer sat quietly in the farm cart, staring at the mob with vacant eyes.

Of the strong pine timbers they erected the gallows tree.

They hauled Christer down from the cart and cut the thongs from his legs; between two miners, he walked slowly to the gallows tree. He looked upon it, his eyes remote.

And Dame Barbro pushed herself forward. Before Christer she stood, her black cloak dropping from her shoulders, her long arm thrust out and the fist clenched, with two fingers extended . . . so to avert the evil eye. "Evil go with you," she said, her voice rough with hate. "Evil be lifted from us all . . . let it go with you into the darkness of death . . . into the pit of Hell . . ."

Christer gazed at her, and said in a strong voice, " 'Thou shalt not suffer a witch to live.' "

And then as they hauled him up toward the gallows tree, his head dropped on his breast, and he said faintly, "Ma Donna . . . ma Donna . . ."

And some said that he repented of his sins and cried aloud to the Madonna, the Virgin Mother, ever merciful, to receive his soul.

But some said that in his last moment, he spoke in his Devil tongue—he spoke my lady's name, ma Donna.

It was not long till dusk. The sun dropped below the rim of the iron mountain. In the grey light, by the black mouth of the mine pit, the stunted pines took on the shapes of nightmare, black and shaggy as trolls. Mist was rising from the hollows in the rocks.

The women began to be fearful. What if Christer now— even now, in death—could call upon the power of Hell to save him? They murmured to one another, pulling their shawls around their heads, in the evening chill.

But one of the miners pointed to the body, the dark cloak upon it hanging limp, upon the gallows tree. "Let ravens pick his eyes . . . let the eagle clean his bones."

And one said, scoffing, "Let his devils rise to save him now."

And then from the mouth of the mine pit, there was, faint as distant thunder, a long rumble of sound. From deep within the mine, a rumble of sound.

And from that black gap in the rocks, a strange mist was rising, rank, sulphurous, curling like smoke.

And the women scrambled for the farm cart; one of them was weeping.

"It be judgment . . . judgment upon us."

But the miners said it was but the foul breath of the mine, a rockfall deep within, and the mine gas rising.

The women said, "It be Christer . . . his soul, uneasy in Hell."

And they mounted the horses in haste, for fear of Christer, and for fear that a gap would open in the trampled earth and swallow them—for this has been seen; the thin crust of the earth splits at times near the mouth of an old mine when a crowd gathers, where men have dug too deep.

Fat Tomas was sweating; his face was grey in the fading light. "So it were . . . the day of blessing the mine. Then did Christer call up his demons. And there were a great rockfall."

And the women turned to Dame Barbro, for she had some knowledge of the Black Art; they knew and respected her for it.

"A strong sorcery." And her voice was harsh. She made the witch sign with crossed fingers. "It be wise if Christer be given the burial. The sorcerer's burial . . . to keep the soul fast to the body. Or the spirit will wander, to trouble us all."

And three of the miners agreed to return in the morning, in clear morning light, and cut the body down. And give it burial in a peat bog, far from the road, in a dark part of the forest. And they would take strong pine stakes, and thrust two through the breast, and one through the loins, thus to fasten the spirit to the body, that it might not escape.

And then they made haste away from Hell Gate mine.

At the manor, my lady was near distracted. We had walked down the path from the Virgin Spring; we found the good maid Anna crouched in the meadow grass behind the barn. She was counting the beads of her rosary; little Anders clung to her, weeping.

And she told of the mob, and how they had taken Christer away. "I know not where . . ."

My lady sent men into the forest to search—perhaps they had not taken him far. But both of us knew, in our hearts, that there was no hope.

It was dark when the two ploughmen returned to the manor and told us of Christer and how they had hanged him on the gallows tree.

"Be not blaming us," said one. "Begging mercy, my lady. There was no helping him. And we'd our own skins to save."

The other said, "He did no hurt that I could see. Though he were strange, not right in the head. But he'd not harm a puppy."

He spoke very loud; his thick fingers were picking at his rough woolen tunic. And I saw that he believed that Christer was truly in league with the powers of darkness. He told of the strange light at the mouth of the mine—"like cloud it were, but yellow as sun."

And he crossed himself and said that Christer would be cut down in the morning and buried as all are who are suspected of sorcery: in a strong pine barrow, in a desolate spot, with stakes through breast and belly.

So I rode with four of my lord's armed men along the dark road, in thin moonlight, to Hell Gate mine.

We had torches; we tethered the horses and picked our way among the rocks. From a distance we saw the body dangling upon the gallows tree. Very tall and black was the tree, and the body a long black shape upon it, the cloak lifting a little in the wind.

We saw it clearly; for behind it there was a strong yellow light at the mouth of the mine. A light untended by man. Like a great sacrifice fire, flaming and sinking, and the strange flames rising again.

And I felt my heart leap. Yet I knew this for what it was, the mine gas, surging from the mouth of the mine, with flashes of flame in it.

We cut the body down. I looked with sorrow upon that noble face, the cheeks sunken now, and the eyes unseeing. I closed them. And we wrapped Christer in his cloak, and rode with all haste to the monastery.

We roused the Abbot. He looked upon Christer with shock. And then with pity. "Truly," he said, "this was an innocent man. And he brought the boon of beauty, such beauty as they cannot know again. And they have destroyed him."

Christer was laid out upon the pallet in the abbey chapel. So he lay in his dark mantle, his face waxen pale in candlelight, as he had in the chapel at the manor, the night we brought him in, the unknown, from the ice.

The Abbot watched by him. And I. And during the night the monks filed into the chapel, beneath the dark stone arches, chanting the office and the psalms.

Before dawn—there were still faint stars in the sky—we buried Christer, in holy ground, beneath a giant oak.

The ground mist was rising, a dark mist, blown by the wind, and full of shadows. If any of the monks saw devils in those shadows, no man spoke of it.

Chapter 20

I will not write of my lady's shock and sorrow at this time. Or of my own.

She began listlessly to sort over Christer's things in the barn. Paints and brushes and powdered gold. All to be sent to the monastery workshop where the monks are ever busy, illuminating the manuscripts for which our abbey is famed.

The great Crucifixion was sent to the Abbot. "A marvel," he said. "A treasure." And the painting was hung in the refectory, where folk even now make pilgrimages to see it, though it is defaced. One corner had been slashed with a wolf knife when the mob crowded into the meadow barn. And one of the men had lifted his smock and made water upon it, like a dog. The monks wished to repair the painting; the Abbot would not allow them to touch it. It hangs today with no mark of brushwork upon it save Christer's own.

It was my lady's right—I thought it her duty—to persecute all who had had a part in Christer's death. But she would not do it. "More violence. Men maimed and hanged. Christer would not have it so."

"The men must be brought to judgment."

"Let God be their judge. And who is to witness, Jon, if these men are brought to trial? Will they bear witness against each other? We have only Anna—her word against theirs. And the two ploughmen."

"My lord would not consider that for an instant. Will you let murder be done and not bring the men to justice?"

"Ah," she said sadly. "Let it end now. Or an endless bloody feud will begin between village and manor. And nothing can bring Christer back."

Yet in the village folk said that his spirit returned. Few would go near the mouth of Hell Gate mine, where still the strange fires burned. And who had cut Christer down from the gallows tree? Some said men of the manor had done it. Others said that Christer had once returned from the dead . . . and now . . .

We kept our own counsel.

There were other rumours. And these troubled me so deeply I could not sleep. I could not speak of these to my lady.

For folk were saying that she had always been with Christer; in his strange, dark moods, he had turned to her. She had never feared him. She had helped him boil his stinking messes; she had been seen stirring the sulphurous brew in the iron cookpots. And she spoke with Christer in his Devil tongue . . . there was communion between them.

In short, they said that my lady was leagued with him and his demons.

Hadn't Christer himself accused her as he was hauled toward the gallows tree? To save his own soul, he had accused her.

For he had cried aloud in a strong voice, saying " 'Thou shalt not suffer a witch to live.' " And then he had said clearly, "Ma Donna . . ."

And when I heard this, I felt that my own heart might choke me, rising like a stone in my throat. Yet how could such rumour harm my gentle lady? I could not see how.

Dame Barbro saw how.

We were in the meadow barn, sorting over Christer's things. A sunny day, but the golden haze of autumn lay beneath the oaks at the edge of the meadow. The scent of autumn was in the air, the smoky smell of mushrooms, of yellow meadow grass, the smell of russet oaks.

We were alone in the barn. None of the manor folk would enter it now. And the child Anders was not with us; Dame Barbro had sent a neighbour to fetch him that morning.

In the barn the air was damp. I lit fires of birchwood in two of the braziers. Birchwood gives a fresh green scent as it burns . . . so Christer would say. So much that he had said came back to me, and I am sure to my lady, rummaging in the chests full of painter's gear. We packed up the little pots of ivy leaf and walnut brown; of buckthorn green and orpiment; of burnt siena. We wrapped in linen kerchiefs the amber tools for smoothing, the fine silver stencils, the palette knives.

Close by the door there was a large linenfold chest, brought down from the manor; my lady opened it and took out glasses and wine; she poured a measure for each of us.

"My hands begin to warm," she said. And I wished that I might hold them, close in my own, to warm them.

She pulled from the chest the long velvet backcloths which Christer used at times, to shield the light or to drape his models. She was shaking them out and piling them upon the wooden bench.

"Ah, Jon," she said sadly. "Not to see Christer again . . . I am thinking . . . do you recall that he said once that the greatest sin is the denial of love?"

"That, and much else. But that above all."

Donna gave me a handful of brushes to wash. I took them with a vial of raw white spirit and a chunk of yellow soap to the little stream; it runs, clear and cold, through the meadow and sinks in moss and wet brown leaves beneath the oaks.

A little wind stirred in the oaks, and sunlight struck through the leaves. But beneath them was shadow, a still green shadow.

I heard a bird call. A shrill, piping sound. And looked up and saw no birds, no sudden flash of wings among the leaves. But Peter.

Peter whistled again. I went to him, and saw behind him the horses. And Kurt, in his dark leather armour. Kurt's face was seamed with weariness; he had, I saw, a fresh scar upon his cheek. But he smiled at me and clapped a hand upon my shoulder.

"Jon. How is it with my lady?"

"She is well. She is here."

"At the manor? She must leave the manor. Before sundown. She must pack a saddle bag, a small bag, no more, and ride to the cloister at Lindhagen. Go with her, Jon. Guard her. Before sundown. My lord is expected then at the manor. Men from the village, from Reyborg and Granholm, will join us soon after moonrise. We will storm the manor. By then my lady will be safe in cloister. The nuns expect her; they will give her sanctuary."

I said nothing; I felt my heart pound in my chest.

Kurt looked at me. "There is no one to trust save you, Jon."

Of a sudden I felt shamed. I had nursed my anger at Kurt since that day at the Virgin Spring when he spoke in anger to my lady. And I had been eaten with bitter jealousy . . . ah, God, I could not help it. But now as he put a hand on my shoulder, I felt the old bond between us.

"My lady is in the barn, Kurt. Alone. No one will come, I think. But Peter and I will watch."

And I saw the light come into his eyes; I saw that the hard lines in his face eased.

I watched him striding across the meadow. My lady would tell me later of what passed between them, yet I did not want to know. I was struck anew with jealousy. And then I thought, yes, it is right. They belong together, the two I love above all.

In the barn Donna was bending over one of the braziers, stirring the red embers. I think there must have been a glow of firelight about her—on her blue cloak, on her cheek, on her dark, shining hair. I have often seen her so. At the sound of boots on the plank flooring, she set the iron poker down but did not look up. "Jon, I cannot manage the fire. I have not the trick of it, it smokes so."

"Let me help," said Kurt.

Donna looked up. "Kurt!" Her hand went to her throat.

"I had to come. I had to come because . . . because I think only of you, my Donna. Night and day. You are always in my heart. And deep in my heart, like scars, the hard words I said to you. I could not come before."

"Kurt," she said again and put out her hands. He took them in his and saw that there were tears in her eyes.

"Ah, God. Ah, Donna, do not weep. I cannot bear it, do not weep. What is it, my sweet, the babe you bear within you, to make you sorrowful?"

"You did not have my letter?"

"I have had no letter, my Donna."

"I wrote . . . Jon took it to the island. I wrote that I would not bear my lord's child."

"You have lost the babe? I am sad for you, my little Donna. But I cannot be sorry."

"I never expected my lord's child, Kurt. It was . . . rumour. Rumour, only. I allowed the rumour to spread because I knew my lord would keep me here, and not send me back to court. I wished to be here. Where I could be near . . . near Christer."

"Now, my Donna, you must leave."

"I suppose so. Now that Christer is dead."

"Christer is . . . ?"

She told him.

"My sweet," he said, and took her in his arms.

But then he said urgently, "You must leave; I have come to tell you this. Before sundown. My lord will come then. The manor will be attacked. You must go with Jon, to the nuns at Lindhagen."

"You will come there?"

"I cannot say when I will see you again. Though I am torn apart with longing . . ." His mouth grew hard then, in his need of her, his love for her, and the pain of denial. He was holding her strongly, but now he released her. "Ride in boy's clothes, if you will, to Lindhagen. Take little with you." And then he said in bitterness, "You will want court dress, I suppose. And the rubies, my lord's rubies."

"Kurt! You do not care for me in court dress?" And then Donna pulled the cloak from her shoulders. She unlaced the bodice of her blue gown and ripped it from her shoulders. The gown lay upon the floor and she stepped away from it, as if she stepped from a still blue pool.

She stood before Kurt in her white linen shift. She pulled the shift away from her throat, from the soft curve of her breasts.

"Is it so that you would have me, Kurt, like any tavern tart?"

"Ah, God . . . would you have the heart out of my body?"

"Yes, Kurt, yes!"

And she took his hand and led him into one of the barn stalls, where sweet dry hay lay upon the floor; she brought the lengths of soft velvet which Christer had used, and spread them upon the hay.

And there in sunlight they lay as lovers, tender, at first, and then caught up in a strong tide of fierce joy.

Afterward, Kurt said, "I will be happy all my life for this hour, my Donna. The thought of you will warm me as I ride, and nourish me in hunger, and heal all wounds."

She brought wine then, and a single cup. She stood before him, clasping the cup with both hands; he put his big hands over hers. Together they lifted the cup and drank.

"Always know," said Kurt, "that you are my true love. There will be no other. I pledge you this. I beg a pledge of you."

"I will love you always, Kurt."

"I will not ask it. I cannot bind you. I am bound to my men, to the cause. I can see you seldom. You belong at court, safe, sheltered. Yes, my Donna, even wearing the rubies. Pledge me now that you will ride to Lindhagen. Start within the hour."

She kissed him and smiled and said, "God go with you, Kurt."

They came from the barn, hand in hand; I saw at once that they had known each other in love. My lady's face . . . ah, my lady looked as if she wore a crown of stars.

We watched as Kurt and Peter rode off; they were soon lost to sight in the deepening shadow beneath the oaks.

Within the hour we were ready. I went to the lower hall where men of the kitchens slept. It was deserted at this hour; I rummaged in wooden chests, and found boy's clothing to fit my lady. A pair of leather britches and woolen hose and smock. A cap of knitted wool. These I stuffed into my saddle bag.

My lady's bag was small, as Kurt had asked. "I have left to my lord his rubies," she said; and the little dimple showed. "I have with me pearls that were my naming gift, some jewels of my mother's, some gifts of the Queen. Kurt may have need of them. All can be sold, if he will, to buy arms and horses."

At the manor stables, the horses were being watered. One of the men said, "It be growing late to ride out, my lady."

"We do not ride far," she said. "I will not take Arab but the roan mare with the white forelock. Jon will ride the grey."

He gave her a hand up; he helped us to fasten the saddle

bags with leather thongs. I suppose he thought we carried some of Christer's things to the monastery, if he thought at all.

But he looked curiously at my lady's cloak, her favourite— the blue cloak with the furred mantle. And I saw with dismay that at the throat it was torn.

It was not long till sundown. Low in the golden sky, the red sun burned, in a bank of sun-streaked cloud. The pines cast long shadows across the road.

We stopped close by the road; there was a thick growth of hazel shrub. It was near dark in the thicket; there my lady changed the blue mantle and gown for boy's clothes.

When she came out upon the road, quick and slender as a boy, I saw that she had forgotten the cap. Her hair lay loose upon her shoulders—all the shining mass of it. So I helped with the cap, for she had trouble. I can see her now, piling the dark hair on top of her head, so that the white nape of her neck showed . . . tucking in the little loose tendrils which escaped, like loveknots.

Touching her, touching her hair, I felt myself to be trembling.

"Now . . ." she said. She handed me a stick of Christer's charcoal. "I will be smudged and black as any chimney boy."

So I stroked her cheeks with charcoal; but nothing could hide the blaze of her blue eyes.

"I am fit now to be your squire, Jon," she said, laughing. "Or Kurt's. When we come to Kurt's island."

"To . . . ? I will not take you to Kurt's island."

"Jon . . ." she said, wheedling, and very sweet. "It is so far to Lindhagen, to the cloister. Two hours, certainly. So far . . . And the roads perhaps full of fighting men. I am fearful."

"I doubt that, my lady."

"That I am fearful? Perhaps not—I am consumed with happiness. And not in the mood for nuns."

"I will not take you to Kurt's island."

"Then I will go alone. I can find the way; you have told me often of it. The sea road, and then the cliff beyond the inlet where Christer was found. The cliff, and the sentinel pine, and the cave with the boat . . ."

"My lady, it is very rough at Kurt's island. A stone ruin, peat fires, coarse food . . ."

"I care not. I will not go to the nuns. I will go where Kurt can find me. When he has time. When he has need of me."

Then she threw her arms around my neck, and put her cheek close to mine. So full of witchery. And I felt that my heart would burst. My hands were fists at my sides, I ached with the need to hold her.

"Jon," she said softly. "I think of what Christer would say. Seize love. Seize life . . . the joy of life . . . even if Heaven must wait."

I thought it likely that Hell would wait.

"Would you forsake your life at court, my lady? Would you break finally with Lord Ivar? If you go to the island, if you seek sanctuary with Kurt, there can be no turning back. You can never go back to my lord."

I knew that Kurt had thought of this, that he would not bind her. If she thought with regret of him, of their passion . . . if she went to the nuns, she could still go back to my lord.

"I would never go back to the manor, Jon. I would be free, free of Lord Ivar! Jon, my dear friend, would you fail me now?"

So we left the road to Lindhagen behind us. We rode on toward the inlet . . . and Kurt's island.

I have condemned myself for this, I have been torn by bitter remorse ever since.

But then my lady rode beside me, laughing, throwing me a handful of kisses, and singing. A song of Peter's.

> "If I should go to Heaven and find
> No trace of thee among the natives there,

Then I would sin and sin,
And seek thee otherwhere."

We saw no one on the road. It was near dusk; I could not
ask my lady to climb the cliff. The rock ledges are perilous
even by day. So we took the forest track, the dark pines closing in on us on either side.

A way of shadows . . .

By the time we reached the shingle beach and the sentinel
pine, it was so dark we could scarce see Kurt's island. A black
fortress of rock, it seemed, against the night sky. Stars were
showing over the tips of the pines; but the moon had not yet
risen.

I had a pine-knot torch; I tended it, though I was fearful of
showing a light . . . to be seen from Kurt's island, where no
doubt his men kept watch. If we should be met by a flight of
arrows . . .

The long, red beams of light shone into the cave. Light
moved on the rough rock walls, thick and furry with fungus.
The boat was there. I dragged it out, and then we tethered
the horses nearby. There was not room for them in the boat;
I would have to come back in the morning, with a large boat
and a lad from the island to help with the horses.

I told my lady to crouch low in the boat. She held the
torch, and I rowed hard. The wind was up; from the island,
over the wind, we heard the sound of the iron bells, a deep
booming. A riptide was surging in the channel. From the
torch, a thin red streamer of light moved on the water . . .
black water, and choppy, crested with foam.

I pulled the boat in on the strip of pebble beach on the lee
side of the island. And saw above me on the rocks the quick
flame of a torch.

It was Jens, old Jens who challenged us. I shouted to him.

"Jon?" He scrambled over the rocks to us. "And a lad with
ye. Come along."

"It is no lad with me, Jens. It is my lord's lady. My lady Donna. From the manor. Kurt would have you give her sanctuary."

If he felt surprise, he did not show it. But he peered at my lady with open curiosity, at her small face under the boy's cap, her smudged cheeks. She looked up at him with dark, shining eyes; she smiled at him.

Old Jens squinted, looking down at her. "Kurt's luck be holding."

He took up her saddle bag then; we followed him, climbing the dark forest path to the clearing in the pines. Here on the windward side of the island, the sound of the bells was loud. And the sound of the sea, crashing and hissing on the rocks. As we climbed, my torch picked out of the darkness a rude headstone beneath the pines. And another. White as bone in the sudden light of the torch.

And I thought of the day long ago when Kurt and I had discovered the island and come upon the old chapel in ruin, and the long stone hall of the monks, the roof fallen, the broken arches overgrown with thorn. And found the old bones wrapped in monk's cloth, and the brown parchment . . . "God hath visited upon us the Black Death."

The old bones had been given burial; the chapel had been repaired, and the long hall of the monks, the old stone refectory. Light streamed from the open arched doorway. Within there was warmth and rude comfort. At each end of the hall great fires blazed on open hearths; torches burned in brackets on the wall. There were stools and chests and a long oaken table; and on the table, mugs and a stone crock of ale. Close by the blazing fires, there were piled wolfskins; on these the men of the island slept.

"All be gone but me," said Jens. "And two of the lads. Six of us here, but the rest be gone to the mainland, north, to Kurt's big farm. They be bringing back food in the morning. Or next day, maybe, the sea be building up fierce."

Jens left us and went to the kitchen, close by and new built of pine timber. There the women slept. Two only were left on the island: the good Ebba, rosy and comfortable, her grey hair tucked under a grey coif. And Gulli, her daughter, fresh-skinned and smiling.

They brought wine and cheese, and a thick cut of fat ham. My lady bade them sit and eat with us, but they would not.

Donna ate but little; she drank a little wine. "I am replete, Jon, filled with happiness. Do not pull so long a face!" She put a hand upon my sleeve and smiled at me.

But then she said, "It is long past moonrise. I think of the manor. Did my lord come . . . to find us missing? Did Kurt come to attack the manor . . . on such a night?"

We were silent, listening to the thud of wind against the casement, the roar of wind in the pines, and the deep boom-ing of the bells.

I would not sleep, I knew it. I would lie by the fire and find comfort, but I would not sleep, caught up in the turmoil of my thoughts.

At last the women showed my lady into Kurt's chamber. They brought a steaming basin of water and linen towels. And Ebba put a hand beneath my lady's chin.

"Ye're weary, I warrant. Ye've a face sweet as a singing bird. Will I brush your hair?"

Donna said she would brush it herself.

"God watch you, my lady. Sleep in peace."

And they left us.

"I will sleep in peace," said Donna, her eyes soft. "In Kurt's chamber."

The room was small but vaulted. A part of the old stone ruin. The walls were stained with damp. But the little win-dow was fitted with scraped sealskin to keep out the chill night air; there were curtains of crimson woolen, bordered with tapestry work in a dull forest green, a patterning of leaves. On an old pine chest there were candles in copper candlesticks—small, steady flames in the dim room. On the hearth, the fire burned low; I built it up.

Close by the hearth there was a great bedstead of carved pine, piled with eiderdowns. My lady stood by the bed. "It is big as a field," she said. "A pity to sleep in it alone."

The high headboard was carved by an unskilled hand; red and blue and green chalk paint had been rubbed into the carvings.

Donna was charmed. "See, Jon, the carving is of Adam with his Eva, and the apple of guilt. Eva seems of a cold nature." And indeed Eva was long of nose, and her mouth prim. In wooden ridges, her hair flowed over her body to cover her.

Donna smiled upon Adam. "How eager he is, for the apple. He leers at Eva . . . in haste, or in hunger. Such great round eyeballs he has."

"An uncertain artist, my lady."

"Yes." And then my lady's eyes grew shadowed. "Poor little Eva . . . so brief a time in Paradise."

In the morning, my lady declared that she had slept well, and dreamt of Paradise. I suppose she meant she had dreamt of Kurt.

I took one of the lads with me. From the small, rocky harbor beneath the chapel we brought a whaleboat round, in rough sea, to the lee side of the island. In the narrow channel, the sea was subsiding. We pulled up the boat on the shingle beach below the great pine.

When we reached the oak grove where the horses had been tethered, they were gone.

They had been fast-tethered; they had not broken loose. They had been cut loose, the leather straps severed with a knife.

Chapter 21

———◆•••▶———

"I blame myself, my lady. I should have gone back last night for the horses."

"How could you, Jon, with the sea so strong?"

We sat at the midday meal, with small appetite.

"I thought they would never find us here," said Donna. "Ah, Jon, I have led you on a troubled path. Truly I am sorry."

"I will follow you always, whatever the path, my lady."

"Dear Jon." And she smiled at me, but then she said sadly, "What if I have led my lord's men to Kurt?"

I said to comfort her, "Perhaps the horses were not found by my lord's men."

"Who else would find them?"

"Sven the poacher. I have seen him on the forest track."

"Surely he will go to my lord."

"I think not. If Sven found the horses, he would hide them for some days in the forest. And then take them by night to the market town. To sell."

After the meal, we roamed the island. And then sat on the rocks above the sea. Donna wore her boy's clothes, for comfort. She sat, chin in hand, deeply thoughtful.

Just before sundown we saw a boat, far out, beating its way

in tossing sea. It was heading for the island. A whaleboat, rolling and dipping, spray flung over the bow. Behind it the red sun was sinking in a heavy bank of cloud. The sea was darkening but veined with foam. Spray spattered the rocks where we sat.

At last the boat tacked into the island mooring, the little haven below the chapel.

Kurt's men, back from the farm.

And Kurt with them.

My lady ran down the steep rocky path to him. The men were making the boat fast; Kurt bent over the ropes. She called to him.

He turned and saw her, in her boy's clothes, her hair tumbled upon her shoulders, her cheeks pink in the sharp wind, and her eyes shining.

"Kurt!"

He stared at her, in disbelief.

"Donna . . . my dear heart . . . you are *here!*" And he seized her hands; the quick flame came into his eyes.

"I have come, Sir Kurt, to be your squire."

"You are not well qualified for that, my little Donna. Peter serves me well."

"I will serve you in other ways, if you will keep me. As . . . as companion of the bedchamber?"

He put a hand upon her hair, upon her cheek.

"I will keep you. As mistress of my heart," he said with tenderness, and kissed her.

But then he said, his mouth tight, "But not here. You cannot stay here, my little love."

"I have left my lord. I will not go back."

"I will make some arrangement for you . . ."

"Kurt, are you not happy to see me?"

"My Donna, can you ask me that?"

And Kurt turned to me. "Jon, it is good to see you. But I thought to see you in Lindhagen."

"Jon is not to be blamed because I am here. It is my fault, Kurt . . . I am sorry to be willful," said Donna demurely. Ah, I knew her in such a mood. "Kurt, do you stay the night?"

"Yes. To see if you give good service." But his eyes were anxious upon her.

"What of the manor?" I said. "Did you storm the manor?"

"No. My lord did not come. We had word that he rode with the Bishop to Lindhagen. A sudden change of plan."

"Ah, then," said Donna. "I am most grateful not to be in Lindhagen."

We sat long before the blazing fire that evening. Donna changed to the blue gown; she sat in a high-backed chair before the wide hearth. And she wore on her shining hair a little net of pearls and pearls in her ears.

Kurt poured Rhenish wine—the best. We told him of the horses.

Donna lifted her wine glass. "But Jon thinks there is little cause for alarm. If Sven the poacher found them."

I glanced at Kurt; he knew I had said this to comfort my lady. His face was much troubled. "Sven would know the horses were from the manor. High bred . . . and their saddles and trappings."

"But he could not know that Jon and I rode them," said Donna.

"Such hue and cry as there must have been at the manor last night when they found you gone—ah, yes, my Donna, Sven would soon hear of it. And he would go straight to my lord's men, knowing that my lord would set the value of my lady above the price of two horses. He would go to the manor in hope of a fat reward."

And Kurt got up to pace before the fire. "It is only a question of time. My lord's men will come to the island. God grant us a little time. By noon tomorrow I will have you off the island. With Jon."

"You will take us to the farm? Where you will sometimes come?"

"No, my sweet. It is rough at the farm, you cannot live so. And there we are under constant risk of attack. It is a rallying point for men of the north shore." And Kurt paced; I saw that his dark hair was now touched with gray at the temples. In firelight, his face was shadowed; the strong lines on it etched in black.

Beyond the casement, the wind was shaking the pines. And I heard the fluting of a fox, so wild a cry in the gusty dark.

But within, the fire was rising and singing. I piled on more wood.

And Kurt said, "I will send you, my Donna, to my lady of Holmen. A friend through the years."

Donna lifted her little chin. "Is she pretty?"

"I . . . I have never considered if she is pretty. She is gentle and good. Her husband and I were schooled together at court. Her oldest son is a true knight, the youngest a squire; he has not yet won his spurs. Both ride with me, and my lord of Holmen himself."

The maids brought in venison, well roasted on a spit, mushrooms in broth, and a spicy cheese pastry. We sat at table.

"Before dawn," said Kurt, "I will leave for the farm. And from there send riders to Holmen."

"We will go with you," said Donna happily.

"No. The roads are full of fighting men. My own, and my lord's. It's best if you go directly from here by sea. I will have a boat to take you off the island by noon . . . God willing. No whaleboat. A strong koster boat in such rude weather. Between here and Holmen, there are some hours of open sea." And Kurt took my lady's hand. "Are you anxious, my little Donna? Good men will be with you. I'd trust Jon in any sea. The trip is rough, but soon over."

A great gust of wind roared in the chimney; the fire flared, and sparks scattered on the hearth. And we heard the tumult of surf on the rocks . . . even there, in the warm hall, we heard it. And the iron clamour of the bells.

My little lady was silent for a moment.

And then she smiled. "I sit and hold court, with the two I love best in all the world. We will be merry." She had seen a lute, lying on one of the chests, left there by one of Kurt's men. A lute of carved beechwood and birch; she took it up and tuned it. "We will have music at court."

As we sat on at table, she sang to us. Her voice was sweet and true, but small. She sang "Of the Monk of Angers," a "monk of mighty thirst."

> "I swear
> He'll bear
> His carcass to eternity.
>
> So stained
> And grained
> With life-preserving wine is he.
>
> He'll keep,
> Don't steep
> His body with embalmer's myrrh.
>
> No spice
> So nice
> As alcohol, I do aver."

And Kurt got up to pour more wine. Donna watched him; the hard lines in his face were eased; he was smiling.

And then she sang "I would sin and sin . . ." And watching her, Kurt's eyes grew dark.

The maids brought in a bowl of apples and hazelnuts and bade us good night.

And Kurt brought out chessmen of bone and ivory and a beechen board. He and my lady played at chess. Their hands kept touching; their eyes met. Donna played well, but she was rash.

At last as she would make a move, Kurt put his big hands over hers.

"No, no my dearest heart, you must not move so . . . don't you see that I will checkmate your King?"

She made a pretense of pouting. "You distract me, Kurt." Then she leaned to him for his kiss and began to collect the chessmen.

"Tell us, Kurt, do you truly have hope of checkmating my King . . . though I call him my King no longer?"

"It is the only way. The King must be utterly routed. He must be driven from Sweden. And with him, those who favour the Kalmar agreement. Sweden is bled white, to serve the Danish interest. The Danish overlords, the bailiffs must go. And Sweden must be ruled, not only by sovereign lords . . . *all* men must have a voice in government. The Bishop's clerk as much as the Bishop. The poorest crofter, the bondman, as much as any manor lord."

Kurt had often spoken so . . . without hope.

"Now," he said, "there is hope. Ours is no longer a rabble army. Ah, we are often quartered in caves, we are bedded in leafy hollows in the forest. Eating the pounded bark of pine, or acorns. Squirrel or fox in the cookpots . . . whatever the men can find. One man in fifty perhaps owns arms or armour. The others fight with mallet or ax. They stuff their jerkins with plumegrass and moss—a sorry shield against the thrust of my lord's arrows. They stop their wounds with dust of the smoking mushroom, and bind their sores with dock leaf."

My lady was looking at Kurt, her eyes dark with pity.

"Yet," he said again, "we have hope. For now strong lords join us. Men of power and vision who see that Sweden will be a sovereign nation governed by Swedes."

"We will never see that day," I said.

But Kurt said, "Yes. But it will take time. And first the Danes must go. The decision will come at Stenborg. We will attack at month's end." He was gazing into his wine cup, his face bitter and intent. "Against armoured men, against the King's mounted mercenaries, we will fight with stronger weapons . . . with the fury of the oppressed, the gut strength of mountain men. And the iron will, if need be, to die."

My lady said softly, "You would give your life for the cause, Kurt."

"Yes. My life. But not yours. I will have you off the island by noon. I believe there is time. You came late to the island last night in rough weather. I think the horses were not found till this morning. Perhaps, Jon, even as you were bringing the boat round to fetch them. My lord cannot know how few we are on the island. I think he will collect considerable force before he comes. By tomorrow perhaps . . ."

At last my lady said, "It grows late." She came to me to bid me good night; she took my hand and held it against her cheek. "God watch you, my good Jon."

Kurt said, "Make ready for bed, my sweet. I will come shortly."

She went into the bedchamber, closing the door. And Kurt and I stood before the fire.

"Jon," he said, and there was anguish in his eyes. "I love her more than my life. She is all my happiness. God grant you bring her safely to Holmen. Yet . . . if you are taken by my lord's men . . . do you know the penalty for adultery? If my lord should find her . . ."

"I have had no occasion to learn the penalty for adultery . . . I regret it."

"I am no master of laws either, Jon. But I know this. We had a case, one of my men, not long since. The man was convicted and hanged. For myself, I care not. I am wanted for so many crimes—arson, assault, breaking the peace on holy days. Inciting to riot, treason. A man can be hanged but once."

I stared into the fire, sipping the last of my wine. "And my lady—what is the penalty for her?"

"It is . . . ah, God, Jon . . . it is burial alive."

I could say no word. I felt that my heart had stopped beating.

"Unless . . ." said Kurt. His mouth was tight with pain. "Unless my lord chooses to forgive her. I think we agree that is not likely."

I looked down at my hands and saw that they were fists.

"So, Jon, my Donna must claim abduction. Rape and abduction, let us add those to my list of crimes. Remember, Jon, if the need arises."

Then Donna opened the door of the bedchamber; she came to us. Her hair was loose and shining; she wore her blue cloak. It was open at the neck; I saw that beneath it she wore only her white shift. On her feet were soft little slippers of miniver skin.

"Kurt, are you coming?"

"I . . . I am trying to think what to do with you, my sweet."

Donna smiled; I saw the little dimple. "Kurt. You do not know what to do with me . . . in your great wide bed with Adam and Eva upon it? You do not know?"

From the bowl on the table she took an apple, bit into it, and offered it to Kurt. He bit it, and tossed it into the fire.

"My little hoyden," he said fondly. He picked her up in his arms and carried her into the bedchamber.

Before dawn, Kurt was away. The wind had moderated, and Kurt was sorry for that. The whaleboat was clumsy, with heavy sails. "Three hours before us, I think, to get to the farm."

In the black sky the stars were still bright. We stood with Kurt on the rocky shore, as the men hauled water casks aboard and mounted the sails. They worked by torchlight; the dark hull of the boat was dipping in the wash of the waves; the red gleam of torchlight shone on black water.

And on Kurt's face, strong and etched with shadow. My lady's face was rosy in the light.

"Take heart, my sweet." And Kurt held her close to him. Two as one.

As I would hold her . . .

"Jon will bring you safe to Holmen," said Kurt. "Even in such rude weather." For the sea surged and broke on the rocks below us, sending up pearls of spray. "Do not be fearful."

"You will come soon, Kurt? To Holmen?" My lady's eyes were bright with tears. She brushed them away and smiled at him.

"When I can. My Donna. My one love, my true love. Always. I pledge you. As God is my witness." He clasped her hands then and held them to his heart. "You should have a morning gift. So fine a gift. And I have nothing now, nothing for you but my heart."

"It is all I would have, Kurt."

The quick flame came into his eyes. But Donna pulled away. In a cleft of the rock dwarf rowan grew, no higher than heather, the bright berries crusted with spray. Donna stooped to break off a sprig of it, a green plume set with scarlet berries. She fastened it into the leather strap of Kurt's gauntlet.

"A talisman, my true knight. Rowan to ward off evil, to keep you from malice and hurt. May God watch you as well."

"I will cherish my talisman, my little Donna. But I have no need of it. Your love is my strength and my shield. And my delight."

He took her in his arms and kissed her. A deep kiss.

And I turned away.

We watched them cast off. The sea was still strong, dark and tossing, and then molten silver, in the early light. The stars were fading; on the far horizon there were red streaks of light.

We watched till the boat tacked behind a rocky promontory and was lost to sight.

And within the hour, my lord's men—forty or more—were upon the island.

My lady lifted her face to my lord's captain. "We will come quietly." Her voice was rough with tears. "We beg you to show us courtesy. We are only seven. Jon and I. Two maids and two lads. And an old man, Jens, who can do you no hurt."

All were taken into custody by my lord's men. On the forest track, horses were waiting. Even our own. Once more I mounted the grey mare, and my lady rode the roan with the white forelock.

The two maids were much frightened; and old Jens lifted his fists and cursed with such fierce vigour that my lady told him to be quiet. And I thought one of my lord's men would strike and maim him. But they showed mercy to us all. Suddenly I knew why. My lord wanted witnesses—in good sturdy condition—when we came to Lindhagen.

For at last we took the road to Lindhagen.

Chapter 22

My lord was in residence with the Bishop, at the Bishop's
great castle in Lindhagen.

My lady was not housed there. She was taken to the nuns
at the cloister. The cloister became her prison. It is strong-
walled; and without the wall, my lord's men were a strong
guard, pacing night and day on the cobbles before the gatehouse. Fifty or more men in iron armour . . . though they
were not permitted inside the holy enclosure.

I was with my lady at the cloister. Not as her priest, her
spiritual guide, to give her counsel and comfort. My lord paid
small attention to my lady's comfort. I was there because I
was a vital witness to her transgression. My lord proposed to
bring her to trial for adultery.

So the cloister became my prison. I was not permitted to
leave it. I slept in the gatehouse with two aged monks who
kept the gate. Most of the time I had a bed to myself, a
wooden cot with a straw mattress, though once I shared my
bed with two mendicant monks, given shelter for the night. I
slept little for both snored, one alto, one treble.

I slept little in any case, so sore was my heart for my lady.

She was given a small room in the old part of the cloister,

above ground, but the narrow window let in only a thin shaft of light; the stone walls were furred with mould. There was a narrow wooden pallet for sleeping. A single woven coverlet. I think my lady must have felt the chill, though she made no complaint. Upon the wall there was an iron crucifix; beneath it burnt a thin pine taper.

There was, in the room, a curious smell—waxen, sour. One of the little novices told me the room had been used formerly for laying out the dead, those who had died of pestilence. I said nothing to my lady of this.

Yet the nuns were kind to my gentle Donna. She was permitted to walk in the walled cloister garden and the orchard, and I with her. It was hoped, I suppose, that I would bring her to consider the enormity of her sin, and to seek atonement in confession before my lord.

Donna was constant in attendance at the abbey church with the nuns. And she was allowed by the Abbess to help with nursing the sick in the infirmary, a task she welcomed.

"For the time goes slowly, Jon. So heavy is my heart."

Yet she did not lose heart. She was convinced that Kurt would find her.

"He must know. He has informers everywhere. He must know my lord is in Lindhagen. Kurt will come. He will storm the castle . . ."

I tried to share her hope.

I took my meals with my lady and the nuns, in the refectory. This was torment to Donna. For as we ate—often a thin bean gruel, blood sausage, or a pallid river fish, and watered beer—there were readings from Saint Birgitta. The nuns were like a colony of doves in grey habit. Stupid, busy, fluttering. And sometimes quarrelsome, as doves are, when confined to the dovecote.

Three of them could read; at table they took turns. So we heard the dictum of Saint Birgitta: "The life of the flesh is bitter as venom."

At this, Donna's eyes met mine, over her pewter mug of sour beer. She put down the cup; I could swear that I saw the little dimple.

The Abbess cleared her throat scratchily. Donna clasped her hands upon the oaken table, disdaining the wooden trencher before her, the meager portion of boiled cabbage and beetroot.

The reading continued. We heard that before each act of marital intercourse, the granite saint had prayed with her husband "to God that He might have forebearance with the sin they thereby committed."

We heard further of how Birgitta had mortified the flesh: "Every Friday evening she would take a burning candle from a crucifix and drip the hot melting wax into her armpits. As soon as the sores began to heal she tore them open again with her finger nails, wishing to bear them perpetually in memory of Christ's wounds."

And: "When Birgitta's husband was away for a night, she would stay awake weeping and praying, scourging her body till it bled."

At this, there was a small murmuring among the little novices at table; they peered over their mugs at my lady, their eyes round and curious. They knew well that my lady had not followed this shining example. When her husband was away, she had consorted with the rebel leader, Kurt.

Donna endured the curious glances, the whisperings . . .

These were torment. But small torment compared to the sessions of the trial.

Twice daily the trial judges assembled in the abbey oratory. A large room of vaulted stone, the ceiling much carved with spires and rosettes, a canopy of stone lace. And the room was so cold that at times we seemed to sit in a vast, dim cavern of ice, wind-cut and echoing.

Braziers were brought, and small fires lighted; but these did little to moderate the chill.

The judges would file in to take their places in the carved choirstalls, settling their robes around them, declaring themselves of solemn intent to probe truth in the matter of my lady's adultery, a sin most grievous and intolerable in the eyes of God and man.

The Bishop of Lindhagen was chief interrogator and judge. He had with him scribes and two learned doctors of theology from the ecclesiastical college in Lindhagen. There were minor churchmen—twelve of these. And a Doctor of Logic, in scarlet robe, with a long neckchain of heavy gold.

The Abbot had ridden over from the monastery in Morby. He sat apart from the others; his old brown cowl was shabby; he kept rubbing his withered hands, stiff with chill. But his eyes upon my lady were sad and tender. I saw that he meant to defend her. If he could.

All stood, until my lord Bishop had taken his place.

And beside him, my lord.

Both sat in high-backed chairs of carved walnut, with gilt rubbed into the carvings.

My lady and I would enter the room, her blue skirt whispering upon the stone floor, her manner modest, her shining hair tucked under a white coif. Beneath it her eyes were dark and enormous.

I would take my place beside her and feel my lord's eyes upon us—the icy venom of his look. As he had loved my lady once, he now hated her. A ferocity of hatred, with deadly intent. He meant to destroy her, as she had destroyed all that he had once held dear.

I thought of the saying among us: "When the wood dove flutters from shelter, the falcon rises and strikes."

My lady and I took the oath. On stiff parchment this was written, and we repeated it, swearing that we would, as God was our witness, speak truth and not obstruct the seeking of truth. We signed the parchment, and wax and flame were brought.

We had not with us our own seals. Our saddle bags had been taken from us. So a hair was plucked from my lady's head—long and dark and silken; and one from mine. These were fixed in the molten wax, and we were each required to press a thumb into the wax.

My lady was permitted to sit; but I stood, facing the assembly of learned ecclesiastics. For my lady was being tried in Church court; she had the right, since she could claim "benefit of clergy." She could read and was made to give proof of this. She read from the thirteenth chapter of Corinthians. Her voice was soft, in this dim stone chamber. But clear, though I heard the little tremour in it.

" 'These three abide . . . faith, hope, and charity. And the greatest of these is charity.' "

She looked up then at the faces of her judges. And observed in them, I am sure, a singular lack of charity.

For she said sadly, "My lords spiritual, you do me honour to attend my case. But the essence of the Christian doctrine is forgiveness. I marvel to see so little in you of an inclination to leniency."

My lord pounced. "Do you admit then, my lady, that you have committed a crime for which you beg clemency?"

"I will not admit to crime. I meant only that I observe that my lords are all very wroth with me."

Lord Ivar said then, "There can be small doubt that you have committed a crime which is hideous . . . unnatural . . . vile."

"Unnatural, my lord?"

My lord regarded my little lady with cold fury. "You will speak again only when you are questioned."

And I was then examined.

"It was good of you, Jon, to go with my lady to . . . to Kurt's island. You have been devoted to her. I have no doubt that you have sought to dissuade her from folly."

So he sought to disarm me. I suppose he thought to find me a docile witness, a monk regarding my lady's sin as vile.

His long fingers were clasped upon the carved arms of his chair. He wore on his forefinger a great sapphire; from it, there was, of a sudden, a blue flash of light. "When my lady was upon the island, was Kurt there?"

"Your men found us alone. But for the serving folk."

At this, my lord looked upon me as if I were a toad.

"We will waste no time on the question. We do not require your answer. Kurt was not there when you were taken off the island. No. But he had been there. We have put the question to the two lads who were with you. They said they could not remember if Kurt was at the island. We took them to the torture chambers in the Bishop's castle. They were not harmed. We merely showed them the rack and the burning oil and the thumbscrews. Their memory was miraculously restored. Kurt was there. They affirmed it, and that there is but one bedchamber."

The Bishop of Lindhagen cleared his throat. I looked at him, at the fat jowls, the small, cruel eyes. At the wet, red lips, the underlip protruding, pouting like a child's. I knew I hated him. His eyes upon my lady . . . upon her throat, where above the blue gown, the little curve of her breasts showed.

He said in his breathy voice, "We ask you, Brother Jonas, only one thing. We ask you to confirm that Kurt slept with my lady in the bedchamber."

"I am not accustomed to entering my lady's bedchamber, so I cannot say what may or may not have occurred there."

"Did Kurt enter the bedchamber?"

"The men slept before the fire in the hall."

"Did Kurt lie down to sleep before the fire and get up later to go in to my lady?"

"I am not very observant when I am asleep. If Kurt had

gotten up from his place before the fire—and I did not see him do it—I would have assumed that he had gone outside to make water."

My lord said acidly, "I am touched by your devotion, Jon, to my lady . . . your effort to spare her the reward of her wanton behaviour. But I must remind you that such efforts can be interpreted as an attempt at mockery of this court. For such misdemeanour, there are . . . suitable punishments."

"Yes, my lord."

"We require a direct answer. Did you at any time observe any evidence on the part of my lady of licentious or unchaste conduct . . . with Kurt?"

"No, my lord." It was true. I had observed in them a deep and tender and surpassing love. But no evidence of licentious conduct.

"Will you swear to this by God's blood, and by the innocence of Our Blessed Virgin?"

"I will so swear."

My lord was not done with me; I knew it.

But the Bishop intervened. He was not concerned with me, but with my lady. "We are well aware that according to the most honoured of Church fathers, Hieronymus, 'Woman is the Devil's gate, the thorn of iniquity; in other words a perilous thing.' " He spoke in commanding tones, and directed his discourse to the clergy, seated in the choirstalls. "A woman is ever prone to weakness and folly, unable to stand fast against temptation. Forever leading the male into the sins of the flesh. Consider the downfall of Adam, tempted by the wanton Eva."

Among the learned doctors, heads nodded in assent.

My lady lifted her hand. The Bishop granted her permission to speak.

"Do you consider, my lord Bishop, that *all* women are, as you say, unable to stand fast against temptation?"

"I think there can be no dispute on the point. We have

ample evidence from Holy Writ, from the Church fathers, from our own observance of life. Woman is a frail vessel. Ever in need of guidance. Ever inclined to the path of waywardness."

Donna was demure. "All women. What then of the Mother of God . . . presumably a woman?"

A buzzing as of angry hornets, among the judges.

The Bishop said icily, "My lady, do not compound your crime with blasphemy."

The Doctor of Theology rose, in his scarlet gown, and said severely, "We are not concerned with the lives of the saints, for these transcend mortality."

The Bishop rapped firmly upon the carved arm of his chair. "We are not here to dispute a point of theology. We are here to determine truth, in the charge brought against my lady. The Abbot of Morby is with us. He has known my lady well and often been her confessor. I suggest that he may tell us a little of her character as he has observed it. If he has seen in her any inclination to willful spirit, to lewd thought, or incontinent behaviour."

The Abbot got to his feet, smoothing the front of his shabby gown. I had never seen him look so grey, so frail. He said quietly, "Do you ask me to slander my lady?"

My lord glared at him.

The Abbot looked beyond him. Old, grey, peering with weak eyes at the assembly of judges, a slight figure in his frayed gown, the Abbot was yet a man to command respect.

He smiled upon my lady. "I suggest, from what I have observed in my lady—her gentleness and her piety—that she was, and is now, the victim of cruel intention. I suggest that at Kurt's island she was the victim of rape and forcible abduction."

I had intended to plead this, if need be. So Kurt had told me.

But the Doctor of Laws urgently wished to speak. He rose,

a dour, sallow man, with dark pouches under his eyes. He stared before him, intoning in a wooden voice. As if he read aloud from some invisible parchment. "It is written in the laws of Dalarna, of Östergötland, and of other provinces: 'Of rape there must be evidence of marks upon the woman. Or there must be witness of *'skrek* and *ansträngningar*,' . . . of 'struggles and screams.' "

The Bishop passed a round, red tongue over his lips.

But my lord said coldly, "It is ridiculous to claim rape and abduction. My lady, with great forethought, had taken her jewels with her. It is clearly evident that she rode to meet Kurt of her own free will, and that with him she committed adultery." He stood over my lady. "You will save the court much time if you admit to it."

Donna was dead white; she put her hand to her throat. But she met my lord's gaze—narrow, icy—and said, "If you believe me guilty of this, you must prove it."

"Let my lady make no further answer as yet," said the Abbot. In those wise old eyes there was much compassion. Donna gave him a grateful look; and I recalled that as a young man he had read law at the University in Paris.

"What firm evidence have you, my lord Ivar?" The Abbot spoke strongly. "Suspicion . . . conjecture . . . but these are not admissible in a court of law. The law says there should be evidence of 'sheets and bolster' . . . 'take bolster and sheets and bring them before the council . . .' The law says further that responsible witness or witnesses must be found. In this case, to confirm that my lady and Kurt were seen together in circumstances which can leave no doubt—no reasonable doubt—that they were lovers."

"I have no doubt of it," said my lord furiously. "On the island together. One bedchamber . . . The two lads have so witnessed."

"But they are of minor age, my lord. And it may be argued that they gave information under duress. Also recall that we do not try the case of a common herdsman's wife. My lady has powerful friends at court; she is a Queen's ward. It is within her right to seek royal counsel."

And I felt a small glimmer of hope.

But my lord said, "Does it occur to you, my lord Abbot, that my lady has now forfeited the Queen's friendship? She has been found with Kurt—sworn enemy to the King. She can look for no help from court."

"That is true," said the Abbot sadly. "I had not considered it. But I insist that this court is a mockery of justice if my lady is tried and condemned without witnesses to attest to her misconduct. If indeed she has been guilty of misconduct. Witnesses must be found."

"I think there will be no difficulty." My lord lifted a long hand to smooth the sandy hair, touched with white at his temples. I saw a gleam of gold from the heavy ring on his finger; the great sapphire held dark fire in its depths. "I have no doubt that my lady's misconduct did not begin on the island. I believe that was not the first occasion. I have often been absent from the manor. I have seen my lady's interest in Kurt. I believe others have seen it. And can furnish evidence—solid evidence—that my lady indulged with Kurt in carnal sin. I will send to the village, and to the manor, to find if any can so witness."

And I felt despair. Witnesses would be found. False, swearing to falsehood, but well rehearsed and recompensed by my lord.

Court was dismissed but resumed on the following morning.

A sunny day. In the oratory long fingers of light struck through the high casements. These were glowing with stained glass—rosettes and medallions of ruby and emerald and blue. As the hours passed, the light moved upon the stone floor and settled upon the faces of the judges, upon their robes. A shaft of violet light struck the front of the Bishop's cassock; a shimmer of topaz lay upon his shoulders.

The learned judges seemed to be wearing motley, the bright diamonds of colour worn by jesters at court.

That we sat in trial court, in judgment upon my gentle lady, seemed a mockery, a dream of evil, a play of buffoons.

A dream from which there could be no waking . . .

For I looked upon my lady's white face. And thought in anguish, my Donna sits on trial for her life. Ah, God, I thought, God help her.

The Bishop opened the session.

I saw that he meant to needle my lady with questions, to harass her, to break her spirit, so that she would confess out of sheer weariness to carnal crime.

"My lady." The Bishop put the tips of his fat fingers together. "Do you swear to answer with truth the questions put to you?"

"I will answer truth . . . when I can give an answer. I cannot answer questions on my state of mortal sin . . . as you call it. I believe that Almighty God is the judge of that and I am not obliged to answer you, my lord Bishop."

The Bishop glared at her. "Do you submit to the rulings of the Church and the word of God as revealed in the Holy Bible? I do not now refer to the question of your adultery—forbidden as deadly sin in the Seventh Commandment. In other matters do you endeavour to follow the precepts of the Bible?"

"I have tried. I am as others are . . . but mortal. And liable to fault."

The Bishop's hands were upon the Holy Book. I can see those hands now—white, plump, with the episcopal ring, set with a great ruby, dark as the heart's blood. "I will read to you from Deuteronomy, Chapter Twenty-two: 'The woman shall not wear that which pertaineth to a man; neither shall a man put on a woman's garment; for all that do so are an abomination to the Lord.' My lady, when you were taken from the island, you were wearing boy's clothes. Boy's clothes! The first step in immodest behaviour. Expressly forbidden by Church law. The first step to license."

"My lord Bishop . . ." And I saw for a moment the little dimple. "I am sorry you find objection to my boy's clothes. Yet you, my lords spiritual, for whom I have great respect, in that you serve the Church—you, every man among you, wear skirts like a woman. I have no objection to that."

I saw upon the Abbot's face a small smile.

The Bishop smoothed his flowing ecclesiastical robe; he snuffled and coughed. "The offense is after all not the offense for which you are under trial. Do you admit, my lady, that carnal love outside the bonds of marriage is a deadly sin?"

Donna's eyes were very dark then, and shining. "Love is a force beyond our control. A force beyond ourselves. I believe that true love is a gift of God. But I assume, my lord Bishop, that you have had no occasion to find out."

The Bishop controlled himself. "Will you admit that your carnal love for Kurt is a grievous sin?"

"I will not admit to carnal love for Kurt. I have not committed sin."

"And, Jon, that is true," she said to me later. "My love for Kurt is not sin . . . but blessing, as Christer would have said. If I have sinned, it was in giving myself to Lord Ivar . . . a commerce without love."

We walked for a little time in the cloister garden, close by the wall. Donna ripped off the stiff white coif; her hair fell upon her shoulders, shining and free. I wanted to touch it.

"To be free, Jon . . . ah, to be free and pounding along the road on Arab. Hard and fast. And you beside me. Chiding me, of course." And she smiled at me.

Then her face was wistful. She put a hand upon the wall, high and built of heavy stone. Creepers grew thickly upon it; to the thick twining stems brown shreds of leaf were clinging. For a moment I had the fancy that I might climb the wall, pulling myself up on the strong woody growth. And my little lady with me.

"In the world outside there is life and love and laughter," she said, sighing.

A grey evening . . . it was not long till dusk. The grass was wet; on the black, twisted limbs of the apple trees, on the crumpled leaves in the grass, there were drops of moisture. Apples lay in the grass, yellow-green, a faint bloom upon them. There was a small pool, leaden grey and faintly shining. On the banks, wild flag grew, the leaves sere and yellow.

And something else, something of evil in this quiet place. The *dvale* grew here, deadly nightshade, the Devil's berry. The stalks were black now, coated with slime and set with black berries. The Devil's herb . . . he is everywhere, the horned god, the Prince of Evil, even here within cloister walls.

My lady said sadly, "Where is Kurt? Why does he delay?"

"He would need a strong force with him. Most of his men are near Stenborg, I think. From there, it is a week's ride, at the least. On the road. But they will take forest ways. Kurt will be careful. He must know that my lord has many men to waylay him."

"Perhaps he has been ambushed."

I took my Donna's hand. "Take heart. Take care as well. Bear with the Bishop, and do not provoke him."

"He provokes *me*," she said. "But I will try to be disarming. Though he does his best to plague me. A fat gadfly . . . with so evil a sting."

At the morning session, the questions went on as before. Donna admitted nothing. But her small face was white with strain. Her hands were twisting in her lap.

My lord said finally, "Nothing is gained by repeating the questions. At the afternoon session, I propose to bring in witnesses."

The Abbot rose then and said wearily, "I marvel, my lord, that you are so anxious to dishonour your noble name."

My lord stared at him.

"An ancient name," said the Abbot. "And illustrious, known throughout the north for probity, for knightly honour, for service to the King. Never a blot of shame upon it."

My lord's hands were tight upon the arms of his high-backed chair. "There is no blot upon it now."

"But there will be. If word spreads that you bring my lady to trial for adultery. Few know of it now, except in the village. And here, in court. If my lady is condemned, the world will know of her dishonour. Your name will be smeared by her misconduct . . . she bears your name. Moreover, my lord, you will be a—I venture to say it—a laughingstock at court. The mature husband and the young bride who could not bear the marriage bond between you . . . who deceived you. And made you cuckold."

I could see that this gave my lord pause. But he said, "It is inconceivable that my lady's crime should go unpunished."

Chapter 23

Court was called to convene soon after the midday meal. I had felt during the sessions as if I moved and spoke in a cruel dream.

And now I felt it more strongly than ever.

Two witnesses waited, standing against the wall.

Dame Barbro—her black cloak limp, her shoulders squared, her pale eyes shining with malice. I felt her gaze like a blight upon me. And upon my lady.

And her companion—old Mother Svenson, in her frowsy bottle-green cloak; upon her head was a scrap of yellow woolen. Her hair was loose, a grey tangle upon her shoulders, like shreds of wool; her small eyes peered like a ferret's. She was snuffling, and drops of water appeared upon her chin.

The Bishop's clerk approached them to swear them to truth. He wrinkled his nose. There was about both so foul an odour, rank as that of a rutting fox.

"My lord," said the Abbot. "These are responsible witnesses? These will witness against my lady? Let him without sin cast the first stone."

For he was well aware of their witchcraft . . . aware too

that they would never be convicted of it. Too many depended upon them, and feared them, in the village.

The midwives were sworn to truth. The clerk submitted the parchment; they repeated after him the oath; they scratched their marks upon the parchment. Each gave up a long, grey hair and pressed a dirty thumb into the waxen seal.

And Mother Svenson spit upon her thumb and wiped it upon her skirt.

Then she shuffled to my lord, squinting at him, and said in her daft voice, "Have ye seen my Svenson?"

My lord said icily, "I have not seen him. Nor do I wish to . . . in this life or the next."

And the Bishop said angrily, "Take your place and speak only when you are required to speak."

Mother Svenson nodded at the Bishop; she waggled a finger. "A hard, cold man. Unfeeling. 'Tis often so with great lords and Bishops. Not like my Svenson."

Dame Barbro seized her sleeve then. "That's nor here nor there. Take your place. Be remembering what ye're to speak when my lord asks you."

My lord made an effort to be genial. "Tell us now, Mother Svenson. Tell the court of the time when you walked in the forest and came upon Kurt Arnison and my lady beside the Virgin Spring."

I felt my heart pound; I glanced at my lady and saw that her hands were tight, clutching her blue skirt; her face was white as ivory. Yet that time by the Virgin Spring had been a time of innocence between them.

Barbro nudged Mother Svenson to speak.

Mother Svenson pointed to my lady. "I seen her. I seen the two of them, my lady and Kurt Arnison, close by the Virgin Spring. I were in the forest picking mushrooms. And looking for my Svenson. I come upon them by the Virgin Spring. And he'd his head in my lady's lap. Lying on the moss beside her, he was, his head in her lap. And she were kissing him. Close as fleas they were on a poor man's shirt. And kissing. So it were with me and my Svenson."

"Your Svenson is not on trial, good woman. No doubt God keeps his soul," said my lord with remarkable forbearance. "You will swear to this. You will swear that you saw my lady and Kurt . . ."

"Aye, my lord. And swear to more. The babe she carried, the babe she lost—that were not yours, I'm thinking. Ye've no cause to sorrow for that, my lord. The babe were Kurt Arnison's, I'm thinking, from what I seen."

"No . . . no . . ." said my lady, on a little gasp of breath.

Mother Svenson peered at her. " 'Tis curious ye could not keep the babe. Ye're young and lusty . . . and Kurt so strong. Afeard of my lord, were ye . . . afeard that the babe would bear Kurt's look upon him? Ah, there be ways to abort a babe if a woman wills it. The Devil's berry be good for that." Of a sudden her face was sly. Daft she was, but she knew how to save her own skin. "I'm not saying the Devil's berry be good. I've no way of knowing that. But some in the village be saying it."

The Abbot was suddenly on his feet. "My lords spiritual, I ask you to consider this as slander of my lady. That she should seek to destroy her child—that is unthinkable. I would swear to this with my last breath. But . . . I suggest that this occurs in the village. That women destroy the unborn babe if they have no means to keep it. Knowledge of this has come to us at the monastery. The Devil's berry is used . . . a potion of it. I suggest that Mother Svenson herself and Dame Barbro are skilled in the mixing of herbs. That both are skilled in mixing the potion of the Devil's berry."

Dame Barbro strode forward, her heavy boots striking hard upon the stone floor. She towered over the Abbot in her rusty black cloak. Her voice was harsh as a man's. "Ye've no cause to be saying that. That be slander of *us*. Ye've no way to prove it. We'd no cause to be giving my lady such a drug. We'd no need. I'm thinking she knew herself the way to be mixing the drug. *Dvale* is everywhere, in wood and meadow, for the picking."

I said roughly, "That is a lie. My lady knows nothing of mixing drugs. It is——"

My lord broke in. "I think you have not been asked for an opinion, Jon. You will be quiet until we require you to speak." He turned to Dame Barbro. "I am deeply troubled by this testimony. What cause have you to think that my lady is skilled in the mixing of drugs . . . that she herself prepared a potion of abortion from the Devil's berry?"

"I were called to the manor, my lord. A night in spring, it were. And the young maid Kari were there, in sore pain and trouble of birthing. I've some skill in that. But this were beyond my skill, I were called too late. And Kari lay upon the bed, white as death, near senseless. She'd been given a potion, I saw that. A potion of the Devil's berry. The mark of it was upon her."

"The mark of it?"

"The sign of it upon her. Her eyes unseeing. The centers black, big and black and bright. Her heart racing. And she'd wake to screaming. And lie back senseless again. Birthing be my business. That, and the laying out of the dead. I've been called to birthing many times, when the woman has taken the Devil's berry. But I'd not give it, so wicked it be."

"You think that my lady gave it?"

"Aye, my lord. I will so swear. There were another, helping at the birthing. Old Marta, from the manor. She told me. My lady held the cup to Kari's lips. And my lady mixed the potion . . . none at the manor mixed it. Saving only her. There be none at the manor could mix it; it be a witchcraft potion. My lady has skill in that, so they say . . ."

"What are you saying? What evil is this?" said the Abbot strongly.

"Folk in the village be saying it." And Barbro's mouth was tight. "Folk at the manor."

Mother Svenson said, "Ye've only to ask. 'Tis well known my lady had skill of witchcraft. She were always with the wicked one . . . Christer the painter . . ."

"Speaking to him in his Devil tongue, helping him mix his wicked broths and brews . . ." And Barbro's pale eyes blazed. "Didn't he accuse her? Himself, he accused her. Called her a witch . . . called her by name, as he hung on the gallows tree!"

"How do you know that? Were you *there*, Dame Barbro?" The Abbot's hands were knotted into fists.

Barbro's eyes were narrow then. "Not I. But folk be saying it. They be talking of nothing else in the village."

My lord said then, "Thank you, Dame Barbro. You will be called again to testify." Then he addressed my lords spiritual. I can see him now. Very tall and spare and proud in hose of fawn doeskin and doublet of green velvet stitched with small arrow points of red silken thread. His eyes burned. In his cheek a little muscle was twitching. "I will withdraw my suit against my lady for adultery . . . for the present. I am deeply grieved by the testimony of these good women. I suggest that my lady must be examined for witchcraft."

"Ah, God . . ." I said savagely. "This is wanton evil."

My little lady said nothing. She was slumped in her chair, her head resting upon the carved armpiece. She had fainted.

Chapter 24

They came in numbers from the village to testify against my lady. They came from compulsion, to serve my lord to whom they owed obedience. And they came for hatred of my lady. They stood before the judges and accused her. I saw in their faces envy of her, brute stupidity, avarice—for my lord had paid them well for their trouble in coming.

Fat Tomas, Sven the poacher, many from the village and from the manor. I saw their faces as Christer had seen them. As he had painted them, in the panel of the Crucifixion.

My lady was constantly urged to confess. The learned doctors pleaded with her; the Bishop thundered at her.

But the Abbot said, "Let her make no reply to such accusation of evil."

And she would say no word except, "I am not guilty. If in the heart of the Blessed Virgin there is pity, let her intercede for me."

I was with her one evening in the abbey church. I knelt beside her as she knelt and took her hand. She looked up at me with piteous eyes. "Kurt," she said . . . her voice was but a whisper. "Kurt must come. I cannot bear more. He must come."

"Come and rest now, my lady." And I walked with her to her cold, narrow room.

My lord was waiting. He was waiting for her most evenings. He said, as he always did, "Are you ready, my lady? Ready to make full confession for your sin?"

"I will not do so, my lord," she said wearily. She was so white and drawn with weariness now that I feared she would faint. I put my hand beneath her elbow to steady her as she faced my lord.

"The good Jon," he said with sarcasm. "Always the devoted priest. That is a stubborn fault in you. Are you unable to see my lady as she is—willful, shaken by lust, far gone in evil? I have no doubt she had traffic with Christer and the horned god he served, the evil one who guided his hand. He painted with more than human cunning."

"I believe my lady to be gentle and good. I will always believe so."

"She has bewitched you. She is—I have no doubt of it—a witch."

I knew my lord did not believe this for an instant.

But now he saw the way to destroy my lady with no loss to his pride. The world would never know that she had deceived him, that he had been made cuckold. He would win a great citation in Stockholm for capturing and causing to be burned a witch.

He had brought with him parchments with my lady's confession. Ready to sign. She shook her head and did not take them; she turned to the small window; her eyes were bright with tears.

My lord said then, "My lady, you have done us a great service. We have word that Kurt is on the road to Lindhagen with some of his followers."

Donna turned to face him; there was light then in her eyes; her hand went to her throat.

My lord observed this. He said in anger, "A great providence. Kurt has been evasive as the stag on the slope of Stenborg. His men move by night on forest paths. No doubt they think to storm the Bishop's castle. So at last they must take the bridge road and first storm the bridge. We will have Kurt at last. The vixen has led the fox into the trap."

Though she was fearful for Kurt, my lady was heartened. She bore the trial the following day with fortitude. She was quiet, she answered nothing, she gazed with remote eyes over the heads of the judges.

In the evening my lord came to her as usual in her chamber. My lady and I knelt in prayer before the iron crucifix; we knelt upon the damp stone floor, and I helped her to rise.

My lord gave me a sour look.

To Donna he said, "You are stubborn. And wanton. And foolish. Your confession is not needed. You will be adjudged in spite of it. So great is the weight of evidence against you."

On the following day this great weight of evidence was presented before the court. My lady was asked no further questions; no witnesses appeared. We were required to listen as the clerks read aloud, in turn, from the thick sheaf of parchments. All that had been said in court, all that the busy scribes had recorded, was read.

"Of my lady Donna's carnal sin with Kurt . . . of her deception . . ."

"Of my lady Donna's traffic with Christer, and her submission to the horned god, the Prince of Evil . . ."

"Of her lapse from the Catholic faith in giving herself to the practice of witchcraft . . . vile heresy . . . an abomination of the faith . . ."

And more.

At the end, my lord Bishop arose. His fat white hands were upon the Holy Book. I saw the dark flash of the great ruby upon his finger. "My lords spiritual, I leave you to deliberate. Court will convene in the morning. I shall expect then a decision. I am confident that you will, as men of probity and professing Christ's holy doctrine, custodians of our sacred faith—I expect you will reach the decision that sin, mortal sin, demands strong chastisement. For such mortal sin as my lady's there can be but one punishment."

My lady and I did not join the nuns at the evening meal. I was with her in her cold chamber; she said nothing. She stood by the narrow window with clasped hands. Rain was spattering against the leaded panes.

At dusk my lord came to us as usual. With my lady's confession. I saw that the parchments were now weighted with heavy seals. The Bishop's seal, and that of my lord.

Donna gazed at my lord, her eyes dark with grief.

He said with impatience, "Do you expect pity from me, my lady? Pity . . . when you have used me so ill?" And then he said savagely, "The reward of your crime is burning. You will burn as a witch in the market square. Already the Bishop's men erect the scaffolding. And if you have hope that Kurt"— he spat out the name—"that Kurt will come to save you . . . your knight in dark armour . . . abandon the hope. An hour ago Kurt's men were surprised in the forest near the Bishop's bridge. Kurt was taken."

My lady's hand went to her throat. I stood beside her.

"A pity," said my lord. "A great pity. We had hoped to take Kurt alive."

Donna swayed, and I caught her. I laid her out upon the wooden pallet, upon the rough coverlet.

My lord looked down at her. His look was cold and full of venom. "The Bishop and I will be in the small office beside the oratory. Occupied with the court papers. We will hope, Jon, that you will at last recall your Christian duty and persuade my lady to sign the confession. We will be in the office for some hours."

I could spare no thought for Kurt now. Kurt, my friend. Though I felt pain like a stab wound to the heart.

I brought water in a basin and bathed my lady's sweet face. She opened her eyes. I knelt beside her as she lay on the hard wooden pallet and took her hands.

"I am cold, Jon. So cold. And soon will be colder."

I went to the small iron brazier; beside it were faggots; I built up the tiny fire.

"Jon, I am so afraid, afraid of the burning. Yet . . . if Kurt is . . . dead, perhaps it will not be so terrible for me to die."

"My Donna. Hear what comfortable words our Lord Christ has said, 'I am the way and the life, and he that believeth in me shall never die.' "

"You are very good, Jon. Can you believe that Christ was, as they say, 'a man of sorrows and acquainted with grief'? Then how can He visit upon us such grief?"

"My Donna . . ."

"Ah, Jon, I thought that I would know . . . surely know . . . if Kurt were dead. Not by any messenger. I thought that I would know of myself, in my blood, in my bones. We were so close . . . though apart. So much a part of one another . . . as light on snow, so that the shining is part of the snow, embodied in it. Or as mist mingles with the sea. Or as a bear's hide covers the bulk of the beast, but all is one."

She was standing now before the iron crucifix, the harsh Christ upon the wall. She gazed up at it.

"Kurt was your friend, Jon. I am sad for you."

"I am glad for our years together. I think now of you, my lady."

Her eyes were wide and dark.

"Do not fear, my Donna."

"Jon . . . you said once that death is a long sleep and a great peace. You said it—do you recall?—that night, the first night in the manor chapel, when we sat by Christer and he lay as one dead."

"Yes. Believe it."

"It is so hard to sleep. Will you . . . will you help me to sleep?"

Of a sudden I said—I could not help myself—"I will help you. I will do it because . . . because I love you."

"Yes, Jon. I know." Donna took my hand and held it tightly.

"Forgive me."

"I think I have often caused you pain, Jon. When I was with Kurt. Forgive me for that."

And suddenly she came to me, came into my arms, and put her cheek against mine. And kissed me then, upon the mouth. "I am blessed, Jon, by your love. I love you, too—not as I love Kurt—a different kind of loving. But my love for you is just as strong."

I will always hold these words in my heart.

"When will it be, Jon? When will I find sleep? Let it be soon."

"Soon." And my voice broke. I was sobbing. Harsh dry sobs tearing from my throat. And I had meant to be so strong . . . so strong to comfort her in her extremity.

I collected myself.

Donna said softly, "There must be no risk to you, no blame."

"I will bear it."

"No. There is no need. Go to the infirmary. There are drugs . . . the gentle juice of poppy. I have seen it. They will think I have taken it myself. They will not think of you."

"My Donna . . ."

"Go now, Jon."

And still I stood there.

"Jon," she said again. "The burning. I am so afraid of the burning."

So I went to the apothecary room—the little room close by the infirmary, where the healing drugs were mixed. The room was dim at this hour; two pine tapers burned. On the wooden shelves there were basins and mortar and pestle, pots of healing salves, and piles of linen bindings. There were herbs spread out to dry, and in the room, the sweet dry scent of rue and rosemary.

And no bustle of nuns. There was one little sister, sturdy and smiling.

"Shall I help you, Brother Jonas?"

She was mixing the evening potion of wine, with a little poppy, for some of the old ones in the infirmary. She reached for a dark glass jar, high upon the shelf. And I saw upon it, in script, on the parchment label: *Papaver somniferum.*

My heart was pounding. "I would like a little wine for my lady. She did not go to the evening meal. She is sorely troubled and cannot sleep."

"Ah, it be wicked . . . wicked what they do to her," said the little nun, lapsing into country speech. Then she touched her coif and collected herself and spoke as she had been taught at the cloister.

"My lady is gentle. She is often with us, helping with the sick. Of great estate—yet she will carry slops and sit with the old ones."

"Yes. I will tell her you said so. You are . . ."

"Sister Anna. Tell her I give her my pity. And blessing."

Sister Anna smiled and left me.

I went to the door of the infirmary. I saw her at the far end of the room, moving among the wooden cots, bringing comfort and physic.

I went quickly into the apothecary. I poured wine for my lady. And took a portion of the poppy and mixed it.

I heard my lady's confession. There was little to confess—but hatred of Lord Ivar. And love for Kurt.

She took up the cup and stared into it . . . into the dark wine. About the rim of the cup there was a white froth.

"It will be . . . quick, Jon? And merciful?"

I nodded, too miserable to speak.

I sat by her. When her hands grew cold, I took them in mine. I wanted to cover her with my body and hold her against the cold. I watched by her a while. I pulled the cloak, with the furred hood, close around her white face. She looked as I had seen her before, as if she were sleeping . . . a soft sleep, a gentle dream.

At last I went to the office where Lord Ivar sat with the Bishop. A fire burned on the hearth; they sat in carved chairs beside it. The Bishop was dictating to his scribe; my lord was examining a large parchment scroll.

He looked up. "My lady is ready? She will sign the confession now?"

"She is . . . my lady is dead."

He stared at me. His eyes were dark with shock. "Dead?"

I felt the hard dry sobs in my throat. "She has taken a draught to bring easeful death."

My lord stared into the fire. In the room there was no sound save the snap and hiss of logs on the hearth.

"She killed herself?" said the Bishop. I saw in his face no shock . . . but bitterness. He had seen himself as a great crusader for the Church. He had hoped with my lord for a great citation from Stockholm.

My lord's long fingers were tapping angrily on the arm of his chair. The muscle in his cheek was twitching; his eyes were like stone. He is in a fury, I thought, because he has been cheated of my lady's death.

He said, between tight lips, "You are dismissed, Jon. I hope never to see your face again. I will bring no charges against you. Though you have constantly sought to obstruct justice in the court, you have constantly defended my lady."

And then he looked at me strangely. "You were devoted to

my lady. Your grief is sufficient penance, I think. Now she is dead."

Dead . . . my little lady. My Donna, I thought, I love you, I will always love you. I have given you freedom from pain, from the agony of the burning, from the scorn in all men's eyes. And freedom from him . . . from Lord Ivar. With death, I have given you all I have—my hope of Heaven and my immortal soul. And I thought, I do not regret it.

And then I went out into the darkness. The sky was deep and remote; there were faint stars. Under the apple trees, I lay on my face in the wet grass and wept.

I tried to pray. I slept a little. And woke, and thought in agony, I have killed her. I mixed the potion. My sweet lady . . . my little love.

I was chosen as surely as Judas was chosen to kill the Christ he followed. Yet for me there had been no choice.

I looked long into the black pool, still and black and silver under the late moon. I could not take that way and so compound my guilt.

I must bear my burden, my guilt.

Soon after dawn, I heard the bells of Matins. I went back to the cloister. I could not bear to look upon my lady. When I left her, the sweet scent of her was still in the room—the scent of dark violets and white.

I went to the gatehouse. There I had left a hooded gown, my empty purse, a pair of sandals. I would leave the cloister.

In the gatehouse I met the Abbot and told him of my lady, that she had taken a heavy draught of poppy and now lay dead.

The Abbot looked at me as my lord had done. He must have seen on my face what my lord had seen—agony, agony. Ah, God, I thought, will there never be an end to that?

He said with compassion, "My grief is as your own."

No, I thought wildly, it cannot be as my own. It cannot be.

The Abbot's thin hands were fumbling at the neck of his gown. I saw that those wise old eyes were dim with tears. But then he said quietly, "I will take care of my lady. I will take the body. She shall lie beside Christer. Beneath the oak beside him."

"I am grateful." My voice broke from my throat . . . so harsh and strange. I felt that I was strangling.

"You must leave now, Jon. Leave the cloister."

"Yes. My lord has dismissed me."

"Ah, yes. We must all leave. Kurt's men storm the bridge. And soon the castle. And Kurt with them."

"Kurt! My lord said . . . Kurt is taken and dead." And I thought with fresh grief of Kurt, my friend. I had given him no thought, in my agony for my lady.

But the Abbot said, "My lord was misinformed. Kurt is alive, leading his men. Two of my men spoke with him only an hour ago. My lord was misinformed."

I will never believe it. My lord lied, I know it, to force my lady's confession. And to give her pain. Ah, God forbid, I thought, that I should meet my lord now. I would put my hands to his throat and choke him.

The Abbot put a hand on my shoulder. "Join us, Jon. On the road by the south gate. I have strong men with me. The town will soon be under attack. Already the Bishop is at the castle; he makes ready for siege. My lord has ridden out with a strong party along the north road, to rally more men from Stenborg and attack Kurt from the rear."

I could not speak.

"We leave within the hour. Come with us, Jon, come back to the monastery."

"I will go alone."

I could not bear to see her go. My Donna. To watch as the Abbot's men wrapped the slight body in the blue cloak. To see them take her away, to follow her. I walked heavily down the long corridor to the cloister kitchen. Where I could not see . . .

My arms, my legs, seemed hewn from stone. My heart was a stone in my throat.

The kitchen was like a cavern, big, dim, with low vaulting, smelling of malt and stale grease.

And deserted. At this hour there should have been a dozen kitchen folk, men building up the fires, a bustle of sturdy women round the bake-ovens, maids ladling out wooden bowls of thin gruel.

The cook fires were dying and soon would be ash. On a wooden stool before the wide hearth one of the novices sat, a small girl in grey gown and rumpled coif. Her face was cupped in her hands; she was weeping.

Another stood by the scarred settle. A plump girl, perhaps fourteen. And wearing no coif. Her brown hair was tangled on her shoulders, her feet were bare.

Where were the kitchen folk?

Where were the nuns to oversee them? And hustle the novices to chapel and chide them for being slovenly.

The plump girl was stuffing her mouth with walnut cake. She looked up at me, her face red and shining. I caught the thick, sweet odour of wine.

"Soldiers be coming," she said, and hiccoughed. "Soldiers to take us . . ."

"Where are the nuns? The kitchen folk . . ."

"Packing the cloister treasure in sacks. The great rich cups, the candlesticks. The men be digging in the orchard to bury the treasure. Soldiers . . ."

Two burst into the kitchen then. Two of my lord's men in iron armour. One snatched up half a ham from the open cupboard.

The other put a hand in heavy gauntlet upon the plump girl's shoulder.

"Have ye wine to spare, lass?" Then he ripped off the

gauntlets and let them drop. He was grinning. He seized the girl and covered her moist mouth with his. He was pawing her buttocks.

I felt no shame for her, no pity. My mind was clouded then as Christer's had been.

I paid them no heed. I had seen on the settle what I wanted.

A tinder box. I stuffed it into my leather purse.

I grabbed a loaf and a cheese, tied them up in my cloak, and slung the bundle over my back.

And snatched up a knife. A long knife, the iron hilt smeared with grease. I stuffed it into its leather sheath and knotted it to my girdle.

And ran.

Men were swarming in the gatehouse and in the cobbled street before the cloister. Men in armour, town folk, women with children tugging at their skirts. I was pushing my way through the mob. Of a sudden a flight of arrows scattered them.

I slipped into the narrow lane behind the cloister. Gabled roofs overhung the lane; these gave me shelter. But above me I heard arrows, striking on the roofs, the leaden gutters.

The cloister bells were tolling . . . tolling . . .

At the end of the lane was the open square. Empty now . . . arrows were striking the cobbles, falling like silver rain. But I must chance it. Across the square was the town wall. And the south gate. Open still, and beyond it, the open road. Ah, God be thanked.

And then I saw, close by the gate against the wall, the scaffolding.

The scaffolding for the witch burning. A high platform of rough pine timbers. Beneath it faggots and piled straw and cauldrons of whale oil, all in readiness.

I thought with anguish of my lady, my sweet Donna.

A fresh volley of arrows. I raced for the scaffolding and crouched beneath it. Suddenly fire arrows were falling. Striking around me, into the cauldrons of oil, into the dry straw, and these took flame. I felt the heat beating against my face. The thick, surging smoke was in my eyes, in my mouth.

Only a little way to the gate. No more than fifty paces . . .

There were shouts on the wall above me. I heard the grating of heavy chain and saw the barbican come down. Thick iron bars, spiked with iron, barring the road, the sunny road to freedom. Dust rose in great coils, like blowing smoke, as the gate struck the roadway.

And then behind it the oaken port came down. A solid wall of oak buttressed with iron, studded with spikes.

I was trapped.

And the Abbot? Still at the cloister . . . and his good men, trapped as well, like animals.

Of a sudden I thought of the postern gate where sheep were driven in. Sheep grazed outside the town walls; at night they were herded into the open grassy space within the walls, for fear of wolves.

The postern gate . . . a low tunnel beneath the wall. The outer entrance was barred with iron at night. But now?

I had one thought—to be free. Free of the town, to join Kurt and Kurt's men. To strike a blow against Lord Ivar. Blood vengeance upon my lord, in the name of my sweet lady.

I had not far to go. I ran, careless of shelter.

I tied up my monk's gown and crawled into the tunnel, on hands and knees as a miner does, worming his way along the rock ledges. And here the rough rock walls sloped over my head, dark and dripping. The smell was foul; I crawled over stones crusted with mud and slick with sheep droppings.

Only a little way, toward the light.

And then I stood in sunlight, in meadow grass outside the town wall. Fire arrows were falling. In the dry grass there were sudden spurts of flame. Beyond was the forest. I ran like a fox to the shelter of trees.

I was gasping, I felt that my heart would burst. But I was unhurt.

And free.

Over my head the strong oaks lifted their branches, arching, entwined, like the vault of a great cathedral. Sunlight struck through russet leaves; between the boughs there were patches of blue and shining sky.

The forest was deep and still. Only the murmuring of leaves. And the sound of rushing water. I followed the sound, moving as a poacher does, parting the brushy thicket, wary of movement around me, the snap of branch and bracken. Here at the edge of the forest some of Kurt's men would be. Bowmen sending the arrows winging toward the town. I meant to find them.

But there might be others. The Bishop's men. Or my lord's men. Searching the thickets to flush out Kurt's bowmen.

Then I heard the rustle of dry leaves. The thin stalks of fern were quivering. I crouched for shelter behind a rock. and saw a fox dart from the bracken. A flash of movement.

I followed the fox. And came upon the stream, curling over rocks, slipping between mossy banks, eddying to form a still, brown pool. I dropped to my knees on the green cushion of moss and drank. And bent to splash my face with cool water.

And felt of a sudden against my neck the cold, flat blade of a knife.

A rough hand came down on my shoulder. A grip like iron.

Then on the face of the pool I saw his image—a big man with heavy shoulders. Dark brows, a dark growth of beard. And not armoured; he wore a thick wadded jerkin and leather breeks.

Over my shoulder he saw his own face. He spat into the pool; the image was blurred.

"A priest," he said roughly. "Be ye Bishop's man then? No room here for a Bishop's man."

God be thanked. "I am Kurt's man," I said strongly.

"Can ye prove it? Many be saying it. Kurt's man, they say, and they be spying for the King."

"Take me to Kurt. He'll vouch for me."

"Kurt be busy." But the big man lifted the knife from my neck. I was crouching still; behind me I heard the rasp of his breathing. He could throttle me, or mount my shoulders, pushing my face into the pool.

"God's truth," I said, "I'm a priest. But I'd not spend my life on my knees. Let me up. Take me to Kurt."

"Kurt's got no time for a priest. Another mouth to feed. Lest ye can fight."

"I'll fight. For Kurt."

"Get ye up then. No tricks."

I got to my feet and faced him. A brute of a man, swarthy and scowling.

"Get along," he said. "Over there to the clearing. We've ways to find out if ye're a spy."

He pointed downstream. And I saw the gap in the trees. Long fingers of sunlight, bars of gold, striking through leafy, brown shadow. Like brazen lances parting the heavy boughs, piercing the leaves.

The big man walked beside me, the flat blade of his knife nudging my shoulder.

In the clearing were a dozen men, with four women. All wore leather or rough wadmal; the men were bending over iron cauldrons. These were big enough for sheep dip and now held heavy oil. Arrows were stacked on the moss; women were twisting strips of woolen and rag; men were dipping the fire arrows. Boys were stacking the arrows and filling leather pouches.

The men looked up at us but did not speak. Then a stocky

man came out of the forest beyond. Thick-set but quick to move, though he wore a heavy buckler of iron plate over his leather jacket. But he wore no helmet; I saw the thatch of red hair, the stubble of red beard. The lines beneath the sharp grey eyes.

And the gap between his front teeth that I remembered. He was grinning.

It was Jurgen, Kurt's steward. I had known him in boyhood. God be thanked.

"Ah, Jon," he said. "Ye're late to join us. What kept you . . . tumbling a girl in the sheepfold that ye've covered yourself with muck?"

I looked down at the smeared front of my monk's gown.

Still the blackbeard beside me held the knife to my back. "A priest," he said; his lip curled back from his teeth.

"Under the priest's gown," said Jurgen, "there's a miner. And poacher. Born to fight."

I had not fitted my hand to the bow in those years as a monk, but my hand had not lost its cunning. Ah, to feel again the strong curve of the bow, the tremour of gut under my finger, the thrust against my shoulder as the arrow took flight. And the gutstring purring . . .

We crouched in hollows in the rocks; among the mossy hummocks; in the thin cover of larch and birch at the edge of the forest. Boys were slipping like weasels between the trees, bringing up stores of arrows. The women brought water in tin cups; we stopped to drink and splash our faces.

I was sweating, and grimed with smoke; an arrow grazed my arm; blood was clotting upon my monk's gown.

I did not feel it. I felt glory. Glory! Sending the arrows out upon the town wall, knowing my hand was sure. My heart pounding, my mouth sour with thirst, my eyes sore and streaming . . . yet in my mind a singing, a savage glory. Blood vengeance upon my lord! In the name of my dear lady . . .

Hour after hour, and no thought but this.

From the wall fire arrows came toward us, but most fell short. Into the grassy space before the wall. Flames were streaking the dry grass and spreading. The heat beat toward us, and rank smoke, and rising wind, spreading the flames. Soon we would have to drop back.

Jurgen moved among us, the sun striking his breastplate; his red beard was like flame itself. He was shouting; we took up the shout.

"Kurt will be King! Kurt will be King!"

He stopped to clap me on the back and spat through the gap in his teeth. "For luck. We're needing that. Forty of us here before the south gate, keeping them busy. Most of Kurt's men be north of town, close by the bridge."

He put a big hand on the head of the lad who worked with me. A towheaded lad, snub-nosed, his face as grimed as ever any miner's was. He was tending the arrowtips with wick and tinder.

There was a lull then, a silence from the wall. And then a great shout. A clamour, the ringing of heavy iron chain upon stone, the thud of heavy armament, the sound like the clash of ironclad cavalry, borne on the gusty wind. Were they sending a party out of the gate to ride us down?

And then great stones and pots of boiling pitch and fire-balls were hurtling over the grassy space toward us. On the wall they had brought up the catapults.

Jurgen lifted his fist in fury. "Hold yer ground! Keep them busy. So long as ye can . . ."

We sent fresh volleys of arrows out. And beside me a great stone crashed; there was the crack and splintering of thin branches, the heart torn out of a young tree, the tree a jagged stump.

And beneath the branches the boy, the towheaded boy, his leg crushed and doubled beneath him, blood spurting from his mouth.

I dragged him back upon the moss and knelt beside him. It was over for him. And I was glad. I looked at the torn flesh, the splintered bone of his leg, the dark blood soaking into the moss. And I was glad for him. What good is a summer day, a day for racing the wind, to a boy with only the mangled stump of a leg?

There were cries from the copse beyond us. In the brushy thicket fire leapt. Fire pots were striking around us. The oily flames were spreading. At the edge of the forest the dry bracken took fire. A wavering wall of smoke shot with flame.

"Drop back!" Jurgen was shouting, climbing over the rocks.

I sent out one last arrow.

In the clearing we took counsel. How many men were missing? Twelve . . . twenty . . . Some of the men crawled into the rocky hollows dragging the bodies out. In the blazing bracken there would be more . . .

Upon the leafy ground we laid them out . . . the stiff bodies, the still bodies. Yet some lived, retching and jerking with pain. I moved among them, cutting the scorched leather from stinking wounds, bathing the streaked bloody faces.

And Jurgen with me. "Ah, the smell of it, the smell of blood and burnt flesh, it brings to mind the springtime. The birthing time, when lamb and colt are born. And the branding of the young creatures." But I saw there were tears in his eyes. "God keep them all, the brave lads. That will never again fondle a lass, or hear the bowstring singing."

And I cannot forget them. Kurt's men. The young ones, the burnt men, shreds of wadmal stuck to the scorched flesh.

And among them an old man, a grey face, the eyes sunken in the sockets, the toothless mouth agape. And deep in the cords of the neck, the arrow embedded. The rush of dark blood from the throat.

A blessing for the dead. For the wounded—only water for parched throats, rags and moss to stanch the flow of blood from raw wounds. We had no physic for them, no wine. Or juice of poppy to ease them.

I thought with fresh anguish of my sweet lady.

The sun was dropping into a bank of cloud. The leaden sky was streaked with a strange pale light. Beneath the trees there was a sudden darkness. The wind was rising; over our heads we heard the roar of it, lashing at the trees.

Some of the men were muttering. "It be early dark. The sun leaving us. A bad omen."

Jurgen was scowling; he was grimed and hoarse, but still shouting. "Omen! I'll hear no talk of omens. Be it bad for us—or for them? Them in the town."

A ruddy man gestured with a blunt thumb. At the bodies laid out upon the ground.

"Bad for us. God be turning His face from us."

"The sun be in God's hands." Jurgen thrust up a fist. "The sun be taking no sides."

The rain began. A sharp spattering on the leaves. A mighty rush of wind. And the rain, in drifts, in gusts, sharp and hard against the skin, a torrent, a flood, a fury of rain.

"God's blood," said Jurgen; his strong face creased in a grin. "The rain be soaking the fires. An omen for *us*."

We huddled on the sodden ground, rain streaming over us, silent and bone-weary.

In an hour the storm had passed. We pushed through the dripping thickets to seek out the bodies in the hollows.

In the bracken still there were rising plumes of smoke, and the smell of scorched leather, the rank odour of burnt pitch.

The slow dusk settled in the meadow. The town wall was black and silent and strong under the stars.

"Come morning," said Jurgen, "we bury the bravest of us. And march north to be joining Kurt."

We built watchfires in the clearing. There was no dry stick or stump in the forest; the dark oaks were dripping. Under foot the leaves were sodden; little pools formed in the moss where a man stepped. But under the trees the men had built a rude shelter—sacking stretched over stripped pine saplings, to keep the stores of oil dry. Left to us were three cauldrons of oil.

We dragged these into the clearing and tended them with flint and tinder; the oil flared up. Strong, singing flames against the chill of night. Streamers of sparks rose and glowed in the dusky air.

The women brought strips of pork rind and sour black bread.

I looked at the men, hunched over their food: dark, shaggy shapes in rough wadmal or sheepskin. Bearded faces, blackened faces in the red glow of firelight. A company of gnomes, they seemed, emerged from the rocky hollows, from the darkness under the coiled roots of the trees, to crouch for a time in ruddy firelight. And then creep back into dwarf tunnels underground to sleep.

Then one of the men drew the sleeve of his sheepskin across his face, wiping his nose and his streaming eyes, sore as my own were with the rank, oily smoke of the fires. And he took out a little harp of birchwood and tuned it, his big hands gentle upon the whispering strings. Then he was singing—a rough voice, but strong and true.

The others took up the song. With darkness behind them, they sat in the red glow of the fires and sang . . . of the strong surge of the heart's blood in battle; of the fierce will to fight and die for freedom.

And I thought, these are Swedes—men of the mines, of the forest, men of the sea. And each will have a voice in the new Sweden . . . if, God willing, our cause is won. I looked at them in their rags and filthy wadmal, at the blackened faces in firelight, and felt my heart swell with pride.

Among them, one in three would give his life, perhaps. The others would fight on, to make and mould the new Sweden.

The man with the harp was coughing. A miner's cough,

harsh, racking—so it is with a man who has spent years in the dark channels of the earth. But then he began a new song. The others were silent to listen, for the words were sweet.

Of spring, and sowing time, and fresh green meadows, of young love and laughter.

Then on the soaked ground the men stretched out to sleep. But one got to his feet and took one of the women by the hand. They went off into the thicket together. A cold bedding, I thought, but the man threw his sheepskin over the woman's shoulders; she took his hand in gladness.

And one of the women came to me. A young one, crouching beside me on the moss. I looked at her, at the dark hair tumbled upon her shoulders, the bent head, the curve of her cheek in the firelight.

And my heart seemed to stop. She lifted her head and looked at me. I turned away from the gaze of her blue eyes.

Donna . . . for a moment, only a moment, she was so like Donna.

And I felt the agony again, a great tearing wave of it, the agony for my sweet Donna.

I would never be free.

"I watched, today. Ye've a sure hand with the bow." The girl touched my sleeve. My monk's gown was stiff and stained with dried blood. "Ye're hurt, are ye?"

I had paid no heed to the wound, so slight was it.

She put her hand upon my thigh and smiled at me. "Shall I help with the hurt?"

"There's no help for it," I said. "I will bear the wound for all time." I heard my own voice, so rough and strange. I felt the harsh tears gather in my throat.

She stared at me. "Is it an icicle ye have there under yer breeks?" And her lip curled. "Or 'tis sinning ye think of, priest? Loving is sinning? To bring a little warmth to men that can be cold in death tomorrow . . ."

But her eyes were fearful. I believe she thought me

deranged. She moved away and I got to my feet, pulling my hood close around my face. The others gave no thought to me; they did not heed my going.

The moon was rising. In the dark heart of the forest, there were night sounds, the rustle of leaves, the crack of branch and bracken as some night creature crept between the trees. Badger, perhaps, or weasel. I climbed the rocks by the stream, slipping on wet moss, twig and briar clutching at my gown.

I followed the cool voice of the stream. A silver sound, water rushing over stones, in still moonlight. I sat on a rock by the pool where blackbeard had found me. Over my head, through bare branches, I could see in the heavy sky the moon, a blind white eye. Like the eye of the Old God, the heathen, the terrible One, the avenger.

A shaft of moonlight struck the black pool. On still water, a cold radiance. Somewhere I heard the voice of a wood dove, mourning, ever mourning, as I must do.

I cried aloud, as Christer had done, "Ah, God who made us, why must it be so?"

Why must I live, when my lady lies dead, the sweet voice forever stilled, the sound of her laughter . . . It was I, it was I, who mixed the wine, with the silken killer, the poppy.

God, why do you let me live? Today fire arrows fell around me and great stones. You struck down a boy beside me.

And I am unhurt. A scratch, only. I would have welcomed death, the dark presence, a solace to enfold me like a cloak, to close my eyes and to stop the pounding pain in the dark heartroot.

I stared into the dark vault of heaven, into the cold eye of the moon.

God, God, let me die.

Yet I knew. With certainty, I knew. I must do penance.

So harsh a judgment upon me: to live, to walk the earth in knowledge of my sin.

I must seek atonement, and I must go alone. And, I thought, I can never join Kurt now. Kurt, my friend. What can I tell him of my gentle lady?

At dawning, when grey light sifted between the trunks of the great trees, I set out. I had no thought of direction; I followed the stream.

The stream flowed down toward Lindhagen, I was sure of it. It would widen and glide at last beneath the Bishop's bridge, where even now Kurt's men would be storming the town wall.

I walked upstream, climbing the rocks, pushing through bracken and briar. I came out of the forest at last and saw before me the great thrust of the iron mountain, the sun strong upon the lower slopes, the deep gashes in the rock face filled with shadow. And the peak veiled in cloud.

I was not far from the monastery. From sanctuary . . .

Nor far from Hell Gate mine.

I know not what impelled me there. I was stumbling; the blood was singing in my ears, yet I went on.

It was close to midday, for the sun was high. But the mine field lay in shadow, the sheer reach of the mountain behind it. Mist was rising from gaps in the rocks.

I saw before me the dark mouth of the mine—deserted now and overgrown with ragged patches of thorn.

And I thought of the night when they had hanged Christer upon the gallows tree, of the strange yellow light at the mouth of the mine, and the gallows black and tall before it. And Christer sacrificed upon it.

And now the gallows was fallen, brought down by autumn storm. The strong tree studded with iron nails, the crossbeam still fast to it, lying upon stony ground.

This, I thought, was the shape of the true cross.

I knelt beside it. And saw that the earth beneath it was green with soft new moss. And the gallows was overgrown with lichen and partridge vine. A green veil, as if in promise of spring.

Small flowers clustered in the moss. White and waxen, the little woodland plant which blooms in the dark and damp of autumn, even in early snow. Men call it the Christmas crocus; they say it foretells new birth and the surge of life in the returning spring.

I was sobbing, without sound. And then it seemed to me that Christer stood beside me, very tall in his dark mantle. And stretched out a hand.

It seemed that he smiled at me. And said, "God so loved the world . . ."

So it would be. I would never go back to the monastery. The ordered life of the cloister, the voice of the bells marking the silent hours, the hours for work and sleep, for prayer and plainsong. The minutes measured out for fellowship. A life of ordered peace, and at last a quiet grave.

I must go into the world. Alone.

Alone. Two years have passed. I am the tall monk on the roads, the monk with bull shoulders, the strength of the miner in him. The monk with strange eyes . . . I know what men say. Men think at times they meet a ghoul upon the road. I wear the brand of murderer, though no man sees it. It is on my heart.

But I find a welcome in the villages, in the wooden crofts beside the road, and on the herder's path upon the mountains. I sign children with the cross; I give such help as I can to the sick; I watch by the dead. I find some comfort in this; and I find, at times, bread, and a warm hearth to sit by.

At times I hear of Kurt. Of his achievement.

I heard of the siege of Lindhagen, the storming of the Bishop's castle.

And of the Bishop's death. Some say he died with courage, with longsword in hand. And others, that he died of rage and spleen, an excess of it, because his world was crumbling.

But my lord lives still on his great estate in Skåne. And there he is secure, safe from attack so long as Skåne remains a province of Denmark. How long will that be?

All men know of Kurt's great victory at Stenborg, the King hunted and driven from Sweden, forever exiled now.

Now Kurt is Regent of Sweden.

I went to Stockholm when he was so proclaimed. On a March day, a day of strong spring sun, I stood on the cobblestones before the palace gates. A great crowd had gathered; around me, the crowd was surging; men were shouting and hoarse, and wild with joy.

"Kurt will be King! Kurt will be King!"

I saw Kurt then, above me on the stone gallery, looking down upon the crowd. He wore his leather armour, black and scarred. But his head was bare; I saw the streaks of grey in his dark hair. He lifted his arms in the old salute, with fists crossed. And he was smiling.

The man beside me clapped me on the back. "A new day," he said. "We'll be seeing a new day . . . us that have been yoked and beaten and mastered by the Danes."

I thought he had the look of the miner: the stubble of coarse beard, the grime deep in the lines of the swarthy face, the strong cords in his neck. And the bent shoulders. He spoke in the harsh accent of the north provinces.

"You're from the iron country," I said. "A man of Dalarna, aren't you?"

"No more. We're that no more," he said, grinning. "A man of Uppland, a man of Dalarna, a man of Grängesberg . . . We're Swedes."

I think of this and my heart beats strongly, as I walk the dark road on bitter nights, when the wind tears at the bare trees and the ice shines in the hollows, and under the moon, the snow is silver, hard-crusted with frost. And I have found no barn or hovel to shelter me.

I think of how we sat in the great hall of the manor. Kurt and Christer and I. And my Donna, the glow of firelight upon her dark, shining hair, upon her cheek, upon the folds of her blue cloak. And Kurt saying then, "All men must have a voice in government. Sweden must be a sovereign nation, ruled by Swedes. There can be no stemming the strong will to freedom."

And I am warmed, though in the iron cold, my breath steams and hunger gnaws at my belly.

Yet Kurt would have me with him. One bitter night I met Peter, by chance, in the old inn in Granholm. We sat at the scarred oak table, stretching our legs to the warmth of the blazing fire. We lifted mugs of ale and spoke of old times.

And Peter told me that Kurt was ever searching, that I might join him.

I gazed into the fire. "He has better men to serve him. And I have found what I must do . . ."

Peter poured more ale. "Kurt's dream is dream no longer. A free Sweden—free of the Danes."

We drank to it.

"Yet," said Peter, scowling, "his work is but half done. That all men should have a voice in government—that is still dream. Men of power conspire against Kurt. Great lords, churchmen, loath to give over to him the reins of power. To Kurt—the rabble rouser, so they call him."

Peter went to stand before the fire. "Go to him, Jon. Often he asks for you. Kurt has need of his friends."

I said no word.

Peter said then, "My lady asks for you. My lady Donna."

I stared at him. Had I heard rightly? No, this was a cruel

dream. Ah, God, the torment of such dreams. Always I saw my lady's face before me. I would wake from such dreams, sweating and hearing her name—her pounding name—like a song of darkness deep in my heart.

"My lady . . ." The words were torn from my throat. "I . . . I have heard that she lives no longer. That she feared the judgment upon her. And took a heavy dose of poppy." My voice died.

"That is true." Peter tapped on the table for more ale. "My lady took a dose of poppy. A heavy dose, yet not enough. Not enough to kill her, we can thank God for that. On the morning the siege began—the siege of Lindhagen—the Abbot found her. He had gone to her chamber to bring her comfort in her extremity. He found her lying upon her cot white and still. But he roused her. He called for wine and physic. She lay ill for some days. The nuns cared for her. Until Kurt found her."

My hand was shaking so that ale poured from my cup, upon the front of my monk's gown. "Until . . . Kurt found her?"

"Six days the siege lasted. Until the Bishop fell, fighting like an old bull before the postern gate. Who would have thought he had such blood-lust in him? And then men of the town opened the gates to us. I can see it now. We rode into the town, a mob swarming upon us. The men raising their fists in the old salute. Bloodied and battle-weary, yet shouting and cheering. Kurt rode like a madman through the mob. At the cloister we found my lady, walking beside the herb garden, the stone walk under the arches. The Abbot was with her. At the sound of boots striking the walk, she turned. Her hand went to her throat in fear, as if she thought to see my lord. And then she saw Kurt and ran to him. He caught her up in his arms."

My heart was pounding. My voice was thick, I spoke like a man dazed with drink. "She lives—she lives now with Kurt?"

"In happiness. Though she cannot wed him. Not so long as my lord Ivar is living. My lady is wife to my lord, in the eyes of God and man. She cares nothing for what men say of her. She is Kurt's handfast love and he is hers." Peter put down his cup. "I have miles before me tonight. In the cold . . . on the snowy road as always. I ride on to Arboga." He put a hand on my shoulder. "Go to Stockholm, Jon. Go to Kurt. And to my lady."

I bade him farewell. And sat on a long time at table, my head in my hands. I had walked the roads in guilt, in bitter remorse, seeking atonement.

But my lady lived. I had not killed her. God be thanked.

Yet the burden was with me still. The burden on my heart. I had conspired to kill her—I, sworn to the service of God. I mixed the cup, the dark wine and the poppy. With intent to kill.

With merciful intent.

But truly from carnal love of my lady. A consuming love. Of that I knew I would never be free. Such love is a deadly sin in a priest.

I thought then of my lady at the trial. As I have often done. I thought of the judgment upon her, of the hard faces of the judges. Stone faces in a dim stone chamber. Of Donna looking up in appeal and saying softly, "The essence of the Christian doctrine is forgiveness."

Yes. And to forgive others is possible. At times.

But to forgive myself? In time could I come to forgive myself?

And so at last find peace?

And I thought, O Lamb of God that taketh away the sins of the world, have mercy upon me. O Lamb of God, grant me Thy peace.

In time could I bring myself to join Kurt? With the knowledge in my heart that I had sought to bring death to my lady? The dark knowledge always between us.

And their happiness always before my eyes. I thought of the quick flame in Kurt's eyes, always at sight of my lady. I thought of him, tall in his leather armour, and Donna beside him, on the dark morning when he left us upon the island. My little lady beside him on the spur of rock, the waves cresting and lashing the rock below us. The red light of the torches upon their faces. And Donna looking up at Kurt with shining eyes.

Of Kurt, holding her close to him, close to his heart. Two as one. As I would hold her.

I heard in my heart his words. "My Donna, my true love. Always. As God is my witness."

No. I could never go back.

I thought of how Christer would say, " 'The kingdom of Heaven is within you.' "

And also, deep in the sorrowing heart, the dominion of Hell.

I have known both with my gentle lady, my Donna.

She is not wholly lost to me. I have seen growing by the roadside dark violets and white.

And I see her face before me on the dark road at night, in shadow, in moonlight, in mist, rising from the autumn woodland. In still pools upon the ice, where the sun strikes. In the movement of leaves, the green darkness beneath the oaks.

I think of her when small flowers star the grass in spring meadows.

> Love knows no season,
> Nor any rhyme or reason,
> Except the season of the heart.

Afterword

The malignant power of the dead has been feared in all parts of the world, in all ages. In Scandinavia it was a common belief that ghouls walked abroad; not every man was content to stay in his burial mound. In Iceland during the Viking Age one stalwart warrior even instituted court proceedings to order his wife's ghost to "cease and desist from haunting him." Stories of dread phantoms are numerous. Spirits appeared in the strange silvery light of Midsummer, in the mist rising from the lakes, in the desolate gorges, and in the dark heart of the forest.

Special precautions have always been taken to keep baleful spirits in their places. The most feared were of those who had died violent deaths, or who had caused one; and those suspected of congress with demons, or knowledge of the Black Arts. It was customary to bury such offenders in a lonely part of the forest, or in a peat bog, with stakes through breast and belly, to keep them in their pine barrows, to keep the soul from leaving the body to plague the living.

One such corpse reappeared recently and may now be visited. While ploughing his peat bog, a farmer in Varberg turned up, in the thick wet peat, a human head. "It had reddish brown hair and an almost black cranium, on which could still be distinguished the remains of skin and a beard. A human body, dressed in a garment of some antique material half rotted away, belonged to the detached head." (Vilhelm Moberg, *A History of the Swedish People*)

Local police were called; a local doctor determined that the man had died from a violent blow on the temple—six hundred years ago.

Peat moss is a natural preservative; body and clothing were in remarkably good condition. "It is the only complete medieval costume in the world," says Albert Sandklef, director of the Varberg Museum in his book *Bocksten Man,* published in 1943.

The way the corpse had been treated also helped to date the body. Three stakes had been driven through it. "Two pointed, slender birch trunks had gone straight through the loins, and a sturdy oaken stake . . . had been thrust through the heart." (Moberg)

Experts have determined not only the time (about 1360) but the circumstances of this man's death. Today Bocksten Man stands in the Varberg Museum, a witness to his own murder.

Even today the modern Swedish word for funeral is *jordfästning* (*jord,* "earth"; *fästning,* "fastening"). In former days men were actually fastened into their graves that their spirits might not wander to trouble the living.

The belief that a bear will not molest a woman "if only she lifts her skirts and shows him that she is a woman" is a very old one in Scandinavia. I first encountered it in *The Story of San Michele* (1928) by Dr. Axel Munthe, for many years official physician to H. M. King Gustaf V of Sweden. Dr. Munthe was traveling through the northern forest with a young girl, a Lapp guide, when they came upon a large bear not fifty yards away; the animal was standing knee-deep in a thicket of bilberries, a twig of berries "sticking out of his big mouth." The Lapp girl, "Ristin, one hand on her axe, advanced a few steps toward the bear. With her other hand raising her tunic she exposed the wide leather breeches which are worn by the Lapp women. The bear dropped his bilberry twig, sniffed loudly a couple of times, and shuffled off among the thick firs. . . . Ristin told me that when her mother brought her back from the Lapp school in the spring, they had come upon the same old bear . . . in the midst of the gorge. . . . He had scrambled away as soon as her mother had shown him she was a woman."

I have since heard similar stories in Finland and northern Sweden and have wondered if this widespread tradition gave birth to the medieval tale of "Beauty and the Beast."

The belief that Satan guided the hand of the artist or of the fiddler is also very ancient in the north. This is shown in an old *nubbevisa,* literally "a song to accompany a nip of liquor." The song tells of Satan playing on his lute, while "all the small devils play upon violins." The scene is depicted on medieval church walls, possibly to warn the unwary of the dangers of dancing to Satan's tune.

The most hated of the Danish bailiffs was the notorious Josse Eriksson, whose crimes and cruelty "to the poor peasants of Dalarna" are recorded in the contemporary *Karl Chronicle.* The habit of "hanging the peasants up to smoke them" is attributed to him. Another bailiff named Olov Stut would compel insubordinate peasants to sit on the stones in icy lake water, stripped naked, so that they died of exposure. Where the Gullspång River flows into Lake Vänern these stones can be seen; they are called *Plågan,* "The Torment."

The Black Death, bubonic plague, was the most dreaded of the great plagues that swept medieval Europe. (The disease is personified in medieval art as a hideous old hag with a broom, sweeping every living soul before her.) As a sanitary measure, walls were often coated with a thick lime wash, even though treasured paintings were forever effaced. (Daniel Thompson, *The Materials and Techniques of Medieval Painting,* Dover, New York, 1956)

As fearful as the Black Death was Saint Anthony's fire, called so because only the monks of Saint Anthony would harbor the sufferers, whose limbs seemed to be consumed by living fire. "There would be a season when the rains were heavy and the summer damp and foggy. The harvest of grain, the rye from which the black bread was made, would be scanty and the seeds spotted with a mildew blight. Then late in the fall some poor fellow would be found with his legs and arms black and shriveled, trying pitifully to crawl to the monastery. . . . People would run from him in terror . . . that day the town was quiet; men and women stayed indoors; no children played in the streets. In hushed voices they murmured that the fire of hell, St. Anthony's fire, moved through the land.

"Soon in one house and then in another and another a child, a man, a woman, would be stricken with the disease. Scarcely a home would escape." (From *The Doctor in History,* H. W. Haggard, Yale University Press, New Haven, 1934)

The blight on the rye (*claviceps purpurea*) was ergot. "Taken in large enough quantities it shrinks the blood vessels for a time until so little blood can flow to the arms and legs that they become starved and die." (Haggard)

"The victim suffered from severe burning pain and cramp in the limbs, followed by a long and painful stage of gangrene and separation." (*A History of Medicine,* Douglas Guthrie, Thomas Nelsons and Sons, Ltd., London, 1945)

"The legs and arms . . . would . . . become frightfully painful. Then they would turn black. Some of the people would die; some would recover; but many of the latter would have lost an arm or a leg which had withered and dropped off. From a few the vicious disease would take both legs, leaving nothing but the maimed trunk and head. . . . Small wonder that people feared the disease." (Haggard)

The disease was often accompanied by frightful hallucinations.

For centuries men have known that this terrible plague was caused by eating bread made with affected rye. Yet the last great epidemic of Saint Anthony's fire occurred in Russia in 1911.

Cruel as the effect of ergot can be, it has two faces; it can be both malignant and benign, as many drugs are. It is used in carefully controlled doses in childbirth to stimulate cramps and contractions of the womb and to prevent hemorrhage. It has been used as a drug to produce abortion. And it is a blessing to sufferers of migraine, when its property to shrink the veins and inhibit the flow of blood to the head can relieve this excruciating malady.

Of the other drugs mentioned in the book, *Papaver somniferum,* the opium poppy, has been in use since the dawn of history. When Jesus was crucified, the Roman soldiers took pity upon their prisoner on the cross and offered Him a strong narcotic. "They gave him vinegar to drink, mingled with gall; and when he had tasted thereof, he would not drink." (Matthew, 27:34) This gall was the juice of the opium poppy, which grew profusely in the Holy Land. (*All the Plants of the Bible,* Winifred Walker, Harper and Brothers, New York, 1957) From the Levant, preparations of the opium poppy were probably introduced into northern Europe by physicians traveling with the armies of the Crusades.

The Devil's berry, *Atropa belladonna,* deadly nightshade, grows throughout the temperate zone; it is very common. In all the Scandinavian languages the popular name for it is *dvale,* literally, "a deadly trance." On occasions it causes hysteria and hallucinations, but its chief property is to cause a dreamlike stupor; so, extracts of it are used in modern medicine to prepare a patient for anesthesia before an operation. The pure chemical agent is atropine, so named after one of the three Fates in ancient Greek mythology, the three aged crones who held in their hands the thread of human life. The oldest, Atropos, severed the thread.

Though the plant grows wild in wood and meadow, it has occasionally been cultivated for its deadly properties. Plutarch tells us that an early king of Troy grew it and other poisonous plants, "making it his business to know their juices." He would then invite guests to a curious entertainment, a banquet at which trays of fruit were passed. Some of the fruit was wholesome, and some was poisoned. It amused him to calculate the odds for life or death among his friends.

Among hallucinogenic drugs, marijuana, hashish, peyote, and certain toxic mushrooms have been used for centuries to induce exhilaration and visions. Like them, deadly nightshade has been employed by certain religious cults, and notably in witchcraft.

So much has been written on "the prevalence of witches" in northern Europe (and elsewhere) that I will mention only two of the many references that I found interesting and suggestive: *The God of the Witches,* by Margaret Murray (Oxford University Press, New York, 1952), with a very full bibliography; and *Witchcraft and Black Magic,* by Montague Summers (Rider and Co. Ltd., London, 1945). The Scandinavian witches had many descendants, among them the forest witch in Hansel and Gretel, the hag Madge in the ballet *La Sylphide,* and Shakespeare's witches in *Macbeth.* Sweden offered a hospitable climate for witches, both real and imaginary. Today in Scandinavia, as Prince Vilhelm of Sweden points out in *This Land of Sweden* (Norstedts, Stockholm, 1946), "paganism lingers hidden among the rocks, and the wind from the big forest is laden with superstition. One stands on the borderland where evil powers have . . . sway. . . ."

On witchcraft trials and the proceedings of medieval Church courts I found valuable material in V. Sackville-West's scholarly account in *Saint Joan of Arc* (Michael Joseph, London, 1948). The Maid of Orleans was illiterate so could not claim "benefit of clergy," but she was examined by churchmen because the accusation was of witchcraft, a heresy against the Church. Since she was among "those who could not write their names" and had no seal of her own, she was required, according to contemporary French records of the trial, to pull a hair from her head and to press this with her thumb into molten wax, to attest that she spoke the truth.

The provincial laws of medieval Sweden give a fascinating picture of the life of the times. And as Prince Vilhelm says, "A juicier . . . Swedish than exists in our old law books is hard to find. Sparks fly from the language like the striking of steel against flint." The law was often written in dialogue, and the language is indeed pithy; an example is this provision for punishment of slander:

"Now someone calls someone else a bitch. 'Who is a bitch?' answers the victim. 'You,' says the first. [The victim says:] 'I take those present to witness that you have called me an insulting word.' [The law concludes:] "That means a fine of sixteen silver pieces every time."

The old laws of all the provinces are so full of provisions for crimes of violence that life in medieval Sweden must have been chancy indeed. Punishments were severe: for setting fires, burning at the stake; in cases of manslaughter, the apprehended murderer was chained to his victim and forced to drag the corpse with him before the assembled council. At such a trial, says Moberg, "hyena-minded spectators no doubt gazed their fill."

Sex crimes must have been very common. All provinces had strong laws on adultery, rape, sodomy, and particularly "whoredom." "For the theft of another woman's bed a woman shall pay a fine of three marks. Thereafter shall she be called a whore." In King Kristoffer's law of 1442: "The best thing a man hath in his dwelling, it is his lawful wife. He who stealeth her from him, he is the chiefest and worst of thieves. Wherefore he who lureth a man's wife from him and runneth away with her . . . let him be hanged above all thieves. Should [the deceived] man not grant his wife her life, then shall she too be brought before the council and be condemned to be buried alive."

Hanging was the preferred punishment for men, but stoning, burning, and burial alive were specified for women—for reasons of "propriety and of chivalry . . . no part of her body may be exposed at her execution." A doubtful chivalry!

On the revival of Christer, I quote from the report of Dr. Samuel Naucler in the Proceedings of the Swedish Royal Academy of Science, 1756, abridged from *Peasant Life in Sweden*, by L. Lloyd (Tinsley Brothers, London, 1870):

"During my stay in the Swedish islands . . . a man 60 years of age was on the 23rd of last March cast away during a storm on a rock. He had drunk to excess and immediately fell asleep, and it was not till the following morning that he was found. He was then carried, as a corpse, into a cottage, when I carefully examined him to ascertain if any signs of life remained. The feet were entirely frozen, the toes blackish . . . with the exception of the big toe on the right foot; the legs, thighs, arms, hands, stomach, breast and countenance icy cold; the jaws were exceedingly firmly closed, the joints quite stiff, the eyes fixed; and when one touched them, they did not wink; no respiration could be observed; neither the pulse not the beating of the heart were perceptible; but as the pit of the stomach (epigastric region) still felt a little warm, I determined on attempting to restore the circulation of the blood, and therefore caused his arms, legs, and thighs to be diligently rubbed with coarse woolen cloths. On the stomach and chest I placed napkins, which at first were only slightly heated but afterwards when it was observed that these parts began to feel warm, I increased the warmth of the napkins. . . . The feet I did not trouble about, because if the man should recover, it seemed more than probable that he would lose them. Here was I in a desert place, far distant from a druggist's and medicines! . . . It struck me that as when housewives have any frozen meat or eggs, they lay them in cold water which draws out the frost, and this without their acquiring any rotten taste, which otherwise happens, the same expedient ought to be tried on the present occasion. But difficulties stood in the way, the man being so frozen that it was impossible to bend any of his limbs, and the feet in consequence could not be immersed in the water-tub. I therefore caused napkins which were frequently changed to be dipped in cold water and placed on the feet. After a time the stomach began to be warmer, but respiration could not be observed until after four hours' labour, when it was about two o'clock in the afternoon. There was then no pulse, nor was it possible to force open the jaws. At about four o'clock however the pulse became perceptible and at half-past six, I was enabled with a silver spoon to separate the jaws. . . . I warmed a little wine . . . poured it . . . into the spoon and gave it to him. So soon as he got it in his mouth, he bellowed like a bull, when the bystanders said he gave up the ghost! But . . . after some difficulty he swallowed the wine. . . . Afterwards he perspired somewhat in the face, and his cheeks became redder. He began to wink when anyone touched his eyes, and . . . to move his arms a little. I then caused him to be laid in a bed nearer the fire . . . a couple of spoonsful of warm wine were likewise administered to him. At eight o'clock he began to speak, thought at first very indistinctly; when he could be understood, we found he was fancying he had been in a forest, where he had . . . a bad attack of colic. . . .

"When I examined the feet, the frost was entirely gone from them and the toes not so black as before; nevertheless, the feet . . . and legs . . . were still very cold. About ten o'clock in the evening he was enabled to move his legs a little and complained of pain. . . . He then ate a small quantity of egg posset and slept tolerably well during the night. On the following morning the feet were warm and they no longer gave him pain. The toes had resumed their natural colour, but . . . were very tender.

"The pulse was then strong and he complained of great thirst. . . . My travelling medicine chest had been left behind at Visby. . . . [But] I caused some gruel to be prepared for him, of which he drank freely. Towards noon the pulse was more quiet. He had a good motion, fell into a mild perspiration, ate a little and slept afterwards.

"In the evening he caused himself to be led to a boat, since without pain he could not walk of himself. Well-contented he now departed for home and thanked me, whom Heaven had been pleased to make the instrument of saving him from temporal and it may be eternal destruction."

I was fascinated by this old report, and so began the story of Christer.

Yet how authentic is the report? The Swedish Royal Academy of Science is a venerable and highly respected institution, thoroughly reliable; but the report was published a long time ago. It is an eyewitness account, not based upon scientific observation, since Dr. Naucler had with him no instruments. Was it really possible by such simple treatment to restore the frozen man?

From the Orient I received a curious confirmation of the report. My son (an airline pilot) sent me a clipping from a leading Tokyo newspaper, *The Asahi Evening News,* dated February 13, 1974. "Returned from the Dead," says the headline; the article tells of a four-year-old boy who fell through the ice while playing near his home in Oslo, Norway. For forty minutes he lay submerged, on the bed of an icy river. Police and firemen observed the accident and noted the time it occurred; frogmen rescued the child, who suffered suffocation as well as extreme chilling (hypothermia); he had respiratory and cardiac arrest; no vital signs were present. Nevertheless two days later he was conscious, asking for his mother and his toys. He was released from the hospital in time to celebrate his fifth birthday. He had shown no sign of cerebral activity when rescued, but now appears to be completely recovered, apparently without physical or mental damage.

I wrote to the American Ambassador to Norway, Thomas R. Byrne, and would like to express my sincere gratitude for his kindness. He sent me a clipping from the Oslo newspaper, which covered the event— *Oslo Dagbladet,* for Tuesday, February 12, 1974. He also furnished the name of the doctor who was responsible for this medical miracle, Dr. Bjørn Lind.

Dr. Lind is the head of Åkerhus Central Hospital, at the University of Oslo. I am deeply grateful to him for his courtesy and kindness. This very busy man took the time to read through Dr. Naucler's report, to reply to my many questions about its authenticity, and to comment upon it.

From Dr. Lind's detailed, very interesting, and gracious letter, I quote some relevant points:

"I firmly believe the report is reliable. The Swedish Royal Academy of Science is a very sincere society, and Dr. Naucler gives every impression of being honest. . . . I believe that the essence of what he is saying is true. . . .

"I think what he found was a hypothermic victim with an extremely slow pulse which he did not detect, and with a respiration unperceivable. The treatment is rewarming, which he indeed did. His sidesteps, trying to cool down with cold water, may actually have been warming, if skin temperature was below water temperature. . . . The temperature [of the "frozen" patient] would never be anything near 0 degrees Centigrade. To make a rough guess, I would say between 20 and 25 degrees Centigrade. . . . The stiffness of the extremities may probably have been due to the rigidity or rigor which follows the hypothermia.

"I take it . . . [the patient] had probably fallen asleep in his wet clothing, on an unprotected cold rock and probably with a cold wind blowing, and these circumstances have lowered his body temperature so much that he has become unconscious. . . . I think it is very probable that he suffered a partial degree of amnesia which probably would decrease as time passes on. . . ."

In part, Christer's amnesia was due to extreme chilling, in part to the blow on the head which he suffered when, at last exhausted, he fell upon the ice.

On conditions in medieval Swedish mines, Prince Vilhelm writes in *This Land of Sweden* (P. A. Norstedt & Soners Förlag, Stockholm, 1946): "[The mines are] described by all visitors in the past as . . . a descent into inferno out of which smoke poured and grimy figures crawled to the top at long intervals. Or else they plunged straight down into the abyss with the aid of a rope." In the same book, the great Swedish botanist Carl Linnaeus has given us this description: "Never has any poet been able to describe . . . [nor] any theologian . . . Hell so terrible as this appears to be. . . . [Into the mines] go *ad metalla damnata laborantes,* labourers condemned to the mines, black as devils, which the soot and darkness envelope with smoke and fumes on all sides. The walls are black with soot, the floor loose with stones, the passages narrow, dug like a mole's, encrusted on all sides . . . the roofs drip with the corrosive vitriol water. Landslides are continually feared . . . the slightest shock . . . could destroy everyone's life without *refugium* for a single one of these doomed beings. Besides I do not know what fear may arise down there . . . or what consuming longing to return to the surface. These *damnati* are stripped to the waist, having a woolen cloth held over their mouths, so that the smoke and dust should not choke them."

Prince Vilhelm has also described the rotting timber in the galleries so that rockfalls were a constant menace; the frayed ladders of rope; and the total lack of any safety measures. "A misstep, a slippery shelf of rock were sufficient to send the miner crashing into an abyss from which there was no escape."

However, there is a macabre and true story about a miner named Fet-Mats Israelson, who lay buried under shale for forty-two years. His body was then recovered and his fiancée recognized him. The body was well preserved by damp and chemicals in the loose shale; it was exhibited as a curiosity for years, when Church authorities finally insisted that it be interred. Richard Wagner made a sketch for a three-act opera based on this event; numerous poets and writers have used the material, among them the Swedish writer Per Hallström, in a famous short story, "Darkness."

In *The Season of the Heart,* all characters are imaginary except for the King, Erik of Pomerania, and his unhappy Queen. When the embattled miners had driven King Erik from Sweden he took refuge in an "impregnable" castle on the rocky coast of the island of Gotland and became a pirate in the Baltic. One historian, Andrew Stomberg (in *A History of Sweden,* Macmillan, New York, 1931), says he was eminently suited to this bloodthirsty occupation.

The character of Kurt is based in part on that of the great Swedish liberator Engelbrekt, "the first Swede" (as the historian Henrik Schück calls him). In Arboga there is a powerful statue of him, showing a man with muscular shoulders and a strong face with deep-set eyes. Often in Stockholm I have walked past the statue of him in Kornhamnstorg. There are in fact more statues of him than of any other ruler of Sweden, though he became Regent for only two years, his amazing career cut short by a brutal murder.

Engelbrekt is celebrated in contemporary chronicles and verses, in later historical novels, in copious volumes by historians, in an opera, and in one of Strindberg's plays. Moberg calls him "Sweden's greatest rebel . . . the very symbol of Sweden's liberties and of our national freedom."

He is as well known to Swedes as George Washington is to Americans, and for many of the same reasons. Although, as Moberg says, "he appears to have left no children . . . [this] has not prevented quite a few Swedes from claiming descent from him."

Yet in all the scholarly disputations, it is difficult to find agreement on the facts of Engelbrekt's life. But it is an assured fact that he was murdered in cold blood.

And it is known that he was a mine owner, though not a very wealthy one; he studied in Bavaria and became a Master of Mining; he was compelled to serve in King Erik's (the Danes') war against Holstein; it is certain that his knowledge of military tactics and his genius as a military leader stemmed from his experience in the field. He had also been educated in noble houses, where young knights were taught the arts of war as part of their basic equipment for life.

From the Danish war, Engelbrekt returned to Sweden fired with revolutionary ideals. He was born to privilege (of the *låg frälse,* the lesser nobility), but he took up the cause of the common people. A contemporary German chronicler, Hermann Korner, states that he took the part of the poor "not out of any overweening pride or lust for power, but out of compassion for those who were suffering."

He dreamed of forming the first representative parliament in Sweden where all classes of society would have a voice. To some extent he accomplished this; in a medieval world where "great lords and bishops ruled," and the common man suffered untold misery and oppression, Engelbrekt laid the foundation for the modern social democratic system in Sweden.

Liberty and equality for all men! In England there was Wat Tyler's rebellion, the wretched poor, gathering in country lanes, with their wretched children, at last a swarming mob, marching in anger upon London. In France, the *Jacquerie,* the "shabby little Jacks," building their barricades in the streets of Paris, tearing up the cobblestones and setting fires. In Bohemia there was the powerful Hussite rebellion. All were strong movements for democracy. But all failed.

And Engelbrekt failed in his first attempts to win freedom for the Swedes. Freedom from the Danish yoke—and freedom from want, from fear and oppression. He tried to negotiate with the King, to put the plight of the common people before that granite monarch, to plead that the hated Danish bailiffs be removed.

At last "in a fit of anger, the King shouted, 'You always complain; depart and never show yourself before my eyes again.' 'It is likely that I shall return once again,' said Engelbrekt, as he left the royal presence." (Stomberg)

And so he did, at the head of a rabble army—men of the mines, men of field and forest. "Throughout the summer and autumn of 1434 the skies of Sweden were darkened with smoke. Armies of peasants were marching through the land, leaving a trail of fire-blackened ruins . . . the bailiffs' castles." (Bertil Waldén) If the King would not order his bailiffs to depart, Engelbrekt's men would use stronger persuasion.

The contemporary Rhymed Chronicle tells us there was no outrage against peaceable citizens, no plunder. "None suffered insult, none was deprived of his property, none lost so much as the value of a hen." Surely a visionary view of a rabble army on the march!

Yet it is also on record that Englebrekt tried always to negotiate, to win his objectives through "peace and parley." If this failed, says the Chronicle, he "carried sword and club through the land."

"Great lords and bishops" were beginning to support Engelbrekt, though their motives were not always altruistic. Many men of power saw in the rebellion the path to more power for themselves.

In Vadstena, Saint Bridget's town, in 1434, the King's Council met. The Engelbrekt Chronicle gives us a dramatic scene: into the Council Chamber came Engelbrekt, alone, unexpected and unannounced, to demand that the Council join in the struggle against the King, and draft an ordinance to depose him.

Lords and bishops refused. So Engelbrekt seized two of them "fast by the throat" and threatened to deliver them to the furious swarm of shouting peasants who waited in the market place. A reluctant Council composed a letter to the King, revoking their oath to him of loyalty and obedience.

A dubious victory. Home again in the strong security of their stone castles, many of these lords declared that they had acted under duress. If they had not acceded to Engelbrekt's demands, "he and his men would have slain them and pillaged their estates" (from the chronicle of Olaus Petri).

The peasant army marched on. Stomberg writes, "Engelbrekt showed extraordinary skill as a military leader; within three months the entire country was practically cleared of Danish . . . bailiffs and the control of government restored to the Swedes." Moberg says, "A natural military genius . . . he also showed himself a political leader of substance. [Over his troops] he . . . exerted a magical influence, [he] knew how to speak to them in their own language."

He must have possessed great personal magnetism—the charisma of the born leader.

We have the evidence of a letter from the powerful Bishop Tomas of Strängnäs who at first bitterly opposed Engelbrekt and his ideals. In the end, the bishop became an ardent partisan; he wrote in celebration of Engelbrekt the famous "Frihetsvisa," the "Song of Freedom."

The letter was written earlier; in it the bishop complains angrily that Engelbrekt is a thief of Church property. "Engelbrekt, a ship's pound of pork in Romtuna Church, that stole Johan Anderson on his behalf."

A "skeepund," a ship's pound, was equal to over four hundred "skålpund," normal poundweight. We can picture a forest clearing, a troop of ragged and famished men sitting round campfires, gnawing on the bishop's roast pork.

The scene is suggestive of Robin Hood, who stole from the rich to give to the poor.

And it poses a question. Who paid for Engelbrekt's rebellion? An army marches on its stomach. The romanticized chronicles of the period emphasize that Engelbrekt was the liberator of the people, welcomed among them wherever he went; his armies were given food and shelter with open-handed generosity. This can scarcely be true, since the rebellion was prompted in part by grinding hunger, by famine and starvation among the peasants. They had little enough to feed their own ragged children, let alone an army on the march.

Several historians have suggested that the Hanseatic League or the German cities furnished Engelbrekt's war chest. I am inclined to agree. At this time King Erik was at war with Holstein and with the League. Both were probably disposed to lend support to the man who led such widespread opposition to the King.

In 1435, Engelbrekt was elected by popular vote to the position of Commander in Chief of all the military forces in Sweden, in effect, Regent of Sweden. The election took place at a meeting in Arboga where "citizens of the towns and the *bonder* [the commons], as well as clergy and nobility sent representatives. This was the first representative meeting in Swedish history in which the commons clearly had a part." (Stomberg)

But other historians disagree!

About Engelbrekt's power, his influence at this period, there has been endless disputation. Erik Lönnroth feels that as Regent he had no political importance, that the Council of State effectively checked his powers. But Nils Ahnlund and Gottfrid Carlsson feel that he remained "the country's standard bearer." And Stomberg says, "He laboured unceasingly and with the force and insight of true constructive statesmanship for the welfare of Sweden."

He was constantly opposed by the aristocracy; "great lords and bishops" hated him and contrived to place beside him as joint ruler one of their own number, Karl Knutsson Bonde, as Earl Marshal, a man from the highest rank of nobility.

The Danish historian Erik Arup writes that Engelbrekt was murdered "to the great relief of the Swedish nobility." "These gentlemen feared the popular movement." (Wilhelm Than) And Olaus Petri states that "some counted it but small harm that Engelbrekt had been rid out of the way."

On the circumstances of his death there is no dispute. Early in 1436 King Erik launched an attack upon Sweden, the country he had sworn to protect and rule with justice and compassion. The King had concluded his war with the Hansa towns; he brought up a huge force and ravaged the east coast of Sweden.

Engelbrekt took to the saddle again. His peasant army rallied. Once more the ragged men were on the march, in the iron cold of the fierce northern winter. Again "Engelbrekt showed himself to be a consummate field commander."

Before the stone fortress of Axvall, the ragged men dug themselves into the snow to lay siege.

And Engelbrekt became "rather ill." (Engelbrekt Chronicle) It is thought that he suffered from rheumatic fever brought on by exposure, by months in the saddle in the bitter weather, the raw wind from the Baltic, "the snows and freezing temperatures of his winter war."

The King declared himself ready for truce. The Council of State summoned Engelbrekt to Stockholm to discuss the terms. Engelbrekt must have had misgivings; "agreements with [the King]," he said, "were not worth the paper on which they were written; he kept no promises and abided by no agreements."

And Engelbrekt was forced to go on crutches; he could no longer mount his horse. He decided to make the journey to Stockholm by boat. On a raw spring evening he stopped for the night, with a few servants, to encamp on an island in Lake Hjälmaren. A bonfire was lit but this did little to dispel the chill.

In the dusk a second boat "struck hard against the land." (Engelbrekt Chronicle) In it was a strong party of armoured men with torches. And the son of an old enemy, the powerful

Bengt Stensson, lord of the nearby castle of Göksholm. He had strongly opposed Engelbrekt, but now their differences had been resolved, and Stensson had declared himself to be at peace with Engelbrekt.

Engelbrekt stood on shore, leaning on his crutches, watching the boat as it grated on the shingle. Recognizing the son of his old enemy, he raised a hand in greeting and pointed out a better place to land.

Måns Bengtsson stepped ashore and shouted, "May I have peace from you in Sweden!" Engelbrekt stretched out a hand in welcome, speaking words of peace. And Bengtsson "struck straightway at him with an axe." The blow chopped three fingers from Engelbrekt's hand.

Engelbrekt lifted a crutch in defense; turning, he tried to flee. His assassin struck again "with wrathful hands," striking a deep wound in Engelbrekt's neck, and then with the axe, cleaving his skull. Engelbrekt fell to the ground and Bengtsson's men rushed up, shooting the corpse "through with many arrows."

The murder was unpunished. The man who ruled jointly with Engelbrekt issued a proclamation that "none might persecute, denigrate or libel [the murderer] for his deed . . . for the sake of peace and quiet in the land." (Ericus Olai)

Some peasants found Engelbrekt's body and took it "in tears" to nearby Orebro church "for greater honour sake."

Before long, Engelbrekt's tomb became a place of pilgrimage. To it came the lame, the halt, and the blind; miraculous cures were reported. As Bishop Tomas wrote:

> Many a pilgrim seeketh it out
> And there of his ill is quit,
> And harmless goeth home.

Legends gathered about the people's hero; but in time his tomb disappeared. It is thought that it was destroyed when the Lutheran faith became strong in Sweden, and relics of popular "saints"—Saint Birgitta's among them—were destroyed.

But on the shores of Lake Hjälmaren a monument still stands, graven with the legend: "Here fell Engelbrekt . . . the Bulwark of Swedish Liberty . . . and Victim of a Vile Murder, April 27, 1436."

But perhaps Engelbrekt's most notable memorial was composed by Bishop Tomas, who once called him a thief. The Bishop wrote in "The Song of Freedom" words which curiously foreshadow some of Shakespeare's:

> If to thine own self
> Thou shalt be true,
> Freedom thou prizest
> More than gold;
> For freedom follows in the wake of honour.

Acknowledgments

————◆•••▶————

Page 34   "The Blessed Virgin brought out a stool;
              'Sit down, little Kari, and rest your feet.' "

From the medieval Norwegian ballad of "Olav og Kari," quoted in "Folk Songs and Visionary Poetry," Chapter 26 in *Scandinavia Past and Present,* published by Edvard Henriksen, Arnkrone, Denmark, 1959.

Page 34   "As well I like thy yellow hair . . ."

From the medieval Norwegian song of chivalry "Bendik og Arolilja," a later version of the old epic poem of Hagbard og Signe. Quoted in "Folk Songs and Visionary Poetry," Chapter 26 in *Scandinavia Past and Present,* published by Edvard Henriksen, Arnkrone, Denmark, 1959.

Page 65   "Witte hath wonder . . ."

Attributed to Bishop Reginald Pecok and found in Douglas Gray's *Themes and Images in the Medieval English Religious Lyric,* London, 1972.

Pages 70–73 The tale of the Sicilian sorcerer is adapted from *The Autobiography of Benvenuto Cellini.*

Pages 155–56 "The Ballad of Little Karin and the Barrel Lined with Nails" is medieval Swedish. The original is found in *Kärleksöden i Norden under Tusen År,* published by Sohlmans Förlag, Stockholm, 1949. I have freely translated the ballad and abridged it. In the original, the wicked King offers Karin successive inducements to abandon her virtue—a grey horse, a gold saddle, half of his kingdom.

Page 230 "Of the Monk of Angers" is ninth century, anonymous, translated by Howard Mumford Jones in *Medieval Literature in Translation,* ed. Charles W. Jones, David McKay and Co., New York, 1950.

Pages 237–38 Quotations from, and about, Saint Birgitta are from *A History of the Swedish People,* by Vilhelm Moberg, Vol. I, Pantheon Books, New York, 1972. I have also relied upon Moberg for the quotation in the afterword describing the Bocksten Man, with "stakes through breast and belly," and for the excerpts from "The Song of Freedom," by Bishop Tomas.

Afterword, pages 285–86 The story of the Lapp girl lifting her skirts to "show the bear that she is a woman" is from *The Story of San Michele* by Axel Munthe, first published in 1928; many subsequent editions.

Afterword, pages 287–88 Quotations on St. Anthony's fire are from *The Doctor in History* by H. W. Haggard, Yale University Press, New Haven, 1934.

Afterword, pages 291–93 Dr. Naucler's report in the Swedish Royal Academy of Science, 1756: I have abridged

the translation of this report from *Peasant Life in Sweden* by
L. Lloyd, Tinsley Brothers, London, 1870.

Afterword, page 296   The quotation from Carl Linnaeus is
from Prince Vilhelm of Sweden, *This Land of Sweden*, P. A.
Norstedt & Söners Förlag, Stockholm, 1946, translated by
Elizabeth Kjellberg.

Afterword, pages 297–301   On subsequent pages I have
used quotations on Engelbrekt from *A History of Sweden* by
Andrew Stomberg, Macmillan, New York, 1931.